EDGE
of
SMOKE

EDGE
of
SMOKE

KARLYLE TOMMS

Fresh Ink Group
Guntersville

Edge of Smoke

Fresh Ink Group
An Imprint of:
The Fresh Ink Group, LLC
1021 Blount Avenue #931
Guntersville, AL 35976
Email: info@FreshInkGroup.com
FreshInkGroup.com

Edition 1.0 2024

Cover design by Stephen Geez / FIG
Cover art by Anik / FIG
Book design by Amit Dey / FIG
Associate publisher Beem Weeks / FIG

Cataloging-in-Publication Recommendations:
FIC073000 FICTION / LGBTQ+ / Transgender
FIC043000 FICTION / Coming of Age
FIC030000 FICTION / Thrillers / Suspense

Library of Congress Control Number: 2023922153

ISBN-13: 978-1-958922-65-1 Softcover
ISBN-13: 978-1-958922-66-8 Hardcover
ISBN-13: 978-1-958922-67-5 Ebooks

DEDICATION

v

This book is dedicated to all those who have been marginalized and mistreated simply because of who they are. It is dedicated to those forced to play a role rather than being allowed to love themselves and be themselves. It is dedicated to all who have felt unloved, ridiculed, rejected, hated, and abused simply for being who they are. This book is dedicated to the unconditional love that needs to be shared with all people and to those who genuinely come to understand that love is the bottom line, for this book about love.

CHAPTERS

STEPHANIE'S NOTE

All I wanted was to be myself and live the life I knew was mine to live. Yet, almost everyone around me tried to mold me into something else. Only one person initially accepted me without trying to change or force me into a mold where others thought I belonged. Only one person stood by me and gave me the courage to be myself, no matter what others thought about me or tried to do to me. I gained strength from her love, compassion, guidance, and encouragement. She didn't try to make me into something she wanted me to be, but she taught me right from wrong and the difference between love and control. I also gained strength from what all the others tried to force me into. I gained strength from what I went through and how I was punished for not fitting the mold they wanted to force me to accede. I gained strength from abuse not only by those who tried to force me into being something or someone who I was not meant to be but by those who sought only to use me as satisfaction for their debauchery and malice.

For my entire life, I fought to learn how to love myself because the abuse and the constant barrage of attempts to change me taught me that I was worth less than other human beings, that there was something wrong with me, and that I was an aberration of nature as well as an abomination to the church. They were not required to love me. They were not required to approve of me, nor were they even required to accept me. All they needed to do was allow me to live without being tormented for not becoming what they wanted me to be. Initially, only one person, one soul of an angel, stood by me and taught me that I was worth loving and that I deserved my place on earth regardless of what others might think of me. That one person taught me I am a certified member of humanity, just like everyone else. I deserve the respect, honor, and dignity that every human being deserves; for we are all part of one humanity. Regardless of our differences, unique traits, or life course, we are all worth valuing and loving as children of the same creator.

Humanity is like smoke. There are varying levels of density and shades as smoke dissipates into and becomes the air, but how do you know when smoke ceases to be smoke and becomes the air? Smoke is only a temporary density of specific molecules that soon fades into the mix of molecules we call the atmosphere. Like smoke, we all eventually ascend into the hidden world of existence beyond this life, where there is no definition of one from the other.

How do you define the edge of smoke? How do you determine what part of the smoke differs from another? Some portions may seem darker than others, but those portions are still smoke. The lighter portions where smoke begins to fade into the air are still the same smoke, and when smoke becomes the air, it dissipates into and becomes one with the indistinguishable whole. The eyes alone cannot discern when smoke blends into the air. Even though the smoke appears separate from the air, it dissolves into the whole and is no longer recognized as distinct or different. Human beings may also seem different from each other, but they are still all human beings. In the end, we all blend into one unified human race despite all the variations that occur. Ultimately, we are all more the same than we are different. In truth, we are more united than separate. In the meantime, human beings keep wanting to create niches and roles that they try to force others into because it helps them to feel safe in their own assigned role, or they resent not being able to break free from their engrained expectations of what it means to be yourself, what it means to be a man, what it means to be a woman, what it means to be religious or even a human being.

When we finally have a society that fully embraces our differences and uniqueness rather than fearing and hating it, allowing people to live peacefully and be who they are without interference and oppression, we will finally have a civilized society.

"Truly, I say to you, as you did it to one of the least of these my brothers, you did it to me." (Matthew 25:40)

DISCLAIMER

There are words and phrases in this book that would be considered offensive by today's standards. However, the terminology was common during the time frame of the story. These words and phrases are not intended to be offensive toward any person or social group but to portray the time's language accurately. An example would be that the term *transgender* did not come into common use until the 1990s.

All characters in this book are fictional, and any resemblance to any person or persons other than the author is purely coincidental as these characters are not drawn from any person known to the author.

If I have misunderstood or misrepresented anyone or anything within this writing, please accept my sincere apology, as no part of this story is intended to be offensive to anyone.

NOTE: Stephanie, the protagonist of this novel, was introduced as a character in my previous book, *The Calling Dream*, as each story presents a character who will become the protagonist of another novel in the *Soul Encounters* series.

CHAPTER 1

HURTING IS LIVING

My so-called mother was a whore. There is no way to deny it. She would fuck anyone for a cigarette. You don't want to know what she would do for a heroin needle in her arm. My wounded heart had no sympathy for her. The abandoned child within my growing skin could not fathom the difference between malice and violent anguish. As an adult, I realized she was also a product of abuse and neglect. Her eyes were not always hollow because of drugs. Her eyes were first made hollow because her soul had been dug out of her childhood and discarded like kitchen garbage scraped from the sink. Unlike me, she had no one. She had no real friends and no one to turn to. She grew up half-black in southern Missouri, a part of the country where almost everyone is white. Growing up in the 1950s, she had nowhere to turn from the torment she experienced at home, in the community, at school, or any playground. The white half of her still could not save her from the word, *nigger*. She learned to isolate, withdraw into herself, and suck any morsel of satisfaction she could find, no matter where she found it. Unfortunately, she found it in drugs.

I don't know that she ever tried to be a real mother to me, but it was not unusual that I was left unattended while growing up in the St. Louis slums of Pruitt Igoe in the 1960s. Even when I was very small, she trusted me to our apartment and the Pruitt Igoe grounds while she ignored the danger, the acrid stench, and the selfish wheedle of the slums where society pitched the unwanted. The vast majority of the time, I played alone with the few toys she might have picked up at some yard sale or out of a garbage can. I dared not go out onto the grounds where I faced dangers from many instead of the one with whom I lived. My toys were likely broken before I ever got them, somebody else's discards. Even for Christmas, if there were anything, I would likely receive something already worn and misused. My so-called grandmother, from down in the Ozarks, might send me a Christmas card with a dollar in it, but that was quickly snatched from my hand for "safe keeping."

It was not easy to be a child, either in our assigned cubicle or the whole of Pruitt Igoe, and I didn't associate any more than I had to. Even if we had been entirely black, there were few places where danger did not overhang, like clouds full of lightning. Pruitt Igoe was unsafe, and my so-called mother was a light-skinned biracial. I was even lighter-skinned than her. I am not sure that she didn't resent me for that. Maybe my father was white, but I didn't know who he was. Our light skin was unambiguous in the almost all-black slums, and sometimes, the hatred that white folks commonly cast onto blacks got dumped back on us in a pecking order of resentment. Those who feel the most devalued try to find someone to disrespect even more than themselves. It probably didn't help that my so-called mother had a penchant for bedding white men.

Pruitt Igoe was a place where white society could shove away all those they didn't want to accept. My so-called mother and I were scapegoats for that, called high yellow, redbone, and other things that were not as kind. We were easy targets for rage that often did not find its way back to where it started. We were neither white nor black, misfits in either culture.

I took a lot when I was growing up. I took a lot from many people of both races. I took a lot in my own home and from the asshole my so-called mother used to farm me out to. He did things to me that she never wanted to admit, even though she had to have known. So, I was tough. I had to be tough to survive. Everyone always told me that boys had to be tough, that I should buck up, and that I shouldn't cry. I was taught that real men, boys growing up to be men, take it and keep going. I did all that, but I was never a boy. I may have been born with male genitals, but I have never been and never will be male. I was strong anyway. I may have been born in a boy's body, but I have always been female, and tough is something that lots of girls have to be, especially in places like Pruitt Igoe.

My so-called mother could not stand that I was a girl. She hated my femininity and tortured me for it every time she witnessed it. Somehow, it was the straw on the camel's back of her shame and self-loathing. That she hated herself was evident, addictions notwithstanding, but her addictions were her way of numbing the anguish she had carried all her life. Within her was the insidious concept that, no matter what, she could never be worth as much as others and never be whole or happy, and she passed that down to me. My femininity was only another mark of shame embedded into her graphically scarred soul.

The first time I saw her with a needle in her arm, I must have been about six years old. I had been playing on my bedroom floor with a three-wheeled toy truck, rolling it over to an old shoe box that I pretended was a beauty shop. I wanted dolls, but she would never give me dolls, and if I happened to get hold of one, she would grab it out of my hands and scream, "How many times do I have to tell you, boys, don't play with fucking dolls!" If she found them, she would pull the heads and arms off them and throw them in the trash. I tried to make sure she didn't see them.

On that particular day, I had been left in our apartment alone. I had a mangled Barbie in my *beauty shop* shoe box, but I quickly stashed it when I heard the click in the lock of our front door. I resented her for what she did to my dolls, but that was only one in a collection of resentments that hardened into hatred, which I carried for much of my life. For a while, I hated her viciously and wanted to kill her. As I grew older, I refused to call her Mom, Mother, or any facsimile of that. Her name was Mable, but I wouldn't even use that without attaching the word *bitch*. I called her *fake mom, so-called mother, Mable-bitch, and occasionally - cunt*, when she couldn't hear me. Over the years, I learned that my hate harmed me more than her. So, after many years and a lot of therapy, I finally stopped hating my so-called mother, but that came long after she was no longer in my life.

After the lock clicked, I heard the front door squeak and heard her come in with some man—not unusual. There were always people, primarily men, in and out of our apartment. If she wasn't buying drugs, she was trying to deal drugs but was never very good at dealing. She used more than she sold, and more than once, that got her in a lot of trouble. I became accustomed to seeing bruises and busted lips, but she was lucky that was all she got. Usually, she whored for drugs and semi-kept it from me, but I knew there were things she did with men in her room, and it was not unusual to see some man crossing the living room buttoning his shirt, trying to pull up his pants or slip his feet back into his shoes. I never really knew exactly what happened in her room until that day.

At first, I paid no more attention than usual and went back to playing, assuming that she would not catch me with what was left of my doll once she went through the living room to her room. The usual sounds of adult banter came through thin walls, but this time, the sound was not as muffled, and I could hear what they were saying. Usually, the door to her bedroom was closed, so only muffled sounds could be heard. However, the unmistakable sounds of adult conversation were evident that day. I didn't understand anything they were talking about, something about a horse and needing a fix. I had never heard that man's voice before. Sometimes, the same men would come around again, but it was not unusual that a man would come through our apartment and never be seen again. None of them had ever stayed for long.

"Come on, Daddy, don't get hairy about it," she said. "Momma just needs a little help with a do-up. I'll do anything you want. Come on, baby. Momma needs a little more than money."

I heard him say something about her being a sleepwalker and that she needed to quit the brown sugar. I heard her pleading, begging like she was terrified that he might walk out. The banter went on for a few minutes. Then I heard him saying, "Okay, okay, okay."

Hesitantly, I went to investigate. I was very careful about it. I learned very young never to disturb her and definitely never call for her. When I called for her, if she came at all, she was in a rage, and her rage was something I didn't want to face. I carefully peeked into her bedroom from my doorway across the living room corner. We had a two-bedroom flat, and both bedrooms opened onto the living room. I had no idea why her door was left open that day. Maybe she had been too drunk to remember to close it, but the sounds were more evident because of it.

I walked silently and cautiously across the corner of the living room to the door of her room. Then I stopped at the doorway, hid behind the door facing, and peeked around. I saw her sitting at the edge of her bed, an old mattress on the floor shoved up under the window. She had a rubber thing around her arm and was sticking a needle into the inside of her elbow. She didn't even notice me. Often, I wasn't noticed. I was more like an object in her way than her child, and as long as I stayed out of her way, she didn't seem to mind too much.

She pulled the needle from her arm and tossed it and the rubber thing onto the floor. The white man with her stood by, watching as she did all this, unbuttoning his shirt and loosening his belt. When she had finished, he asked her if she was ready. She pulled her skirt off and scooted back on her mattress with mismatched sheets and blankets strewn about. She glanced at the door, and I darted back behind the wall. I stood there for a long time, trembling with fear that she might have seen me and would come out raging, but she never came out.

When, at last, I peeked around and watched, the man's pants were off, and he was thrusting his pelvis into her pelvis. She seemed to have almost passed out and barely noticed what he was doing. I felt a dull shock, a numb emptiness as I peeked. I watched the way one might watch a coffin lowered slowly into the dark ground. The man looked up, saw me, got up, walked naked across the room, and closed the door. Startled, I darted quickly back to my room.

A few minutes later, I heard a deep and muffled groan. A little while after that, the man came to the door of my room as he was tucking in a Hawaiian shirt that was buttoned only halfway up. His thick chest hair crawled around the edges of the thin fabric. I pulled back into the corner because I was deeply frightened of most adults, especially men. Almost all of them would hurt me.

He quietly strolled toward me. "Hey, how are you?" he gently said. "It's okay. I'm not going to hurt you. Would you come over here?"

He made several attempts to coax me before I hesitantly did as he instructed and walked up to him. He placed his thick hand on my head and muffled my short hair. I looked up at him, then back toward my so-called mother's room. I didn't know what to say. At the time, I didn't know what any of it meant. I only knew that I felt almost sickly strange. I had never seen the man before, nor had I ever seen adults doing what had just happened in my so-called mother's room. I felt intimidated, but I somehow knew I was safe with him. I don't know how I knew since I had never been safe around any of my so-called mother's acquaintances, but I knew he was one of the few adults who would not hurt me. He was different. His demeanor was different.

The man reached down, placed huge hands beneath my armpits, picked me up, and I allowed it without struggling. He put his arm under my ass to support me, pulled me to him, and hugged me. I was small for my age, and he could pick me up as though I might have been a four-year-old. No man had ever hugged me before, and not many women. Any man I had encountered had either ignored me or abused me. My so-called mother never hugged me unless it was a show for the cops or child protective services. This man felt warm, and the hug felt comforting. The scent of woodsy cologne filled my nostrils, and I turned my nose to his neck for a better whiff. Before that, I don't remember being genuinely hugged by anyone except Miss Mattie, my friend who lived down the hall. Her hugs were warm and affectionate. This man's hug also felt affectionate, but it was a very different experience from hugging Miss Mattie.

I had confusing, odd feelings about this stranger. The touch of his skin was different. His body was different, thick and muscular, unlike Miss Mattie's skinny frame. It felt reassuring. He had a different energy, a distinct essence of protection and strength. It was not at all like the essence of a woman. The only way I had ever previously been touched by any man was violent and abusive, but somehow, I felt guarded by this stranger. Despite what I had just seen him do to my so-called mother, I felt safe.

He carried me to our ripped and raged second-hand sofa, sat down, placed me on his knee, and put his arm behind my back. There was nothing else to sit on in our living room except that old sofa. Our decrepit black and white TV sat on top of a packing crate on the opposite side of the room. There were no pictures on the walls; the only thing that adorned our apartment was a clock hanging on a nail beside my so-called mother's bedroom door, but that had fallen off the wall.

"So," he said, smiling. "You live here?"

I nodded my head.

"What's your name?"

"They call me Stephen," I whispered, "but I don't like that name."

"Oh, your name is Stephen," he goaded with a deep, echoing voice. "That's a good, manly name, isn't it?"

I said nothing. He didn't ask why I didn't like my name, and I didn't tell him. Besides, Mable-bitch had wailed the hell out of me when she heard me say that I preferred to be called Stephanie.

"So, Stephen," he said, reaching his other hand into his opposite pocket and pulling out a clean brown wallet. "Do you think you could do something for me?"

I stared at the wallet. Then, he nudged me off his knee to stand in front of him. He reached into his wallet and pulled out a twenty-dollar bill and a five-dollar bill. He first handed me the twenty.

"Now when your Momma comes to—ah—wakes up." He sweetened his deep voice. "This is for her. You make sure she gets it. Okay?"

I nodded. Then he handed the five-dollar bill to me.

"This one I want you to keep, just a little bonus for your troubles." He placed the bill in my palm and folded his huge, warm hand over my fingers to close them around it. His hand felt tender and reassuring. I loved the feeling of it. No one, except Miss Mattie, had ever touched me with such tenderness, but her hands were scrawny and thin.

"Now don't tell your Momma I gave you this. It is our little secret, and who knows, there might be more where that one came from someday. You just give her the twenty, keep the five, and that'll be our little secret. If she doesn't remember, tell her *Mike* left her the twenty for services rendered. Can you remember that? Services rendered?"

I nodded.

He got up, placed the wallet in his hip pocket, and walked to the door. He turned back to me just before he left and said, "I might come back to see you someday. In the meantime, take good care of your momma. She's gonna need it."

He winked at me and walked out the door.

After Mike left, I returned to my so-called mother's bedroom and peeked inside. She was still lying flat on her back, mostly naked and unconscious. Maybe what she wanted from heron was to be unconscious. Perhaps her feelings and experiences were so overwhelming that she didn't want to feel anything at all. Maybe it was her way of being dead before she was dead.

I knew to leave her alone. I learned early in life that the last thing I wanted to do was disturb her when she was out. I probably wouldn't have been able to rouse her if I had tried, but I dared not try. Too many times, I had been pulling on her arm, trying to wake her, when the other arm came hard across my head, knocking the crap out of me.

I returned to my room and placed the five-dollar bill on my tattered dresser beside the door. I hid the twenty in my hiding place, where the baseboard pulled loose from the wall at the corner of my bedroom. There was a little hole in the plaster behind it. So, I could stuff small things in there, and Mable-bitch would never know. I had learned to take care of myself. There was often no money in the house to buy anything to eat, but I sometimes lifted a bill from Mabel's purse if she had it. Most of the time, she didn't, and she never knew if she had money or she didn't. When I had a stash, I could buy something to eat if I could get Miss Mattie to take me to the store. I hid the food I bought, too. If I didn't hide it and she asked, I would say Miss Mattie gave it to us. Besides, it was not unusual for Miss Mattie to bring a casserole or something. Miss Mattie knew how my so-called mother was and always shared what she had. She knew my so-called mother would trade food stamps or commodities for drugs, and we were soon without. So, I learned to hold back. If we went through what we had too soon, there might be a few days when there was nothing to eat. I learned to manage my hunger. Later in life, that helped me keep my thin, womanly figure. I learned to starve myself before I was seven years old.

After I hid the money, I continued to play with whatever I could find. One of my favorite games was pretending I was a princess in a grand magical kingdom where the king and queen were both kind and gentle people like Miss Mattie. In my imaginary kingdom, I had all the best new toys, including Barbie dolls that had all their arms and legs and all the accessories. I could go out into the castle courtyard and play with magical creatures like dogs and cats that could talk or pink goats that could fly, and I always had the most beautiful things, the finest outfits and shoes, and the most wonderful delicious things to eat. After I met Mike, he became the king of my fanciful kingdom, and Miss Mattie was the queen.

I would drape a sheet around when I played and pretend it was a sequined gown. I cut up the centers of toilet paper rolls, colored them with crayons, and ran string through them to make my necklace. I used some rusty scissors I found to cut around the corner of a cardboard box and make a tiara. Although she had some costume jewelry and a few nice outfits, I didn't dare use any of my so-called mother's stuff. She would snap into a rage over the littlest thing, and it only took getting caught one time using one of her blouses as a dress to realize that I should never do that again. I did my best to stay out of her way. When I was little, I was terrified of her rages. As I grew older, I discovered I could rage just as well as she could, and I began giving it back. Our screaming, violent fights became more like street fights than something between a mother and her child.

Several hours after Mike left, I heard her stir in the other bedroom. Then, she got up, staggered to my room, and stood leaning on the door facing staring at me. She was still only partially dressed, but her arms were now in the sleeves of her blouse. It didn't matter. She rarely bothered to dress around the apartment anyway, and sometimes she sat around totally nude, especially in the summer when it was hot, and we had only a fan to cool us. When I realized she was at the door and looked up, she hissed, "What the hell are you looking at?" A smirking grin stretched her mouth.

My so-called mother could have been a beautiful woman, but she ruined any chance of that. Drugs put bags under her eyes and deepened the sockets. The sinking skin of her face created craters around her cheekbones. Most of the time, she never ate enough and looked more like a starving dog than a human being. My so-called mother had short, curly hair. She liked to keep it cut short, almost like a man, because "I don't have time to deal with that shit!" She usually cut it herself rather than waste a dime on a coiffure when the money could be devoted to drugs. She also clipped my hair close to the scalp for the same reasons. Sometimes, she wore a hat "Like my momma did." She could look pretty when dressing up and putting on some makeup and jewelry, but that was usually only when there was a family services meeting, or she was trying to hook up with a new trick.

Her mother was white trailer trash from the Southern Missouri Ozarks near the Arkansas border, and her father had been black. She grew up in the primarily white Ozarks down at the south end of Missouri, and because she was biracial, she didn't have a very good time of it. There were only a few black folks in the area, and when they married, they often had to marry a white person or someone out of the region if they didn't want to marry kin. There were some second-cousin weddings, I'm sure. In the 1930s through the 1950s, there was a separate cemetery for black people outside of town because they weren't allowed to bury a loved one next to a white person. At that time, there were still sundown laws where no black person was allowed to be seen in town after dark. The only white people who would associate with them had already been cast out by their own. Mable-bitch said my so-called grandma and grandpa were married, but I never knew my grandpa. My so-called grandma told me he died, but Mable-bitch said he was in prison because he had killed some man in a bar fight. I never knew what was true and what wasn't. It seemed like Mable-bitch would rather lie than tell the truth, and often, a story didn't match itself from one telling to the next.

My so-called grandma was meaner than Mable-bitch, and I was thankful we didn't visit very often. She wouldn't come to St. Louis because she couldn't stand the idea of a big city and being around all the traffic and people. I had not seen her more than two or three times in my entire life, which was fine with me. She lived in a nasty old trailer on some back road in the sticks. I didn't like visiting because it was filthier than our apartment at Pruitt Igo, and she always got in a fight with Mable-bitch. She would also slap the hell out of me, sometimes right out of the blue, just because she felt like it.

I stopped asking about my father. Mable-bitch would just say, "I fucked a lot of men. How am I supposed to know?"

I rarely said anything back to her. I was too scared to say the wrong thing when I was little because it might make her rage. She would scream, call me terrible names, throw things, or pick up whatever was near and hit me with it. So, I didn't say much to her at all. You might think I would become beaten down and timid. Instead, I built my own rage that could stand up to just about anyone or anything. I built a blaze of burning fury around my tender heart that almost anyone could fall victim to, even for the slightest thing. I could cuss as big as she could, like a tobacco-chewing truck driver, before I was eight years old. She taught me well. As I got older, I gave the rage right back to her claws and teeth, but when I was little, I kept my mouth shut most of the time because she could still hurt me.

After standing at my doorway for several minutes, glaring at me, she suddenly noticed the five-dollar bill on the dresser. She crossed to it, snatched it from the dresser top, and screamed, "Where the hell did you get this? What the fuck! Are you stealing my fucking money?"

"Mike," I said quickly. "This guy named Mike said to give it to you—for services rendered."

"Mike?" She smirked as though not initially remembering who he was. "Oh … oh, yeah … told him he could fuck me for twenty bucks and a hit of dope. Lying mother fucker! Bastard stiffed me … in more ways than one." She giggled a little, apparently thinking that she had made a joke. "Fucker comes around again, see what he *ain't—gonna—get!*" She folded the five-dollar bill lengthwise over her middle finger and waved it around her crotch like a magic wand. Then, she shoved it in her blouse pocket and said, "You hungry?"

I nodded. The truth is, I had not eaten all day. Lots of times when she was stoned, I could easily go the whole day without eating anything unless I snuck out and went up the hall to Miss Mattie or I had food stashed somewhere. Miss Mattie would always feed me, but my so-called mother didn't like for me to go up there. I think she might have been suspicious of Miss Mattie. She might have been afraid that Miss Mattie had reported her to protective services before, and maybe she did, but Miss Mattie also saved both our asses on multiple occasions, mainly by feeding us. Who knows if she turned my so-called mother in? Still, there had been so many times that child protective services should have taken me out of there but didn't. When they finally did, it was too late to have prevented the toxic effects that would haunt me for life.

"Come on." She said.

She turned, headed toward the kitchen, and I followed. We had a little galley kitchen with crappy cheap appliances. She didn't actually cook. So, the oven was most often used to store things. Sometimes, she would pull all that stuff out and bake something, but most of the time, it was just another space to stuff crap or hide drugs. We used the burners on top of the stove to heat canned soup sometimes, and if her fortune were to shine on me, she would scramble some eggs. Most of the time, I just got bologna or hot dogs eaten cold from the refrigerator, if there were any. If I was lucky, I might find some bread. I learned to eat it, mold and all, rather than letting it go to waste. I didn't go to my stash unless I knew she would be asleep, away, passed out, or I couldn't get something from Miss Mattie.

She went to the kitchen and began digging through cabinets. Some cabinet doors had been ripped off the hinges, and all the cabinets were past due for a coat of paint. Roaches scrambled. She pulled out half a bag of macaroni, threw it on the counter, and went to the refrigerator. "We ain't got shit!" she exclaimed as the refrigerator light spread an alien glow onto her face.

She grabbed a bottle of catchup and a bottle of mustard from inside the refrigerator door. One slimy hotdog was left, and it was way past time to throw it out. She pulled that out and threw it on the counter as well. Then she put a pan of water to boil and threw the macaroni in. She squirted catchup and mustard into the bottom of another pan, tossed on black pepper and salt, and mixed in water. She cut the hotdog into little pieces and threw that in, too. After the macaroni had cooked, she drained the hot water into the sink using a pan lid to hold the pasta. She picked up the little pieces of macaroni that fell into the sink and threw those back into the pan. Then she dumped the ketchup, mustard, and hotdog mix on top of the macaroni and stirred it in the pan. She put some of it into a little bowl and handed it to me with a spoon and a glass of water.

"There you go—enjoy," she said as though she had just made a five-star dinner.

I took it back to my room and sat on the floor to eat. She grabbed what was left in the pan and carried it to the beat-up couch in the living room. I heard her flip on the TV and twist the knob, trying to find a channel. What came out of our old television, with the crappy rabbit ear antenna, was often more static than entertainment. Even the wads of foil wrapped around the rabbit ears didn't help much, but she watched it anyway. She watched it spellbound, especially when stoned. Sometimes, she would smoke a joint while she watched television. I guess it made the static more entertaining. One night, I saw her smoking a joint, gazing at the smoke rising off the tip. She watched it like it was the most fascinating thing on earth. Then, as if talking to some unknown entity or apparition in the empty room, she said, "You ever notice there is no edge to smoke?" Her eyes rolled around the smoke patterns as they rose and dissipated into the room. "There ain't no edge. You can't ever tell where the air begins and the smoke ends. Smoke or air, air or smoke? You can't tell."

When I finished my little bowl of macaroni, I took the dish back to the kitchen and set it in the sink, which I could barely reach. Then I returned to the living room and asked, "Can I go see Miss Mattie?"

She looked around the room for the clock that had fallen off the wall. "What the fuck time is it?" she asked.

When she realized the clock was lying on the floor with the battery popped out, she exclaimed, "Fuck!" Then she got up and went to her bedroom to look at her alarm clock, plugged in, and set on the window sill. She only needed an alarm to get me up and ready for school, but even with that, she overslept more often than not.

"2:42?" I heard her say. "Fuck! It's dark outside. Baby, Miss Mattie is gonna be asleep. It's too late to be going down there."

Disappointed, I turned back toward my room.

"You should be asleep too," She said as she returned to the living room. "Go get in bed."

My bed was a few blankets folded on the floor with a sheet over them and a rank and stinking worn-out pillow.

"I don't feel sleepy," I pleaded as I walked toward my room.

"I don't fucking care," she exclaimed. "Go lay down."

"Okay," I replied. "But I don't think I can sleep."

"If it wasn't so fucking far, I'd call Jake and have him come get you," she smirked. "You could stay with him. You wanna go see Jake?"

Jake didn't live at Pruitt Igoe but in an old house a few miles away. My so-called mother didn't have a car, and the phone was often cut off because she didn't pay the bill. Sometimes, she would hook up with somebody who agreed to drop me off at Jake's. Sometimes, Jake would just show up and ask her if she needed him to babysit me for a while. Sometimes, she would borrow somebody's car or call Jake if she had remembered to pay the bill. She would get rid of me as often as she could. Jake never hesitated. He was always happy to see me, but I had good reason for never being happy to see him.

"NO!" I exclaimed

She knew I hated Jake and had to have known he did things to me, but she didn't care. He was some man she had befriended, probably over a drug deal. He offered to babysit for her, and she didn't want to admit why this strange unmarried man would offer to take care of her kid so often. He told her he loved children, but I doubt he ever told her what he really meant by that.

I hated Jake. He was a skinny redneck with stingy thin mousy brown hair and arms that looked too long for his body. He had a thin nose and beady green eyes that sunk back into his skull like the eyes of a demon peeking from inside. He was about the same age as my so-called mother and only wanted to keep me because he wanted to do things to me—things that sickened me. It still brings disgust to my memory. He did things that hurt. He liked to hurt me.

When he brought me back home, my so-called mother never asked why I had cuts, blisters, and bruises around my ass and between my legs. She would smear a little salve on it and say, "Baby, you got to be more careful." She never questioned anything Jake did, and Jake was a sick bastard, to say the least. It seemed like the more he hurt me, the more he enjoyed it. He took pictures of me, too. Sometimes, he put the camera on a tripod and took pictures of himself doing things to me. Sometimes, he would take photos of me with other kids and make us do things with each other. If I could have found a way to kill him, I would have, but I was too little back then to accomplish something like that. Sometimes, I wanted just as much to kill my so-called mother. Thoughts of murder should not be in a child's mind, but when you grow up in torment, it can seem like your only option other than killing yourself, and I thought of that, too.

There was this older black boy named Ronza from Pruitt Igoe, and Jake made me do stuff with him, too. He was maybe about fourteen or fifteen and much bigger than I was. I don't know how Jake teamed up with Ronza, but often, Ronza would be waiting for us in Jake's car when he picked me up. Ronza seemed to like it. He liked it as much or more than Jake did, and then, if I weren't very careful, Ronza would corner me somewhere around Pruitt Igoe and do what he wanted.

I started hating Jake early on. I was about three or four years old when my so-called mother started leaving me with him. It was convenient for her. She didn't have to deal with me. She could get rid of me and do whatever she wanted. She didn't care what Jake was doing. Sometimes, she would leave me at his house for two or three days. It never mattered to her as long as I was out of the way. At least the ugly mother fucker fed me.

I was thinking about Jake and how much I hated him when my so-called mother brought my attention back to the moment.

"I'm sure Jake would like to see you." She grinned.

"I'm going to go lay down," I said.

"Okay," she teased, "but you know Jake is always open to taking care of you."

"I'm going to go lay down," I said again. Then I went to my room and curled up on the blankets. I stuffed the thin pillow under my head, closed my eyes, and pretended to be exploring all the different rooms in my princess castle. Soon, I fell asleep.

CHAPTER 2

REVEALING THE SHADOW

I woke the next afternoon, a Monday. The TV in the living room was still on, and I could hear the mid-day news show that usually played around noon. I got up and went to the living room to see my so-called mother on the couch, head propped on the arm of the sofa, sound asleep. Rather than risk waking her, I went to the kitchen to see if I could find something to eat. I had just opened the refrigerator when I heard a knock at the front door. I came back to the living room, but my so-called mother never moved. Then I heard the knock again. The third time, it was louder.

Finally, she stirred, "WHAT!" She yelled, "WHAT THE FUCK?"

Then she rolled off the couch into the floor and got up from her knees. She waved me back toward my room, staggered to the door, and opened it with the safety chain still in place.

A man stood on the other side of the door. I couldn't see him, but I knew it was a man's voice when he said, "Mrs. Saunders, Mabel Lynn Saunders?"

"No," Mable-bitch lied, "There's nobody here by that name." She started to close the door again when the man shoved a book between the door and the frame.

"Mrs. Saunders," he said calmly. "We've met before. I know who you are."

"What the hell do you want?" She exclaimed.

"It has been two weeks since Stephen has been in school, Mrs. Saunders. I need to talk with you about this."

"Oh ... Ah," she lied again. "He's been staying with his grandma down at Thayer."

My so-called grandmother lived a few miles outside Thayer, Missouri, a tiny town on the Arkansas border.

"Is he in school down there?" the man asked.

"Oh, yeah—yeah, she has him in school," she continued to lie.

"Maybe we might call down there and ask about that." The man continued. "What is your mother's name and phone number?"

"Oh, she ain't got no phone." She told the truth that time.

"What is her name?" he asked.

"Ah … Milly, Milly Saunders." She lied again, at least on the first name.

"Well, then," the man continued. "Maybe we need to call the school district down there and ask if Milly Saunders has Stephen in school. What's the name of the school?"

"Thayer Elementary." She told the truth that time. There was only one school in the town, and the man could have looked it up without asking. "Yeah, go give them a call. They'll tell you he's fine."

The whole time this was going on, I stayed at the door of my room where the man couldn't see me. I knew if he came in, she would want me to hide somewhere or sneak out the back and down the fire escape. I did what she wanted when I was little rather than face the consequences.

"I'll give them a call," the man said, "but you need to understand that it is important to have your child in school if you want him to have any kind of a chance for a future. Kids without an education don't make it much further than Pruitt Igoe. You don't want your kid to end up like you, do you?"

"Nah, they got good schools down in the Ozarks," she returned. "They got safe schools down there. Besides, he likes staying with his grandma." That was the biggest lie she told all day.

The man left and didn't come back that day.

Mable-bitch had me out of school about as often as I was in, if for no other reason than sleeping off a drunk or a high. Still, I learned. I was smart, and I wanted to learn. I caught up quickly, and Miss Matte helped me with my homework. Even when I wasn't in school, I would take my books down to Miss Mattie's apartment, and she would help me with the lessons on the lesson plan. When I was little, I liked school, but it didn't take long for that to change. Kids soon began picking on me and calling me *sissy*, usually worse, because I walked like a girl, I played with the girls, at least the ones who would let me play with them, and I wore girl's clothes as often as I could get away with it. It might be no more than a stolen scarf that I tied around my neck, but it was enough to prompt the bullying. Sometimes, I would borrow clothes from some girl. Sometimes, I would steal things. Eventually, I started daring them to bully me because I dared to be myself. I had already developed a "fuck you" attitude when I was small, perhaps a tenacious side effect of growing up at Pruitt Igoe.

I learned to shoplift from my so-called mother. She rarely went anywhere without taking something that didn't belong to her. If she got caught, she used me as an excuse to talk them out of calling the cops. She would tell them that she was only stealing for me, and as a poor single mother, she had to be out of jail to take care of me. She would plead that she didn't have anybody to help take care of me. Sometimes, she would offer to pay and say she didn't realize she was walking out without paying. Sometimes, they bought it. Sometimes, the police were called anyway. More than once, child welfare was called in, and more than once, they threatened to take me out of the home, but they never did, not until there was no choice left for them.

Obviously, my so-called mother wasn't much of a mother. Miss Mattie was more of a mother to me, and even though I didn't know my father, Mike became kind of like a father to me, at least the closest thing I had to a father in those days. The first time he returned after I caught them together, she chewed him out for stiffing her on twenty bucks. I was playing in my bedroom when I heard him say, "I left you the damn twenty dollars!" Then, it must have dawned on him what I had done, and he started backtracking, "Well, hell. At least, I thought I left you a twenty. You mean it was a five? I could have sworn I pulled a twenty out of my wallet. Tell you what, baby. I'll make sure you get a fifty this time."

When I was little, I didn't know that horse and brown sugar meant heroin, but I learned quickly. She took him up on it, and the next thing I knew, I could hear them fucking in her room. I soon learned what they were doing, and Mike came around often enough—maybe every couple of weeks. There were plenty of other men in and out of our apartment, but Mike was the only one who came back consistently, and he was the only one who treated me decently or even paid any attention to me. The others could not have cared if I lived or died. That first time he came back when she jumped on him about the money, Mike came to my room after he had finished fucking her. Then he stood at the doorway, grinning at me.

"You little shit!" He grinned. "You took your Mom's twenty and left her the five."

I didn't say anything.

"Buddy, you know that ain't right," he said as he crossed the room to me. "Stiffing your mom for money ain't the right thing to do."

He picked me up again and hugged me. He may have come by to fuck Mable-bitch, or rig her up with dope, but he never hurt me, and he did nice things for me. Most of all, he hugged me. I loved it when Mike hugged me. He never did any of the horrible stuff Jake did to me, and I learned to appreciate him. I looked forward to those brief moments of affection from him. I would look forward to hugging him and feeling the bristle of his five o'clock shadow against my cheek. I looked forward to smelling the cologne on his neck. I looked forward to seeing Mike as though he were a rare piece of candy to be savored for as long as possible. He would usually leave me a little money, not more than a dollar or two, but he never left my so-called mother's money with me again. He made other arrangements.

When I was a little older, I told him I hid money from her because she would spend it all on dope, and we wouldn't have any groceries. After that, he started bringing a bag or two of groceries. Sometimes, he would even get into the kitchen and cook steak or shrimp for us. Those were the most elegant meals I could have imagined as a child. When Mike was around, I felt loved and pampered.

The first time he walked in with groceries, Mable-bitch asked, "What the hell are you doing?"

"You know you are awful skinny, Momma," He replied. "You might need to put a little weight on those bones, give me a little cushion for the pushin', and that kid of yours could also use an extra pound or two."

The more Mike came around, the more I looked forward to seeing him. I think I liked him more than my so-called mother did, but she definitely looked forward to seeing his money and the dope. I looked forward to Mike's groceries, hugs, and the treats he would bring almost every time he came: candy or a trinket toy. When I got older, I began to have feelings for him. Maybe it was because Jake messed with me that made me start having attractions early, but I was having sexual feelings, especially feelings for Mike, by the time I was nine or ten years old. I didn't want anything to do with Jake, but I started having fantasies about Mike. My fantasies ceased to be that he was the king in my magical kingdom and began to be about having him as my husband, living together in a beautiful house in a nice neighborhood as husband and wife, and having him come home from work to make love to me.

After I went to bed at night, I would imagine Mike doing with me what he did with my so-called mother: a moving hug that lasted a long time. That was my concept until I was old enough to understand male-to-female sexual intercourse. What Jake did was completely different from what Mike did with my so-called mother. I knew Mike would be gentle. I knew he wouldn't hurt me like Jake and Ronza. One day, when I was older, I tried to get with him.

When I was ten, Mike didn't pick me up to hug me anymore. He put his arm around my shoulder and pulled me to his side. Sometimes, he would lock me in a headlock and muss my hair, boy play, I guess. It didn't bother me. I relished any contact I could have with him. One day, when Mike came by my room to say goodbye, he put his arm around my shoulder and gave me a sideways hug. With my head under his arm, against his ribs, I reached down and started rubbing my palm across his crotch. It didn't take a second for him to say, "Whoa, buddy! What are you doing there?"

He immediately reached down and took my hand away from his crotch. "Stephen, what are you doing? Don't be doing stuff like that," he said.

"But I want you. I love you," I pleaded.

"What!" he exclaimed. "What the hell?"

Then he caught himself and stood back away from me for a moment. It wasn't as though he was repulsed, but more like he was shocked, not knowing how to respond. He was quiet for a moment, in deep thought. Then he shook his head.

"Oh man! … You're queer … Jesus! I should have known by the way you priss around so much. I … Jeez. I'm sorry, I didn't mean to give you the impression that I—I—Jeez, Stephen, What's up with this?"

He got down on one knee and held me back from him at arm's length with his huge hands over my shoulders. He looked like he was struggling with what to say. Then he said. "I love you too, kid. I do, and … I guess it's okay if you're queer, but you can't be doing stuff like that. You try that with the wrong dude, and you are going to get the shit beaten out of you or worse. That sort of thing repulses guys, and a lot of them—"

"But I only want you," I interjected.

"Jeez, you can't," he challenged. "I don't want to hurt your feelings, but you're a little boy. Even if I was queer, I—I couldn't be with you like that. It's not right for a grown man to do that with a little kid. You just don't do that, a grown man with any little kid? I mean, as much bullshit as I do, I couldn't do that."

I stood there wondering if I should tell him, wondering what he would do if I told him about Jake and Ronza. What would he do if he knew how they would force me to do stuff I didn't want to do? I didn't want him to know about that, partly because I thought he might not love me anymore. I thought he might judge or blame me and think I was bad because I let them do that to me. I hated them, but I hated myself too because I deduced that I had let it happen. I knew my so-called mother knew. She had to have known. She didn't give a shit. There is no way she couldn't have known what Jake was doing to me, but I also knew she would deny it. I knew that Jake had given her money, and I wondered if he had paid her so he could take me. I couldn't tell anybody. I was confused and angry about all of that. I knew I didn't want that, but I wanted Mike to love me.

Tears began to drift down my cheeks. "But I love you," I pleaded.

He reached over with his thumb and rubbed a tear from my cheek.

"I love you too," he said, "but that doesn't mean we can do what you want to do. Jeez, kid. That's not love. What I do with your mother is not love. That's just—" He sighed. "Love is something you feel for somebody in your heart, not in your—"

"You love me?"

"I do, kid … I do," he responded. "I love you, but I can't do that with you. You may not understand why that would be wrong right now, but that would be very, very wrong."

"More wrong than giving dope to her and doing it with her?" I questioned with sincerity while nodding toward my so-called mother's room.

He exhaled and looked down, "I deserved that … I know what I have been doing with your Mom is terrible, and I have already been thinking about stopping that, but yes, more wrong than that. I don't know if I can explain the difference between lust and love. I don't know that you are old enough even to understand. I truly do love you, but I don't lust for you. What I do with your Mom is lust. It's just physical, not love. You are different. When I hug you, that's love, and that's real. Even if I could desire you, you are too young for anyone to do that to you, and I would never want to hurt you."

"But I need you," I continued to plead.

"Stephen … it just isn't right," he replied. "I mean, I'm no saint, but having sex with little kids is totally off the list. That's a bridge I just won't cross, even if I did lust for you. You just don't do that crap. You don't hurt kids. It's at the top of the list for totally wrong things. No little kid should ever have to experience the confusion that something like that causes. No little kid should ever be deliberately hurt."

"Doesn't it hurt when you do that with her?" I asked. "Sometimes, you yell like it hurts."

"Oh, my God!" he exclaimed, slapping his hand to his forehead. "I've been such a jackass! Damn! What the hell? No, it's not like hurt. It's different, but shit, you shouldn't even know about that! I'm such an idiot!"

"I thought it was supposed to hurt," I quietly replied. "Doesn't it kind of hurt when everybody does it?"

Then he realized that my confusion was already there. "Stephen, has someone done something like that to you?"

I stared at him and said nothing.

"Have they?"

I was not about to answer his question. What would he do if I responded to that question? Would he judge me, blame me? I already felt like it was my fault. I felt like I should have done something to stop Jake and Ronza, even though I couldn't think of what that might have been. Would he try to kill them if he knew? Even though I wanted to kill them myself, I didn't want Mike to get in trouble. My silence and dejected look told him the truth I could not utter, and tears welled in his eyes. He said nothing but continued to look at me. His face filled with compassion.

He was about to say something when I asked him, "Do you love my mother?" I almost choked on having to remove the 'so-called' prefix.

Again, he sighed deeply. "No … actually … No, I don't, not really. What I do with your mom isn't anything like real love, and I know it's wrong. It is like the temptation of forbidden fruit, but it's just … It's a distraction from my usual boring life, from coming home and having a list of chores to do after a long day at work and nobody in the family considering what my day might have been like or what I might want or need. With your mom, there are no real demands on me. She's convenient for me. She never tells me she's not in the mood. She lets me do whatever I want as long as I drop a few bucks, but it's not love; it's an escape. It just … kind of meets my needs."

I knew Jake and Ronza didn't love me, and I damn sure didn't love them. So, I knew physical contact was not love. I just wanted more from Mike. I wanted more than a hug; I wanted some kind of bodily communion with him. I wanted the long and enduring naked hug that I thought he had been giving to Mable-bitch. I knew he wouldn't hurt me. I just wanted to experience more of him. I wanted to touch him, continue touching him, and have him touch me.

"But you love me?" I asked.

"Yes, I do love you," he said. "Despite all this shit you live in, all that I denied you had been going through, I think you're a good kid. I don't know how, but you are. I believe in you, Stephen. I like you. I like who you are, and I care about you."

He didn't know that I stole things. He didn't know about the screaming fights I had with Mable-bitch as soon as I thought I was big enough to start slapping her back. He didn't know when I stood over her bed with a butcher knife, watching her sleep and wanting to drive it through her heart. He didn't know about the stuff going on with Jake and Ronza. He might have started suspecting that day, but he didn't know for sure. He didn't know that I had tried to stop it. I might have gotten big enough to fight my so-called mother, but the first time I tried fighting Jake, he nearly strangled me to death. The memory still haunts me, seeing him over me while I was on the floor with his hands around my neck. He raged so hard that his slobber fell with drooling globs into my face and mouth, "LISTEN YOU LITTLE MOTHER FUCKER, YOU TRY THAT AGAIN AND YOU ARE NOT GOING TO FUCKING LIVE! YOU GODDAMN WORTHLESS LITTLE PIECE OF SHIT!"

When Jake brought me home that night, he told Mable-bitch that the red marks on my neck must be from some sort of rash. He didn't mention the knot on the back of my head where he had beaten my head into the floor, and she didn't ask. Nonetheless, I knew I would be big enough to beat him one day, and I had mentally registered that I would kill him when I was old enough.

"If you love me," I continued pleading. "Do with me what you do with her. Lay down with me. I want to feel as close to you as I possibly can."

"Jesus Christ!" He exclaimed. "Oh my God! I can't believe I'm having this discussion with a ten-year-old!"

He stood up and started to pace back and forth in my room. He paced for a while. Then, he turned back to me. "Stephen! Don't ever say that again! Don't ever say it to me, and don't ever say it to anybody else! Okay? … Jesus! It's not right, and I can't have people thinking things like that." The palm of his hand went to his forehead as he paced again. "Did I make you queer? Did I do something to make you queer? Oh, God, I hope I didn't do anything to lead you on!" He turned back to me. "I can't do that! I just can't, not even if you were a girl. You are still a little kid! I could never do that with a little kid! How do I get you to understand? Even if I had those kinds of feelings for you, it still wouldn't be right."

"But I am a girl." I affirmed, "When I grow up, will you do it with me then? When I'm an adult, will you make love to me?"

"Oh, Christ … no! Stephen, no! I can't be with you that way!"

"But you said you love me."

He stopped, wiped his hands over his face, and quietly pleaded. "Please don't tell anybody we had this discussion—Okay? Please—especially don't tell your mom or anybody else. People will get the wrong impression. If you tell anybody about this, they will think I'm a pervert, even if I didn't do anything. You say things like that, and people are gonna think I'm guilty of molesting you even though I didn't do anything!"

He walked back to me, bent over, and took my shoulders with both hands. "Please," He pleaded. "Can you promise never to repeat that to me or anyone else? I do love you, but I love you more like a father, like I love my kids."

"You have kids?" I asked.

His face turned red, crimson at the cheeks. Again, he sighed and turned his face away from me. "Yes … I have three kids. I'm married. I have a wife."

"Where are they?" I asked

He hesitated. He didn't want to tell me. I could see the misgiving on his face. Perhaps, for a moment, he thought about lying to me. His face went through a multitude of expressions as he decided what to say.

"I have a house in Ladue," he said, finally.

"Isn't that where the rich people live?" I asked.

"Some might say that," he said. "I don't consider myself rich, but some might say that."

"Why do you come all the way over here, out in the slums? Why would you want to have anything to do with my … mother?"

He sighed again. "Call it an addiction. Call it boredom. I'm not into drugs. I know better than to do that shit, but I also know better than to give it to your mom. I should know better than do half the shit I have been doing. I risk everything when I come over here. Call it forbidden fruit. It turns me on because it is something I'm not sup-posed to do, something I don't have to beg for, something I can't get at home. I guess I'm drawn to the excitement of it; maybe I like not having responsibilities for a while. I score a hit of dope for your Mom, or I give her money, and she—"

He stopped saying anything. He let go of my shoulders and stood up. "You know what?" He said as he turned away from me and threw his arms up. "Fuck this shit! Fuck what I have been doing, what I've been ignoring. Fuck my stupidity and my selfishness! Fuck it! I'm done! I should have been done a long time ago! I should never have started this shit!"

He turned around, "You shouldn't even know anything about any of this, and this is not a discussion I should be having with a little kid.

You should never have been exposed to what you have already been exposed to. I would never let my own kids see what I've let you see, and I know it's got to be worse when I'm not here. The look on your face tells me that it's worse when I'm not here. I don't know why I've done this. I guess it just feels like there are no rules or boundaries here, and I made the mistake of thinking it was okay—even for you. I've denied what this was doing to you. I wasn't raised this way. I know better, but there are so many rules and boundaries where I come from that I got tempted by the idea that there could be a place where rules don't apply. I didn't stop to think that there is a reason for some rules, and when certain rules don't apply, things get out of control, like rules about what happens to little kids."

He sighed, slapped his hand hard on his forehead, and said, "JESUS! I wouldn't talk to my kids the way I am talking to you. They have never seen this side of me. They have never seen the kind of life you live, the things you've seen, and the truth is, you deserve better. If I'm honest … if I'm really honest with myself … and I do care about you, I have to ask myself why I am letting this happen to you. Why am I letting myself participate in what has been happening to you? I have to ask myself why I'm not doing something to get you out of here. I've ignored you. For all the years I've been coming here, I've ignored what I was doing to you by having this thing with your mom. A hug on the way out or a few groceries doesn't cut it. That wasn't taking care of you. That was just another way of paying for what I wanted."

I stared at him with hollow confusion. I didn't know what to say. Some of the things he was saying didn't make sense to me. I watched as he made some kind of transition right before my eyes, as though he became a different person. I watched as shame consumed and overwhelmed him, a flock of vultures picking at his soul. I watched as he repented.

He stood there rubbing his face with his hand. Then, in a moment, he said, "You know what? Enough! Enough of this! It's not right, and I should be totally ashamed of myself for all of it! I know better than this! I—KNOW—BETTER! I would never allow my kids to go through a tenth of what you go through. I would never let them see anything like what you see every day. It's not fair! It's not fair to any child! It's not fair to you!"

He started pulling open the drawers of my dresser. "Pack up your clothes!" he commanded. "I'm taking you with me!" Then, he walked forcefully out of the room, and I heard him in the other bedroom, yelling, "Mabel, get up! Get up, we need to talk!"

She moaned. "Whaa … Leeeeave me alone."

"GET UP, DAMN IT!" he yelled. "GET THE FUCK UP!"

"I'm stoned," she slurred.

"I DON'T GIVE A FUCK!" he exclaimed. "Get the fuck up. We need to talk!"

I heard her whine, "Leave me the fuck alone!"

"NO, I'M NOT GOING TO LEAVE YOU ALONE!" he yelled.

I heard a scramble and a scuffle.

"What?" she yelled back, "Okay, WHAT! WHAT THE FUCK? WHAT?"

"YOUR KID DOES NOT NEED TO BE GROWING UP IN THIS BULLSHIT!" he raged. "He doesn't need to see even half of what you and I are doing, much less whatever the hell goes on when I'm not here!"

"What the fuck has gotten into you?" she yelled. "Go away!"

"What has gotten into me is that—I'M DONE!" Then, he went on. "I HAVE FINALLY COME TO MY FUCKING SENSES … FINALLY, AND MAYBE, JUST MAYBE, I'M FINDING MY MORALS AGAIN! You see—" He softened. "I have been coming around here for several years. I come in every few weeks, get my rocks off, and pretend I don't see anything that's happening around here. I pretend like what we are doing is okay, that what *you* are doing is okay, and I never stopped to think about what all this bullshit might be doing to Stephen. To do this, I had to pretend that none of this was having any effect on a little kid who deserves BETTER THAN THIS BULLSHIT!"

There was a pause in the discussion when I heard her laughingly mumble, "You've lost your fucking mind. Go home."

"No, Mabel," he said, calming his voice. "I think, instead, I am finding my fucking mind. I am remembering my morals, and I'm beginning to face how fucking selfish I have been to take advantage of you and your kid just because my life was boring, just because I got a thrill out of getting my rocks off with a whore. Hell, I don't know what I've been doing over the last few years. I don't know what this is, and I don't know how it has affected Stephen, but it has done something to him. I don't know what to call what we've been doing around here, but I know it's fucking wrong; it has affected Stephen, and it has got to stop!"

"Fine!" she needled. "Get out … I don't fucking need you! You ain't the only fuck I get, and you ain't my only hit of dope! You ain't nothing but a fuck and a hit of dope to me, anyway!"

"No," he replied calmly, "Unfortunately, you ain't nothing but a fuck and a hit of dope. There is absolutely nothing more to you than that. If you ever had a soul, heroin has taken it. You have sold your soul to the devil for a needle in your arm. You don't give a shit about anything but that damn needle and the dope in it! You damn sure don't give a shit about your own kid."

"Get the fuck out!" she screeched.

"No, not yet," he replied. "I want something first. I want something from you."

"What?" she gnashed sarcastically. "You wanna climb in my pussy again, just one more time?"

"No," he said. "I want Stephen."

"WHAT THE FUCK?" she yelled.

By this time, I had moved over by my bedroom door and stood slightly behind the door frame where she couldn't see me, but I could see the two of them.

"I want Stephen," he said again. "I will adopt him. I'll have an attorney draw up the papers. You sign over parental rights, and I'll take him to live with me. I'll make sure he is fed, properly educated, and treated like a little boy should be treated. I'll even fucking pay for him if you want. What do you want? Ten thousand dollars, twenty? Would that be enough to purchase your child?"

"Oh, now you're into little boys?" she laughed. "You got a queer side, queer for kids. Okay—okay. You want to take him now, and then, we can work out a deal."

Mike slapped her hard and yelled, "No, you stupid cunt! I don't have a queer side! I have a fatherly love for a little boy who has put up with way too much shit for way too fucking long, and the fact that you would be willing to whore him out is fucking pathetic! From the looks of him, you probably already have! I need to get him the fuck out of here!"

"Give me a fucking break!" she laughed again while rubbing her hand on the sting in her face. "You can't be fucking serious! What the hell are you gonna tell your pretty little *white* Ladue housewife? Hey, Honey … I brought this little high yellow, nigger kid home to raise 'cause I felt all sorry for him. Don't ask where I got him. Okay—okay—I got him from the bitch I have been fucking and doping up over at Pruitt-Igoe. I bought him on the … *slave* … market. You know, 'cause it ain't like you can pick up a little half nigger kid down at the dog pound, right?"

He drew back to slap her again but held himself and lowered his hand. "I'll figure something out," he responded quietly.

"What?" she taunted. "Are you gonna tell her you fucked some black woman and got her pregnant ten years ago, that she died or something, so you had to bring your biracial bastard kid home? How the hell do you think your prissy little *white rich-bitch* wife is gonna respond to that? My kid would be about as acceptable in your family and neighborhood as a fucking turd in a punchbowl!"

When she said that, I wondered, for the first time, if Mike might actually be my birth father. Maybe he had come around and been so good to me because he really was my dad. Perhaps he was trying to take me because he was my real dad.

"I know some people who can care for him until I can figure something out," he reasoned. "I'll figure something out."

Then he yelled over his shoulder, "Stephen, get your bags packed! You're going with me today."

"OH, FUCKING BULLSHIT!" my so-called mother screamed.

With that, she came up off the bed in a rage, hitting and clawing at him. Mike shoved her back. Then, she grabbed the neck of an empty vodka bottle on the window sill and broke it against the window facing. She began jabbing it at him, and he backed out of her room. She pointed the jagged edges at him, threatening him with repeated jabs as he cautiously backed into the living room.

He yelled again, "STEPHEN, GET YOUR CLOTHES!"

Mike glanced over his shoulder toward my room as I hid behind my door and watched. He backed toward my room while keeping an eye on Mable-bitch, exclaiming, "Stephen, go ahead and get a bag packed! I'm taking you out of this shithole!"

He grabbed his coat off the sofa and swung it at her, knocking the bottleneck out of her hand. When it flew across the room and shattered in the corner, he turned and walked toward me.

She was right behind him, grabbing at the back of his shirt, screaming, "YOU ARE NOT GETTING MY KID, YOU FUCKING BASTARD!"

He turned around and pushed her so hard she fell back onto the floor cutting her hand on shattered glass. Then, she got up and came at him, again with screaming rage, clawing at him, slinging blood onto him. He grabbed her and threw her down on the sofa. Then, he was on top of her, holding her down while she kept tearing at his shirt.

"YOU FUCKING SELFISH CUNT!" He yelled. "YOU DON'T DESERVE THIS CHILD!"

"GET OUT!" she screamed. "GET THE FUCK OUT OF MY HOUSE!"

"I'M NOT THROUGH WITH THIS, GODDAMN IT!" he shouted.

Then, I screamed with wretched terror. "STOP IT! STOP IT!"

When he heard me, Mike suddenly became calm. He caught himself, let go of her, and stood up. "Yeah," he said, turning around and wiping his hand across his mouth. "Yeah … ah … you're right. I should leave now. I shouldn't act like this, doing this kind of thing in front of a kid. I can't be letting you get to me like this." He had scratches across his neck where she had clawed at him.

He reached over and grabbed his sheepskin coat off the floor. "I'm sorry," he said. "I got a little carried away, there. Ah … yeah … I need to leave."

I had stood there watching all of this silently until I had become completely overwhelmed. It was not the first time I had seen my so-called mother get into a screaming fight with some man, but it was the first time I had seen her get into it with Mike. I didn't care about those other men, but I loved Mike. Still, I was too shocked to cry. I didn't want what I was seeing. I didn't want Mike to be upset, and I especially didn't want him to leave, but I could do nothing. So, I watched in silence.

Mike turned to me as I peeked from behind my door. "I'm sorry, Stephen," he said. "You have never seen me act like this. I'm sorry. I … Ah … I am going to figure something out, okay? I will. I will figure out how to get you out of here and get you a better life, okay?"

My heart ached for him. I wanted to run to him and throw my arms around him. I wanted to leave with him, but I knew my so-called mother would have gotten on me just like she had been on him, and it would only have gotten worse.

"GET THE FUCK OUT!" she screamed.

Mike turned and gave her a look of pure malice. He said nothing but looked at my so-called mother as if he could have killed her at that moment.

He turned back to me one last time and said, "I really do love you, Stephen—like a father loves his child. I'm sorry. I'm sorry for everything I've done. I'm sorry for everything that's happened to you. I will make it up to you. I will find a way. I promise."

He walked straight to the door, opened it, and left without saying anything else. At that moment, I knew I would probably never see him again. There was an emptiness that gripped me. Suddenly, my soul felt void, as vacuous as the deep recesses of space, as though a hole had been torn in my heart that nothing could ever fill. A numb grief invaded me, pushing away any semblance of happiness I had ever felt. After he left, I stood staring at the closed door for a long time, savoring the memory of his hugs, his smiles, and the sensation from the last time he touched me.

Mable sat on the couch nervously, giggling.

CHAPTER 3

THE OTHER SIDE OF HELL

Numb, hollow grief engulfed my soul, and I could not sleep. I felt like I had lost my best friend, but I still had one friend and needed comfort. The day after Mike left, I went up the hall to spend an afternoon with Miss Mattie. I loved her place. It was a sanctuary, solace, an eye in the hurricane of my life. She always kept everything neat and clean, and you would seldom see a roach, unlike our apartment, where roaches hurried frantically every time a light was turned on. Miss Mattie's apartment practically glistened with cleanliness and smelled of pine cleaners. The air felt fresh to breathe, unlike the stagnant dark halls of Pruitt Igoe or the rancid filth of our apartment. Just outside her door was squalor, but in Miss Mattie's home, there were little Dutch figurines, clean and polished with meticulous care, devoid of dust and cobwebs. Beautiful pictures were hanging on the walls, and although things might have shown the chip and wear of age, her home had charm and tranquility.

Miss Mattie had made popcorn, and we watched a Saturday afternoon movie on her dented, used black-and-white TV. I couldn't tell her what had happened, but she knew something was wrong.

Several times, she had looked over at me, an eyebrow raised, and said, "Child, you feeling awe right? You ain't lookin' right."

"I'm okay." I lied to her.

Most of my life had been torment and turmoil. I had learned to have a good poker face, but Miss Mattie could usually see through it. Yet, despite all the terrible things that Jake and Ronza had done to me, I had never told anyone. I easily kept that secret from everyone else and never let my tormented heart be exposed, but I had never experienced a broken heart before, not for love. When Mike walked out, my heart shattered like a bullet through crystal. I tried to put on a good face, but Miss Mattie saw through it.

"You sure you okay, baby?" She asked, "'Cause I ain't never seen you mopin' round like dis."

"I'm fine, Miss Mattie," I reassured, faking a smile. "I'm good. Let's watch the TV."

"Mmmm-hmmm." Miss Mattie paused and stared at me with a look that said she knew I was lying. Then, she let it go and went back to watching television.

Miss Mattie looked after me like nobody else. She was an old southern Creole woman from Louisiana, old enough to be my grand-mother. She was skinny and had terrible teeth, but she was constantly nagging at me to eat, and she would feed me, especially if she knew we didn't have any food at home. I knew she had moved to St. Louis from New Orleans, but I didn't know how she ended up at Pruitt Igoe. I was just thankful that she was there. She was the only person I could truly count on. I came to get her once when this guy was beating Mable-bitch, and she ran that asshole out of our apartment with her pistol. Miss Mattie told him, "You can get gone by de doe o' by a bullet, but either way, You is gonna get gone!" She was my only protector and always had my back. Yet, I didn't want to put any more on her than I absolutely had to. Plus, I didn't know how she might react if I told her what had happened with Mike. I had never really told her about Mike, only that Mable-bitch had a regular friend who was good to me.

After we watched the movie, Miss Mattie packed a couple of sand-wiches in a brown paper bag. She saw me to the door and gave me the sandwiches and a hug before sending me back down the hall. It must have been about six o'clock in the early evening when I finally headed home. I went back down the dark hall and noticed that the front door of our apartment was not shut all the way. Often, when I came home, I had to knock on the door, over and over, to get my so-called mother's attention because, even with my key, she would still have the safety chain latched. Sometimes, I had even sat in the hall waiting for her to wake up from a drug stupor, but on that day, the door was, strangely, cocked slightly open without the safety chain attached.

I slowly pushed the door open, feeling a nervous tingle under my skin. I called for her as I entered. "Mabel? Mabel?"

Something felt wrong, and my heart fluttered as I stepped over the threshold. The apartment was silent, and she did not respond. It was not unusual for her to be passed out, but I would usually hear something, some groan or snore, if not the incessant music from the clock radio she kept on the window sill behind her bed. The silence called the ticking clock to resonate in my ears, battery replaced, hanging back on the wall by her door, and it kept a constant haunting rhythm. *Click ... click ... click ... click ...*

As I walked through the living room, I tossed the sandwich bag onto the couch and noticed that the door to her room was also slightly open. Her door was usually only closed when she had a man in there, but I would have heard some mumbling or rumbling if a man had been with her. Instead, the odd silence lingered. As I neared her bedroom door, I noticed blood on the Asbestos tile floor and sensed the iron-like stench filling my nostrils. It had rolled into the living room from under her door. My heart began to pound as I neared the door. I tried to convince myself that some blood might not have been cleaned up from that fight with Mike the day before, but I knew better. This blood was too fresh and plentiful. It drifted across the floor like a slow red river. Large burgundy footprints led through it toward the kitchen and the fire escape.

When I came to her door, I had no choice but to step in the red mess or leave. My grungy tennis shoes displaced bits of hemorrhage, and when I nudged the door open, the scene shocked and terrified me. To this day, the image is burned into my mind as though it had been seared there by a branding iron. Despite all the times I had stood over her bed at night with a butcher knife in hand, fantasizing about stabbing her to death, I don't think I had ever imagined what an actual stabbing might look like. She lay there, half on and half off her mattress, her head lying on the floor and her eyes staring into blank space. This time, I knew she was neither sleeping nor passed out. This time, I knew she was gone. Blood splatters surrounded her and pooled on the floor from stab wounds in her neck and chest. Her body was full of wounds, and her face had become ghoulishly pale with every drop of blood drained.

I stood, frozen in time, looking at this with no thought, just an image that would forever burn into my consciousness. As much as I had wished her dead for years, as much as I had wanted to kill her myself, I could not have imagined what impact that moment would have on me. It felt like my breath stopped, but I must have been breathing, for the smell of blood became revulsion in my nostrils. I felt nauseated, but I didn't move. I just stood there, seeing that moment as though it were a photograph, a snapshot in time taken by the camera of my mind. The room was silent, but I heard the ticking of the living room clock. Even as the clock ticked, one second into the next, it felt like time stood still.

I don't know how long I stood there. Finally, I turned slowly, silently back toward the front door. Part of me wanted to run, screaming and horrified, but shock took precedence over terror. I knew I had to tell someone. I knew I had to get help, and the only person I knew to tell was Miss Mattie. I walked zombie-like down the hall from our apartment to hers in the darkness of the Pruitt Igoe, where the lights seldom worked or had been knocked out by vandals. I could hear the vexatious thud of boom boxes, the buzzing clatter of televisions, and human babble rattling in my ears, suddenly noticeable and clear after having ignored it during all my years in that hell. I walked quietly and slowly, smelling the caustic stench of poverty and filth that had been my home. Every breath contained the lingering smell of blood mixed with feculence. My nausea begged attention, but I swallowed hard, held the contents of my stomach, and walked.

That felt like the longest walk of my life. So many times, I had taken it before when it seemed like seconds that I sprinted up the hall with a grin on my face, looking forward to the simple joy of seeing Miss Mattie open her door to me.

When, at last, I reached Miss Mattie's apartment, I knocked almost too quietly to be heard. Inside, I could hear the sound of her TV and the sounds of the evening news. She did not respond, and I knocked again.

The TV sound quieted, and Miss Mattie came to the door. She opened it with the safety latch in place and said, "Who's out, dere?"

"It's me," I replied, saying nothing more.

She opened the door, looked at me, and exclaimed, "Lord, child. What's de matter?"

"You have to come," I said quietly.

"Honey, what in de world is goin' on?" she pleaded. "Ya look pitifully awful."

"Come, please," I replied softly with a rasp.

"Let me get my key," she said as she disappeared inside her apartment. I heard the TV shut off. Then, she returned and bent over to lock her door.

"Baby, you awe right?" she continued. Then she looked me up and down. "Baby, what's dat on yo shoes?"

I said nothing. I knew she would follow me. I turned down the hall back toward our apartment.

"Do I need my gun?" she asked.

I said softly, "Just come."

When we got to our apartment, I walked through the open door and straight toward my so-called mother's bedroom.

Behind me, I heard Miss Mattie scream, "OH, LORD JESUS! GOD OF MERCY!"

She grabbed me from behind, turned me around, hugged my face to her bosom, and began to cry, "Oh, Lord of mercy! You should never be seein' notin' like dat! Notin' like dat, my poor baby!"

She then hurried me back across the living room. "Come on!" she commanded. "Don't touch nothin'. You didn't touch nothin', did ya?"

Miss Mattie half pushed and half dragged me through our apartment door into the hall. "Come on. You gonna stay wid me!" she exclaimed.

We went hurridly back through the hall, where she fumbled nervously with the key to her apartment, shaking as though a frigid wind had been blowing against her. When she managed to unlock the door, she pushed me into her apartment and commanded, "Sit down, child." She pointed to the sofa.

I did as I was told and sat on the edge of the sofa, staring, disconnected, numb, watching the lamp light glow off her Dutch figurines.

Miss Mattie locked the door and went to her phone on the wall near her kitchen. She grabbed the phone book and turned to the front page where emergency numbers were printed. Then, she began to dial that old black rotary phone, with each dial popping restlessly back to the original position. She stood restlessly, mumbling, "Come on, come on, come on."

Then she said, "Yeah, yeah! Dis Mattie Laroquette over at Pruitt-Igoe. I need to repoat a murder."

Various electronic gibberish filtered through the receiver. She said, "No! No, I didn't commit no murder. Dis woman I knows was murdered in her apoatment. I needs fo de po-leece ta come right away."

The conversation went on for a minute or two. I knew Miss Mattie was answering questions, but I didn't pay much attention. I stared at a knickknack on her coffee table, suddenly made fascinating by the need to feel numb. I had seen it before, but the little Dutch girl figurine seemed to be the most fascinating thing in the world, and I couldn't stop looking at it. In dull silence, I glared at the blue and white ceramic that glistened in the pale light.

After she got off the phone, Miss Mattie came to sit by me on the sofa. She hugged and kissed me on the cheek and exclaimed, "Oh Lordy baby. Oh Lordy, no child should ever be put through anything like dat."

"What do we do now?" I asked softly, still staring at the Dutch girl figurine over the squeeze of her arms.

"Now we wait fo de po-leece ta come." She replied without loosening her hug on me.

As we waited, she periodically got up and fidgeted around the apartment. Then she would come back to sit next to me, pat my hand, rub my hair, or hug me. I kept my gaze on the figurine.

After what seemed like a grueling expanse of time, there was a knock at Miss Mattie's door.

She went to the door and called, "Who's dere?"

"Detective Charles Brighton, St. Louis Police," the voice responded from the other side.

Miss Mattie opened the door without keeping the safety chain latched, and exclaimed, "Come in, detective. Please, come in."

A somewhat chubby white man in a brown suit came through the door. He appeared to be in his mid-forties and was as clean-shaven as I had ever seen a man. His face looked like he had cut down into the rose-colored splotches that peppered his cheeks. His hair was a pale brown with infiltrating streaks of gray, and he had a pair of wire-rimmed reading glasses over his nose. He carried a notebook in a metal case. Behind him was another man, also dressed in a suit, a black one. He was taller and a little thinner than the first man. Behind him, I could see uniformed police officers standing in the hall.

"And you are Mattie Laroquette?" he asked.

"Yes, sir," she replied.

"We understand there has been a possible homicide," he said as he entered the room.

"Yes, yes," she said. "I don't know what you need to do here, but I need somebody to stay wid dis baby whilst I go show you de scene."

"Is there anything we need to be concerned about?" Detective Brighton asked. "Anyone in the apartment, any weapons or animals?"

"No, Sir," Miss Mattie replied.

The man in the brown suit motioned to one of the uniformed officers waiting in the hall. That officer entered the room to stay with me while Miss Mattie led the others to our apartment. His excessive friendliness repulsed me.

"Hey, buddy," he grinned like the outer edges of his lips were tacked to his ears. "How are you doing?"

I stared at him momentarily and went back to staring at the figurine. Words felt like too much work, as though speaking a congenial reply would have taken more strength than I had. Besides, I did not feel the least bit affable and never liked being called "buddy."

When, after several tries, he couldn't get a response out of me, he just sat there while I continued to stare at the ceramic Dutch girl. I don't know where my mind was. I don't know what I was thinking. Maybe I wasn't thinking anything at all. A mental void would have been preferable. The image of my so-called mother dangling off the edge of the bed amid the splatters of drying burgundy pools kept rushing back into my head. The smell of her blood seemed stuck in my nostrils as though still drifting across the floor. I looked down to see it crusting around the edge of my shoes. Maybe I was staring at that little Dutch girl to block the image. It didn't work.

Then, the guilt began. I had often wished her dead and wanted so intensely to kill her that maybe I had somehow manifested it. Perhaps I had gone down there in a daze while Miss Mattie was still watching the movie and stabbed her to death without remembering that I had done it. I stared away from the Dutch girl and looked at my clothes. There was no blood on them, only blood around the edge of my shoes where I had tracked remnants of flesh up the hall. I turned toward the door and looked for evidence of crimson footprints. I must have stopped making tracks by the time I got to Miss Mattie's apartment. Blood was on my shoes, but nowhere else. Did that mean that I didn't stab her? Still, there was the nagging thought that I had wished it into existence. I felt tears beckoning, but I battled them back behind my eyes. I felt myself trembling inside, as though every cell in my body was vibrating. As much as I had hated her, my so-called mother had been my consistent companion. *She wasn't all bad,* I thought. *Sometimes, she could be nice, I guess.*

It seemed to take forever for the cops and Miss Mattie to return. I sat there feeling light-headed, having forgotten that it had already been about six o'clock when I went home. I somehow had not realized that night was falling. The clocks in Miss Mattie's apartment were the only things to break the silence except for the occasional sounds of voices in the hall. I imagined the residents of our slum stretching their necks around doors or over the heads of others to get some curious, morbid information about what must have happened.

Miss Mattie had several clocks, and one of them was a kuku. They ticked, almost together but not quite, and each one made a slightly different sound. I was startled when the kuku announced the hour, even though I had heard it chime hundreds of times before. Through the window of Miss Mattie's place, I could see police lights faintly flashing against the night sky. The bored cop picked up magazines and old newspapers and pretended to be interested. He thumbed through them between glances of an authoritarian eye on me. Finally, we heard a click of the door, and Miss Mattie came in with Detective Brighton.

"I think he gots a grandma somewhere down in Southern Missouri," she said as she entered the room. "But I can keeps him till arrangements be made. I wouldn't mind keepin' him fo my own, far as dat go. He really ain't never had much other dan me anyway."

She rarely referred to me as "her" in the company of others, but when we were alone, she honored my wish to be referred to with female pronouns. Miss Mattie was the only person who recognized me for who I was. She was the only one who called me Stephanie and referred to me as "she" and "her," but when talking to that man, she acted like I was a boy. She knew he wouldn't understand.

"We have already radioed to have someone from family protective services come pick him up," the detective replied. "We will try to locate his family in the morning. In the meantime, although I'm satisfied with your answers during our interview, you remain a person of interest in this case. You are not to leave the city or engage in any activities outside your normal routine. We will continue to be in touch with you about this. We are likely to have further questions as the investigation progresses.

"Yes, Sir," Miss Mattie responded. "You wants me ta go down and gather up a few of his things fo de protective services person?"

"No," he replied. "No one is to go in or near that apartment while the investigation is going on, and I will have a guard posted there until we are satisfied with the evidence we've gathered. I'm sure child protective services will have some clothes he can wear."

The door stood open behind him, and one of the officers approached the door. "Hey, Charlie," the cop said. "You might want to take a look at this."

The cop had a plastic bag, and he was wearing rubber gloves. He reached into the bag and pulled up a jacket and a shirt, both with blood on them. I immediately recognized the coat. It was Mike's sheepskin leather jacket.

"Hey!" I yelled as I ran for the door. "That's Mike's coat! Where did you find Mike's coat? Is he okay? Did they kill Mike, too?"

The man in the brown suit grabbed me and held me back.

"NO!" I screamed. "DID THEY HURT MIKE? THOSE FUCK-ING BASTARDS BETTER NOT HAVE HURT MIKE! NO! NO! NO!" Tears rolled over my cheeks and dripped into my mouth.

It was one thing to see my so-called mother lying in blood splatter. Although the sight had completely abhorred me, part of me didn't care that she died, but I couldn't deal with the idea that someone might have hurt Mike.

"Baby, calm down," Miss Mattie implored. "Please, child, come here."

She reached out a tender hand to touch my face. Detective Brighton held me, but she urged him, "Here, let me have him. I'll make sure he don't cause no trouble."

She pulled me gently toward her, and I sobbed into her arms. "Miss Mattie, they hurt Mike! They killed him, too!" I didn't remember, at that moment, that Miss Mattie had no idea who Mike was because I had never told her his name. Although I loved and trusted her, many things that went on in Mable's apartment, I deliberately kept from her.

Miss Mattie gently tugged me toward the sofa and sat down, holding me while she cooed, "I'm sorry, baby. I'm so sorry."

Behind us, I heard Detective Brighton ask, "Where did you find that?"

The cop replied, "It was thrown into a dumpster behind the building. It looks like there is blood on the inside of the coat, like maybe the suspect put it on to cover the blood on the shirt. The shirt has quite a bit of blood on it."

"Tag it and file it as evidence," Detective Brighton ordered. Then he approached the sofa where I was still sobbing in Miss Mattie's arms.

He kneeled beside the sofa and said, "Stephen, can you tell me who this Mike fellow is?"

"Did they kill him?" I asked without raising my head from Miss Mattie's bosom.

"I don't know," Detective Brighton replied. "If he is in danger, it might be important for us to find him. Can you tell me who he is?"

"He used to come and see my mother," I replied.

"How long had he been coming to see your mother?" The detective asked.

"Maybe a couple of years," I replied.

"Were they close?" the detective asked, "boyfriend—girlfriend?"

"No," I responded. "He just paid her to let him fuck her, but he was my friend."

"He was your friend?" The detective parroted.

"Yes!" I growled as I raised my head and glared at him. "Out of all these no-account mother fuckers who were in and out of our apartment, he is the only one who was ever nice to me. Not even my so-called mother was nice to me. I'm glad the fucking bitch is dead!"

"You wanted your mother dead?" the detective asked.

Miss Mattie interjected, "This child was with me all afternoon, sittin' here watchin' a movie. Don't go thinkin' he had somthin' to do wid dis."

"Mattie," the detective responded. "Right now, I don't know what to think or who to believe, and it is my job to try to find out as much as I can to start putting a case together. Right now, as far as I am concerned, anyone could be a suspect."

The detective turned his attention back to me. "Stephen, you said Mike used to come see your mother. So, he stopped coming to see her?"

"I guess so."

"When did he stop coming to see her?" the detective pressed.

"Yesterday," I responded.

"Why did he stop coming to see her yesterday?" the detective continued.

"Because they had a big fight over how she treated me, and Mike said he would take me away from her." I felt the tears welling up again. My voice trembled. "I wish he had."

"What happened during that fight?" the detective continued.

"They just got mad at each other, and Mike walked out," I replied.

"How bad did the fight get?" he pressured.

I was starting to feel suspicious and distrustful, "I don't know," I lied.

"Well, were they yelling at each other?" the detective interrogated. "Did it get physical? Were they violent? Did he hit her?"

"You ask too many questions!" I yelped and buried my head back into Miss Mattie's chest.

The detective sat in the chair next to Mis Mattie's sofa. He paused for a long while, glaring at us, deep in thought. Then he asked her. "Did you know this man?"

"No," Miss Mattie replied. "I never met de man. Never knowed nuttin' bout him till jes now, cept Stephen tole me she had a regular visiter. Lord, she had men in and out o' dat place all de time. Some of dem roughed her up, but far as I know, dis Mike fella never caused no problem, least not none I was told about."

"Men in and out?" The detective pressed.

"I hate ta say anythin' bad bout her." Miss Mattie started to reply.

"SHE WAS A FUCKING WHORE!" I screamed. "My so-called mother was a fucking junkie whore! She would have fucked a dog if she thought it would get her a shot of dope!"

"Stephanie!" Miss Mattie scolded and caught herself. "Ah … Stephen … you don't need to be talkin' like dat, specially 'bout yo Momma."

Detective Brighton sat watching the dynamics of communication between us. He didn't say anything if he noticed that she had called me Stephanie. "Stephen?" he questioned softly.

"What? What the fuck!" I exclaimed. "Leave me the fuck alone!"

"I'm just trying to figure things out, okay?" he said gently. "May I ask you some more questions?

"You will anyway!" I snapped.

He sighed softly before asking, "Do you know Mike's last name?"

"Foster, maybe," I replied.

"Was he a black man?"

"No, Mike is white."

"Do you know where he lived?" the detective pressed.

"He said he lives in Ladue."

Brighton's eyes popped wide when I said that. The expression of shock and surprise was unmistakable. Then he caught himself, returned to his poker face, and continued. "How long have you known Mike?" he pestered as he jotted notes into his folder.

"I've known him a few years, maybe since I was six," I replied. "He was always nice to me."

"How old are you now?" he asked.

"Ten."

"So, four years. How often did you see Mike?" he continued.

"He would come around every couple of weeks. Sometimes, we wouldn't see him for a month or so, but usually once or twice a month."

"Did he do more than just spend time with your mother?" the detective pressed. "Did he also spend time with you, do things with you?"

"Usually, he would just spend time with my so-called mother, but he never left me out. Mike was good to me. He brought food. He never left without coming to see me and never left without hugging me." Imprisoned tears began to rattle the bars of my eyelids, and I buried my face back into Miss Mattie's bosom.

The detective questioned Miss Mattie, "And you say no one knows who Stephen's father is?"

"Not far as I knows," Miss Mattie replied. "You thinkin' dis Mike fella might be Stephen's daddy o' somethin'?"

"Seems odd that he would be the only one of all the men to take up with the boy like that," Detective Brighton replied.

He turned back to me.

"Stephen, is there anything more you can tell me about Mike?"

"I was in love with him," I replied.

"You … you … were *in love* with him?" Brighton pondered with bewilderment. For a moment, it was as though he was hesitant even to ask the next question. Maybe he wanted to avoid the question entirely. Finally, he went there. "Did he spend time with you the same way he did with your mother?"

"NO!" I yelled. I stared at him for a moment, then continued. "I wanted him to, but he wouldn't. He said he couldn't because I'm a little kid, and no grown man should ever be with a little kid that way. My fucking so-called mother's so-called dipshit friends didn't seem to mind! They did shit to me all the time, and she fucking knew about it! They paid her for it!"

Miss Mattie's shock was vocally evident when I said that. A quick chirp came out of her. Then, she started to say something but held back.

"Your mother had friends who did things to you," he asked. "Did Mike know about that?"

"No," I replied. "I never told him. I couldn't tell him."

"So, this didn't have anything to do with why he wanted to take you away?" he asked.

"No," I responded. "He loved me, but he never knew about that. Maybe he suspected it, but he only knew about stuff she did to me, and that's what the fight was about. He said I deserved better than growing up in Pruitt Igoe with a drug whore mother. He said he loved me, but like a father loves his child. He said he wanted to adopt me and take me out of here, but he didn't love me the way I wanted him to."

Detective Brighton let out a very long, deep sigh.

"Did your mother know you felt this way about Mike?" he asked.

"NO!" I ripped back at him. "Do you think I would fucking tell that cunt something like that! She would have ripped my fucking head off! I never told her! I never told anybody that I felt that way except Mike. Mike never knew till yesterday. He told me he couldn't be with me that way and needed to get me out of there. Then, they got into a fight after I told him how I felt. The truth is, my so-called mother didn't give a shit about him or me. She just wanted her fucking dope. If he had wanted to do things to me, she would have cared less as long as she got money or dope. She whored me the same as she whored herself. She would have let him do whatever he wanted if he paid her. She let men do things to me before, but Mike never did anything. He didn't want to do those kinds of things to me. He would never hurt me on purpose. The only way he ever hurt me was when he left yesterday, but he said he was going to come back for me."

"Baby," Miss Mattie interjected with shock, "I never knew nuttin' bout mens doin' things to you like dat. I never knew. I'm so sorry, baby. I would have done somethin'. I would have tried to stop dat." She trembled and wiped tears off her face.

"Did you tell Mike about the other men hurting you?" Detective Brighton went on.

"No! I told you, no! I couldn't tell him. I would never want him to think—" I fell silent and dropped my head.

"Would Mike have hurt your mother?" the detective asked.

I glared at him in silence. "I don't want to talk anymore." I felt annoyed with the detective and guilty that I had hurt Miss Mattie with what I had revealed.

Detective Brighton waited a moment, "Do you think Mike could have been angry enough to kill your mother?"

"I told you! I'm not talking anymore!" I hissed back at him. "You find out if Mike is okay! I need to know that Mike is okay! He wouldn't kill anybody! Mike would never kill anybody!"

Miss Mattie leaned back and sighed. "I could use a glass o' tea. Would you like a glass o' tea, Detective Brighton?"

"No, thank you," Detective Brighton replied. "I have a lot more questions to ask, but it's late, and I'm sure everyone is tired. We have a lot of work to do, and some of it will just have to wait. "Would you mind coming to headquarters tomorrow to answer a few more questions?"

"Sho, detective," Miss Mattie replied, "Just let me know what time."

"I will call you tomorrow and let you know what time to come in." He endorsed.

Detective Brighton turned to a cop who was standing by the door. "Carson," he commanded. "Has Family Services gotten here yet?"

The cop turned and stuck his head out the door. He briefly interacted with another cop in the hall, then turned and said, "Yes, Sir. They have been waiting for you to finish your questioning."

"Send them in," Detective Brighton ordered.

The cop opened the door, and a pudgy, auburn-haired white woman with a round face and pert lips came in. She was also holding a folder. A large, dark-headed man with a football player type of build came behind her wearing jeans and a pale blue button-down collar shirt.

"I'm Doris Mansfield," the woman announced, "from the Missouri Department of Family Services."

"Yes," Detective Brighton responded. "This is the child we called you about."

"What the fuck are you talking about?" I yelled.

"Family services will take you into foster care until we can locate your grandmother." The detective responded.

"NO!" I screamed. "I didn't fucking do anything wrong! You can't put me in jail! I didn't do anything!"

"No-no-no," The detective attempted to comfort. "No one is going to put you in jail. This is about getting you into a temporary home until we can find a family to care for you."

"I'm not going to my so-called fucking grandmother!" I howled. "She's worse than my Goddamn, bitch whore mother! She is a mean old cunt, who lives in a trailer that's nastier than Pruitt Igoe, and I won't live with her! I'll stay here with Miss Mattie."

"Well, unfortunately, Mattie is not next of kin," The detective tried to explain, then glanced at Miss Mattie, "and you are not a foster parent either. Is that correct, Mattie?"

"No, sir. I means yes sir, dat is correct," Miss Mattie replied. "I jest love dis child."

"Then, son." Detective Brighton turned back to me, "You have to go with family services."

"NO!" I screamed. "I'M NOT FUCKING GOING WITH THEM! I'M GOING TO STAY WITH MISS MATTIE!"

I jumped off the sofa and ran into Miss Mattie's kitchen at the back of the apartment. Behind me, I heard Miss Mattie plead, "Please, sir. Let me talk ta her—um—him."

The next thing I knew, she came sauntering into the kitchen behind me as I was frantically trying to open the window to the fire escape. I would have been out the back and down the fire escape if she had not installed safety latches.

She first said, "Baby, I knows you scared."

I turned from my efforts and looked at her, tearfully pleading, "I don't want to go with them. I don't know them. I don't have anybody but you."

"I know, sugar." She softly continued. "I know dis be harder dan anything you has ever had ta do, and de Lord knows you has been through hell."

I stood there looking at her with begging eyes.

"Baby, don't cause no scene now. Don't give dese good people no trouble. De only want ta help you."

"But what about you, Miss Mattie," I cried. "They are gonna take me away from you. I'll never see you again. What if the killer comes back and kills you, too?"

"Oh, sugar," she continued. "I'm sure we are gonna see each other again. Can't nobody break apart love dats real."

She walked over to the backside of her kitchen and put a comforting arm across my shoulders.

"Ya knows I loves ya, baby," she went on. "Ole Miss Mattie ain't gonna go nowhere. Gonna be here fo you till de day she dies."

"How do you know?" I sobbed. "It's like I'm losing everything all at once. I'm losing everybody. My so-called mother wasn't much, but at least she was there part of the time. Mike is gone. I'll probably never see him again if he isn't dead, too, and now they are taking me away from you."

"Baby, ya ain't losin' me," she soothed. "Lord brought us together, Lord gonna find a way to keep us together. Ya watch."

"I want to stay with you now." I implored.

"I know, and I wants you to, but we gotta do what de law says, and de law says, right now, ya gotta go wid dese peoples."

"What are they going to do with me?" I searched.

"Sugaa, I don't know," she truthfully replied. "But it has got to be safer dan dis place. It has got to be safer dan livin' down dare wij yo momma. It may not be de same. It might be really different, but at least we know it won't be Pruitt Igoe."

I looked at her, my expression pleading for a different answer.

"Come on," she implored. "Let's go talk to dese nice folks."

I stood for a moment, silently pleading. Then, she took my hand and led me back to her living room. The round-faced woman and the big football guy were still standing by the door. Detective Brighton had sat down in a chair by Miss Mattie's coffee table.

Miss Mattie led me through the living room to the family services woman. "Ya take good care o' dis child, now," she said. "I loves him mo den my own kin."

"Do you mind if we ask you a few questions first," the family service woman inquired.

"Sho," Miss Mattie responded.

"May we sit down?" Mrs. Mansfield requested.

"Sho," Miss Mattie replied as she motioned them toward the sofa.

When they sat, Mrs. Mansfieled opened her folder and proceeded to make sure she had as much correct information as possible.

"Can you tell me the child's full name?"

"Stephen Christopher Saunders."

"Date of birth?"

"January 11th, 1960."

"Mother's full name?"

"Mabel Lynn Saunders."

"Maiden name?"

"Saunders. Ta my knowledge, she wasn't never married."

"Any knowledge of where his father is or any next of kin?"

"He ain't never knowed his daddy, an' only next o' kin I know bout is his grandma down on the south end of Missouri somewhere."

"Does the child have a teddy bear or any special toy he would prefer to take with him?"

"Ask de child."

Mrs. Mansfield asked me, "Stephen, do you have any special toy or something you would like to take with you?"

I looked at Miss Mattie, hoping she would give me an answer. I didn't have anything unless it might have been one of the broken dolls left back in the apartment, and I didn't want any of those, even if they would have let me dig them out of hiding.

Suddenly, Miss Mattie said, "Ya know, deres dat lil pilla' dat you likes so much, dat lil decoration pilla dats on my bed. Ya member you was admirin' dat? Would you like ta have dat?"

I nodded, not remembering what she was talking about.

Miss Mattie hopped up and went trotting to her bedroom. She returned with a little black and white pillow embordered with the silhouettes of a gentleman and lady from Victorian times. They faced each other in the black outline on a white background with black and white lace sewn around the outer edge. She handed it to me. I accepted and pulled it to my chest.

I had commented, one time, that I thought the pillow was pretty, but I had never thought much about it after that. However, just knowing that she was giving me something of her own meant more than anything else had ever meant. I hugged it, knowing it might be the only thing that could remotely substitute for a hug from Miss Mattie.

"I embordered dat pillow years ago befoe I ever left Na Olens," Miss Mattie interjected. "I'll tell ya bout dat, someday."

I held the pillow to my chest. Just knowing that it came from her, that she was sending a little piece of herself to comfort me, meant everything.

The family service woman asked a few more questions, and then I quietly went with them, doing as Miss Mattie had implored.

Before I left, Miss Mattie gave me a big hug and a kiss on the cheek. She said, "Now, I know you gonna has some challenges. I know dis ain't gonna be easy, but you listen ta me. You be good. You do yo best ta follow da rules and do as you told. You try to keep dat temper reeled in, and try ta be nice ta deze peoples. Dey tryin' ta help you. Now, you gonna do you best to behave yo self?"

"Yes, Ma'am," I courteously replied.

She hugged me again and said, "I know dat ya will, and ya knows dat I'm gonna love ya, always, no matta what."

Tears streamed down my cheeks, and I hugged her as tightly as I could for as long as I could before I finally had to let go. Then, I turned to wave goodbye and see my last image of Miss Mattie, her face wet with tears grieving as I was grieving. She forced a smile and waved to me.

Guided by one of the cops with a flashlight, I walked between Mrs. Mansfield and her hefty bodyguard down the access stairs at the end of the hall. The lights on the stairs, as usual, were out. In respect for Miss Mattie, I resisted the urge to dart away and seclude in one of my hiding places on the grounds. When we got to their car, the bodyguard guy sat in the back with me while Mrs. Mansfield drove.

CHAPTER 4

THE SLATE WIPED CLEAN

It was well past midnight. I had sat for the entire trip with Miss Mattie's pillow hugged close to my chest. Then, the car pulled into a circular drive in front of a red brick house with white columns that were two stories high. I didn't know, at the time, that it was Greek Revival architecture, but it was the fanciest thing I had ever seen outside of a magazine or a TV show. I had no idea what architecture was, much less Greek Revival. Apparently, the family at this home had been called regarding fostering me during my crisis.

Lights were shining down from the top edge of the porch onto the red brick façade, and the white columns had light reflecting on them from the bottom and top. The sidewalk was lit like runway lights at an airport. There was never that much light around Pruitt Igoe. We were lucky if the street lights worked, much less any of the building lights. When we pulled into the driveway that circled in front of the house, a woman with bleach-blond, permed hair descended the porch steps and pranced down the sidewalk dressed like she was going out to some special event. She had a string of pearls around her neck and what I thought to be gaudy jeweled rings on her fingers. She must have been in her mid-thirties. She was slender, like a fashion model, and came down that sidewalk like she was about to meet some foreign dignitary. It was a surreal transition from stepping in my so-called mother's blood early that evening to stepping out of a car at a St. Louis version of a Greek temple. I learned later that the house was in Ladue, in the same neighborhood where Mike lived. The irony of that later baffled me.

The blond woman opened the car's back door with a gigantic smile, "This must be the child," she practically swooned. "What is your name, sweetheart?"

"Stephanie," I replied.

That grin quickly moved from congeniality to smirking confusion. "Stephanie?" she queried. "Why, that's a girl's name. You are surely not a young lady dressed as a boy."

Mrs. Mansfield intervened. "This is Stephen Christopher Saunders," she explained. "I don't know why he called himself Stephanie."

"Yes, hmmmm," the blond woman went on. "You had me confused there for a moment."

Mrs. Mansfield got out of the driver's seat and came around to my side of the car. "Stephen, this is Gertrude McNeil. She is a state-approved foster parent, and this will be your home, at least for a little while."

"Looks like something out of a movie," I commented as I scooted out of the seat and stood before the blond woman. I noticed that her tits, neatly packed into and held up by a bra, met me at eye level, but the round collar of her dress, draped neatly around her neck, covered any evidence of cleavage.

The bodyguard guy scooted across the seat and out of the car on the same side behind me. Then, he stood there and never said anything. It seemed he was just there to ensure I didn't hurt anyone or run away.

"Well," the blond-headed woman commented, "We are quite proud of our modest home." She appeared to have a well-rehearsed, fastidious gleam about her as though every word she spoke had been neatly scrubbed and handed out like clean dishes from a shelf.

I didn't know what she meant by "modest," but looking back, the home was anything but modest, especially by any of the standards I had ever encountered.

"May we go inside?" Mrs. Mansfield implored. "I have a few things I need to brief you about."

"Certainly," Gertrude McNeil responded. "It is a bit chilly out here, and me without my sweater. Yes, follow me."

She pranced up the sidewalk like a debutant at her own personal ball. She glided up the steps onto the flat brick porch as if she had been trained for a show, high heels precisely matching the width of each step. Then she opened and held the white door. We walked single file into the house with Mrs. Mansfield leading. I was in the middle, and the bodyguard followed behind me. When I reached the door, Mrs. McNeil noticed my blood-stained shoes. "Sweetheart, do you mind removing those shoes and leaving them on the porch before coming into the house?" she asked. "I will get you a better pair that you can keep."

I had forgotten about trekking around in blood. When I looked down, my shoes were disgusting. The blood had dried around the edges of the crappy thrift store tennis shoes. I didn't blame her for not wanting me to wear them in her house. I didn't want them on my feet, either. As I pried them off my feet, toe to heel, my mind snapped back to my so-called mother's blood drifting across the floor. There was a moment of nausea. I closed and blinked, trying to blink that memory out of my mind and the nausea out of my stomach. When I had removed my shoes, Mrs. McNeil also motioned for me to remove my socks, as well, and go into the house in my bare feet. The football guy followed, but no one else had to remove their shoes. I don't know what happened to those bloody shoes. I never saw them again. I never wanted to see them again.

"Stephen," Mrs. McNeil questioned immediately after having pulled the door closed behind her. "Would you like to have a glass of chocolate milk?"

With Miss Mattie's pillow pulled tightly to my chest, I looked at her curiously and said, "I guess."

"Follow me, sweetheart." She looked as though her smile had been painted on. Considering her lipstick, perhaps it had been.

I followed her as she pranced by a set of stairs that descended from the second floor toward the front door. The stairs had white spindles and a walnut handrail curled at the bottom. Each step was a bullnose walnut plank, and the front of each, between the planks, was painted white. She brought me to a set of white French doors leading into a room without windows. It was painted forest green with a white trim. A white chair rail was around the room; the wainscoting painted an even darker green below it. A large walnut table in the middle of the room would probably seat at least ten people. Surrounding it were walnut chairs with looped backs and cushions of green and tan stripes. An ornate chandelier descended from the tray ceiling and hung a few feet above the tabletop. She pulled out one of the chairs and said, "Sit here, dear." Then, she left by pushing open a white side door across the corner from the French doors. She propped it open to reveal a large tan and yellow kitchen. There was a tan, tiled island in the middle of the kitchen, and across from it was a white porcelain sink with a window above it.

I turned back toward the dining table and looked around the room at the ornate landscape paintings in gold frames that seemed to call one to meander across European pastures. There was an opulent walnut sideboard with a silver tea set on top and two large white vases on either side filled with yellow flowers. I had never seen anything like it in person and had barely ever seen anything like it in magazines. Shortly, she returned with a crystal water glass full of chocolate milk and set it on the table with a small napkin beneath it.

"Be careful not to spill any on the table, sweetheart." She said, smiling, "and be sure to always set your glass back onto the napkin, not on the table. Do you think you can do that?"

"Yes, Ma'am," I said softly.

"Do you think you will be all right to sit here and sip your milk while I speak with Mrs. Mansfield in the next room?" she asked.

I nodded and watched her walk back through the French doors toward the front of the house. Her hips swayed side to side, a walk that looked more rehearsed than natural. Through the window panes of the French doors, I could see the front door and part of a living room on the opposite side of the stairs. The bodyguard guy had come to stand just outside the French doors where he could watch me. I took the glass in hand to get a drink of chocolate milk. It was like ambrosia, a sweet solace to a horrible day, a tingling in my brain as creamy dark comfort covered my tongue. There had been only rare occasions that I had gotten treats like that, and only from Miss Mattie. Perhaps my enjoyment had something to do with having only popcorn and iced tea with Miss Mattie the previous afternoon.

From the living room on the other side of the stairs, I heard Mrs. McNeil exclaim, "Oh, my word! Poor child!"

I sat there looking around that beautiful room, feeling like I had a whole reservoir of tears behind my eyes, but I couldn't cry. I felt numb and lost like I had never felt lost, when I had been lost for my entire life. I simply sat staring at some object or another as I heard the voices from the front room, most too faint to comprehend. I didn't care what they were saying, anyway.

After a while, I heard the front door open. I noticed the bodyguard guy was missing from his post, and the blond woman was closing the front door behind him. When she closed and locked the door, she returned to the room where I was sitting. She came to my chair and squatted beside it. She placed her warm, red-nailed hand on my cheek and said, "Bless your heart, poor child. You have been through the torment of Satan."

I didn't know what to say or what to do. I sat staring at this strange woman. She seemed nice enough, but I had learned at Pruitt Igoe to suspect everyone. I only sat and looked at her. Then, she stood and said, "Come on, let's find some pajamas for you and get you to bed. She took my hand and led me through the kitchen to a door at the back of the house that opened into an enclosed back stairwell. Beside the stairwell, I saw a large dark room with sofas, toys, and a console television. There appeared to be a door on the other side of that room, but it was difficult to determine in the darkness. She led me upstairs to a bathroom near the stairs and said, "This is the children's bathroom."

I looked in to see pink tile across a counter which was perpendicular to the door. It had two white porcelain sinks. Above each sink was a large medicine cabinet that had sliding mirrored doors. On the other side of the counter was a white porcelain toilet, and on the other side of that was a fancy white dresser that sat below a window outlined with white curtains with pink rose prints. A shower curtain with similar rose patterns was pulled to one side of a white porcelain tub directly across from the toilet. Cabinets on either side of the tub had two small white doors with pink glass door knobs. Pink tile surrounded the room halfway up the wall and covered the shower tub enclosure just past the height of the shower head. Above the tile, the wall was painted an even paler pink. The white sinks, tub, and toilet were all spotless, glistening in the light like Miss Mattie's Dutch figurine.

"Honey, you are going to need a shower before bed," she explained as she led me into the bathroom. "Over here is your shampoo." She pointed to a tile shelf inside the shower. "And there is a bar of soap, as well. I will get you a towel, hang it beside the tub, and get you a washcloth. Then, while you are cleaning up, I will find some pajamas that might fit you. Okay?"

She opened the cabinet door under the counter and pulled a large brown paper bag from a stack inside. She opened the bag and said, "When you get undressed, I need you to put all your clothes in this bag, including underwear. Then, just set the bag outside the door. Okay, sweetie?"

I still had said nothing. I looked at the bag, looked up at her, and took it from her hand.

She opened one of the little white doors beside the tub, reached up, and pulled out a large, plush, white towel. She hung it on the bar that she had shown me. Then, she handed me a washcloth, and as she was leaving, smiled and cooed sweetly before pulling the door too, "If there is anything you need, just come tap on the bathroom door. Okay?"

She closed the door, and I stood momentarily with the bag and washcloth in my hand. I stared at the back of the door for a very long time. Then, my bladder told me there was something I had been neglecting for hours. The top lid of the toilet was down over the seat, something I had never seen. I lifted it, pulled my pants down, and sat on the toilet seat to pee. When my bladder had emptied, I did as she requested and stripped to complete nudity, putting each piece of clothing in the bag as I removed it. Then, I set the bag outside the door and stepped inside the shower.

Although the plumbing fixtures were much fancier and significantly cleaner, they functioned like those I had been used to. I reached for the soap and silently washed under the trickling water. My mind kept snapping back to walking into the apartment and finding my so-called mother in a scene worse than a horror film. The memory of the smell filled my brain as though it was right there in the room. The fragrance of soap and air freshener only seemed to blend with and be overpowered by the smell of blood. Even though I smelled it, I knew it could not be there, but I felt as though I was still standing in her blood, staring at her murdered remains. Deep sighs went through me, and I dropped the soap as I trembled. Breathing became difficult, and I found myself panting as my chest tightened. I knelt on my knees on the tub floor, placed my head down on the porcelain, and cried.

I began to realize how terrified I was. Jake had tortured and frightened me my whole life, but I knew what to expect. I had learned how to deal with him, but at that point, in the pretty pink and white room, there was no one left, no one I knew, not even Jake or Ronza. The slate of my life had been wiped clean. There was no more apartment, no more Pruitt Igoe, no more so-called-mother, no more Mike, no more Miss Mattie. Nothing was ever going to be the same. I was being drawn into an unknown world where I didn't know the rules, where I didn't know the people or what they were like, and where I didn't know what to expect or what would be expected. I felt like an alien setting foot onto an unknown planet, totally alone.

At some point, there was a tapping on the bathroom door. "How are you doing in there?" Mrs. McNeil said from the other side of the door. "It has been quite a while. Are you about done?"

I could not respond. My tears had become silent, replaced by my heartbeat throbbing in my ears. As she tapped, it was as though the sound had come from a great distance, as though I could barely hear it, as though I heard it echoing from some far-off place where time didn't exist.

Next, a man was picking me up from the tub basin. The water had been turned off. I felt hands under my armpits, lifting me. My body was limp.

"Stand up," he instructed as though his voice echoed. "Come on, stand up."

"Should we call an ambulance?" Gertrude McNeil questioned.

"Let's give him a moment," the man said.

I felt my awareness returning, and the muscles in my legs began to form into a position to hold me up, but my knees kept shaking, and my legs felt weak.

"I'm sorry, I'm sorry, I'm sorry." I heard myself frantically chanting. "I'm sorry, I'm sorry, I'm sorry, I'm sorry—"

"Shush, shush, shush," I heard the man say. "Can you stand up now?" His hands were still under my armpits, and I was facing him. He was a handsome man. His short, dark hair had a bit of a curl to it. His body was slender but muscular, with a chest as bare as a dolphin's back. He only wore pale blue silk pajama bottoms with no top, and I noticed that Mrs. McNeil was standing behind him with a worried look on her face, holding what must have been the top of his pajamas. "Can you stand up now?" he asked again.

I nodded, barely feeling my head move, my wet hair dribbling water across my face.

"Jake," Mrs. McNeil said. "I'm going to step out now so you can help him dress."

The name "Jake" echoed through my mind like an alarm. *Jake! Jake! Jake! Jake!* Suddenly, I was not seeing a handsome, kind man who had helped me to my feet, but I saw the face of Jake Carter, my tormentor.

Instead of a kind man, I saw a man who had done nothing but torture and torment me. I began slapping him away, flailing my arms about, frantically trying to escape.

"NOOOOOOOO!" I heard myself howl. "NOOOOOOOOOO!"

"Stop," the man said gently. "I need you to stop, okay?"

I continued flailing my arms and backed up into the corner of the tub, as far away from him as possible. My feet slipped from beneath me, and I fell into the back corner of the tub, hitting my head as I came down.

Mrs. McNeil immediately turned around.

"Oh, my Lord!" She exclaimed. "I don't know if we will be able to handle this one. He probably needs to be in the hospital."

The man stopped reaching for me. He turned to Mrs. McNeil and whispered, "What's his name?"

"Stephen," she whispered back.

He turned back to me and said, "Stephen, I know you must be really scared. My wife has told me that you have been through a lot. Yeah? You've been through a lot? I want you to know that I won't hurt you. Okay? My name is Jacob McNeil, and I will be your foster father. Okay? We just want to help you get ready for bed so you can rest."

I pulled myself up, squatting away from him, trembling, staring at him, terrified, while I sucked back short snippets of breath. Jake Carter's face kept flashing back and forth over the kind man's face. One face flashed, and then the other. I felt nauseated again and felt my body going limp.

Then, there was darkness, a blank space where nothing existed. It was not as though I passed out. Time ceased to exist. Time erased itself. I had no awareness, no recollection. Maybe I had died while still alive, but all memory stopped. For a very long time, there was nothing.

Suddenly, one day, I was sitting in the lounge by the backstairs of the McNeil house, which had been set aside for the foster kids. I heard a newscaster say, "There has been an arrest in the murder case of Mable Saunders, who was stabbed to death a few weeks ago at Pruitt Igoe. Police have arrested a man from Ladue named Mike Foster and charged him with the murder."

I leaped off a sofa where other kids had been sitting beside me and ran to the TV, shouting into the screen, "NO! NO! HE DIDN'T DO IT! MIKE DIDN'T DO IT! MIKE WOULDN'T KILL ANYBODY!"

I continued screaming and began pounding on top of the TV set with my fists.

The next thing I knew, the man who had previously been across from me in the pink and white shower had his arms around me, saying, "Stephen, Stephen, Stephen. Calm down, now. It's okay."

"NO!" I screamed, fighting him as he pulled me to the floor, wrapped his arms and legs around me, and held me. "THEY WILL HURT MIKE! DON'T LET THEM HURT MIKE! MIKE DIDN'T KILL HER! MIKE DIDN'T DO IT!"

"Shush, shush, shush—" the man whispered into my ear as he held me firmly from behind while I squirmed on the floor. "Come on, Stephen. Relax for me now, okay?"

"MIKE DIDN'T KILL HER! I KNOW HE DIDN'T KILL HER!" Long streams of tears rolled off my face and into the shag-carpeted floor. I could hear myself crying. I could feel the anguish in my heart, but my face was numb, and even though I was fighting to break free, my body was numb, and my muscles did not want to respond.

I heard Mrs. McNeil's voice as she stood at the door between the kid's lounge and the kitchen. "That guy had a sheepskin coat handmade by a leather craftsman in Manchester who always brands and numbers his work. The craftsman verified that he had made it by special request for that Mike guy. His shirt had her blood all over it, and blood was inside the coat. They found that guy's skin cells under her fingernails where she had scratched him, probably trying to fight him off. Oh, he did it, all right. No doubt, he did it."

"NO! HE didn't! He … couldn't … do it!" I moaned, feeling my voice go weak, feeling my body go limp, and my awareness slipping, once again, into silence. I was hearing myself but barely able to hear my own voice, even though I knew I was screaming and crying.

Again, everything went blank, completely blank. It was as though I ceased to exist, falling into a deep sleep without dreaming.

CHAPTER 5

STRAIGHTEN UP

I felt a slap on my knee, a sharp, slight sting of pain, and suddenly became aware.

"Stephen! Stop saying that! You are not a girl, and your name *is NOT* Stephanie! Now, straighten up. We are almost to church!" Mrs. McNeil called from the front seat, hissing at me like an angry cat.

I was in a van, in the middle of a wide padded bench seat behind the front seats. Mrs. McNeil had turned around from the front passenger's side and had slapped me on the leg. Mr. McNeil was driving. There were kids on either side of me, and after that split second of awareness, I flew into a rage.

"DON'T YOU EVER FUCKING HIT ME AGAIN!" I screamed. I came out of my seat into the front, pulled her bleached blond, perfectly permed hair, and started hitting her as hard as I could.

Mr. McNeil immediately yanked the steering wheel and pulled the van to the curb. Shortly, Jake McNeil pulled me from the van onto the sidewalk and had me down on my back. He was on top of me with my hands forced back over my head onto the concrete. He sat on me and held my wrists down while I was screaming, cursing, and spitting.

"Stephen," He said with a firm but calm voice. "I need you to calm down, okay? I need you to relax. This is not how good kids behave."

I heard three short bursts of a police car siren, whoop, whoop, whoop, a sound I had become familiar with around Pruitt Igoe. When we heard it, we often scurried like rabbits, looking for a hiding place. A jolt of fear dashed through my heart. Then, I could see a policeman standing over us, the sunlight shining around his head, causing me to squint.

"Is everything all right here?" the cop asked.

"I'm just trying to get this child to calm down after a temper tantrum." Mr. McNeil said calmly, barely looking over his shoulder where the policeman stood.

"Yeah, I saw your van lurch over and thought you were about to hit the corner of that building." The cop commented. He glanced around the area as though inspecting and brought his gaze back to me. "What's the matter, son?"

"FUCK YOU!" I screeched. "I AM NOT YOUR FUCKING SON!"

"Nope, my son would never disrespect me or dare to talk to me like that 'cause he dang sure wouldn't like the consequences." The police officer looked down at me with a snide glare. "Maybe you should be thankful you are not my son."

Mrs. McNeil had come to stand next to the cop while Mr. McNeil continued to hold me down. She pulled out a compact, stared into the tiny mirror, and tried to stick strands of hair back into place.

The other foster kids had their faces pressed to the van window, displaying astonished glares like they were watching a freak show. They were all white, so-called well-behaved, but they weren't so well-behaved, just favored. I was the problem child. I was the "colored" child.

"Jake, I don't think we are going to be able to continue this." Mrs. McNeil said, staring down at me and folding her compact to a close. "I don't know that we can keep him anymore. He is too out of control. Lord knows what his … *heritage* … and the slums have done to him. We are going to have to have him placed in some kind of treatment facility or something."

"Agreed." Jacob McNeil affirmed as he continued to hold me while I squirmed beneath him. "I hate to do that," he went on, "but we may have to. Do you think Pastor Simmons might be able to offer us some suggestions?"

"It's worth a try, honey," she endorsed. "Maybe we can talk with him after services today."

Jacob McNeil looked down at me. "Are you calm yet?" he asked.

I had stopped squirming and was not entirely unappreciative of the physical contact. Even if he held me down because of a fit, it was the next best thing to a hug. It was male contact, a semblance of affection, which I had come to crave. Even though he did it for discipline, Mr. McNiel never really hurt me. He just held me in place for a while until I could recoup.

"Fuck you!" I exclaimed, not wanting him to get up too soon.

"That doesn't answer my question, Stephen." He continued.

"Stop calling me Stephen!" I demanded

"That's your name." he returned. "It's the name on your birth certificate, and last I heard, anyone with a penis and testicles is classified by all the laws of nature, the laws of God, and the United States legal system as a male. You are a boy, Stephen. You don't have a vagina; you have a penis, and no matter what you wish or desire, nature has spoken. God made you that way, and that is simply how it is. Your insistence on anything else doesn't change the facts or alter God's will."

I lay there on the pavement, staring at him.

"Can I have your assurance that there will be no more fit throwing if I let you up?" he asked.

"Can I have your assurance that your bitch wife is not going to hit me anymore?" I retorted.

"First of all," he admonished. "I'll thank you not to call my wife those terrible names. She deserves a lot more respect than that. Second, I am not in charge of her choices, but I will ask her, Okay? Now, here is the deal. I can sit on top of you for the rest of the day if necessary. Gertrude can take the rest of the kids to church, and you can go without lunch or dinner, or you can give me your word, and keep your word, that you will behave. Then, I will let you up. Otherwise, I'll sit here until you decide you can control yourself better. However, there will be punishment for this when we get home."

"Tell her to quit hitting me!" I demanded.

"Oh, for heaven's sake. We will find some other way of discipline." Mrs. McNeil acquiesced from behind him. "Not that anything we have tried has worked. If he can't behave, then we will have to send him to some secure facility where they have the staff to control him. I've had enough!" She paused and took an exasperated breath. "Stephen, I will do my best not to hit you again."

"Have you had enough, Stephen?" Jake McNeil said as he returned his attention to me. "Do you want to meet with Pastor Simmons? Maybe he can arrange a meeting with Ronald Dennison, that TV preacher you like to watch. I've heard he's coming to preach here soon."

"Whatever you say," I replied. No one knew I liked watching the TV preacher because I thought he was cute. I had not known, until that moment, that he was coming to town, but certain memories began to filter back into my mind. That incident was my reawakening, my return to awareness from a long, dark void.

"Are you going to behave?" he asked.

"As long as she doesn't hit me again," I continued to bargain.

"Oh, for Heaven's sake!" Mrs. McNeil exclaimed from behind him. "Fine! I've told you I will try not to hit you, but you need to know, *young man*, that you do not rule this family, and you are going to have to learn to behave appropriately!"

"*Oh, for Heaven's sake! Fine!*" I mocked.

"I have your word, no more violence," Mr. McNeil asked.

"I won't be violent toward anyone if they are not violent toward me first," I replied. That had not been entirely the truth, but at that moment, I was willing to agree to it.

"Okay," he said as he began to loosen his grip on my arms.

I lay there without moving as he slowly let go and lifted his hands from my wrists.

"Don't get up too soon," I teased and grinned at him. "It's kind of sexy having a man on top of me."

With a sudden disgusted look, he moved off me and stood up. I continued lying there. Finally, I rolled over onto my side and started to get up.

"Looks like you folks have this under control," the cop interjected. "I guess I'll be on my way, but it sure looks like I'll be the one dealing with that boy in a few years if he don't straighten up. I know the kind. Seen it my whole career. You can mark my words. That boy's headed for the pen."

"Thank you, officer," Mr. McNeil commented. Then, Mrs. McNeil parroted him.

"*Thank you, officer,*" I sassed, parroting them.

The cop walked back to his patrol car, shaking his head toward the ground, then drove off. The rest of us loaded back onto the van and went to church.

That incident shocked me out of the darkness, and my memory began to return. Apparently, I had lived almost a year with these people and remembered practically none of it, but I knew their habits and routines. I even had my eleventh birthday while under their supervision. I was told that I had a birthday party, but I could only remember tiny pieces of what might have been my birthday. Almost everything from when I had heard the TV news announce that Mike had been arrested for murder to that moment was blank. Until Mrs. McNeil had slapped me on the knee, It seemed I had not existed. Yet, I somehow knew what would come next at church.

We slinked in and sat quietly in a row on the same pew at the back after being made late by my tantrum. Somehow, I knew the routines of the church service. I knew and sang the hymns, though I had no memory of ever having attended church or having sung hymns. My so-called mother certainly never set foot in a church, and although I knew that Miss Mattie attended church, she had never taken me, but there I was, singing hymns like I had grown up with them.

Suddenly, I was aware again, and apparently, I had been giving these people hell since they took me into foster care. So much for my promise to Miss Mattie. On that day, I didn't know how much I had forgotten, but more memories came back to me as time went on.

Even before she had been murdered, I had begun to insist that my so-called mother call me Stephanie, and I had been tearing violently into her when she refused. My violence escalated whenever she went into a rage, and I gave her back as much or more than I got. I had become fed up with her, fed up with neglect and abuse, and fed up with being called names. Long before she was murdered, I had become fed up with everything about her and my so-called life. Apparently, I continued that behavior in foster care. Apparently, in the past year, hatred and resentment had infected my mind and kept festering into eruption with the McNeils, but this time, I was with an upper-middle-class, church-going family from Ladue. I had transferred the resentment for Mable-bitch and Pruitt Igoe onto practically everyone else, and the bitterness of having lost the only two people I had ever cared about was a recipe for disaster.

A few days after the van incident, Mrs. McNeil brought me into the church to see Pastor Simmons. I sat in his ornate office across from his huge dark walnut desk, staring at him the way I stared at almost everyone. As I sat there, a few unfocused memories began to return. Being in Pastor Simmons's office felt like a *'here we go again'* scenario in which everyone was determined to convince me that I was a boy and that I was somehow delusional to think I was a girl. For some reason, they seemed to believe that my violence came from my insistence that I be called Stephanie, in conflict with their absolute refusal to do so. They had no apparent clue what ten years of every kind of abuse possible had done to me or how it had affected the fight or flight reactions programmed into my subconscious. They seemed to have no clue how much witnessing my so-called mother's murder had affected me, much less how much I was tormented by being taken away from Miss Mattie and Mike. It seemed as though they didn't care about any of that. All they cared about was that I stop insisting that I was a girl.

A memory returned of a Christian counselor, some fat, frumpy older woman who thought, like all of them, that she could pray me out of it. Lord knows, she prayed. She had put her palm on my forehead and rebuked Satan. All of them prayed that I would come to see the error of my ways, that I would change and become like them, and that I would somehow become a *"normal"* boy, whatever that means. That wasn't going to happen because I was not a boy. I didn't want it to happen because I knew it wasn't true, and even if I had tried, I knew I couldn't make it happen. It wasn't some game that I could stop playing. It was a way of being. Nobody seemed to understand that. They all had it in mind that they knew what normal was and that they, alone, knew how I needed to be. Nobody ever asked what would make me happy. Nobody ever prayed for me to love myself and know that God loves me as I am without trying to force myself into some mold that society or the church concocted for me. They were like my so-called mother, insisting that I be male. They just did it without physical abuse and failed to recognize that shaming me for something I couldn't change was also abuse. No one seemed to care that I was miserable, that I often didn't want to live because I couldn't live the way they wanted me to be.

I couldn't see Miss Mattie or Mike anymore, and I couldn't see many options other than dying. Sometimes, I lay in bed at night contemplating how to kill myself. I felt like I had lost everyone who loved me, and I felt like everyone else thought I was a freak of nature. If something was so horribly wrong with me, I was terrible just for being who I was and an abomination of humanity, then I needed to die. Right? Why not kill myself and spend eternity in the hell they so much believed in when I was already in hell, and I couldn't see any way out? I don't know why I never tried it. I had plenty of plans and opportunities, but Miss Mattie instilled hope in me. Even if they didn't let me see her, I knew she still loved me. I knew, at least, that Miss Mattie accepted me for who I was, even if no one else would.

In those days, it wasn't so cool to accept your gender identity or any attraction outside of what was considered heterosexual. No one had accepted me except Miss Mattie. Even if I accepted it in myself and knew that Miss Mattie did, society did not allow it. For the most part, and in most circles, it wasn't acceptable to love yourself the way you are, not if you were outside the limits of heterosexual, gender-congruent expectations of society, especially as defined by the church. Instead, you could only love yourself, according to them, and only if you could fit yourself into the mold that they determined for you. Even if I had never been a girl, if I had never questioned having been born with male genitals, even if I had never been attracted to men, I was made different from the rest of the world by being born a half-breed between two races. I had been changed by growing up with abuse, raised by a drug whore mother. Nobody seemed to consider that I was affected by spending my formative years in an environment of drugs, filth, abuse, and boundaryless sex, and it would become an indelible part of my personality for most of my life. I would always have to fight the temptation to become like my abusers, to let their hatred form me into a hateful person. Deep down, I wasn't that either. I was infuriated by my life experiences, but my core was honorable. It seemed that no matter where I was or who I was around, I was always out of place, a square peg in a world of round holes. They didn't get it. At the time, neither did I.

For whatever reason, we are what we are. Nobody ever questions that we are not born speaking our native tongue, but we learn it in the formative years of our lives, and it becomes so ingrained in us that we can't even imagine not being able to speak it. We don't choose to speak it; it becomes part of our identity. No one sees that you can learn a different language as an adult, but you could never be as comfortable speaking it as your native tongue. Attraction and gender are like that, even if you were not born into them. You could pretend to be straight, even marry and have children, but that would never change who you really are. Just as you could learn to speak a different language, that would not change the original tongue that was engrained into your mind, programmed and wired into your brain, and no one would want to be forced to learn a foreign language. There might be things people could pretend to be, but that could never be as comfortable as being themselves. It did not matter if I was born a girl in a boy's body or if something developed during the formative years of my life or in the womb; I was what I was. They all wanted to figure out a cause for it, like it was some kind of disease like they could cure it, but who we are is not a disease. I didn't have a disease, and the true me was something I could not change. The bottom line is that I was what I was. Still, they insisted that I could not be who I was and expected me to learn to be different when my brain formed and solidified in the first three or four years of my life. The only thing that had saved me from total insanity had been Miss Mattie. She had been my anchor in the storm, the one piece of sanity that I could cling to, and her memory, as well as the hope of seeing her again, was one of my very few comforts and the only thing that kept me moving on.

So, at eleven years old, I sat there almost a year after my so-called mother had been murdered. I sat in the office of the pastor of a huge church who was determined to convince me that I could suddenly recognize that I was a boy by the miracle of prayer. All of what they perceived to be the *"delusion"* of a female inside a male's body would—*poof* … disappear. I knew it would not go away, but I went along with their charade as much as possible. What else could I do? This blue-eyed, gray-haired, skinny old man sat across that polished walnut desk and smiled with what he thought was the love of Jesus. Maybe it was the love of Jesus, but I couldn't help thinking that if Jesus really loved me, he would love me the way I am and not try to make me into something else, or that if God really loved me, he would have put me in a female body in the first place. The whole concept was confusing. Yet, they seemed to be totally convinced.

"They tell me that you are a fan of Pastor Ronald Dennison," Pastor Simmons said, smiling.

I looked at a painting mounted to his right of Jesus hanging from the cross, a spear piercing his side, blood dripping as he gazed at those kneeling below with an anguished and suffering expression. I was hard-pressed to understand how such a gruesome scene was supposed to represent love and compassion. I noticed that everyone depicted in the painting were white. Did that mean that Jesus was only for white people?

"I like to watch his show," I replied, thinking about how cute the preacher looked on TV. I certainly was not going to mention why I liked the show.

"Would you like to meet Pastor Dennison?" he asked. "He is going to be coming to speak at our church, and I think I might be able to arrange a meeting with him if you would like."

"Sure," I responded. I didn't realize Pastor Simmons had called this Dennison guy before he ever talked to me about it.

"Stephen," he went on. "We are hoping that Pastor Dennison might be able to help you."

"You mean, make me into what you want me to be," I contested.

"Well, we don't want to make you into anything you are not," he argued. "We just want to help you be comfortable with how God made you."

I sat staring at him, thinking to myself—*Whatever.* I had learned to let them talk and say nothing in return. They tried to get me to speak, but they wanted me to parrot back what they wanted me to say, not what I actually felt. If I had played the role and pretended to be a good Christian boy, they would have been happy without ever knowing or admitting the truth, but I couldn't do that. I couldn't pretend for them. Why should anyone have to act or play a role that someone else wants them to play when that is not who they really are? It doesn't matter if they think it is wrong; no one should be forced to put on a show for others because they don't like who you are.

We sat in silence for a time, staring at each other. Finally, he said, "Okay, I will let Pastor Dennison know you agree to meet with him, and we will see about making arrangements for that. You know, he is coming to speak to our congregation shortly."

"Okay. Yeah, you told me that," I replied nonchalantly.

"All right, Stephen. That will be enough for today. Let me take you back to Mrs. McNeil." He rose from his desk and came around to my chair. He reached his hand toward me and motioned me to go with him. When I stood, he put his hand on my back as we walked out the door. I had mixed feelings about men touching me. On one hand, I loved the sensation of a masculine touch. On the other, I always had suspicions that it could lead to abuse. Sometimes, it just felt … icky. I must admit that even though I was attracted to men, I was also afraid of men. The only man I had ever really trusted was Mike. Before foster care, he had been the only man who had never hurt me and the only one who had been the least bit truly affectionate with me. Mr. McNeil had never abused me, and I liked him in a way, but I still didn't genuinely trust him. He wanted me to play along and pretend to be a boy, just like everyone else.

Mrs. McNeil was waiting in the hall. She looked at me and said, "Stephen, go wait for me by the door. I will be there presently."

I went down the hall and stood by the door that led to the parking lot behind the church. They stood by Pastor Simmons's office, talking in whispers, assuming, I guess, that I could not hear them, but my hearing was excellent.

"If this doesn't work," she breathed a whisper. "I think we may have to ask the state to place him in a specialized orphanage or a reform school or something. We simply can't deal with his behavior anymore."

"I know, I know," Pastor Simmons whispered back. "I don't think I have ever seen a more troubled child, but I think we have to try anything we can to reach him for his sake and the bidding of the Lord."

"It has gotten ridiculous." She continued. "He sneaks into the girl's room and steals dresses. Jake has caught him dancing in the bathroom mirror, wearing one of the girl's dresses. He absolutely insists on being called Stephanie, no matter how much you correct him, and insists he be referred to with the pronoun *her.* He can become violent if you don't comply with that wish. He has thrown things, broken things, attacked the other children—attacked us. Pastor, it is just wearing us out. We have been taking children from troubled homes for years and have never had this problem before. I feel sorry that he lost his mother and went through that horrible experience, but when he repeatedly becomes violent, it just gets overwhelming to try to deal with him."

"Have you checked into other options?" Pastor Simmons asked.

"We have talked to state family services, and they have offered to place him in a different home, but I just don't see how that will do any good. He would continue the same behavior there, and then it would be a different family dealing with it."

She stopped speaking, took an exasperated breath as she glanced in my direction, then continued. "The state can do whatever it wants, I guess, but it seems to me that he needs some kind of specialized treatment. Do you know of anything, any program we might be able to send him to?"

"Well," Pastor Simmons hesitated. "Based on the work of Dr. Irving Bieber, some programs have been developed to help boys like Stephen. There is a thing called aversion therapy that they believe can help these homosexuals convert their attraction to women. I'm not sure how that might work for a boy like Stephen, who is convinced that he is a girl, or how it might work for a child that young. I am also unsure how young they might accept children into the programs or if it is just for adult homosexuals who realize they need to change their attraction."

"All I know is that we have to do something," Mrs. McNeil glanced in my direction again, but I had my head down as I piddled with one of the drawstrings around the waist of my jacket. I didn't seem to be paying attention, but I heard everything.

"Can you get us some information about a program for him?" she continued. "I'm sure we will have to clear it with the state, but I think family services is about as exasperated as we are."

"I will see what I can find," Pastor Simmons responded. "Then, if this meeting with Pastor Dennison does not accomplish something, we will take steps to get him some additional help."

"Thank you, Pastor Simmons," she affirmed as she turned to walk down the hall toward me with her high heels clicking against the hardwood floor.

"Come on, Stephen," she said as she neared me. "Time to go home now."

"My name is Stephanie," I whispered under my breath as she opened the door to the parking lot. I followed her to her car. The van was only used when they had to haul all the kids around, but if something required us to be transported individually, they used one of the two family cars. On the drive back to their house, I didn't say anything, nor did she.

A total of seven foster kids were in the McNeil home. There were four boys and three girls. *I considered* four girls and three boys since I should have been counted as a girl, but they called me a boy and made me sleep in the boy's room. The boys' and girls' rooms had bunk beds on opposite walls. So, they had room to take in another girl, which they eventually did. I had the bottom bunk nearest the door in our room, beneath this kid named Efren, who had been taken into foster care after his father had beaten him so severely that he ended up in the emergency room. His Dad had almost killed him, and he had gotten a broken nose and a cracked skull and spent several weeks in the hospital. You could still see the crook in his nose even though the rest of his face had healed, and that crooked nose made him snore terribly. He was always getting headaches and clogged sinuses. He was very timid and winced whenever someone raised a hand to scratch their head or moved suddenly. One of the other two boys, Carl, was about a year older than me and thought he could be mean, but he had never met anyone as mean as Jake Carter, and I had learned how to defend myself with the meanest fucking redneck of them all. We got in quite a few fights while I was there because he was always making fun of me.

"You're not a girl, jerk wad!" He would taunt me when the adults couldn't hear him, "But you are a sissy little queer."

I had to show him this sissy little queer could kick his ass on more than one occasion. If there was nothing else Pruitt Igoe had taught me, it was how to fight. A lot of that, I learned through trial and error, what would get some asshole off me and what wouldn't. A kick to the nuts generally worked very well. I was not opposed to fighting dirty if I had to, and if that required kicking your balls up to your tonsils, I was okay with that, and I never backed down. Still, Carl would push it as far as he could, when he could. He was determined that he was going to beat me. He thought he had an advantage, a head taller and maybe fifteen pounds heavier than me. Perhaps he thought that mop full of red hair and a face full of freckles was also an advantage, but I didn't think it made him look mean. To me, it made him look like a Raggedy Ann doll. He kept trying, even though he kept failing. It must have been an embarrassment to get his ass kicked by a "sissy little queer," almost as embarrassing as getting his ass kicked by a girl. Technically, he was getting his ass kicked by a girl, and most of the girls I knew back at Pruitt Igoe could have nailed his ass to the baseboards just as easily as I could.

The other boy, named Bill, was about my age. I heard that his parents locked him in a room and starved him to punish him, and that went on till some of his teachers began to get concerned about how much weight he was losing and made a report to family services. He had gained it all back at the McNeil's and then some. If he didn't get caught, he would sneak away food the other kids didn't eat and carry it back to the boy's room. He had hidden rolls and pieces of pork chop that barely had any meat left on the bone. Still, he chewed on it until there was nothing left but bone. He tried to hide and eat his stash so the other kids wouldn't tell on him, but we knew, and the adults also knew what was happening. They would periodically flip his mattress, scrounge under the bunk, and go through his drawers. It was not uncommon for them to find something rotten under his mattress or a half-eaten box of cake mix that he had swiped from the cupboard hidden behind the chest of drawers. I knew how he felt. I knew what it felt like to go hungry, but I was determined I would not get fat. I had to keep my girlish figure, so I carefully watched what I ate. I didn't mind going hungry for my cause. After all, I grew up hungry and knew how to control my eating. On the other hand, Bill had belly fat that drifted over his belt, and food seemed to be more like a drug to him than the necessary evil it had become for me. Maybe having it deliberately withheld from him made him want it even more. Unlike me, starving was not a choice but a punishment. Besides, Miss Mattie had fed me, so I had a different perspective on food. Now and then, I would save him something that I chose not to eat.

One of the other girls was thirteen. Her name was Cathy, and she wore the same size dress as me. At first, I tried to get her to let me borrow a dress, but she wouldn't. Then, I tried to bargain with her that I would do her chores if she let me borrow a dress. Still, she wouldn't.

"We're not supposed to trade chores," she said. "Mrs. McNeil wouldn't let us do that. Besides, you are not a girl and are not supposed to wear dresses."

I tried giving her a ten-dollar bill one day. I had stolen it out of Mrs. McNeil's purse. However, instead of Cathy recognizing that she could profit, she assumed it must be stolen and told on me. Then, I got restricted to my bunk for a week even though I returned the money.

So, I finally snuck into Cathy's room, stole a dress from her closet, and snuck it into the bathroom to try it on and admire myself in the mirror. I was doing a fashion walk in front of the mirror when Mr. McNeil opened the door. He didn't even knock. The lock had been removed from the bathroom door on purpose. So, none of us could lock ourselves in the bathroom. One of the other kids must have told, and Mr. McNeil didn't look surprised. After having me in the house for a year, there wasn't much that surprised him. He just made me take it off and return it to Cathy. Then, I was restricted to my bunk for two weeks.

Being restricted to my bunk meant I had to stay within a two-foot radius. The door to the boy's room had to be left open so they could check on me, and if I needed to go to the bathroom, I had to come to the door and call for one of the adults, which included the maids, to escort me, even though the bathroom was right next to the boy's room. Mr. or Mrs. McNeil, their primary maid, Symone, or Jill, the other maid, would walk with me to the bathroom, then stand outside to escort me back to my bunk when I finished. I could read, but I was not allowed to play with any toys, watch TV, go outside, or do any of the things the other kids did. The TV was downstairs anyway. During those times, I read more and more and began enjoying books. When Mrs. McNeil got tired of hearing me call down the hall to ask the meaning of a word, she brought me a dictionary. I then read the dictionary, and I began to learn a lot of new words.

When I wasn't reading, I cuddled with Miss Mattie's pillow. They had tried to take it from me once. Mrs. McNeil claimed it was too feminine for a boy. I threw a screaming fit and told her it was the only thing I possessed that had been given to me by the only person who loved me, and if she took it, I had nothing and no reason to live. There must have been some pity in her heart that day. She let me keep it. Maybe she realized I meant it when I said I would have no reason to live.

Heather and Cindy were The two youngest girls, five and six years old. I never paid much attention to them. I knew one of them was there because her father and her grandparents were killed in a big car crash, a head-on collision with a drunk driver, and her mother had such severe brain damage that she couldn't take care of her kids anymore and had to be put in a nursing home. The family had been on their way to a weekend getaway and had left the kids with a babysitter when it happened. I guess nobody else in the family could take them, or maybe there was no other family. I heard her brother got put in a different foster home, but I didn't know. Kids only heard rumors, and none of us had any actual choice. We never knew the whole truth, even about our own situation.

The McNeils didn't have any kids of their own. I guess Mrs. McNeil couldn't have babies, so they made up for it by taking in foster kids. I'm not sure why they didn't just adopt kids, but they seemed to think taking in foster children was their Christian duty. I liked Mr.

McNeil. Although he manhandled me a few times when I was blasting off, he was still fair and reasonable. I even overlooked that his name was Jake, but I never called him that. I didn't want to utter the word, for one thing, and we were instructed to always refer to them as Mr. and Mrs. McNeil, anyway.

I guess Mrs. McNeil was a good person, but I didn't get along with her. She was constantly on me about something and did not take well to my stealing. Not only did I steal Cathy's dress, but I also stole bits and pieces of Mrs. McNeil's makeup and jewelry. I had to be careful about the makeup. I was most likely to get caught with that. So, I would put it on, briefly admire myself in the bathroom mirror, and quickly wash it off, lest I get caught. Mrs. McNeil would eye me with precision to see if there might be a hint of rouge, God forbid, lipstick. If she caught me wearing it, I would be restricted again, but after learning to enjoy reading, I didn't mind the restriction. So, why not? I read classics like Mark Twain and Charles Dickens, modern children's stories, and more adult types of work when I could get hold of them. I read *A Clockwork Orange* and ordered that with my saved allowance from a book catalog I got at school, but I don't think the McNeils knew what it was about and never bothered to thumb through it. If they had, I'm sure there would have been some type of punishment; the book would have been confiscated, and they would have thrown a fit with the school that an eleven-year-old could order such a book from a school book catalog.

I didn't know, at first, that Mrs. McNeil's jewelry was costly, but apparently, it was. It didn't look much different from some of the costume jewelry that Mable-bitch had, but at the time, I didn't know the difference. The McNeil's usually kept their bedroom door locked, but once, when the maid had left the door open while she went downstairs for more cleaning supplies, I managed to sneak in. I quickly lifted a necklace with a quarter-sized green cut stone as a central pendant and little clusters of green and white stones set in gold on either side. It had a gold chain that latched in the back and was also inlaid with green and white stones. It was a couple of days before Mrs. McNeil realized it was missing. When she discovered it was gone, she screamed and went absolutely frantic.

"JAKE! JACOB!" she shouted from their bedroom as they were getting ready to go to some fancy shindig. "MY EMERALD NECKLACE IS GONE!"

I heard Mr. McNeil say, "I'm sure it is around here. Are you sure you put it back in your jewelry box the last time you wore it? You had mentioned maybe keeping it in the closet one time."

"IT—IS—NOT—HERE!" she yelped. "I ALWAYS PUT IT BACK IN THE JEWELRY BOX!"

I immediately became the prime suspect when they had exhausted their hunt for it. They came to the boy's room, insisted that I must have taken it, and tore everything apart: my bunk, drawers, and the wardrobe designated for Efren and me, but I was not so stupid as to leave it in a conspicuous place like that. While living with my so-called mother, I had become quite good at hiding things.

When they didn't find it with me, they questioned the maids and threatened to fire them if they found either had taken it. Not long after that, Symone quit. I guess she didn't like being accused of things she didn't do. Then, they had to go through a few weeks of interviews before they hired another maid, and in the meantime, Jill was stuck with everything by herself. They hired an older black woman named Mildred. I always called her Miss Mildred out of respect, but nobody else did.

I overheard Mr. and Mrs. McNeil arguing one night. Mrs. McNeil wanted to report the necklace stolen and turn in an insurance claim. That's when I discovered that it was worth several thousand dollars, and I can't say that I wasn't tempted to run away, sell it somewhere, and use the money to finance a trip to run away, lose myself, and live my life my own way. However, I knew it was important to Mrs. McNeil, and as much as she pissed me off, I decided I had to return it. Besides, I knew Miss Mattie would tell me that stealing was wrong. There had been times when we were at a store together, and she would eye me over her shoulder as I lifted something from the shelf, just as I had seen my so-called mother do. "Put dat back," she would say. "Ya ain't gots ta be stealin' stuff." Her voice echoed in my mind, "Ya ain't gots ta be right ta do de right thing. Even if ya thinking a doin' wrong, ya can still do right."

So, the next time I had a stealth opportunity, I left the necklace under a sweater in Mrs. McNeil's walk-in closet. Days later, she finally picked the sweater off a shelf and spotted it there. A gasping shout came out as if she had lifted the sweater off a snake.

Mr. McNeil dashed in to see what was wrong and found her standing there holding the necklace, "See, honey," He told her. "I knew you would find it. I told you that you probably had just misplaced it."

"I—*DID NOT*—MISPLACE IT! I *DID NOT* LEAVE IT UNDER A SWEATHER IN THE CLOSET!" she yelled.

Mr. McNeil said nothing in reply. He was prone to take her drama in stride.

Then, I heard her prancing around in their room, complaining, "Now we have to give the money back to the insurance, and I was hoping to buy a new necklace."

She came to me later and pulled me aside from the other kids.

"Stephen, I know you took my necklace!" she lectured. "I don't know how you did it, and I don't know how you hid it where we couldn't find it, but I know you took it!"

I stared at her and barely tried to hide my grin.

"Now, you listen to me," she continued, "and you listen to me good, *young man!*" There was no hint of gratitude in her voice that I had, at least, given the necklace back. "I will find a way to punish you for this," she babbled on, "and you need to understand that doing things like this will send you straight to *HELL*! As if all your hoopla about being a girl were not enough to send you to hell in the first place, you're a thief and a liar, and you will probably end up like your pathetic mother! I had always heard that black people are lazy and thieving. Now, I am beginning to believe it. Do you want to go to Hell, Stephen? Is that what you want? Do you want to burn for eternity in the pits of Hell? That will happen to you if you don't repent of this evil. Do you honestly think living like your worthless mother is the way to spend your life? Look what it did for *her*!"

As she bantered and bitched, I stood there listening while she bent over with her glistening red polished fingernail pointing in my face about half an inch from my nose. I continued to fight a grin. When she finally finished and permitted me to rejoin the other kids, I said, "I'm glad you got your necklace back, but my name is Stephanie, and I am a girl, and it doesn't matter what you think. I will never be like my so-called mother. You can think whatever you want, but you will never understand and never know who I truly am."

She groaned through clenched teeth, cast her eyes to the ceiling, and exclaimed, "Dear Lord, please help me!"

CHAPTER 6

RETURNING TO LOVE

After Pastor Simmons had *spoken* to me, the days seemed to go by quickly. I didn't cause trouble and went along with the routine that had been established. Then, on a rainy Saturday in March, I was instructed to shower, dress, and come back downstairs after breakfast. Usually, on Saturday, we were allowed to be a little lazier. We generally had breakfast a bit later in the day, and then we could play, lay around, watch cartoons on TV, read, or relax unless an outing had been planned. Excursions included the zoo, the St. Louis Arch, and other things. Once, we went to this big Indian mound just over the river in Illinois. I loved those times, and I appreciated that I was getting to do things I could never have been able to do when my so-called mother was alive. On that Saturday, however, I was to meet with the TV preacher, Pastor Dennison, and he was to speak at the church that night. Since he wasn't to arrive until the afternoon, I spent the morning watching cartoons with the other kids.

Mrs. McNeil had arranged to drop me off at church at about two o'clock after everyone had lunch. I thought about the meeting all morning and decided that I was going to fuck with this Pastor Dennison guy and do everything I could to work his nerves. I thought it would be fun, and besides, I figured the only risk was another scolding by my caretakers. By then, I had started messing with almost everyone who determined they would try to change me other than the McNeils or Pastor Simmons, and I had become immune to their lectures. I was not going to be the good Christian *boy* they wanted me to be, and unlike living in the McNeil home, I had nothing to lose by fucking with the preacher's head, a stranger who had no authority over me and to whom

I owed nothing. I was slightly enamored that he was a good-looking, rich TV personality, but even they have to take a shit.

I had been lectured, prayed over, had hands lain on me, and all kinds of things done to *fix* me from what they saw as this terrible obsession with being a girl. They focused all their attention on that and my attraction to boys, well, actually, my attraction to men. Most boys did nothing for me, but I had begun to take notice of some of the teenage boys who attended church. Mr. and Mrs. McNeil and Pastor Simmons had made changing me their primary focus. Instead of looking at the fact that I would wake up screaming with a nightmare about every other night, that I didn't trust anybody, would startle at a pin drop, or that I would still sometimes wet the bed at eleven years old, they focused on making me into a heterosexual boy. Nobody seemed to realize that I was filled with rage and fear because of what I went through at Pruitt Igoe, not because of my "confusion" over my gender identity. I was frustrated with all the attention over my gender. I felt pressured by their determination, and I felt like an outcast surrounded by other kids and adults who fed and housed me but wanted my compliance as payment for their generosity. No one there had ever tried getting to know how I felt. They simply wanted to tell me what to feel. I felt more alone than ever. I had no one who truly loved me anymore, understood me, or genuinely tried connecting with me. I knew the McNeils only pretended to love me. To them, I was either a project because they thought it was their Christian duty or taking care of me compensated for the fact that Mrs. McNeil couldn't have kids. They also received funds from the state.

So, Mrs. McNeil took me to the church that afternoon and walked me to the door, holding her umbrella more over herself than over me as rain pelted the pavement. She left me under the canopy over the back door, knocked on the door, and turned to walk back to her car without a word, as though she had just dropped a library book into the slot after hours. After she left, Pastor Simmons's secretary came to the door, brought me to her office, and I stayed with her until this

Pastor Dennison guy arrived. By that time, I had dried off mostly. The storm made this Dennison guy late, and Pastor Simmons had gone to pick him up at the hotel. When they returned, I got paraded out into the hallway like a state fair pig on display for the judges. Dennison looked even more cute in person than on TV, and I definitely enjoyed the view. However, I still was not pleased with the idea that this television preacher was supposed to pull off some miracle and make me into a boy.

He walked up to me, extended his hand, and said, "How do you do? You must be Stephen. I am Pastor Ronald Dennison."

He reeked of some cologne that had been far too liberally applied. It smelled pleasant, but there was far too much of it. His black suit, white shirt, and paisley tie made him look business-like but also accented his dark hair and glistening blue eyes.

I said, "I know who you are, and my name is Stephanie."

"Pastor Simmons tells me you like to watch my television broadcast." He grinned as though basking in his notoriety.

"Yes," I replied flatly and let go of his hand.

The next thing I knew, I was herded into a room with him where we could *talk*, and I found myself alone with the TV preacher. I noticed he was more nervous than a startled cat, and I thought, *What a big bunch of bullshit! They bring around this miracle preacher who is supposed to save me, and he is more nervous than I am.*

Of course, I was nervous. For all I knew, he would get me in that room and try the same shit that Jake Carter did. Although I was attracted to him, I didn't want to be forced or hurt like that. It took a lot to trust any man, even if I was attracted to him. As long as he didn't hurt me, I would have been okay with whatever. I knew the sex game, or at least I thought I did, but I had been introduced to it by sick assholes who touched me that way long before anyone should have. I knew I liked the feeling of sex when it didn't hurt. I had not yet realized that I was too young to understand what sex was really about. I knew a lot more than most kids my age, but the abuse had presented me with a distorted idea, and I now understand that I was having sexual feelings sooner than I should have. I assume that was because of the abuse.

They put us in this room with a couch under a window covered in a floral pattern with red roses and other flowers I didn't recognize. I went over, plopped myself on the couch, and stared at him.

He pulled over a red wing-backed chair and leaned toward me. "So, Stephen," he grinned again, "Tell me about yourself."

"My fucking name is STEPHANIE!" I shouted. I grabbed my crotch, got hold of the junk between my legs, and yelled, "I'M NOT SUPPOSED TO HAVE THIS! THIS IS NOT THE BODY I WAS SUPPOSED TO HAVE!"

He got even more nervous, so I tested him. "My mother was a fucking drug whore. She would hump a fire hydrant if she thought it would get her a hit of dope! She was a cunt, and I hated her! She deserved what she got, and I wish I had killed her myself!" Oddly enough, my hatred for Mable increased for a while after she had been killed.

He started stammering and then began praying, "Blessed Jesus, lift up this child—" He never got to finish.

"STOP THE FUCKING PRAYER SHIT!" I screamed. "YOU PEOPLE THINK THAT'S THE ANSWER TO EVERY FUCKING THING! WELL, IT'S NOT! YOU'RE NOT PRAY-ING BECAUSE YOU GIVE A SHIT ABOUT ME! YOU DO IT BECAUSE IT MAKES YOU FUCKING FEEL BETTER! WHERE WAS YOUR STUPID GOD WHEN I WAS IN THE FUCKING SLUMS WITH A FUCKING DRUG WHORE MOTHER?"

I watched him squirm and sputter. Finally, he said, "I'm sorry, Steph—Stephanie." I was shocked that he actually used my real name! No one had done that except Miss Mattie unless I had beaten it out of one of the other kids. No matter how big a fit I threw, the McNeils or Pastor Simmons absolutely refused to call me Stephanie.

He gathered himself and said, "I do care about you."

I doubted that. Even though I felt slightly more comfortable when he used my real name, I still didn't trust him.

"And where are you going when all this is over?" I asked. "Back to your cushy life where you get lots of money from preaching on TV, and you don't have to deal with kids like me! Nobody cares about me! The damn foster family doesn't care about me! It is just something they do because they think God wants them to, and maybe the state pays them to take care of me. They would just as soon see me sent to some program for bad kids somewhere as to really care about me. The state doesn't care about me! I'm just a problem they have to deal with because they can't justify throwing me off the back of a truck somewhere."

He sat back in that tall red chair and asked, "So, why did you agree to talk to me?"

I stepped over, ran my hand up his leg toward his crotch, and said, "Because I think you're sexy."

"Please don't do that." he sputtered as he squirmed nervously and pulled my hand off his leg.

"Does it make you nervous?" I teased. I felt such a sense of power doing that, knowing that it made him squirm. Now and then, I needed to feel powerful. I needed to feel like I was in control. When you have had your control stolen from you, even dominion over your body, you feel an urgency to get the upper hand any way you can. I often tested how much control I could get away with before being put back in my place.

"Yes, it makes me very nervous," he replied honestly. "Now, please sit down."

I'm not entirely sure why I did it. I never tried anything like that with Jacob McNeil, even though I thought he was attractive. Besides, I knew he would have reacted entirely differently, and I could risk getting kicked out and sent to an orphanage. Maybe I needed to feel some sense of power over an adult, especially when I saw that he was already nervous. Perhaps I was halfway hoping that he would take me up on the offer of seduction. I remembered Mike telling me that I could get hurt if I tried it with the wrong man, but this man looked more scared of me than I was of him. I valued Mike's warning, but there I was, coming onto this adult, this TV preacher, this big wig. Maybe I hoped he would let me touch his dick, but my hand never reached his crotch. I respected his honesty and that, like Mike, he was not aggressive in setting his boundaries.

I sat back down, glared at him, and said, "You know men have fucked me before."

"Dear God!" he exclaimed. Then he began apologizing that anyone would do that to me.

I told him about Jake Carter molesting me when I was little, at maybe four or five years old, and how it hurt initially, but I got used to it. Then, I asked him, "Why don't you want to fuck me?"

"Because it's wrong!" he snapped immediately.

My mind returned to the day Mike gave me a similar lecture.

When I asked Dennison why it was wrong, he said, "It does things to a child's mind. Sex is something that you need maturity to understand. Adults struggle with it, and most people can't have sex without getting their emotions involved, which can be very powerful or overwhelming, and it's too much for a small child to understand."

"I understand," I said as I pulled a stick of gum from my pocket and plopped it in my mouth. "You get the urge, you get off, then the urge comes back, and you want to get off again."

"Did you want someone to do that to you when you were four or five?" he asked.

I had never thought about that before, but I knew the answer. The first time Jake had messed with me, I didn't know what he was doing or why. It felt strange and wrong, confusing and painful. It hurt like hell, and it felt frightening because there was nothing I could do to stop him. For a long time, I thought it was a punishment for something I had done wrong. Why else would he hurt me like that? Later in life, my therapist told me that little kids don't have the cognitive development to realize the volition of adults. She told me that kids often think of abuse as their fault. At first, I thought it was punishment, but I soon came to have a venomous loathing for Jake.

I pondered for a moment before I answered his question. "I've always liked men, but the first time it was that asshole bastard Jake who did it. He made me do it, and it hurt. He liked it when it hurt. I fucking hate him! He's not a real man!"

"Well, that's the other thing that makes it wrong," he explained. "It is never okay to do something against another person's will or to hurt someone, and children do not have the cognitive maturity to make a decision like that."

"There were a couple of times, with other guys," I continued, "that I did it, and I liked it, but they were like kids my age, maybe a little older. I wanted it, but I don't like it in my butt. I want it in my pussy. I have a pussy like other girls, but mine is under all this other stuff. Mike would never do it, though. I wanted Mike to do it, but he wouldn't. He came and fucked my whore mother, but he wouldn't fuck me."

He said almost the same thing that Mike had said. Listening to him, I could see Mike in my head, hear him explaining that it is wrong for an adult to do that with a child. Until I became an adult, I never really understood that they were right and that my attitudes about sex were a product of my abuse. However, at the time, I didn't know. I thought I should be able to do whatever I wanted with anyone who wanted me, but Mike and this preacher didn't want me sexually. They saw a child in peril acting out the only thing she knew and refused to take advantage of that. Looking back during my adult years, I respected both for that. Even though I thought I wanted them, my abuse and immaturity could not make sense of it. Making sense of it would only come after some time in therapy.

I explained to the preacher that I liked for men to touch me, and I didn't feel the same when a woman touched me. I didn't dislike having a woman touch me, but I preferred the touch of men. After telling him about Jake Carter and coming onto him, only to have him turn me down, I asked him directly, "Have you ever been molested?"

"No!" he snapped back like I had said something wrong.

I watched as his face turned cherry red, flushed, and anxious.

"Then, shut up," I commanded. "You don't know what you are talking about."

"Well, I do know right from wrong," he said. "It is simply wrong to hurt people, and doing something like that to a child, even if he thinks he wants it, is also wrong."

"Well, what that bastard Jake did was wrong," I complained, "because it hurt, and he wouldn't stop. He deserves to die, and I'm going to kill him someday. If it takes me the rest of my life, I will find him and kill him for what he did to me!"

"If the foster care got you away from Jake, I'm glad," he comforted. "Certainly, what Jake did was wrong, but killing people is also wrong."

"The state kills people," I argued. "They call it the death penalty. I would save the state the time and money if I killed Jake myself."

"That's different," he explained. "The state doesn't kill people out of hate and vengeance. The state executes people after they have been found guilty through the justice system."

"As far as I can tell," I countered. "The justice system never did much justice for me."

"Well, it's the court's decision," he continued. "It's not just one person being vengeful."

I considered that he was right. The courts have juries and judges and take into account many things, but I also knew the courts had convicted Mike for killing my so-called mother when I was sure there was no way he could have done it. At least, I had convinced myself that he couldn't have done it. I didn't really know, but I determined that Mike had to be innocent. By then, Mike had been sentenced to life in prison, and I had no hope of ever seeing him again. As much as I wanted to kill Jake, I also wished I could find a way to prove that Mike was innocent, but I had no idea how I could ever do that.

Still, the courts are more than just one person being pissed and getting revenge because another person hurt them, but sometimes they convict innocent people. They had to be wrong about Mike. I knew how he got Mable-bitch's blood on his shirt, but I also knew that the courts had compelling evidence.

I eyed him carefully, wondering if there might be a chance that he would do something with me; even though he had made it clear that he had no interest, I was still interested in him. I didn't realize that my sexual acting out at the time was due to having been molested. As the years passed, I lost interest in sex almost all together. However, that day, I decided to give it one last chance.

"Jake likes pretty boys," I challenged and changed the subject, "sissy boys like me, but I never wanted to be pretty for him. I wanted to be pretty for Mike, but Mike didn't want me like that. I want to be pretty for you."

I reached into my pocket and pulled out a tube of lipstick that I had stolen from Mrs. McNeil. I wanted to test him and see what he would do. I entertained the idea that applying it might change his mind, turn him on, and he would do things with me if he thought I was pretty. Regardless of what the abuse had taught me or what I thought I knew, I still had a child's reasoning.

"WHERE DID YOU GET THAT?" he yelled immediately, suddenly more anxious than he had been throughout the whole interview.

"I stole it," I said, applying lipstick to my lips.

"STOP IT!" he demanded. "GIVE ME THAT!"

"No! It's mine."

He grabbed a tissue and shoved it in my direction. "WIPE THAT OFF YOUR LIPS, NOW!" he commanded.

His face was suddenly flushed, cherry red again, and he looked like he had just witnessed my so-called mother's stabbing. He began breathing like a panting dog, and he was sweating.

"You look sick," I observed.

He fumbled to open the door and shouted into the hallway, "PLEASE! PLEASE!"

Pastor Simmons came running up, "Pastor Dennison! Are you all right?"

Pastor Simmons led him to a bathroom off the hallway, where he fell to his knees and began heaving vomit into the commode.

"I don't know what is wrong with me," he said. "I just suddenly became deathly ill."

"My lipstick made him puke," I giggled while watching the spectacle at the open bathroom door.

Pastor Simmons then ordered his secretary to take me *aside.*

She took me back to her office by the back entry at the other end of the hall.

"Stephen," she scolded. "It doesn't cost you a thing to be nice to people, and everybody needs a little compassion now and then."

"What about me?" I questioned. "Don't I need a little compassion?"

"Yes, you do, sweetheart," she smiled and said. "Maybe you might get more compassion if you gave a little of it now and then. Did you ever think about that?"

I had never thought of it like that, but I realized that she had a point and logged the lesson into my memory that maybe you might be more likely to get compassion if you give it. That would be a challenge.

"It's my fault the preacher got sick," I announced.

"No, honey, it's not your fault," she countered. "But you could have been nicer to him when he got sick."

"No, it is my fault," I argued. "He started getting sick when I put on my lipstick."

At that time, it didn't occur to me that he got sick because of something he was battling within himself, not because of anything I had done. It takes a while to mature into the understanding that another person's behavior is not about you but is about what is happening inside them. In later years, I pondered whether he had been so anxious because he might have been grappling with some conflict within himself that others didn't know. When I turned eighteen, he sent me a letter and explained everything.

"Speaking of lipstick, sugar," The secretary fluffed, "you may think that looks pretty, but it doesn't look pretty on a boy, and there are times when we need to be proper and put aside our whims. You have to dress for the occasion. Right? Now, let me get that." She pulled a couple of tissues from a tissue box on her desk and began wiping the lipstick off my lips.

She treated me better than most, so I tolerated her, usually, but I didn't like when people put their hands on me and tried to control me. Still, I let her wipe my lips without creating protest.

About the time I had my lips wiped clean, we heard Pastor Simmons calling for her to bring me back into the hall.

She wrapped one arm around me and marched me back into the hall.

"Get your hands off me!" I yelled at her and slung my shoulders away from her. I could only take so much handling before it became overstimulating.

Pastor Simmons scolded me, "Stephen, we need for you to behave in a civilized manner."

"Fuck you!" I snapped back.

Pastor Dennison waved to Pastor Simmons. "Please," he said. Then he walked up the hall toward me, knelt eye to eye, and said, "I know you are angry. I don't blame you for being angry. I would be angry if I had been through even part of what you have been through. I know you don't trust anybody because of what you have been through. I don't blame you. I know it's hard to believe that anyone really does care about you, and I can't fix that, but has there ever been anyone you trusted? Has anyone ever cared about you who hasn't hurt you?"

I stared at him silently for a moment. No one else had ever bothered trying to understand how I felt since I had been taken into foster care. He was the first since Miss Mattie. No one had ever asked me that question. All they wanted to do was change me into what they thought I should be. I thought about Miss Mattie, how she had always been there for me, how I missed her. Then, a feeling of deep sadness came over me.

"Miss Mattie," I said, finally. "Miss Mattie was always good to me, but they took me away from her and put me HERE!" I felt both grief and anger. I felt like I would cry, but I determined I would not let that happen. Anger helped to keep me from crying, and despite being a girl, I had learned, especially at Pruitt Igoe, that tears indicated weakness, something you never wanted to show in that environment.

He noticed that I was fighting tears and reached to take my hand.

"I'm sorry," he said softly. "Have you gotten to see Miss Mattie?"

"They won't let me see her!" I exclaimed.

He turned to Pastor Simmons and said, "Who is this Miss Mattie he is talking about?"

"She is an old Negro woman who lived near him in the projects," Pastor Simmons answered.

"Why hasn't the child been allowed to see her?" Pastor Dennison asked.

"She is not kin," Pastor Simmons responded. "Since she lives in the projects, we question whether it would be appropriate for him to see her. Who knows what she is really like?"

Pastor Dennison turned back to me and said, "Tell me about Miss Mattie."

"She is the only person who ever loved me." I found it difficult to hold back the tears. "Now, she might as well be dead, too. She took care of me most of the time. She brought us food and fed me. When my mother had some man over, was into her shit, or passed out, I would go see Miss Mattie, and she would take care of me."

He asked Pastor Simmons if Miss Mattie had been given the option of fostering me when I was taken into state custody, and Pastor Simmons told him there was no way of doing that because she was not next of kin. Listening to them, I realized they could have placed me with my so-called grandmother at Thayer. I didn't know why they hadn't. Maybe it was because she didn't want me, or the state figured she was no more fit to take care of me than my so-called-mother—and she wasn't.

Pastor Simmons told him that I was so light-skinned that they figured I should be placed with a white family and that he didn't think it was appropriate for me to continue being raised in the poverty and squalor of the slums. He didn't even realize how subtle racism seeped through his words even though he pretended otherwise.

Pastor Dennison argued that it would be better for me to be raised in a poor home where I was loved than a wealthy home just because the conditions were better.

Then, Pastor Dennison asked me if I wanted to see Miss Mattie, and of course, I wanted to see her. I had missed her since the very day they took me out of Pruitt Igoe.

When I nodded a yes, he said, "There is no time today, but with permission, I will take you to see her tomorrow before I go back to Nashville."

Pastor Simmons continued to admonish him not to take me to Pruitt Igoe, and he said, "Yeah, though I walk through the valley of the shadow of death, I will fear no evil."

That night, the McNeil's dressed all the foster kids like little designer ducks and took us to hear Pastor Dennison speak at Safe Harbor Church. A crowd was at the church that night, and there was barely enough room to fit everyone in what was already a gigantic church. I hated church. It bored the crap out of me, and I couldn't see much use for it. The only solace that night was that I got to sit near the front and watch Pastor Dennison prancing around while he gave his sermon. I always enjoyed watching the cute guys, but my feelings changed toward him when he had been compassionate and understanding with me. There was no longer any sexual yearning. That had been replaced by gratitude.

They got us up again the following day to attend the early church service. Then, a little after 10:00 a.m., Pastor Dennison arrived at our house to take me to see Miss Mattie. As was the usual practice, after getting home from church, I had changed out of my church clothes into casual clothes.

When Pastor Dennison rang the front doorbell, Mrs. McNeil rushed around to open the door like she was inviting a dignitary into her home. They usually gave the maids Sunday off, but even if they had been there, Mrs. McNeil would have waved them aside so she could open the door for the dignitary preacher.

"Oh, my word!" she gushed. "Pastor Dennison, what an honor to meet you, and have you come to our humble home? Such an honor." She motioned toward Mr. McNeil, who had come to stand behind her. "This is my husband, Jacob McNeil." She always used his formal name when introducing him to others, and the truth is that I cringed a bit when I heard her call him Jake.

Mr. McNeil stepped up to shake hands with Pastor Dennison, and I stood by the front stairs, waiting.

Pastor Dennison spotted me standing there, "Oh, Steph," he called. "Good morning. Are you ready to go?"

He had compromised between Stephen and Stephanie, and I was okay with that. Unlike the others, at least he was making an effort.

"Pastor Dennison," Mrs. McNeil continued to gush. "Are you sure you wouldn't like to stay and chat for a while, maybe have some coffee?"

"Thank you, Mrs. McNeil," he responded. "That's a very kind offer, but I have made a promise to Steph, and I have a very tight schedule that gives me only a little time to honor this promise and get back on the road to Nashville."

With that, you could see the disappointment and jealousy crawling over her face as though I was taking her spotlight and robbing her of time with the Pastor. Even though she had asked for this and requested that the Pastor speak to me, you could tell that she wanted more spotlight for herself, and she had never, for a moment, expected that he would come to their home and take me to see Miss Mattie.

"Very well," she acquiesced. "You fellas had better be on your way then." She waved me toward the door and Pastor Dennison.

"Do you know when we might expect your return?" she questioned.

"I'm not sure," Pastor Dennison replied. "I would say send out scouts if we are not back by sundown, but I hope to have him back and get on the road by at least 3:00 p.m. at the latest, hopefully sooner. I'll drop him off at the church. That will be more convenient for my drive home, so I won't have to drive him back out here. Pastor Simmons agreed to be there, and we may have some discussions before I go back."

He smiled at her as I met him at the door. She was almost hand-wringing and gleaming even though her disappointment was evident. Then he nodded to Mr. McNeil, who was calm about the whole thing, and we turned to leave.

We descended the front steps and crossed the sidewalk to the circular drive where his rental car awaited. I had seldom gone through that door since having been delivered by family services on the night my so-called mother was murdered. The family primarily used the back entrance near the garage, especially for the children.

The Pastor's rental car was parked right by the sidewalk with the passenger side door aligned with the walk. I got in as he walked around to the driver's side. When he got in and started the car, he looked over at me and smiled. "Are you ready for this?"

"I couldn't sleep last night," I said. "I haven't seen Miss Mattie in a year. I have missed her so much. I hope she is still there. I hope she is okay."

After such an extended period, I couldn't be sure she would still be there. A lot could happen at Pruitt Igoe in a month, much less a year, and for all I knew, Miss Mattie might have been murdered, too. I consoled myself with the hope of seeing her.

He put the car in drive and pulled away from the McNeil house. "I hope so, too," he said.

I began giving him instructions to Pruitt Igoe, and when we got near, I suggested that he needed to park several blocks away and that we walk the rest of the way. I didn't want anyone spotting and getting ideas about that new car.

He locked the car, and we walked about ten blocks to Pruitt Igoe. You could see and even feel the condition of the neighborhood deteriorating as we got closer. The sidewalks were cracked, and trash was amassed along the curbs. We had no sooner set foot on the Pruitt Igoe campus than here came Ronza, sideling up to me, putting his arm around me, and acting like I was his girlfriend. I tried to get rid of him, but he kept on. Then Pastor Dennison turned to him, took this ominous stance, and pretended to be a cop.

"I am Officer Ron Dennison with the St. Louis police investigative unit," he proclaimed with a deep, ominous voice. "I am here with this young man on official police business!"

I thought people weren't supposed to lie, especially preachers, but I definitely enjoyed the show. I didn't dare laugh out loud, but inside I was laughing my ass off as I watched Ronza back away, jabbering, "No, hey … I'm just playing."

I felt the urge to taunt him, but I didn't. When we walked on, I said, "He's an asshole."

I got the pastor through the campus to our building. Then, we had to take the stairs to Miss Mattie's apartment because the elevator, as usual, didn't work. The place had the same acrid stench, but it bothered me even more after being away from it for so long. I guess I had gotten used to all those clean, sweet smells that wafted about when Miss Mildred sanitized the McNeil house.

When we knocked at Miss Mattie's apartment, she cracked the door slightly open but kept the burglar latch on.

"Who are you?" she asked Pastor Dennison, her tone intense. "Ya ain't got no business here!"

"Miss Mattie, it's me, Stephanie," I called.

Then her penetrating stare at Pastor Dennison came off him and went to my level, where it melted like warm butter.

"Oh, Lord, a mercy!" she declared.

She fiddled with the lock as quickly as possible, opened the door, and hugged me. "Child! I have missed you. I thought I was never gonna get to see you again!"

As soon as she was done hugging me, I introduced her to Pastor Dennison.

"Dennison, Dennison," She pondered, "Wait a minute! You look familiar. You not Dennison, dat TV preacher? No, man like dat ain't gonna be comin' round no place like Pruitt Igoe."

"Yes, Ma'am," he said as he reached out his hand to shake hers. "Pastor Ronald Dennison."

"De Lord, a mercy!" she exclaimed again, a smile crawling across her face like a wiggling worm.

He explained that he had brought me to visit her, and she invited us in. They chatted, and she introduced her full name, "Mattie Larouquette, Lar—ro—quette, like Larry, oh, and a cat. Creole from Louisiana."

She motioned both of us in to sit down and immediately asked if I had breakfast. I told her I had half an apple for breakfast and wasn't hungry. The truth is, I had given most of my breakfast to Bill. I knew he would want it and was trying to ensure I stayed trim. I tried to explain that I didn't want to get fat, but she insisted on feeding me and the pastor.

"You are skinny," I observed as I defended myself from her renewed and previously constant insistence that I eat.

"I ain't skinny 'cause I don't eat," she rebutted. "I'm skinny 'cause I'm skinny."

She insisted on making a cheese sandwich for me and for Pastor Dennison. When she went to the kitchen to make it, I told him how she had always taken care of me. She had consistently fed and protected me and even ran off this man who had been beating my so-called mother. I had gone to get her, and she took her pistol down to our place and ran him off, telling him he could get gone by the door or by a bullet, but he was going to get gone either way.

Miss Mattie returned with sandwiches and apologized for making them with government cheese, but Pastor Dennison smiled and said, "You know, I grew up poor, and we would get commodities sometimes. Personally, I think government cheese is some of the best cheese."

Miss Mattie started asking questions about the foster home and how the McNeils treated me. I exaggerated how many kids there were and how difficult it was, but what I did not exaggerate was that I didn't want to be there, and I didn't feel welcomed or loved there. I didn't exaggerate about how I was treated for being different and how the McNeils insisted that I never use the name Stephanie.

Miss Mattie tried to get me to understand that I would never have a time when everyone liked me, that I would always have to deal with being different, and that there would always be people who would hate me for no good reason. She said I had to forget about the ones who hate me and find the ones who love me.

She began asking Pastor Dennison what was going to happen to me. He explained that I would probably live the remainder of my childhood in state custody, that I was going to get put into a specialty home, a reform school, or something if my behavior didn't improve, and she immediately began admonishing me that I had to behave so I didn't get put in one of those homes.

I started crying. "I might as well be in one now," I whimpered. "Nobody loves me, and nobody wants me! I might as well be dead! Everybody thinks I'm a freak!" I had always felt safe about crying with Miss Mattie. She never accused me of being weak for shedding tears.

Miss Mattie got up and came to sit beside me. She put her arms around me and said, "Now don't say dat, baby. You know old Mattie loves you no matter what."

"But I'm a freak of nature!" I cried. "I probably should be killed and fed to the pigs like some of the older kids say."

"Honey, you ain't no freak," she comforted as she rocked me back and forth. "You is de way de good Lord made you. Don't ever be ashamed of dat."

"But God made me a boy!" I continued crying. "I don't want to be a boy! I'm not supposed to be a boy! I'm not a boy!"

"Baby, you are eleven years old. Dats what you is. You don't have ta have all de answers right now. You got time." She turned to Pastor Dennison then and said, "Pastor, is dere any way we can keep dis child from going to one of dem homes?"

Contemplation expressed on his face, a deep wondering, perhaps considering various possibilities, and then he asked, "Would you want to keep him?"

I was shocked by that question. I couldn't believe he actually asked her that instead of insisting that I had to be raised in a Christian home where they would always insist that I was an abomination and that I had to become a straight man to be worthy of society and the love of the Lord.

"Oh Lord, Yes!" she exclaimed. "If I knew dat I could give dis child a halfway decent life, I would be happy to raise her. I have practically raised her already. Lord knows she has been through hell already. I just wish I could take her out of dat. I know she gotta deal with dis idea dat she ain't really no girl. Dat's gonna be hard enough when she around people dat loves her. It's gonna be even more hell if she have to be around peoples dat don't."

The pastor pondered again. You could see the wheels of thought rolling around his head, mapped by his affect. After a while, he said he would do whatever he could to help and try to find a way for me to stay with Miss Mattie. My heart jumped at even the slightest hope that he could ever accomplish such a thing. I had no idea how he could ever pull off something like that, but I would rather have lived with Miss Mattie in a ditch than live in the most opulent home on earth where I felt like a burden and a project.

He said he might be able to arrange something like that. He said he might be able to manage it financially but didn't know if he could manage it legally.

The hope alone made my spirits soar.

When the time came for us to go, I didn't want to go. I begged to stay. I begged him to let me stay with Miss Mattie instead of returning to the McNeil house, and my resistance was intense.

Miss Mattie got me by the shoulders and said, "Ya listen here Miss Hot Stuff. You had your visit. De Pastor was kind enough ta bring you over ta see Miss Mattie, and you need ta be kind enough ta straighten up and do right by him. Miss Mattie is all kinds of proud she got ta see you, but right now, you gotta put on dem big girl panties and do da right thing."

"But I don't want to go," I cried.

"Now, ain't nobody in dis world dat always gets what de want. You got ta go, and don't you be causin' no problem fo de good Pastor."

Pastor Dennison then bent over to talk to me, "Stephanie," he said, shocking me by calling me by my real name. "You have my promise that I will do everything I can to help you get back to Miss Mattie, but it will take time and planning, okay? Right now, we have to go back."

I finally, hesitantly, ceased my defiance. I knew I had no choice. When I agreed to return with Pastor Dennison, Miss Mattie said, "Now you behave yourself when you get back dare. Ain't no cause for actin up even if peoples make fun of you. You meet meanness wid kindness. Dat's how it works. Fo every mean thing de say ta you, you say three kind things ta dem. De world ain't won by meanness, child. It's de meek shall inherit de earth. Just like Dr. Martin Luther King Jr. said, 'We must learn ta live together as brothers or perish together as fools.' You keep dat in mind, now."

I listened to her. I always listened to her. I had needed and missed her wisdom. She could make sense when nobody else could. She could reach my heart the way nobody else ever had. As much as I wanted to cling to her and never be apart from her again, we said our goodbyes, and I went back with Pastor Dennison.

On the drive back, I asked him, "Why are you doing this? Why are you going to try to fix it so I can stay with Miss Mattie when every other church person I ever met wanted me away from her and wanted to turn me into someone like them?"

He sighed and looked down briefly, then back at the road.

"You know, I'm not really sure," he said. "You connect me to something. I don't know what, just yet. It's like we have met on a level I can't explain. I feel almost fatherly toward you. There is something in you that I see in myself, and I'm not sure what that is. I just feel a need to help you, and even though my morals say you should be raised in a Christian home with Christian values, my heart says you should be raised with someone who loves you no matter what, with no conditions, no requirements, just love."

He reached over and gently squeezed my hand. My heart pounded, but not from the thrill of attraction or fear that he would hurt me. It felt comforting, fatherly, warm, and good.

"I am going to have to clear this with my wife," he continued. "I'm going to have to talk to my legal team and look at my finances, but I feel like this is a gift I want to give you."

He moved his hand back to the steering wheel, and I sat there looking over at him, saying nothing.

Then, he said something I didn't expect, something I had never heard from an adult before. I could have sworn I heard a warble in his voice as though he was about to cry, "Maybe," he paused briefly, "Maybe, I wish I could have grown up in a home where I was accepted and loved without expectations. You know? My momma gave me that, but Daddy?—"

He shook his head a little and glanced away.

I didn't know what to say, but I knew something had happened between us, something I had not felt since the day Mike sat me on his knee. I only sat there quietly, feeling a bond that could never have happened if he had even remotely responded to my abuse-fueled attempts to seduce him.

"Are you okay?" he asked as we pulled into the church's parking lot.

"I'm a lot better now," I said.

CHAPTER 7

LIBERATION

After my visit with Pastor Dennison, life with the McNeil family continued, as usual, and what I didn't know was that, behind the scenes, the McNeils had continued to pursue this idea of so-called conversion therapy of sending me away somewhere so I could be transformed into the perfect little Christian boy they thought I should be. It didn't matter how well-behaved I was. They still felt it was their Christian duty to change me. I had made a promise to Miss Mattie that I intended to keep, so I tried to be friendly and behave well. Most of the time, I was pretty good at it, but there were occasions when my pot boiled over and, at the very least, unsavory words were spilled. I certainly had learned to cuss at Pruitt Igoe.

The McNeils just couldn't understand that my angry behavior had nothing to do with confusion over my identity and everything to do with the trauma I had been through. Nights when I woke up screaming were comforted briefly and passed on. It felt more like they wanted me to get over the nightmares than to give me any genuine loving comfort. Of course, I wasn't the only kid who woke up screaming in that house. Pretty much all of us had nightmares, at least occasionally, some of us more regularly than others. We all had fear and anguish festering in subconscious vats of memory scorched by trauma. Our dreams would symbolically tell what waking reality would not. The McNeils had no concept that pushing and pressuring me to conform to a mold they defined as appropriate also stressed me and triggered pent-up rage that had been collecting inside since I was small. The pressure of not being allowed to express my true nature was excruciating. I constantly felt like a dam that was about to break, not only with pent-up anger over years of trauma but with an overwhelming sense of self that they demanded I suppress. Pastor Simmons had given them some phone numbers and contacts regarding the idea of converting me, and they had begun soliciting the state to approve the "therapy" for me. Thankfully, that all took time.

I did my best to live up to what they expected, not because they expected it, but because Miss Mattie had admonished me. I got up, dressed as I was expected to dress, tried to be pleasant with the other kids, and followed the prescribed behavior of doing my chores, going to school, doing my homework, and going to bed on the schedule that had been prescribed for all the kids. I even ignored the "Sissy little queer" and other taunts from Carl.

As frustrating as everything was at home, going to school was not a walk in the park either. I had been picked on and ridiculed before, but at least in the post-bussing era, some black kids attended school at Ladue. Of course, there were racial tensions, but my bullying was not just about being black. The whites classified me as black, and the black kids classified me as *high yellow* with a silver spoon in my mouth because I lived with a wealthy foster family. I couldn't win. There had always been taunts such as, "Hey faggot! You've got more swish in your ass than a washing machine!" After something like that, there would be a round of laughter as the perpetrator was goaded on by his companions. I got that same kind of harassment from the black kids. White kids or black, none of them knew that I didn't mind that I had swish. I loved my swish. I loved everything that indicated my femininity because that was my true nature. It took hard work to put on the swagger of a boy. Even if I tried, I would soon slip back into being myself, and it didn't make any difference anyway because I was still considered to be one of the unworthy kids; those who, because of their history, background, or differences, were regarded to be of less value and were singled out by those who had the arrogance of belonging. Sometimes, those kids were physically intrusive, a shove or stiff flat fingers suddenly shoved up my ass from behind, driving my jeans into my butt crack, or a thump to the nuts. Sometimes, they would get overtly violent. Not one of the boys could beat me up on his own because I had learned to fight in an environment where you fought to survive. I could nail any of them individually, but when they ganged up on me, that was a different story. I couldn't beat them all. I was lucky that Mrs. McNeil would drop us off and pick us up from school. So, I didn't have to be around a bunch of them after school or on a bus, and I was careful throughout the day to stay within the visual range of a teacher, some of whom made half-assed attempts to protect me. It didn't help that my foster care roommates often joined the bullies and shared secrets that could be used to fuel the fire of intimidation. None of it made me want to be a boy.

Despite the bullying, I felt increasingly uncomfortable in my boy's body as I matured past thirteen. For one thing, I grew hair under my arms, in my pubic area, and on my legs. I hated it, but Mr. & Mrs. McNeil forbade me to shave my legs and underarms. Most of all, I hated hair on my face, even if it was just a few scraggly chin hairs. At least I was allowed to shave that. I despised anything and everything that made me look like a boy. Sometimes, after a shower, I would stare at myself in the mirror, wondering how I ended up with this body, knowing this was not the body I was supposed to have, knowing that despite my increasing hair and developing genitalia, I was not sup-posed to look like this. No one seemed to understand this except Miss Mattie. They all thought that it was caused by not having a father in the home and by growing up in the slums with a drug-addict whore mother. They were wrong, but I knew I could never prove it to them.

Even if my boy's body was transitioning into a man's physique, I was still feminine, and in the 1970s, feminine men and boys were despised. The Stonewall riots that began the Gay Rights Movement had only been in 1969, and most people, myself included, had never even heard of them, much less had paid them any attention. It wouldn't have mat-tered anyway. Gay or transgender people were seen by almost everyone as unacceptable, especially transgender people. If the bullying was not overt, it was subtle and passive-aggressive. Even teachers who never said anything out of line, on the surface, had that course microaggression of disapproval on their faces, the roll of eyes, or the underhanded comment that I needed to "man up." I kept my promise to Miss Mattie and, most of the time, quietly smiled when I recognized some subtle dig or putdown.

I was beginning to think I would never get out of there, out of the McNeil home, and never be allowed to be myself. Then, on an early June morning, just after school had turned out for the summer and halfway through my thirteenth year, a car pulled into the front drive of the McNeil home. It was a very nice car, a brand new, olive green 1973 Lincoln Continental. Mr. McNeil had been sitting in the living room reading the morning paper and sipping his coffee after breakfast when, from the front window of the living room, he saw the car pull into the circular drive.

Usually, at the McNeil home, the only things that pulled into that front driveway, besides invited guests, were delivery trucks or the mailman. This was different. All the kids were in the back of the house finishing breakfast, and we didn't know what was going on in the front until there was a doorbell ring, unusual at 7:30 a.m.

Mr. McNeil had been peeking out the front window at that Lincoln when a skinny old black woman got out and began ambling up the front sidewalk. By the time she rang the doorbell, Mr. McNeil had already crossed to the door to intercept and opened the door just as she rang the bell. He opened the door to find Miss Mattie standing on the threshold.

"I'm sorry," he said without waiting for her to speak. "You must have the wrong address. The Nelsons are hiring a maid. That's two doors down." He had never met her but assumed that she could only fit his expected role of a black woman in those days. Lord knows no elderly black woman should be calling at the front door of a home in Ladue at that hour of the morning or any time unless she was looking for housekeeping work. It didn't occur to him that someone looking for a maid's job would not likely be driving a brand-new Lincoln or wearing designer clothes.

"Oh, I don't has de wrong address," she smiled. "I am Miss Mattie Laroquette, and I am here ta take cus-to-dy of my chile, Stephanie Saunders."

Miss Mattie stood at the threshold decked out in an aqua-colored silk dress with a crew neck, blouson sleeves, and pleated skirt, that had obviously been purchased at a high-end store, another sight white people never unexpected to see in Ladue.

"You mean Stephen Saunders?" Mr. McNeil questioned, although he knew exactly who she was talking about.

"You may call her dat, an dat might be her legal name, but I have always knowed her as Stephanie."

"I believe you must be mistaken," Mr. McNeil responded. "We have legal custody of Stephen Saunders through the Missouri State Family Services Department."

"Not according to dese court papas," Miss Mattie confronted. "I have de papas right here."

As soon as I heard her voice, I dashed toward the front as Mrs. McNeil commanded, "Stephen! Sit down!"

Kids were not allowed to question or interfere in the affairs of adults, not in the McNeil home. So, any action conducted at the front door was to be ignored, and usually, we did, but this was different. For the past two years, I had tolerated the McNeil home just as Miss Mattie had requested. I had obeyed and tried carefully not to create any trouble. On that day, however, I reverted to the old Stephanie.

"Fuck you!" I exclaimed. "I'm going to see Miss Mattie."

Mrs. McNeil, wisely, did not try to stop me, and by the time I reached the front of the house, I found Miss Mattie reaching into her purse to retrieve papers for Mr. McNeil.

"Miss Mattie!" I yelled as I ran toward her.

Mr. McNeil raised his hand in my direction and shouted, "Stephen, Stop! Stay right where you are!"

"Fuck You!" I shouted as I continued toward her.

"Stephanie," Miss Mattie comforted. "You jest relax, darlin'. We awe right."

I stopped mid-way to the front door, and Miss Mattie continued to dig into her purse. She pulled out a large manila envelope and handed it to Mr. McNeil.

"According to dis right chere," she went on, "I am now de sole legal guardian of one Stephen Christopher Saunders. Dat's da legal name, but I calls her what she wants ta be called."

Mr. McNeil took the envelope from her and opened it with apparent disbelief. He stood momentarily reading and said, "This has to be a mistake."

"Ain't no mistake," Miss Mattie affirmed. "You member dat Pastor Dennison who come ta bring Stephanie to see me bout two years ago? Well, he done fronted de money and hired de legal team ta get me dem papas. He set up a Trust fo Stephanie and everythin'."

"Give me a moment," Mr. McNeil replied with terse congeniality.

He then took the papers to the living room, left Miss Mattie standing at the open door, and sat down to read them. I observed his disrespect, but it was common for white people who didn't seem to think anyone other than another white person deserved their courtesy.

No sooner did he move when I ran to Miss Mattie to hug her.

"Oh, it is so good ta see you, baby," she exclaimed as she wrapped her arms around me.

Mrs. McNeil had come to stand behind me.

"Won't you come in?" she said to Miss Mattie with formal congeniality and courtesy, becoming of her position as the lady of the house but unexpected by me. She extended her nail-polished, ring-adorned hand with her arm locked straight at the elbow to shake Miss Mattie's hand.

Only then, with a courteous handshake, did Miss Mattie step over the threshold into the foyer. "Thank you, kindly," she said, "fo allowin' me inta your lovely home."

Mrs. McNeil stepped behind her and closed the front door.

"Please, come in and sit down," she said as she motioned Miss Mattie toward the living room.

"Thank you very much," Miss Mattie replied as she moved toward the living room and sat in a chair adjacent to Mr. McNeil.

He sat in his leather broad-armed lounge chair, intently reading and taking no notice of or ignoring the movement around him.

"Stephen, please sit down," Mrs. McNeil told me as she motioned to the sofa across from Miss Mattie. "I need to go to the back and tend to the other children."

I was surprised at her behavior. As a rule, the children were only allowed in the front living room during special occasions such as a visit from family services or some formality and would have been run out if caught there any other time. Perhaps this was a special occasion. I sat on the sofa as instructed.

Mrs. McNeil walked past the stairs and the foyer to the kitchen entrance next to the formal dining room and called through the kitchen for Miss Mildred to finish the children's breakfast and take them upstairs. Next, she returned to sit at the opposite end of the sofa from me. Then, she remained silent, legs crossed at the ankles, her hands demurely folded on her lap. She made no effort at conversation.

In a moment, Mr. McNeil released a long sigh. He turned the papers over and held them on his lap.

"Everything seems to be in order," he said. "However, do you mind waiting until 8:00 a.m. when my attorney's office opens? I want to call him to confirm the legalities of this?"

"Dat's no problem atoll," Miss Mattie confirmed as she sat with her purse across her lap, her arms folded over it and her legs crossed at the ankles in a lady-like position just like Mrs. McNeil.

I had never seen her like that. I had never seen her in such nice clothes, with a nice purse and elegant shoes that perfectly matched her dress. She even had on makeup. When she smiled at me, I real-ized she had a complete set of pearly white teeth instead of the few scraggly pieces of teeth that I had always seen before. I didn't know what to think. She was transformed, and yet she was still the same Miss Mattie.

"Mattie, would you like a cup of coffee?" Mr. McNeil asked without daring to use the word *Miss* in front of her name. "It will be about another ten or fifteen minutes until my attorney's office opens. In the meantime, I also need to call my job and tell them I will be a little late this morning."

"A cup o' coffee would be very nice," Miss Mattie responded.

Mr. McNeil said, "Coming up." He rose from his seat. He would have been more likely to call the maid to do it than to get it himself, but Miss Mildred was the only one on duty that morning and she was finishing with the other kids.

"I'll get it, Darling," Mrs. McNeil said as she waved him to sit back down and left for the kitchen.

Mr. McNeil leaned back in his chair, opened the papers again, and looked through them intently as though he might have missed something the first time.

"How you been?" Miss Mattie grinned and ogled me over her purse.

"Okay," I grinned back. "I've been trying to do like you told me. I've been trying to go along and not get in trouble."

"You a good girl," She smiled. "Now, we gonna get you outta here."

"Where?" I asked.

"Oh, actually, I been lookin fo houses in dis neighborhood." She grinned again. "I don't want you ta hafta change schools."

I grimaced when she said this. She didn't know the trouble I had been having in school, but I didn't want to say anything about it in front of Mr. McNeil.

When she affirmed looking for houses in Ladue, Mr. McNeil's eyes popped over the papers, glancing at her with a brief look of shock. He glanced over at me and then poured his eyes back into the document.

"In this neighborhood?" I questioned. "Where did you get that kind of money?"

I didn't want to live in Ladue, and I didn't want to keep going to that school. I hoped that someplace fresh might yield better treatment, but it wasn't likely in those days.

"Dat preacher man," she responded. "Dat TV preacher, Pastor Dennison, what brought you ta see me. You member he said he was gonna try to find a way fo us ta be together? Well, he done set up a big Trust Fund an' everythin', a million dollars, an' on top o' dat paid fo all dem legal fees, hired lawyers, an all, and we gots a housin' budget separate from de Trust dats enough to buy a place right cheer. Baby, we got enough money now ta live as fine as dese peoples, jest you an me."

Mr. McNeil looked up. "I understood that Pastor Dennison abdicated his ministry," he said. "There had even been some lawsuits against him after he gave his last sermon a couple of years ago. He still had enough to leave a Trust that large?"

"I guess so," Miss Mattie responded. "He still had enough money ta do dis fo us, or he got it worked out wid dem lawsuits. Pastor Dennison set up de Trust, an' soon as it look like dey was gonna grant de custody, he let me access it. I went an bought us a new car, got some new clothes, and got me some dentures." She looked over at me and smiled with her new pearly white teeth. "Now we gonna go do da same fo you Stephanie, cept fo de car and de dentures." She snickered. Her nose curled, and her eyes lit up as she shot me that familiar smile that I had not seen for far too long.

Tears came to my eyes. I ran across the room and hugged her in her chair. "Thank you, Miss Mattie!" I declared.

"We need ta thank dat good preacher," she said as she raised one hand and patted me on the arm.

Mrs. McNeil brought in a silver tray containing a carafe of cream, a sugar bowl, and a little white porcelain cup on a saucer. Reflections caught the dark coffee in the cup and glistened as she set it on the coffee table.

"I don't know how you like your coffee," she said. "So, I brought the works."

"I takes it black," Miss Mattie replied. "But thank ya fo de fixins."

Mrs. McNeil sat back in her previous spot and assumed her previous position. She appeared unhappy and I assumed it was about serving coffee to a black woman instead of the other way around. That was her choice. She didn't have to do it, but at the time, she was more committed to formality than her white privilege.

"So," Mr. McNeil queried as he lowered the paperwork again. "How did all this come about?"

"Like I was tellin' Stephanie," Miss Mattie replied. "Da TV preacher man done it. Dat Pastor Dennison."

"No, that's not what I'm asking," he said. "How did all this come about without us knowing about it?"

"Guess de preacher man and his lawyers kept it hush," Miss Mattie replied. "Guess dae didn't wont ta take de chance on nobody interferin'."

"Well, isn't that interesting," Mr. McNeil responded as he glanced at me while I was standing beside Miss Mattie's chair. "So … well—"

"Preacher man didn't want ta complicate it anymore dan it had ta be, I guess." She continued smiling.

"Well, I—I hope the two of you will be happy together," Mr. McNeil spoke with a very businesslike tone. "I have to say, though, that it is an *interesting* action for Pastor Dennison, or any Christian pastor, to take. I never would have expected that a man of God might opt for a child to be taken out of a home where he would receive the encouragement to be who he really is and where he could be raised in a wholesome Christian environment. From talking to Stephen, I understand that you indulged him in this fantasy that he is a girl."

"I didn't indulge her in nothin'," Miss Mattie came back at him. "I let her be *who* she is. I don't think it up ta me, you, o' anybody else ta decide who Stephanie is. I think dat is up ta da Good Lord an Stephanie. God gave her life to her. It don't belong ta you, me, o' nobody else."

"But you acknowledge that it is a choice," he argued.

"I acknowledge dat it is a decision fo Stephanie to be true ta who she really is o' ta try to fit into somthin' dat she ain't," Miss Mattie retorted. "If she don't want ta try to fit inta something dat she ain't, den ain't nobody's right ta try ta make her. What I don't acknowledge is dat she can change what she is on da inside jus 'cause peoples tells her dat's not who she supposed ta be. You tell her she a boy, make her wear boy's clothes, den de inside don't match what's on de outside."

"Who … *STEPHEN* … *really* is, Mattie," Mr. McNeil lectured. "is a boy—born a male, with all male parts and male hormones. Look," he gestured toward me. "He's even growing facial hair. He's a boy. That's what he needs to accept, not some wild fantasy probably caused by not having a legitimate father in a home where he also lacked parenting from his mother."

"I think daze a lot 'o things peoples don't understand, even doe dey thinks dey do. You don't know, any moe dan anybody dat de Good Lord didn't make her female on da inside and male on da outside fo a good reason. I figures anything de Good Lord do is fo good reason. I don't spect ya ta understand. She da only person dat knows what it feel like ta be her."

Mr. McNeil rolled his eyes and glanced at the clock above the doorway to the foyer. "I have some phone calls to make," he said.

He picked up the phone receiver on a table between his chair and the sofa and began dialing. We could faintly hear the ringer as he listened for someone to pick up. When someone answered, he said, "Good morning Debbie. May I speak to Mr. Davis, please? I assume he has made it to work." There was some jabber on the line, then a pause, and in a moment, we heard him say, "Mark? Hey, good morning, Jacob McNeil. Listen, something has come up with one of the kids, and I will need to be a little late today." There was more jabber on the line. Then he said, "I think I can probably be there by ten." There was more jabber. "Yes, fine," he said. "See you then." He placed the receiver back on the phone and glared momentarily in our direction.

Mr. McNeil rose and said, "Be right back." Then he went into his office off the living room, under the stairs, on the opposite side of the dining room. We heard a drawer open and close. Then, he returned to the living room with a leather-bound personal address book. He sat back down, thumbed through it briefly, and said to Miss Mattie, "Do you mind if I hang on to these for a while?" He waved the legal papers briefly in the air.

Miss Mattie nodded toward him. "Dat's fine. I'm sho dae is mo where dem come from."

He ignored her comment and gazed at a page in the address book. Then, he picked up the receiver and dialed other numbers. In a moment, we heard a jabber that sounded as though it came from a higher-pitched voice. "Good morning," he said. "Would Mr. Gunter be in yet?" Then there was more jabber. "Yes," Mr. McNeil replied, and there was a moment of waiting before he said, "Mr. Gunter? … Good morning. This is Jacob McNeil. I wonder if I might take a moment of your time." The jabber returned. "Well, I have papers presented by Mattie Laroquette regarding one of our children. The papers state that she has been granted sole custody of the child. I was previously unaware of this and just need some advice on how to proceed." There was more jabbering on the line. "It appears to be legitimate. It has a court seal signed by Judge Mathew Richards of Clayton County." After more jabbering, "No, it does not appear, at least on initial inspection, to be forged, and I have no reason to believe it would be." After a little more jabber, he said, "No, I don't want to try to tie it up on the courts. Wouldn't that be the responsibility of family services?" There was a bit more jabber—then, "No, I haven't called them yet. Okay then … all right."

Mr. McNeil hung up and said, "If you don't mind, I have one more phone call I need to make." He glanced at another address in his book, then dialed the number as he looked back and forth between the phone dial and the book. "We heard the ringtone. Then jabber came from the line. "Yes," he said. "May I speak to Doris

Mansfield?" In a moment, he said, "Oh, she was planning on calling me? Okay?" There was a pause, and then, apparently, Mrs. Mansfield got on the line with him. She was the same family services worker who had taken me into protective custody on the night my so-called mother was killed. She had continued to make periodic visits with me since then. "Oh, you received papers, too," he said. "So, this is legitimate?" More jabber came across. "So, it's settled? Does she have full custody? Okay. Okay. What would you recommend as next steps?" The line continued to chatter as he listened. "All right then. We will turn the boy over to her."

He hung up the phone and looked directly at us. I was still standing next to Miss Mattie's chair, and she was holding my hand.

"Well, I guess this is it, then," he sighed. "Stephen, you want to go upstairs and start gathering your things?"

"The name is Stephanie, mother fucker!" I exclaimed as I turned toward the stairs.

"Stephanie!" Miss Mattie scolded. "Now, you watch your mouth, young lady! Ain't no cause to be unkind ta dese good folks dat dun give you a wonderful home fo' da past two years."

I turned to see her sitting there with one hand over her purse and the other raised with a finger pointing in my direction. She had a stern and angry look, something I had seldom seen from her, but I knew she meant business, and my heart sank at the idea of disappointing her. Mr. McNeil was sitting with the papers and his leather address book held to one side by his leg.

"Now, you pologize ta Mr. McNeil fo' bein' unkind and disrespectful!" Miss Mattie commanded.

I looked at her and then at him. I didn't want to apologize. I had two years of being pissed. I had two years of frustration for constantly being told I had to act and dress like a boy. Still, I also had two years with a secure roof over my head, good food to eat, and trips to the zoo and the parks, as well as two years of living in a clean home with no roaches, no stench, and no threat of who knows what lingering outside the door. For the most part, it had been a safe and comfortable environment.

I bowed my head and stared at the floor, feeling the shame of Miss Mattie's scolding run through me. The last thing I wanted to do was displease her, and I knew I should not have been ungrateful. "I'm sorry, Mr. McNeil," I said, still bowed, not wanting to look at him. "You have been very kind to me, and I appreciate all you have done for me."

"Apology accepted," he said softly.

"Now go on up dere and get ya stuff," Miss Mattie commanded.

I turned and ascended the stairs, knowing that this would be the last day I would spend in the McNeil house.

As I reached the staircase, I heard Mr. McNeil exclaim, "Well, that's a switch. He does appear to respect you and mind you. Nobody else has been able to accomplish that."

"All dat it takes is some genuine love an acceptance," Miss Mattie replied.

He rolled his eyes and leaned back in his chair.

Mrs. McNeil followed me up the stairs. Miss Mildred had brought the other kids up the back stairs to their rooms after breakfast. Mrs. McNeil walked behind me to the boy's room. When we entered the room, Mrs. McNeil announced, "Children, Stephen will be leaving us today. He has a new guardian and will be going to live with her." She seemed trite and stilted. One could read the resentment in her body. Even though she had wanted to get rid of me and there would be more peace in her house without my presence, Miss Mattie was somehow stealing her show and thwarting her plans to convert me into a heterosexual male.

I ignored her and began digging through my dresser for clothes. Then I turned and asked, "Is it okay if I take these?"

A look of shock went across Mrs. McNeil's face, first shock, and then she melted into sympathy. "Oh, sweetheart," she sweetly proclaimed. "of course, you can take your clothes. We bought them for you. We are not going to send you off with just what you have on."

Despite her intensity and need for perfection, she was not evil and could be sincerely caring. I was an adult before I understood that disagreement does not have to mean disrespect, and if someone sees the world in a completely different way, it does not make them wrong or terrible, just different.

"I really don't want them," I said. "They are boy's clothes, but I'm going to need something to wear till I can get clothes that are more fitting for a girl."

The sympathy froze into a look of irritation, and the internal battle of whether to chastise me or let it go was apparent. Finally, she let it go. "Go ahead and pack your things, Stephen. You are welcome to take them. Put them on the bed, keep them folded, and I will get you a bag."

She left the room and returned shortly with a couple of black plastic garbage bags. She tossed them on the foot of the bunk and said, "Here, put your things in these."

The other kids related to me very differently on that day than ever before. They were quietly staring at my proceedings. In some ways, it felt like they envied me. Carl sat on his bed, gawking, not with the usual animosity on his face, but what I read as perhaps longing or disappointment. As luxurious as the McNeil home was, as well cared for as we were, it felt a bit like a prison to all of us, and it felt more like the McNeils were caretakers or guards rather than parents. We didn't have real parents anymore. Some of us had never had parents, some had parents who had died, and some had been removed from abusive parents. We weren't loved the way other children were. We weren't made a priority like kids who had stable parents. We were housed, clothed, fed, and detained. We were a charity burden for a couple who saw it as their Christian duty to accommodate and provide for us. They were doing a very good thing, and later, I realized they deserved more credit than I had given them. I only wish the provisions could have come with more love and acceptance with less control.

It was probably good that Mrs. McNeil couldn't have her own children. She couldn't relate to children, although she wanted to and thought she could. Maybe she thought she was being a mother to us, but she didn't understand kids like Miss Mattie. She was far too rigid and unmoving. Something was missing in her. Even though she was nothing like the drug whore that my so-called mother had been, she was still disconnected and essentially unrelatable. Mr. McNeil came close to being the father we needed, but he was still only a supplement. He connected with us much more than she did, but it seemed like he only went along with keeping foster children because she thought that might somehow make up for her barren womb. Maybe she was cold because she knew that none of us were her flesh and blood and that she could never have that. I don't know why they didn't consider adopting.

After I stuffed my things into the garbage bags, Bill approached me and said, "I think I'm going to miss you, Steph." He compromised between Stephen and Stephanie for the first time, just as the TV preacher had done. He had been screamed at too many times for calling me Stephen, but he had never complied with my demands before.

Carl sauntered up to me, stuck out his hand, rehearsed like a good ole boy, and said with anemic drama, "Good Luck, Man."

I looked at his outstretched hand and felt a cheesy grin cross my face. Then, I moved past it, hugged him, and kissed him on the cheek.

"Shit, man!" he exclaimed as his once outstretched hand wiped my kiss off his face. Mrs. McNeil scolded him for his language, and he responded with a subdued and pitiful "Sorry."

Efren hugged me from the side.

I started to pick up my bags, and Carl said, "Here, let me help you with that." Then he grabbed the other bag.

I looked over at him and smiled. "Wow," I teased. "There really is a gentleman beneath that cocky act you put on."

He shrugged.

Last, I grabbed Miss Mattie's pillow from my bunk and tucked it under my arm. It had remained on my bed the whole time and had been my only true comfort when I awoke from nightmares or felt the overwhelming sadness of missing her. It had been my only comfort when I felt alone, ridiculed, rejected, and rebuffed. It had been my lifeline to the one I knew who truly loved me. Now, it, too, was going home.

The girls were standing in the hall. The two little ones said nothing, but Cathy simply said, "Bye," as I walked past.

Carl helped me carry my bags downstairs. From behind, I heard Mrs. McNeil telling Miss Mildred she could go ahead and strip my bunk. So, as soon as she had gotten rid of the trash from Pruitt Igoe, it was time for clean-up and the room sanitized for some other discarded child.

We came down the stairs and set the bags by the front door. Then Carl gave me a quick and light fist bump to my shoulder and went back upstairs. His response to me probably had as much to do with sadness that I was leaving instead of him. Miss Mattie got up and came to the door, followed by Mr. McNeil. He had set his leather-bound address book by the phone and apparently gave the papers back to Miss Mattie while I was upstairs.

"Well, I guess this is it," Mr. McNeil proclaimed as though he had stolen the line from some hokey John Wayne movie. He plopped his hand on my shoulder, a move that must have been the good ole boy standard gesture at the time.

"Yeah, I guess so," I glanced back at him. Despite my attitude, I knew that I was going to miss him. He had been more than a disciplinarian. He had given me a sense of comfort and security. He let me know that he had things under control, and even when he was trying to get me under control, he still did it in a fair and comforting way. Even when he held me down during my fits, he never hurt or took advantage of me. He kept his cool and never spoke to me in a demeaning way other than his insistence that I was a boy, which he never realized was demeaning. Even though I knew he was never pleased that I could not be the boy he wanted me to be, he never overtly degraded me. Even though he insisted that I be called Stephen, with the pronoun of he, I knew he was playing out the role that he thought was his

Christian duty. That's just the way he saw things. My feelings became a mix, and I felt sadness. Despite all my fits and challenges, I knew, at that moment, that I would miss him.

Mrs. McNeil had descended the stairs and stood beside him.

"Well, Stephen," she lectured one last time. "I hope we have given you, at least, some sense of morals while you were here." I guess she figured that Miss Mattie had never taught me morals. Perhaps she thought that black people or slum dwellers could not muster morality, but Miss Mattie was probably the most moral and forthright person I ever met.

"Yes, Ma'am," I replied while fighting the urge to tell her to go fuck herself.

She moved over and hugged me quickly, coolly, and hesitantly.

I quickly moved away from her hug and threw my arms around Mr. McNeil. I laid my head sideways across the middle of his chest. I knew this would be the last time I would feel him close to me. Even when he had been holding me down in my rages, there had been a comfort in having him close, and despite my anger, I had felt safe with him restraining me. It had felt as much like affection as it had discipline. He placed his arms around me one last time and gave me one last comforting and fatherly squeeze.

I turned to Miss Mattie and said, "I think I'm ready to go."

"Well, come on, den." She smiled as she reached to pick up one of the trash bags.

I grabbed the other bag, opened the door, and stepped onto the porch. Then, I threw the bag over my shoulder and began marching down the steps and sidewalk, refusing to look back. I did not wait for Miss Mattie.

Behind me, I heard Miss Mattie say, "I wanna thank ya'll fo takin sech good care o' my baby fo me."

"We were happy we could be here for him," Mr. McNeil responded politely.

I cinched the bag a little tighter over my shoulder, fought the urge to yell, "It's *HER*, mother fucker," and kept walking.

CHAPTER 8

THE PROMISED LAND

Miss Mattie had obtained a motel room about fifteen minutes from the McNeil house with a room on the second floor overlooking a walkway into the parking lot. It was a typical bare minimum establishment. When we arrived, she made me take all my clothes and put them in the closet and the dresser. It did not matter that it was a temporary cheap motel. Miss Mattie wanted my things organized. Of course, I didn't know we might have to stay for a couple of months to secure permanent housing. Still, sharing a cheap hotel room with Miss Mattie was a thousand percent better than sharing a room with three boys at the McNeil residence.

"Where are all your things?" I asked.

"Baby, dae ain't much dat I wanted ta keep, but most of dats in storage. I gots my new clothes all hung and folded, and dats what I'm tellin you ta do. Put yo stuff away, cause I knows dey didn't teach you ta be messy at dat fancy house over dere, did dey?"

"No, Ma'am," I replied politely.

"Dat's yo bed over dare."

She motioned to the bed by the wall opposite the door and closest to the bathroom. I went over, plopped down on the mattress, and rubbed my hands across the floral cotton coverlet as though it were fine silk. Since Miss Mattie had been given access to my Trust Fund, she could have gotten a fancy hotel or a temporary rental, but she still had a conservative way about her. Those fancy dresses she bought from high-end department stores were likely all from the clearance rack. Still, they presented a stunning difference from what she had to wear when she lived in the projects. She would later splurge on me as we had never been able to splurge before, but she also remained very conservative with money.

"I've never had a bed this big," I mentioned.

"Well, you gonna have a nice bed and a room ta ya self, soon as we can get us a house." She grinned as she spoke and sat on the opposite bed facing me. "Pastor Dennison is providin a housin budget separate from de Trust, an it's enough ta get us a house in Ladue, maybe not one o' de big ones, but a nice one, so you don't have ta change schools."

"No!" I wailed. "I didn't tell you before, but I don't want to live in fucking Ladue! I don't want to go back to that school."

"Well, dats where you been livin fo almost two years. Dats where you been goin' ta school."

"Yeah, and I don't like it!"

"I don't wants you to be goin' through too many changes. You done been through 'nough," she argued. "Ya needs ta be consistent."

"How are we going to find a house in Ladue?" I asked. "They don't want black people living there, and I've never felt welcomed at that school. It doesn't make any difference what school it is; they are still going to bully me, and I will probably get bullied more at Ladue."

"Well, de school you been attendin is a good school, and you needs a good school," she continued. "So, you put ya things away, and we will drive back over, an I'll show ya what we gonna do."

When I had finished putting all my stuff away, and after lunch at a nearby café, Miss Mattie and I returned to the car and took the fifteen-minute drive back to Ladue.

"I been drivin' round de neighborhood ova dare fo a couple of weeks now, an I think I have found jest what we want," she commented over the steering wheel.

When she drove, Miss Mattie leaned forward in the seat with her chin almost touching the steering wheel. Her bony, thin fingers gripped either side like she feared falling out of the seat if she didn't hang on. She drove as slow as a snail and constantly checked every direction, head darting back and forth, angling her neck to see the rearview mirrors before she made a turn or changed lanes. She looked up into the rear-view mirror and spotted a car that had been tailgating us.

"Yeah, ya thinks ya can get up all on my tail like a breed dog, don't ya?" she quietly commented as if the other car driver could hear her. "Get a little closer, and ya can sniff my butt." Miss Mattie began signaling to change lanes when the car behind us sped past with the driver yelling and flipping the bird. Miss Mattie had to jerk back into the original lane so we didn't get hit. "Speed on cat shit!" she exclaimed. "You jest another turd ta get covered."

I laughed with vigor, and she didn't even turn her face from the road to glance at me.

"What you laughin' at, giggle butt?" she teased.

"I have never heard you talk that way, for one thing, and you're going too slow." I snickered. "No wonder they are trying to run you over."

"Well, I ain't no Speedy Gonzalez," she returned. "You gots ta be careful, 'specially when ya my age, and ya ain't done dat much drivin'. I passed de drivin' test. Dat's all dat mattas."

She took an exit near Ladue and began weaving through the streets until she came to a stop in front of a house that was a combination of red brick and stone. It was almost entirely brick but had the outline of a stone fireplace in front. It also had stone accents around the windows, at the corners, around the foundation, and above the front door, which could be seen through a small porch landing. The perfectly manicured lawn sloped toward the city sidewalk, where stone steps led to a walkway straight to the porch steps. Across the porch, the front door was made of thick dark boards in an arched European style with a half-moon window. A real estate 'for sale' sign stood at the edge of the lawn near the steps.

"Dis actually on da edge o' Ladue, but still Ladue. Still in de same school district, so you can go to da same school dat da McNeil family had you in." She turned in her seat to look at the house. "Whatcha think?"

"It is very nice," I replied.

"I ain't seen da inside of it yet," she commented. "When I calls da real estate company, dae tells me dat all de realtors is busy. Dens dae hangs up on me."

I turned from gazing at the house to look straight at her. "You know why, don't you?"

"Cause I talks like an ole' black woman from da south," she laughed. "I is an ole' black woman from da south. I know dese white folks don't want nobody like me in dere neighborhood. Dat's awe right. De gonna find out."

"You want to buy *this* house?" I asked. "You don't think we will have some trouble in this neighborhood?"

"Yes, I wants dis house," she returned.

"Why?" I asked. "We don't have to live here. Why don't you look at buying a house in a neighborhood where we look like most other folks, where they are not going to resent us for living there?"

"Cause I wants dis house," she said calmly. "Pastor gave me plenty o' cash money ta buy it, an dat's what I'm gonna do."

"How?" I questioned. "If you can't get the real estate company to even talk to you, how are you going to buy it?"

"Well, I been thinkin' bout dat," she mused. "I been thinkin' maybe dat lawyer dat de pastor hired might help me out a bit. Been thinkin' I might give dem a call, cause Pastor gonna buy a house outright fo us, long as it's in budget, an dis one is."

"But why this one, Miss Mattie?" I pleaded.

"Cause you has already had two years ta get used ta livin' in dis area, livin' in a nice home, an I don't see no reason why we shouldn't just keep on wid dat. Sides, you done already been through too many changes."

"But I don't care," I continued.

"Baby," she said as she reached her hand over and laid her palm across my arm. "You has been through too much already. You ain't never had nothin consistent in ya life, an I don't want ta put you through any more changes dat we don't have ta put you through. Sides, you and me both been through so much po dat we deserves a lil bit o' rich. As far as I knowed, I woulda' had to lives de rest of my life po and in places like Pruitt Igoe. Now I don't has ta, and I ain't gonna."

"I'll be okay … we'll be okay," I argued.

"I know you is strong," she responded. "But I think da more stability you has in ya life, da better ya chances to heal from all ya been through."

"I'm healed," I disputed. "I'm fine. I'm a lot better now that I know I'm going to be living with you."

"Baby, ya ain't fine," she continued. "A kid don't go through what you been through widout it affectin' her. I know you has had to be tough yo whole life. I knows you had to be tough jest ta live at Pruitt Igoe, and I knows you had ta be tough ta deal with yo Momma and her caryin' on, but even tough needs a rest sometime. I jest wants ta give you as much stability and consistency as I can. Now, I know social services has had you in therapy since all dat happened, and we gonna continue wid dat too."

I was about to respond when we heard a tapping at the window on her side, and both of us nearly jumped out of our skin. Miss Mattie let out a brief little yelp and turned around to see a policeman standing at the edge of the car. My window was down so we could look at the house, but Miss Mattie still had the window up on her side. The officer was motioning for her to roll down the window. She had turned the car engine off and had to restart it to use the power windows. At that point, the officer knocked angrily on the window as though he thought she was about to drive off and put his hand on his gun. "Roll down the window!" he angrily commanded with a loud and threatening voice.

"I'm tryin'," she exclaimed.

He angrily knocked on the window, then started shouting, "Get out of the car, NOW!

As soon as she the car started, Miss Mattie turned around and pushed the power button to lower the window. "Yes, officer," she said politely. "Somethin' wrong."

"What are you doing out here?" he fumed.

"Well, we was admirnin' dis house," Miss Mattie replied. "We was thinkin' we might wants ta buy it."

A smirk crossed the officer's face as he said, "We had a complaint that there were some suspicious-looking people parked out here in a green Lincoln. The person who called said they had seen this Lincoln cruising around the neighborhood for the past couple of weeks as though casing out houses to rob. You think because this house is empty, you can case it out and see what you can steal?"

Just as Miss Mattie began to answer, I sassed, "Suspicious as in black? Black equals thief?"

"Let's see your license," he demanded of Miss Mattie.

"What the hell?" I exclaimed. "We are just sitting here!"

"Sush, Baby," Miss Mattie quickly interjected. "You let me handle dis."

By this time, a second officer had come up behind me on my side of the car.

"I told you, I need you to step out of the car," the first officer commanded.

"Yes, sir," Miss Mattie calmly responded. "But I needs my purse ta gives ya my license and registration. It's ova here in da back flo boad."

"Get out of the car, now!" He commanded again.

"Yes, Sir." She replied and began to make her way out of the driver's side.

The other officer opened the door on my side and commanded, "Young man, I need you to step out, too."

"I'm not your fucking young man!" I ripped.

"Stephanie!" Miss Mattie scolded. "Just do as you are told, darlin'."

The first officer asked Miss Mattie to place her hands on the car's hood, and she complied as he requested. The second officer asked the same of me.

"Why?" I questioned.

"Baby, just do as you told," Miss Mattie instructed from over the car's hood.

I put my hands on the car and spread my legs as instructed. The next thing I knew, I felt the cop's hands moving over me, and I snapped. "What the fuck!" I exclaimed. "Get your fucking hands off me! You got no right to be putting your fucking hands on me!" I swung around and began kicking and fighting the way I had at Pruitt Igoe, the way I did any time I felt threatened.

Miss Mattie instinctively turned to come around the car, calling, "Baby, No! Calm down, now."

The first cop grabbed her and began wrestling her arms behind her back.

Again, time disappeared as it was prone to do whenever I snapped into a rage. I don't know what happened after that. The next thing I knew, we were both cuffed and sitting in the back of a police car, and Miss Mattie's car was being impounded. I had cuts and bruises and my body ached.

From there, we were taken to the police station, and family services had been brought in again. I had been placed in a stark, white, windowless room with a policeman standing, hands folded over his crotch, at the metal door. Then, that round-faced, auburn-haired Doris Mansfield from family services got escorted in.

She smiled as she entered the room and pulled up a chair facing me. "Is everything okay?" she asked with her sweet sing-song voice.

"Well, that's a fucking stupid question!" I snapped. "Does everything fucking look okay?"

"Stephen, I know you are upset, but you don't have to yell or curse. I can hear you just fine without that. Can you please tell me what happened?" She sat her round ass on an adjacent metal chair and leaned slightly in my direction.

I remembered multiple times she had come into the McNeil home when I was accused of stealing or when I had acted up. She had always been fair and honest with me. She had won my trust. She even compromised on calling me *Steph*. At first, she hadn't been able to get a word out of me, silence, denial, or at last, maybe a "Fuck off!" Still, she persisted with what I came to know as sincere congeniality. I had learned, over time, that I could open up to her.

"Miss Mattie drove me over to look at this house she wants to buy near Ladue, so I won't have to change schools. We were just sitting there looking at the house and talking about it when a couple of these mother fuckers," I nodded toward the cop standing by the door. "came up and started fucking with us."

"We are just wondering if Ms. Laroquette is going to be able to manage your behavior," she said without blinking an eye. "She's an elderly woman, and you tend to lose control. That is concerning for us."

"There was nothing wrong with my behavior until these assholes came up and started messing with us, putting their hands on me!" I defended. "They wouldn't even give Miss Mattie a chance to explain or even get her driver's license out of her purse."

"Can you explain what happened?" she asked.

"Miss Mattie and I were just sitting there parked, talking about the house she wants to buy when this cop comes and knocks on her window and scares the crap out of us. He said there had been a complaint about *suspicious people* in the neighborhood. The next thing I know, she is getting dragged out of the car, and so am I, and Miss Mattie is telling me to do as I'm told. I did. I put my hands up on the car and spread my legs, just like the cop said. I was fine till the mother fucker started feeling around all over me like some pervert. That freaked me out. I can't stand anybody putting their hands on me like that. If I don't know somebody is going to touch me, I freak."

"Putting his hands on you?" she questioned.

"Yeah!" I went on. "He told me to turn around and put my hands on the car, and then, from behind, he started feeling all over me like the mother fuckers who used to molest me. I fucking snapped. I didn't know what the hell he was going to do."

"He was frisking you," she commented. "Didn't you ever see that done to anyone arrested at Pruitt Igoe? They check for weapons when they arrest someone, but I can understand how that might upset you."

"No, you don't!" I demanded. "You don't fucking understand. You're white, you have never been molested or abused, and you never lived in Pruitt Igoe! You never had to constantly watch every fucking corner, every movement from anywhere, every day because you never knew what some mother fucker might do to you or when they were going to do it! You also don't know what it is like to deal with fucking white cops when you're not white! Do you think those asshole cops would have treated *you* like they treated us if you had been sitting just looking at the house? Would the neighbors have even noticed if they had seen you driving around the neighborhood for a couple of weeks? Hell, no! Why? Cause you're white! They would have thought nothing about you being parked there. Miss Mattie didn't do anything wrong, and I didn't do anything wrong. They fucking harassed us!"

"Well, you did attack an officer," she debated. "And the report states that Miss Laroquette also resisted arrest and fought the officer."

"Fucking lying bullshit!" I countered. "She did no such fucking thing! That's a fucking lie! She was telling me to calm down and cooperate. She was doing everything that the cop told her to do. She reacted when I freaked out, and I freaked out because the mother fucker behind me started grabbing me! Miss Mattie tried to come around the car because she was worried about me, and that's when the mother fucking cop attacked her and started twisting her arms and shit! She's an old lady, for Christ sakes!"

Mrs. Mansfield took a deep breath. "Well, Ms. Laroquette has contacted an attorney, apparently hired by Pastor Dennison. Since she has no priors, and since you are a minor, he will probably be able to get the charges reduced or dropped. Still, Stephen, you must understand that if you don't manage your behavior, the state can still override the custody granted to Miss Laroquette if there are any more incidents. You can still be taken back into state foster care."

I glared at her. "It's not fucking fair!" I heard my voice begin to quiver. "She is the only person who ever loved me. She is the only person who has ever tried to help and care for me, and you want to take that from me—again!"

I felt warm tears drifting across my face, tracks of sensation rolling to my chin. The thought of losing Miss Mattie again was more than I could handle.

"Please," I pleaded. "You can't take her from me again."

Mrs. Mansfield looked down at her wringing hands. The anxious dilemma was no doubt affecting her, as well. "We'll do our best, Steph, but you must maintain control. If you can't maintain control, we may have no choice."

"I'll try," I pleaded, with liquid anguish drifting from my eyes, "but you don't know what it does to me when somebody comes at me, when they put their hands on me, especially if I don't know they are going to do it. It's like I can't control myself at that point. It's like I'm an animal fighting for its life like some kind of force takes over me, and I have to fight to survive."

"May I touch your hand?" she asked as she leaned in my direction. I nodded affirmation, and she placed her fat little hand over mine. "I know you have been very hurt." She went on, still holding her palm over my hand. "I know this has to be extremely difficult for you, and as difficult as it might be for you to believe it, what I want most is for you to be happy, safe, and well cared for. I know your happiness may be a very tall order given all you have been through, but you are stronger, Stephen, than even you realize. I want you to know that I am putting my faith in you. I have faith that you will figure this out and learn how to control yourself better so you can have a better life than the one you were dealt at birth."

I looked up to find her staring straight at me. Big brown, serene eyes looked directly into mine. She had a gentle smile on her face, and I felt comforted. I believed her.

"Do I have your promise," she asked, "that you will do your best to manage yourself and keep your behavior under control?"

"Yes, Ma'am," I replied, darting my eyes away from hers. I couldn't handle eye contact for very long. I promised her, but the truth is, I never really knew when I might fly into a rage, what might trigger it, or how to stop it once it started. Sometimes, I didn't even realize what had happened until after it passed.

In a few minutes, I was escorted to the main lobby of the police station. Miss Mattie was there with a man in a business suit. They were sitting in chairs against a wall near a plexiglass window that had a cop sitting behind it.

Miss Mattie stood and came to hug me. "Baby, you all right?" she asked as she threw her arms around me.

"Yes, Ma'am," I replied as I hugged her tightly.

"I wants you ta meet somebody," she said, momentarily pulling away from our hug.

In a chair against the wall sat a white man who was probably in his late forties. I had noticed him sitting next to Miss Mattie when I had been escorted in but paid him no attention. He wore a charcoal gray suit with a lemon-yellow shirt and a red, yellow, and gray striped tie. He was dark-headed, with thick eyebrows and a dark beard line that indicated even though he might have shaved that morning, he needed another shave by afternoon. He stood as she escorted me in his direction.

"Dis here is our attorney, been hired by Pastor Dennison. He gonna help us out wid all dis. Name be Walter Riggs." She held her arm toward him as though inviting me to enter a corridor.

"Hello, young man," he said and extended his hand for a shake.

I realized he was very tall, and when I shook his hand, it was large and meaty. His handshake felt warm and comforting, and his hand completely engulfed mine.

"Walter Riggs," he affirmed, even though he had just been introduced.

"Hi," I said and lingered in the sensation of his huge, warm hand as he let go of the contact. "It's nice to meet you, but I prefer not to be called a man."

"Mr. Riggs gonna get us dat house," Miss Mattie interjected.

I suddenly felt angry. "What? I don't want that fucking house!" I exclaimed. "Especially after what happened today!"

"Why not?" Miss Mattie countered.

"Why the fuck would I want to live where they will call the cops just because they see an old black lady and a kid sitting in a car?" I countered.

She grinned, "Well, I can tell ya. I want dat house now more dan ever, and dats exactly why I wants it. Dat's exactly where we needs ta live. We needs ta live right dare where dem white folks can see us comin' and goin' every day. We needs ta live where dae ain't got no choice but to deal wid da fact dat we is dare and dey has ta see black folks livin day in an day out jest like dey do, where dey can see we is good neighbors. Besides, I tole you, you needs ta live where you can stay in de same school, be round da same chilren' dat you been round fo da las two years. You needs to make yo place in de world stead o' lettin' somebody else tell you what yo place is. If black folks don't stand up and take a place in society, den society always gonna cast us to da side. Now, Mr. Riggs ... gonna help us get dat house."

I had never seen this side of Miss Mattie, this feisty, fighting side. I had never seen her fired up, determined, and obstinate.

The charges were dropped, resisting arrest, disorderly conduct, public nuisance, anything the crooked cops had trumped up against us, all dropped. I guess Mr. Riggs was a pretty good attorney. He contacted the realtors and the homeowner himself and got us the house. He may have had to threaten a lawsuit, but I didn't care how he did it. He looked after everything and saw to it that the wishes of the TV preacher were put into place. He managed the trust fund until I turned eighteen, but even then, I asked him to continue as my advisor. In time, we had established a comfortable relationship.

My life had always been transition and change. It had never been what I expected it to be. My relationships changed, and I met people I never expected to meet. Some relationships were supportive, and some were not. Some would last, and some would not. Regardless, there are always marks on the heart from all our experiences. Our memories never exist without impact; often, there is a mix of effects and associated emotions.

In the summer of 1972, while living with the McNeils, I watched TV news broadcasts about the demolition of Prutt Igoe. There were videos of the buildings imploded with explosives, dozers pushing the remains into piles, and trucks hauling them away. I had emotions I didn't expect. On the one hand, I was glad to see it gone and be free of the threat that I might one day have to return there. However, the buildings could be destroyed, the remains hauled away, but nothing could haul away my memories. Nothing could carry away the impact of the lives that were lived there or those who died there. Along with gladness was a sadness that I couldn't explain, ripping at my heart like something pleading to come in, begging to hide, praying never to be seen again.

By the end of July 1973, we were moving into the brick house with stone accents in an all-white neighborhood at the edge of Ladue. By that time, I was more than ready to say goodbye to the hotel room, going out to eat three times a day, most days, or ordering room service to eat. We had no sooner begun to carry stuff into the house when Miss Mattie insisted that I sit down and write a thank you letter to Pastor Dennison for creating this life for us. I didn't know why he did it, but I was extremely thankful to have Miss Mattie back in my life and a wonderful home for us to live in. He sent a congenial reply and said he would write back and tell me all his reasons when I was eighteen. In the meantime, he affirmed that I needed to be in the care of someone who loved and accepted me.

The house had hardwood floors in every room except the bathrooms and kitchen, which had tile. To the right of a foyer, as you entered the front door, a wide archway led to the living room on the right, which had a brick and stone fireplace on the front wall with windows flanking it on either side. A larger window was at a right angle from the fireplace opposite the archway, and it overlooked our driveway into the neighbor's front yard. To the left of the front door, also with an arch, was a formal dining room appointed with expensive dark wood paneling and chocolate brown drapes with a floral print of green, burgundy, and yellow gliding off the windows to drag on the floor. A large window at the front of the house created a view from the dining table into our front yard. Directly across from the dining room window was a smaller arch leading to a large kitchen, and it had silly little flapping swing doors that looked like something you might see in a bar scene of a Western movie. Those swinging doors looked incredibly out of place compared to the elegant accents in the rest of the room. Except for the thick wood paneling in the dining room, almost the whole damn house was painted eggshell white. Everything was white except the hardwood floors, the tile in the kitchen and bathrooms, and the wood framing around the doors and windows, which matched the wood floors. A small hallway parallel to the kitchen led to an elegant main suite behind the living room. The en-suite bathroom had a Jacuzzi tub adjacent to a walk-in closet as big as my whole bedroom at Pruitt Igoe. Dark walnut stairs with a squared railing led from the living room upstairs, with three more bedrooms and a central bathroom with double sinks. I chose the bedroom at the front of the house with a dormer window overlooking the street. If I had been inclined to crawl through that window, there was a straight drop into thorny holly bushes landscaped at the front of the house. My bedroom was closest to the bathroom, off the hall between my room and the other two upstairs bedrooms. The two of us certainly didn't need four bedrooms, with two full baths and a little guest bath under the stairs, but there we were, nonetheless, with Miss Mattie in the master suite downstairs while I had the entire second floor to myself.

Within three months, the white walls were gone, and the dark wood on the window and door frames and the rail of the stairs had been painted an almost snow white. Miss Mattie hired painters to come in and paint white trim throughout the house, around the baseboards, doors, windows, crown molding, and stairs. While at it, she also had all the doors painted white. The stupid-looking swinging doors between the kitchen and dining room were removed, restoring the arched opening between the dining room and the kitchen. The living room had been painted the color of creamed coffee, as was the dining room across from it, but the dining room paneling retained the texture of the boards. Miss Mattie had them rehang the same drapes as they matched the coffee color. I had selected a dusty pink for my bedroom, and Miss Mattie had her bedroom painted robin's egg blue. The other bedrooms were left white. The kitchen was a pale avocado with harvest gold appliances, popular in the 1960s, but Miss Mattie had it changed to all-white. She left the avocado-colored tile backsplash and countertops. Still, she painted the rest of the room a pastel version of avocado green and had all the cabinets painted white with new colorful porcelain knobs and drawer pulls. Then, the house of white became a house of color.

Miss Mattie brought some of her things out of storage, but we also bought exquisite new furniture. We had a huge dark brown, almost black, leather sofa facing the fireplace with a matching love seat adjacent to it, a matching reclining chair, cherry wood side tables, and a coffee table. We also had a cherry wood dining table that seated eight. It was all dark but brightened by colorful and energetic abstract wall art and white trim. In that big beautiful house, there were only the two of us. Neither of us had friends or connections, and the place, which wasn't nearly as big as the McNeil house, could still feel cavernous and lonely. Since we had no friends or family, we didn't need a dining table that seated eight, but Miss Mattie insisted we would make friends. However, that was not going to be easy.

There were times when we knew the neighbors were staring at us, scoffing at us. Maybe those were the same neighbors who had called the cops on us. Miss Mattie insisted that we always smile and wave at our neighbors whenever we saw them. Yet, either of us could come out the front door to check the mail and wave at a neighbor on either side just to get a disgusted look and no wave back. This black family of two had invaded their pristine white neighborhood. We stood in defiance. Miss Mattie parked her Lincoln in the oversized detached garage at the back of the house. The driveway led beside the house directly into the garage, and beside it was a privacy-fenced backyard with a giant oak tree sheltering it. The tree provided lovely shade in the summer and dropped leaves to allow sunlight into the back windows in winter. Miss Mattie hired a yard worker to care for the mowing and leaf cleanup. A large deck in the back was accessed through the kitchen. We bought nice deck furniture and a grill and often ate outside at dinner during the warmer months. Miss Mattie created beautiful flower beds around the deck and at various spots around the house and yard, which she insisted on tending to herself. It would have been a wonderful place to have a backyard party if there had been anyone to invite. Miss Mattie once asked the McNeil family and the foster children for a Sunday afternoon backyard picnic, but Mrs. McNeil politely declined. That I had expected.

Miss Mattie had never gotten close to anyone at Pruitt Igoe except me. I certainly could not think of anyone there that I ever wanted to see again. The different problem in our new neighborhood was finding others willing to associate with us instead of keeping toxic people away from us, as we had tried to do at Pruitt Igoe. Despite having lived in Ladue for two years, I hadn't made friends at school, and even if I had met someone, the twenty-dollar question was whether their parents would allow them to hang out with me. Neither Miss Mattie nor I wanted to associate with the criminal element we had left behind, and our new neighbors thought of us as the criminal element. We were lost souls for a while. We were lost between two worlds. Like the Jews of Exodus wandering in the wilderness, we had left subjugation behind but had not really crossed into the promised land.

CHAPTER 9

OLD SCHOOL

August in St. Louis can be like the steaming fires of hell. Winter can crack you like a Christmas candy cane, but summer melts you like a candle. I was about to return to school at the end of August 1973 and wasn't looking forward to it. Since we moved into the house, it had been just Miss Mattie and me, except that she had hired a maid. After several interviews, she hired Symone, who had been the one who quit the McNeil family after Mrs. McNeil accused her of stealing the jewelry I had stolen. I never made a point of confessing to or apologizing to her until she became our maid, and then I felt it necessary to tell her what had happened.

"Oh, I knew that," She said.

"Why didn't you rat me out?" I questioned.

"You know, by then, I was already too fed up with Mrs. McNeil, and she had no right to come accusing me. I figured she deserved what she got. I also figured you would give it back eventually. I mean, what's a twelve-year-old going to do with a five-thousand-dollar necklace? It's not like you could have pawned it."

Symone and I had previously had a reasonably cordial relationship, and I didn't want anything to mess that up. They say confession is good for the soul, and I think my admission and apology improved our relationship. Besides, Mrs. McNeil should have been the one to apologize to her, but I knew she never would, and Symone told me that she never even let her know that she had gotten the necklace back.

Symone came twice weekly to vacuum, mop, polish the floors, dust, clean the kitchen and toilets, and do laundry. Miss Mattie was aging. So, doing all the housework was becoming too taxing for her, especially in a house three or more times larger than her little apartment at Pruitt Igoe. However, when Symone was off, she would do what she could and was not opposed to putting me to work either. Work was not something I had ever been accustomed to either at Pruitt Igoe or at the McNeil house. When I was with my so-called mother, there was no cleaning or only a half-assed pick-up of scattered trash occasionally. The McNeil family always had one or two maids who came in daily, and the children were only expected to make their beds, put their clothes in the hamper, and pick up their things. After washing the clothes, the maids placed them in our drawers and shared closets. So, when Miss Mattie expected me to clean, there was some initial resistance.

Miss Mattie would tell me, "Now I can't do dat cause I can't bends over like you wid yo young bones, and it need ta be cleaned."

"So, who's going to care?" I would protest. "Symone will be back in a couple of days, and she can clean it then."

Miss Mattie chided me, "Jest cause you is poor don't means you gots ta be nasty and jest cause you is rich don't mean you gots ta be lazy. Everybody got a part ta do in dis world, an you needs ta be learnin' ta do yo part. Dey might come a time when we can't afford no maid, and you don't wants ta go back ta livin' like filth, do you?"

I did what she told me to do, but Miss Mattie and I were both grateful that the Trust Fund provided sufficient income to hire helpers. Despite Pruitt Igoe and being born into poverty and filth, I ended up living in the lap of luxury with servants to take care of me. My so-called mother's murder had literally cast me from one financial extreme to the other. In more ways than one, it was the best thing that ever happened to me. Without it, I would never have lived in beautiful homes or met the TV preacher. He never would have set up a Trust because he felt sorry for me, and I never would have been able to live with Miss Mattie. I didn't care why the preacher gave us the money. I was just glad to have it and be back with Miss Mattie, fuss or no fuss. Besides, sometimes I kind of enjoyed fussing with her.

The only thing I knew for sure was that I didn't want to have a male body. I wanted to find some way to look female and not feel frustrated with a body that didn't fit or feel like who I was. I wanted a "sex change." That's what they called it in those days. Gender reassignment was not a term used until much later. I discovered that it was possible to have the surgery when I started going to the public library to research whatever I could find about anyone who might have been like me, especially because I had never known anyone like me. I wasn't even sure if anyone like me existed.

Later in life, I came to realize how things that seem to be happenstance can completely alter the course of our lives. Whatever brought my path across the path of Pastor Dennison totally transformed my life, and I never ceased to be grateful for it. I didn't ask about it when I was a kid, but I later discovered that the income the TV preacher had set up would support me comfortably for the rest of my life if I didn't squander it. The annual interest alone was enough to keep me in a lifestyle better than most. I would never have to work if I didn't want to, but I felt I had to give back. I just didn't know how or what. At that time, I didn't know a lot.

Probably the most important gift I had gotten from the McNeil family was that I had become a reader and learned to look things up. I got in trouble a lot, banished to my bunk, like that was actually going to bother me, and the one thing I was allowed to do was read. I discovered stories and fiction, which I loved, but I also found the joy of reading to learn new things. Before that, I barely knew how to read, and I had a lot of catching up, but I caught up and spent a lot of time in my bunk just reading. Because of my previous lack of education, I spent a lot of time reaching for the dictionary and learning the kinds of things that Mable-bitch had caused me to miss. What McNeils had initially intended as punishment had become a pleasure. I learned to enjoy reading and learning new things.

By the age of thirteen, I had long enjoyed the public library. Miss Mattie would take me there almost any time I wanted to go, and that's where I began to research people like me. I discovered information about people who had transition surgery. I read about Christine Jorgenson and how she had it done in 1952. I learned that the surgery had been performed in Germany as far back as the 1920s. Most of the literature was very negative about it and cited it as a disorder, but still, I knew I wanted the surgery. I thought about what incredible courage it took for Christine Jorgenson to go through the surgery and face the public before I was ever born. I realized from reading about surgeries done in Germany in the 1920s that what I was experiencing was nothing new and had probably happened since the dawn of humankind. I realized that I was not the only one, and simply knowing that made a massive difference in how I felt about myself. I had no idea how it could happen for me, and things were difficult for transgender people, especially in the 1970s in conservative Missouri. However, I finally came around to asking Miss Mattie about it.

We sat on the back deck during an evening cooler than usual for August. Yet, I could still feel sweat dripping down my torso from under my arms. Miss Mattie loved to be outside as often as possible and hated being "cooped up" inside. She had spent most of her time in Pruitt Igoe cooped up in her apartment. So, even if it were a bit too cool or warm, we would spend time on the deck as often as possible. Besides, she had grown up in New Orleans before air conditioning. The heat and humidity never seemed to bother her. We learned that we had fewer problems with bugs when we left the electric lights turned off in the evening. We were sitting at our deck table with only the light of a few citronella candles when I finally got the courage to speak.

"Miss Mattie, I want to be a woman?"

"Well," she pondered. "I suppose you will grow into yo womanhood."

"No, that's not what I mean." I wondered how I should present the discussion. Finally, I decided to be direct. "I want to get rid of this male body so I can have a female body?"

I saw her eyebrows rise as the dim light from a candle shimmered on her face. That look made me wonder if she had ever considered such a thing. I realized that because of her age and possibly her lack of education, things that were possible in more modern times might never have seemed possible in her time and that she might never have heard of such things. She hesitated momentarily as faint distant voices from some neighbor's backyard gathering wafted over the fence, "I don't know if dat be possible, sugar. You might be able to dress like a woman an live like a woman. I knows you feels like a woman, but I guess all of us just stuck wid de body dat we came wid."

"I heard there is a surgery," I said.

"Where'd you hear dat?" she queried with curiosity and surprise lingering on her face.

"Well, actually, I read about it at the library."

"All right, den," she smiled. "What you got ta say bout it?"

"I found out that Johns Hopkins does the surgery, and there is this doctor out in Colorado named Stanley Biber who started doing it in 1969."

"An' we ain't at neither of dem places," she replied. "Den, you gotta start back ta school in a couple of weeks. Dat an't something we can do while you in school. I don't even know if dat's legal."

"Yes, it is legal," I responded. "They are doing it."

"Well, you can't do dat and go ta school at de same time." She argued. "If anything, we would have to wait till next summer, and den … how you gonna explain somethin' like dat when you goes back ta school de next year?"

"I have been bullied my whole life, Miss Mattie. I'm used to it. What difference would it make? They are going to pick on me and make fun of me anyway. Even if I don't have a girl's body or dress like a girl, I'm still feminine, and they pick on me just for being different. Anybody different who doesn't fit what they think someone should be gets ostracized, shamed, and abused. Can't you see that?"

"Yes, I see dat. So, what you figurin'?" she asked.

"I figure, from what I have read about hormones and body development, the younger I am when I start female hormones, the better the chances of developing a female physique. Even before the surgery, I need to find a doctor who can give me female hormones."

"Lord child," she debated. "You think we gonna find a doctor round St. Louis who would do somethin' like dat?"

"We won't know till we try." I pleaded. "Please, Miss Mattie. This is really important to me. Can we at least try to find a doctor who will start me on hormones?"

"Well, what do you think is gonna happen if yo balls is still producin' men's hormones and you takin' female hormones at de same time?"

"I don't know," I considered. "but I am willing to go ahead and have my balls cut off."

"Lord, child." She seemed flabbergasted. "You, only thirteen years old. Dat is too young ta be thinkin' bout stuff like dat. Wait till you is growed up ta think bout stuff like dat."

"But I've already started growing facial hair, Miss Mattie, and I'll be fourteen in January. The longer I wait, the more my body will look male. These damn balls will start shaping my body into a man's body. I don't want a man's body. I'm not a man. I don't want to look like a man or feel what a man feels."

"Dis is complicated," she replied.

"Will you at least ask around about it?" I implored.

She leaned over and blew out one of the candles. "Yeah, I see what I can do, but I'm telling you, dere ain't no doctor in dese parts gonna give female hormones to a thirteen-year-old boy."

"I'm not a boy!" I argued.

"I know, sweetheart, but as far as da rest o' de world, all dey sees is a boy."

"You are my legal guardian. Maybe, with your permission, they might do it. Speaking of which, I don't want you just to be my guardian. Please adopt me, Miss Mattie. I don't want my so-called mother's name anymore. I want to change my whole name. Instead of being Stephen Christopher Saunders, I want to be Stephanie Christine Laroquette."

She smiled in the dim light of one remaining candle. "Now dats somethin' I can look into. I'll ask Mr. Riggs bout it. Come on now, let's blow out dat other candle and go back inside where it be cool."

A couple of weeks later, I started the eighth grade at middle school, which meant getting up in the morning before the sun had even climbed over the horizon or had spread any light across my bedroom window. I hated alarm clocks, and I hated having to drag my ass out of bed before the light came through the window, but Miss Mattie was relentless about getting me up for school. She insisted that I set my own alarm in my room, "cause it's yo responsibili-y ta learn ta discipline yo self like a grown woman."

If I had not descended the stairs within ten minutes of the alarm, Miss Mattie would climb to the second floor and pester me until I got out of bed. If I protested too much, she kept a fruit jar full of marbles in the freezer overnight, and she would toss those under the covers in bed with me. I came up off those cold marbles in anger a few times, to which she scolded, "Na you jest settle right back down dare, missy! I jest tryin ta get you ta actin like de adult you gonna be in jest a few shoat years. Peoples dats growd up gets outa bed when de oughts ta, and de don't make no fuss bout it."

I got to the point where I could hear her coming up the stairs with that glass full of cold marbles in hand, and I was out of bed, and headed downstairs before she ever opened my bedroom door. I tried locking the door once, but apparently, she had a key. I had not had any better luck at the McNeil house. There, Mr. McNeil would come to drag me out of my bunk by my feet, stand me up, and march me to the bathroom, where he would splash cold water in my face. The other kids weren't as bad about not getting up as I was. It seemed like all I wanted to do was sleep. Even with nightmares, sleeping seemed preferable to being awake. After all, when I lived with Mable-bitch, I slept whenever I felt like it, and sleeping was one of the ways I could avoid her, but the days of sleeping whenever I felt like sleeping any time, day or night, ended when Mable-bitch was murdered. I suppose, after the McNeils, I tested Miss Mattie to see if she would indulge me, but she absolutely would not.

Miss Mattie always had breakfast ready before I woke up and insisted that I eat. I never could figure out why Miss Mattie wasn't fat because she cooked about everything that could be cooked practically every meal and ate what looked like vast amounts. We could have grits or fried potatoes, bacon or ham, biscuits, white gravy, jelly, butter, milk, pancakes, or many other options for breakfast. Every morning, she ate a full plate or more and still looked like she could blow away in a crisp wind. It may not have been a fact, but I felt like I would soon be the size of a truck if I ate a third of what she ate, and I always envied her metabolism. The one good thing about breakfast was that she began giving me coffee when I became a teen.

I would have been happy to have just the coffee and no breakfast, but she insisted that I eat a "few bites" of everything, and she would point it out if I missed something.

"You ain't had a bite outta dat biscuit."

"Miss Mattie, I don't want it."

"I don't care. You needs ta eat. Now, take a few bites."

"It's too much," I complained. Still, she insisted that I eat.

Finally, I would snatch the biscuit off my plate, take one bite, and slap it back down.

"Now, dats mo like it." She smiled like I had completed some incredible feat as she ignored my sullenness.

Being awakened before the sun came up, notwithstanding, I was not looking forward to going back to school. I knew with middle school, there would likely be new students who might have transferred in. If I only had to deal with the ones I had met in elementary while living at the McNeil house, I could handle that, but I wasn't sure how I might have to deal with strangers. I figured if Carl were still in foster care, he would be there, but he wasn't there. I had no idea what had happened to him, and in a way, I was relieved. I could have handled him and most of the kids I had been in school with because I knew how to read them. Still, something happens in middle school that makes kids different. Competition begins with puberty, and often, people you thought you knew are no longer as they were before. I thought I knew who to stay away from and who would at least be reasonable or congenial. Still, when ego, insecurity, and the frantic search for identity take over, some kids become cruel when trying to define their imaginary dominance and a false sense of importance, even if they hadn't been cruel before.

Even though I had known some kids from elementary, I had no friends. I was the weird kid who insisted on being called by a girl's name and would sneak in the application of lipstick or a woman's scarf, at least until one of the teachers spotted it and made me take it off. No one, even if they had known me before, wanted to be associated with the "fem freak." More than once, I had been taken to the boy's bathroom with some male teacher standing over me, forcing me to wash the lipstick off my mouth. Even the teachers, especially the men, seemed to look at me with disgust. I was made to use the boys' bathroom, even though I didn't feel comfortable or safe there. I tried to drink as little as possible so I wouldn't have to pee, and if I had to, I always tried to hold it until everyone else had cleared the halls for class, but there were times when I ended up soiling myself trying to avoid the boy's bathroom. This made me even more of a target for ridicule. Pubescents have little sympathy. If I could hold it long enough, I would run to the girls' bathroom just before class started, close the stall door, and try to do my business as fast as I could. When this made me late for class, I would get jeers and laughter from the kids who had figured out what I was doing and lectures from the teachers for walking in after the bell rang. Middle school was merely a different kind of hell.

Miss Mattie would argue with me about putting on feminine things or makeup for school. At home, she didn't care and had no problem buying girl's clothes for me, but when I went to school, she admonished me, "Baby, don't draw no mo attention to yo self dan you has to. Fo folks like us, attention, most o' de time, ain't no good thing."

Yet, I would sneak a tube of lipstick into my backpack or a pair of clip-on earrings. By the time of Christmas break that first year in middle school, Miss Mattie had allowed me to grow out my hair, which was crinkly curly, more than wavy, and pale brown with tones of red. In those days, after the hippie movement, many boys wore their hair long, and even in the 70s, when hair got a little shorter, men still had longer hairstyles. So, despite school dress codes, I grew it long, and because the regulations weren't enforced that well, I got away with it. For Christmas, Miss Mattie took me to get my ears pierced so I could start wearing pierced earrings. After that, she even allowed me to dress fully as a girl when we dined out or went to a store. I was delighted when restaurant servers and store clerks didn't seem to realize I was born with a boy's body. However, if on the following day we happend to run into someone who knew me from school, I could catch hell, depending on who it was.

At school, things were different. Everybody knew. When you demand that everyone call you Stephanie and you put on lipstick, it is evident that you are different. I guess I was inviting bullying from those who couldn't accept me. Yet, it wouldn't have made any difference if I let them call me Stephen and never put on anything girly because I was a feminine boy anyway. I was accustomed to some asshole shoving me in the hall and yelling, "Get away from me, faggot!" I tolerated when some clown Like Glenn Tucker got up in my face, grinning like an idiot, while he taunted, "I heard that you and Gary Watson had fun playing butt plug under the bleachers. Is that right? Did you get your butt plugged? Were you letting old Gary pack your fudge for you?"

Gary was a skinny nerd kid who got picked on almost as much as I did. His sin was being a thin, lanky, intelligent bookworm whose clothes often seemed too big or too small. There was no indication that he was gay, but that didn't matter to the assholes. They harassed anyone they considered to be low on their totem pole.

It helped, only a little, that there had begun to be gender-bending musicians and singers like David Bowe in the early 1970s. I bought some David Bowie t-shirts, hoping they might justify how I had chosen to dress and perhaps make me look cool. Still, I had decided long before middle school to be myself and fuck them if they couldn't handle it. That's a tall order for a thirteen-year-old, especially when self-esteem and insecurity seem to be the primary struggle for early adolescence. Yet, I had been through the refiner's fire of Pruitt Igoe, where grit had better be your exterior and determination had better be your core. So, I walked into school at the start of the Spring semester sporting my little gold teardrop earrings. My curly hair, almost shoulder length by then, was tucked behind my ears so my earrings would show. I was very proud of them. Still, nothing negated the underlying feelings of unworthiness from being abused, impoverished, black, and transgender.

The reaction was as expected. Girls scoffed and rolled their eyes. The boys were meaner, but I was there. I wasn't going away, and I strutted my new style through the halls like a glamour queen. Still, they continued to harass me, and it got worse. I would have some guy shove or spit on me, and they decided it was hilarious to de-pants me at my locker and start shouting, "Oh my God! She's got a dick!"

They did it as much as they could get away with it, but sometimes, they were called into the principal's office, just like I was. I was also not above revenge, like picking the lock on the locker of the clown, Glen Tucker, who got in my face about Gary Watson. I filled it so full of fake dirty Kotex that it all fell out when he opened his locker. For that, I stayed up almost all night and smeared each one with dark red tempera paint. When the embarrassed fucker turned around after trying to kick them out of the way, he saw the paper I had taped inside his locker saying, in big red letters, "Oh, No! Glen is on her period again!" I was also not above sneaking up behind some snotty little, hoity-toity bitch and slapping chewed bubble gum into her hair. There had been more than one occasion when an embarrassed Miss Mattie had marched into the principal's office to retrieve me and admonish me in the car, "Chile, jest cause dey do you wrong don't mean you gots ta do wrong. Even if dey, wrong, you can still do right. You gots ta rise above dis now. You don't rise above it; you jest like de are, and dey gonna take you down." I, therefore, changed my approach from revenge seeker to smartass.

A few days after the locker incident, Glen found me in the hall, got up in my face, and growled through gritted teeth, "I know you put that shit in my locker! You better watch your ass, Saunders!"

To this, I said, "Well, technically, if you think about it, no one can watch their own ass. I mean, it is behind us. Right? We don't have eyes in the back of our heads. I don't know about you, but I can't see my ass, try as I might, look over my shoulder, bend over to my knees. I just can't see it. Well, not without a mirror. I could, I suppose, install rearview mirrors on my shoulders, but still, I wouldn't be watching my actual ass, only the reflection of my ass in the mirror, but when you walk away, I can watch your ass—asshole."

He was dumbfounded. "What the hell is that supposed to men? You better not be coming onto me faggot!" The inane look across his face indicated that his mind was having difficulty fully comprehending what I had just said. After a pause, he said, "Just watch your ass, Saunders."

"As soon as I can figure out how to watch my ass, I'll let you know," I replied with a shit-eating grin stretching across my face. "In the meantime, if you can figure out how to watch your ass, please let me know. I'll bet you've never seen yours, either. It's a little large. Want me to take a picture for you?"

Crimson embarrassment crossed his face, and he merely turned and walked away. As he walked, I said, "Oh, look! There goes a big ass now."

There was no one in school I trusted, not one student or a single teacher. It felt like all of them were against me. Even if I had been white and born rich, they would still have been against me for being feminine and attracted to boys, but I was a biracial "fem freak" from the ghetto. I was everything they despised.

CHAPTER 10

A TRUE FRIEND

I never expected to have a real friend, but that January, just after I turned fourteen, I looked over in my first-period class to see a new kid sitting at the desk next to me. At first, I only glanced and thought I saw a boy. Her dark hair was cut short, almost in a boy's style, like a Twiggy cut, with a little extra length on top, and she was wearing a boy's flannel shirt tucked into jeans with a broad, red woman's waist belt and tennis shoes. She had no makeup on, but she didn't need it. She was gorgeous. This white girl's face had trim and classic lines that were stunningly beautiful. She had on small gold hoop earrings with diamond inlays. I noticed those, and I was envious. Then, I realized she had Goldilocks titties, not too big or too small. Those perfect titties were only slightly hidden beneath a black camisole with her red and black plaid flannel shirt unbuttoned down just below what would have been her cleavage. A sultry, sweet, and musky scent lingered on her. Wait? Was that men's cologne? My curiosity peaked. She was different, not like any kid I had ever seen before. I worked up my courage, smiled, and whispered, "Hi."

She turned, met my eyes, and scanned my face with her brown eyes. She didn't seem to be the least bit bothered that I had a sneaky hint of lip liner, was wearing teardrop earrings, and had long, curly hair. Then, she smiled and said, "Hi."

My heart fluttered a bit at the realization that she was a kid my age who didn't scoff at me, scorn me, or roll her eyes in disgust. At first, I wondered what might be wrong with her because she certainly did not act like any kid at school. I was about to start a conversation when we heard the teacher clearing his voice before he announced roll call.

The pig-faced, gravel voice, forty-something tenured asshole was doomed to spend his life teaching high school English. He began calling our names, and we each answered, "Here." When he reached the name Joan Wilson, the new girl returned, "Here." Then, I knew her name. He had already forced me to answer *Stephen Saunders* alphabetically in roll call. I knew it would do no good to correct him. If I tried, he would argue, and I could be getting detention rather than having my name pronounced correctly. Miss Mattie was still in the adoption process, and legal proceedings were underway to change my name to Stephanie. Mr. Riggs had been given some difficulties about it, and there had been some legal delays. Even if my name had been changed, I doubt the teacher would have agreed to pronounce it as legally defined, and the same argument would have been applied. I didn't have the authority to contest it, and I was trying to behave as well as possible for the sake of Miss Mattie so Doris Mansfield would have no excuse to put me back in state custody. Still, I was known to act up a little. I could get away with more acting up after my adoption had been finalized.

I practically didn't hear anything else after the roll call. My mind contemplated this Joan Wilson. I reveled in the hope that we could become friends and wallowed in sweet, immature fantasies. I couldn't wait till class was over because I wanted to talk to this new girl who had responded to me with congeniality instead of the usual putrid scoff of disgust. Was that a put-on, some ruse to trick me so she could stab me in the back later? That would have made sense. I never knew what to expect of most kids, and I usually didn't trust so readily, but I felt something different about her. Maybe I desperately hoped she would become a friend. Certainly, I sorely needed friendship at the time, but I also feared letting anyone get close.

Before the next class, We barely had enough time in the hall to introduce ourselves and plan on sitting together in the cafeteria at lunch. She didn't even flinch when I introduced myself as Stephanie Larouquette. Since the adoption papers weren't complete, I still had to go by my so-called mother's name, but I used my real name anywhere it was not required. When she introduced herself as Joan Wilson, I said, "Yes, I know. I heard it in roll call?"

Her eyes glittered as she smiled cordially, "Funny, I don't recall the teacher calling Stephanie Laroquette, but I wasn't paying that much attention." Of course, she had been paying attention. I knew she was. I was sitting beside her, watching her look toward different students when their names were called. She could not have missed my—less than enthusiastic—response to the call of Stephen Saunders.

"I'll explain later." I smiled and rushed to my next class.

When lunch came, I spotted her at a table near the cafeteria wall, a bit away from other students. Maybe she was just shy about being the new kid in school, or perhaps she was a loaner like me. Nonetheless, she was beautiful, and I had already seen boys eyeing her. She saw me carrying my tray and waved to me. I sat down, and before looking at my food, I said, "Wow! I feel like I've known you my whole life, like I already know you." That immediately felt like such a stupid thing to say, but she didn't shame me about it as others might have.

"Maybe you do already know me." She grinned. "Maybe we knew each other in a previous life or something."

"You believe in things like that?"

"Sure, why not?" she responded. "It makes about as much sense as all that other stuff."

I derailed from the discussion of past lives. "You're the first person I've met here who didn't make fun of me or completely avoid me."

The clanging noise and buzz of conversation in the echoing cafeteria created a kind of privacy that allowed the type of conversation that I had never had with any other kid.

"Why would I do that?" she responded. "You're an American, aren't you? You have a right to be who you are. Freedom is freedom, right?"

"Wow!" I said again. "Who are you, Joan Wilson? Where did you come from? Nobody thinks like that around here."

She had taken a bite of her Salisbury steak just before the question. I watched her chewing, holding her fingers over her mouth, trying to make space to answer. I had spoken to her like a sneaky server who asks if you're enjoying the meal right after you've taken a bite.

After taking a sip from her cardboard milk carton, she answered. "My family is from L.A. My Dad got a job, I don't know, some management position at Anheuser-Busch Brewery. I don't exactly know what my Dad does, but he is an executive. My Mom is a doctor, but my Dad makes more money than she does. She is back in L.A. closing her medical practice. Then, she will look into transferring her license to Missouri, and she'll move here after she has finished all that, probably this summer sometime, maybe sooner. I assume she will try to start a practice here or maybe join one. She likes family medicine. My dad brought my little brother and me to get settled and enroll in school."

I immediately felt intimidated. I was sitting across the table from a kid with one parent, a doctor, and the other in upper management, but I felt like a slug from the ghetto. Beneath my projected persona of anger and defiance, I was still an insecure kid who was a product of tyranny, poverty, and abuse. I had been devalued so much by almost everyone that I questioned having much worth at all. I might not have survived if it had not been for Miss Mattie. Yet, despite thinking that Joan and her family were superior, I continued to muster my courage.

"But who are you—you, yourself?" I continued. "I've never met anyone like you."

"What do you mean, who am I?" she inquired. "I'm me. What you see is what you get." Her mouth twisted into a goofy smile, and I giggled.

"What about you?" she returned. "Who are you, and where did you come from?"

I leaned over and whispered, "I came out of my mother's hooch." Then, we both giggled.

"Is that all?" she smiled.

I hesitated because I was so used to rejection, because I was ashamed of where I came from, and because she was so cool and from a sophisticated family. What if she looked down on me like everyone else did? She came from the type of background that had produced the kids who had mistreated and degraded me.

"It's a very complicated story," I replied, looking down at my plate, feeling ashamed of poverty and having a drug whore mother, among other things. "I usually don't tell people much about myself, but a lot of people around here have found out anyway."

"It's okay," she returned. "You don't have to tell me until you're ready, and you don't even have to tell me at all if you're never ready."

"I'm scared to tell you."

"Why?"

"I don't come from money and class like you do."

"First," she answered, "I don't come from money and class. Second, so what?"

"So, usually, kids like you treat me like a nobody."

Her voice was soft and comforting. "I don't believe there is such a thing as a nobody."

Looking up at her, I saw those big brown eyes gleaming at me. I took a deep breath and decided that I might as well tell her. If she became a backstabber like the others, I wouldn't be any worse off than before. I called on my strength and said, "My so-called mother was a drug whore, and she was murdered when I was ten."

"Oh, Wow!" she exclaimed. "Oh, my God!"

I stared down at my tray. I didn't raise my head and felt unusually vulnerable. I could not bring myself to make eye contact at that moment. The risk of her displeasure seemed to mean more than all the bullying.

"They blamed my friend, Mike, for it," I continued. "They sent him to prison for life. They put me in foster care, and then I met some TV evangelist who felt sorry for me and left a Trust to take care of me. That's why I'm in school here in Ladue instead of some run-down part of town. I got out of foster care last year, and now, I live with the only person I would ever call a real mother, an old lady who used to live up the hall from me in the projects. She is going to adopt me. Her name is Miss Mattie Laroquette. That's why I use the name Laroquette."

She didn't say anything. She just sat there. I could feel her eyes on me, and I hesitated to look up, but her silence made me raise my face to look at her. I couldn't quite make out her expression. She just seemed to stare in silence. Her look was not necessarily shaming, but it was intense.

"I'm sorry," I said after a pause. Then I picked up my tray and started to leave.

"Wait!" she called as I stood and turned away. "Please don't go. Please sit back down. I—I just didn't know what to say."

I turned slowly back to her and sat down. "I'm sorry," I said again.

"No, you don't have to be sorry," she comforted. "What should you be sorry for? I'm sorry you ever had to go through anything like that. I'm sorry about my reaction. I guess I am just shocked. I mean, you see things like that on television, or you hear things on the news, or read about things, but I've never met anyone who has ever gone through something like that."

"You see why I usually don't tell people," I said.

"Yes," she sighed. "I definitely get that."

"A lot of people know anyway. The teachers know. Other kids from foster care have told what they know, but they didn't know most of it. I get treated badly enough without telling anybody all my business, but most of them know where I came from and despise me as much for that as they do for being a girl."

"Why?" she inquired.

She didn't even flinch when I referred to myself as a girl, no argument, pushback, or ridicule, just a sincere question.

"Look at me," I responded. "Do I look like I fit in here? Olive skin, lip liner, earrings? If I could, I would wear a dress. They hate me for all of it. They hate me for expressing who I am. They hate me for the color of my skin. They hate me for where I came from. Nobody else like me attends school here. A few black kids get bussed in, but they aren't like me either, and some of them bully me, too."

"So?" she said. "You're you. Just be who you are. Fuck them!"

"So, things like that don't go over very well around here," I reflected. "Nobody wants to let you be yourself; some kids can be pretty cruel."

"I get that," she said. "I've been picked on a bit about dressing like a boy, but usually, it is just teasing more than anything else. Some guys get turned on by it. Others take it as a challenge like they are going to prove themselves if they can make it with a lesbian."

"You're a lesbian?" I questioned.

"Well, not really—maybe," she replied. "I don't know. I guess I'm not a real lesbian because I also like boys, but I find girls attractive. Maybe I like boys more than girls, though, but I don't know for sure. Maybe I like girls more than boys. I guess I'm attracted to both, but I would rather fall in love with someone's mind and soul than their body. It doesn't really matter to me if they are one gender or the other, but guys can get controlling, sometimes."

I glanced around the cafeteria to see if any of the assholes were sitting near. This seemed like a very private conversation in such a public place, but there we were having it, and no one seemed to care. No one was sitting close enough to hear, and they were all engaged in their own conversations anyway. I had long become used to sitting alone in some part of the cafeteria, separated from the others. They seemed to like it that way, and so did I. The less I had to deal with them, the better.

"So, do you feel like you are a boy?" I pressed. "I mean, you seem to like dressing sort of like a boy."

"No, not really. I'm a girl. I like being a girl, but I like dressing like a boy. I like masculinity, but femininity, too. I like girly things, and I'm not unhappy with my body. So, maybe I don't quite fit the mold either."

"I've always known I was a girl," I returned. "Even though I have a boy's body, I'm not a boy. I have the wrong body. This is not supposed to be my body. I've never felt comfortable in my body."

"You don't want your body?" she asked.

"Not like this," I explained. "I know I have to have a body, but I want to change it. I want to make it female. I want my body to reflect who I really am."

"So, you are a girl in a boy's body?" she asked.

"I guess you could say that, but that doesn't exactly describe how I feel," I replied. "It's like I'm stuck with this, but it isn't me."

"See, that's why I think about things like past lives, 'cause what if you are a female spirit? Maybe you were a woman in your past life, but this time, you got in the wrong body or something?"

"You think that is how it happened?" I asked. "I don't know why I'm like this. I just am."

"We're going to have to talk more about this," she smiled. "You have a lot to teach me."

"I feel like you have a lot to teach me," I affirmed. Then, I asked, "Do your parents know you like girls that way?"

"Well, no, not really," she replied. "Mom and Dad know I like to dress sort of like a boy, but the topic of being attracted to girls has never really come up, and they have heard me make comments about cute boys. I just never really talked with them about it. I mean, they would probably be cool with it, I guess. I have amazingly cool parents. My Mom used to be a hippie, I guess. She even met Ram Dass once, but the subject of my attractions has never really come up."

"Who is Ram Dass?"

"It's a long story. Some like hippie guru or something."

"Miss Mattie knows all about me," I interjected. "We talk about everything."

I had barely eaten anything off my tray, not that it was appealing. Lunch was about to end, and we had to get to our next class. Joan continued eating during the conversation, but I let my food go cold.

With an initial goodbye, each going our separate ways, my first revelation about myself to another student weighed heavily on my heart. Even though she had been receptive and kind, a part of me always endorsed any exposure or vulnerability as potentially dangerous. Still, other than Miss Mattie, I had never had a friend, and the idea of having an actual companion and confidant contradicted my trepidation.

We discovered we had a few classes together, including the first class after lunch. So, we continued to sit together for that first hour after lunch, and each sent knowing glances back and forth. Soon, we were becoming dear friends. The more time we spent together, the more relaxed we became, the more we cut up. She started standing up to the bullies with me, but the bullying changed from some guy shouting, "Get away from me faggot," to shouting, "Which one is the girl?"

Nonetheless, guys couldn't seem to help being attracted to Joan. At thirteen, she already had the perfect woman's body but was usually dressed in boys' shirts and jeans. None of the male attire could hide her boy-enticing curves or the wafting femininity that seemed to permeate the air around her. In fact, the male clothing kind of accentuated it. Sometimes, she would wear some lacy and frilly-looking blouse, barely covering those perfect titties with dress slacks and spats. Sometimes, she would wear khaki slacks, rarely women's slacks, but even more rarely, a dress. She always looked elegant and sexy. The school dress code insisted that dress and skirt lengths could be no more than an inch above the knee but said nothing about whether girls could wear slacks or jeans. The school attempted to cite the dress code to make me cut my hair, but after Miss Mattie marched into the administration office with our attorney and had an intense meeting, they decided my hair was acceptable.

The bullying continued to be regular and was all but ignored by the teachers and administration. One day, around the middle of the semester, we were being pestered by some asshole asking, "Which one is the girl?" Joan turned around, ripped open the snap buttons of her cowboy-style shirt, showing her bra, and shouted, "Does this answer your question, mother fucker? Guess what? Both our dicks are bigger than yours!"

We both got after-school detention, but so did the asshole who taunted us. There were seven of us waiting out our sentence on that detention, not all for the same reason, but it was worth it. For the first time since Mike and Miss Mattie, I had someone on my side and, best of all, someone my age. We continued to grow close, and soon, we were spending the night at each other's houses and doing things together on the weekends.

Our parents, of course, had been called in on the bra flash incident. This was when Joan's Mom met Miss Mattie, and they hit it off immediately. Her Mom had closed her practice early and moved to St. Louis just after Spring Break in late March. I was surprised to see this elite white woman chatting with Miss Mattie in a friendly and accepting way. Perhaps it helped that Joan's parents had both been involved with the civil rights movement when they were getting their education back in the sixties. Her parents and Miss Mattie were coming at Principal Slater with the same argument, "Why are you letting these kids pick on our children just because they are different? What are you going to do to protect our kids from being bullied? What do you expect them to do when they get pushed to a breaking point?"

Joan had the most fantastic parents, but her Dad remained a little aloof and standoffish. Her Mom didn't seem to care at all that I was a girl or that I was attracted to boys. She was highly informal and down to earth. She insisted that I call her by her first name, Amanda. I respectfully called her Miss Amanda. Joan's parents treated me kindly, but I couldn't help feeling that her father didn't really approve of me and just tried not to rock the boat. He never said anything cruel or derogatory, but I never felt he fully accepted me.

Neither of them cared about race. Miss Mattie and I were invited to dinner at their house, and she had them over to our house for dinner. For the first time, I began to feel normal, like I was part of everyday family interactions. I had never met people like them before. Joan also had the coolest little brother named Jeremy. He was about ten, a typical boy, a jock, and more into sports than I thought anyone could be. Yet, when it came to accepting people as they were, he took after Joan and his Mom. He was never anything but sweet to me. They all maintained a live-and-let-live perspective and never tried to change anyone. They let Joan be who she was and let me be who I was. I didn't even know people like that existed, but apparently, L.A. was slightly different from eastern Missouri in the 1970s. At least some people from L.A. were open and accepting.

Since Joan's mom was a doctor, I began to wonder if she might be willing to place me on female hormones, but I didn't dare ask. Still, I lay in bed at night thinking about it and thinking about how I could make my body congruent with my soul.

CHAPTER 11

FROM A GIRL TO A WOMAN

I continued to read everything I could find related to gender. That spring, I read that birth control pills were made from female hormones, could maybe suppress male characteristics, and help me start developing female features. It wasn't that I wanted to be a woman. I already was a woman. I just wanted my external appearance to match my internal feelings. The question was, how would I get hold of birth control pills? One day, I asked Joan, "Since your mom is a doctor, do you think she would prescribe birth control pills for me?"

"Why do you want those?" she asked.

"Because I read that the hormones in them can maybe help me to develop like a girl."

"Jeez, I don't know." Joan winced. "That's not exactly like prescribing you an antibiotic for an ear infection or something, and doctors aren't supposed to prescribe to their friends."

"I just have to get my hands on them," I begged. "The older I get, the more I'm going to look like a man. I don't want to look like a man. I'm not a man. Do you think you could at least ask her?"

She mulled it over for a moment. "I've got a better idea. How about I talk to Mom and tell her that I've started having sex and see if she will get some for me? Then, I can give them to you?"

"Oh, Wow! Would you? That would be the greatest thing."

Joan did ask her mother, and in a few days, she began bringing the pills to me, one at a time. She had to keep the package at home, so her mother would think she was taking them, but every school day, she brought me one, and since we usually spent time together on the weekends, she would bring one to me then, too. She would give me two if it looked like we had to miss a day of seeing each other.

She snickered when she brought me the first pill. "Mom insisted that I also make the guy wear a condom. So, she gave me condoms, too. Mom said there are a lot of things I could get besides pregnant, and the more protection I have, the better, but she also does not want me to be promiscuous. We had to have this long talk about sex, sexually transmitted diseases, responsibility, yap, yap, yap. She said she wants to meet the boy I'm sleeping with. I don't know how I'm going to get around that. She also scolded me that I'm too young to be having sex and tried to talk me out of it, but she knows she can't control my decisions, and she would rather have me protected than get in trouble."

"But she still let you have the pills?" I asked.

"Yeah, my mom is cool."

Joan managed to put off introducing her mother to the imaginary boy she was supposedly sleeping with and continued to bring me the pills for the rest of that semester and throughout the summer. "If push comes to shove," she said. "I'll just tell her you and I have been having sex and decided to date."

"Oh my God!" I exclaimed. "Do you really think she would buy that? I mean, wouldn't that be worse? She knows I like boys too."

"I don't know, but stranger things have happened. What if you were a lesbian on the inside?"

"We could tell her you are having sex with Glen Tucker," I teased.

"Oh! Gag me!" she spouted while sticking a finger in her mouth. "I would rather have sex with a chimpanzee."

"Maybe you would be," I giggled. "Glen's actual species has not been confirmed. Maybe we could hire some kid to pretend he is your boyfriend. Maybe, Gary Watson. Do you think he would go for that? I have more than enough allowance to pay him."

"Jeez, do you think my Mom would buy that? I could tell her I'm into the intellectual type. She would probably think that was cool."

"Let's deal with it if we have to," I said. "Maybe we won't have to."

Joan continued to bring the pills; apparently, her mother didn't pressure her about the boyfriend. I think she told her mom that she was dating Gary Watson and that he was extremely shy. We got away with it for a while.

For a few months, I really couldn't tell any difference, except in my moods, which were all over the charts, and this added to the emotional turmoil that I continued to grapple with because of bullying and trauma. My nightmares got worse, and I felt like I was always angry. If I wasn't angry, I was crying. I began snapping at Miss Mattie over absolutely nothing. Sometimes, I would feel down and depressed, like I didn't want to try anymore, like there was no use or reason for going on. On those days, I wanted to stay in bed all day, but Miss Mattie would have none of that. "I don't care if ya depressed," she said. "Ya needs to get up and get movin'. Don't do nobody no good ta just lay round all de time. Ya has ta fights depression."

It took about six weeks for Miss Mattie to notice the change in my behavior and she asked me, "Ya all right, sugar? Ya ain't been actin' right lately."

"What the hell do you mean; I an't been acting right? Is there something wrong with me? Am I growing fucking horns or something?" Then, I burst into tears.

"You see dat right dere, is what I'm talkin' bout." She responded calmly. "You ain't never talked to me dat way, and what you doin' crying so much all of a sudden? I know puberty gonna be messin' wid ja head, but Lord child, you ain't actin' right at all."

"Well, this is how I act, and so what if I cry!"

"Ya ain't never talked ta me dat way," she scolded. "Even goin' through all dat mess you was goin' through, ya still acted respectful ta me, most o' de time. Now, I don't know what be goin' on. Must be dem hormones goin through da change."

"What the hell do you mean, hormones?" I snapped back, paranoid that she might have figured out what I was doing with the birth control pills.

"It happen' to us all when we get ta dat point in life.", she explained. "Happens again fo women in menopause. Hormones make us all go a little crazy till we gets through it. Den, some peoples don't never stop bein' crazy." She snickered at her little joke.

There were a lot of factors at work with my mood and attitude, not the least of which was that I felt guilty for deceiving her and that I was paranoid that I might get in a lot of trouble if I got caught. My so-called mother would have fucking beat the hell out of me if she had seen me doing something like that. I didn't think the hormones had started to work yet, not that I could tell, but I was looking for physical changes. The changes were subtle. I was still growing some facial hair and could see no indications of breast development, but my skin seemed softer and smoother. I had no idea how I would explain it when the facial hair stopped, and my breasts started to develop. My nipples had gotten hard as rocks, and I had started getting scared that I might be getting breast cancer. My nipples felt like they had little knots in them, and I had all but convinced myself that I had breast cancer. It would have been my just due for having deceived Miss Mattie and Joan's Mom.

"Well," Miss Mattie continued explaining. "You know dere is times when we go through de changes when dem adult hormones starts kickin' in. It messes wid ya. You actin' like you is havin' hormone surges."

"I am *NOT* having hormone surges," I growled back at her.

"Den, what is it?" she persisted. "What is causin' you ta get all riled up deez days?"

I hesitated to say anything. Finally, I confessed. "I think I have breast cancer."

"What in de world make you think somehin' like dat?" She raised those curious eyebrows of hers.

"I have lumps in my breasts, Miss Mattie, in my nipples. They are hard, like tumors are starting. I think I might die."

"Hee, hee, hee, hee." She giggled and put one finger across her upper lip. "Dat ain't cancer, baby. Dat's normal. Normal fo girls and fo boys."

"But I have lumps in my nipples!" I began to cry.

"Baby, let me see." She got up, came across the living room, and commanded that I raise my blouse.

I complied, and she leaned over, looked at my nipples, squeezed around on them a little, and asked. "You ain't got no lumps nowhere but here?"

"No, just under my nipples."

"Den, it's normal. Boys and girls both get some hardnin' o' de nipples when they start dae teens."

"Are you sure?" I questioned.

"You don't believes me, you can go ask Joan's Momma. She a doctor, ain't she?"

"Okay," I accepted.

I didn't confess anything to her and kept taking the birth control pills. Then, late in August, just before I would start my ninth-grade year, I was wearing a loose t-shirt and working in the kitchen, helping her prepare dinner when she glanced over at me from the side. We were standing parallel at the sink. I was peeling potatoes and handing them to her so she could cut them up for frying.

I felt her eyes on me and turned to see her staring directly at me.

"What you got dere?" she interrogated.

"Ah, potatoes?" I responded, knowing that she wasn't talking about potatoes. "I've almost got them all peeled."

"Nah, I mean, what you got dere under dat t-shirt?" she continued, and her bony finger waved around in the air toward my chest. "Somethin' happen' dere?"

"I don't know what you're talking about?" I replied.

She stepped over, grabbed the bottom of my loose t-shirt with both hands and pulled it straight around my waist, tight over my chest, outlining my developing tits in the fabric. "Dis be what I talkin' bout," she said.

I looked down at my tightened t-shirt, creating a crease between my slightly developing breasts.

She raised one hand and circled a finger around my chest. "Mmmm hmmm," she moaned.

"What?" I felt my face flush. I knew I had been caught.

"Where did you get dem titties?" she insisted. "You got somethin' you needs ta tell me?"

"Titties?" I questioned as though she didn't know what she was talking about. I had noticed them, too, but I kept it to myself. I had been wearing loose clothing, trying to hide them, but I had admired them in the mirror for several weeks, hoping they would get bigger.

"Ain't no boy I ever knowd grows titties like dat, less he was real fat or somethin'," she pressured.

"Maybe I am growing into my womanhood like you said."

"Nah, dat ain't growin' into yo womanhood," she pried. "I don't know how you got dem titties, but I'm thinkin' we needs ta get da doctor ta take a look at cha. I know you is a woman on de inside, but somethin' ain't right dat you be growin' titties."

"NO!" I screamed and ran out of the room.

"Stephanie!" Miss Mattie called after me. "Child, you come back here and talk bout dis!"

"LEAVE ME THE FUCK ALOOOOONNNNNNNEEEE!" I yelled as I ran up the stairs to my room. I ran in, slammed the door, locked it, and threw myself on my bed. A few minutes later, I heard a light tapping at the door and Miss Mattie's voice from the other side. "Baby, you know you gonna have ta face dis. Ain't no runnin' away. Ain't no pretendin'. You gonna have ta come clean. How did you get hold o' dem hormones you been takin'? Ain't right if you bought dem on da street. Even if dae ain't hard drugs, you never know what you be getting' when you buyin' somethin' on de street."

I buried my face in the pillow and yelled, "Go away!" Even then, I noticed that my voice had also started getting higher.

I had no idea how I was going to explain anything to anybody. I had not, exactly, thought it through.

"Baby, we gots ta talk bout dis," Miss Mattie pleaded.

"I don't want to talk about it!" I whined.

"Okay, den," she retreated. "But sooner or later, it gots ta be talked about. If you doin' somethin' ta cause dis, den it might also be hurtin' yo health. If you ain't doin' somethin' ta cause dis, den de doctor needs ta take a look at it anyways, cause it mean somethin' ain't right."

I said nothing in response, and after a very long pause, I heard her going back down the stairs. I stayed in my room the rest of that evening and didn't come down for dinner. Miss Mattie left me alone.

I pretended it never happened the next morning, and she let it go. I didn't know until later that she had called Joan's Mom to ask questions about it. And Miss Amanda put two and two together. The next thing I knew, all four of us, Miss Mattie, Miss Amanda, Joan, and I, were all sitting together to have a discussion about it. This occurred around the dining table at Joan's house.

"So," Miss Amanda began, "Miss Mattie tells me you have been growing breasts. Is that right, Stephanie?"

Joan and I both barely looked up but glanced at each other.

"Ansa de woman," Miss Mattie ordered.

"Yes, Ma'am," I said quietly.

"Now, isn't it curious," Miss Amanda continued, "that this all came about after I started getting birth control pills for Joan? Do either of you have anything to say about that?"

"Okay!" Joan caved. "I've been giving Stephanie the birth control pills to help her start developing like a woman."

"Honey, do you have any idea what kinds of consequences something like that could have?" Miss Amanda said with compassion. "Do either of you?"

"I have to do this," I pleaded. "Please, I have to. Can you prescribe real hormones for me?"

Miss Amanda sat back in her chair. "No. It wouldn't be ethical of me to do something like that. I mean, if it was a prescription for a cold or something, fine, but we are talking about a very detailed and possibly dangerous therapy regimen, to begin with, and I'm just too close to you for it to be ethical of me to prescribe like that. Stephanie, I know this must be very important to you, but you will need more than I could do for you, anyway." She looked over at Miss Mattie and back at me.

There was a long and uncomfortable pause when Miss Mattie said, "You know anybody dat could help her?"

"Let me ask around," Miss Amanda said. "I'll see what I can find out. In the meantime, Joan, my dear … you are grounded for a month, young lady. There is no contact with Stephanie, nothing but staying in your room unless you are permitted to come out. Is that clear?"

"Yes, Ma'am," Joan quietly responded.

"Well, I thinks dat maybe I can give dat same punishment ta Stephanie, den." Miss Mattie chimed in.

"Does this mean I have to stop taking the birth control pills?" I asked.

"Not yet," Miss Amanda said. "I don't want you just suddenly to stop taking them. In the meantime, I will see if I can find a referral to an endocrinologist."

I breathed a sigh of relief. A month without seeing Joan would be punishment, but it also meant I would have plenty of time in my room to read. More than anything, it could mean I would finally get the help I needed.

A week later, I started my ninth-grade year. I would soon be fifteen and knew I was becoming a woman. I didn't want anyone to take that from me, but I was also afraid that the house of cards I had been building could collapse at any moment. Other kids at school began to notice the changes in my body, especially the boys. Even though I wore loose-fitting clothing to hide the changes, the taunting became more extreme. I had always invited it, to a point, because I demanded that I should be allowed to be myself and express myself however I wanted. I had not considered how extreme their scorn could become. Joan did whatever she could to step in, but there were times that she endangered herself by doing so. I tried even more to avoid the boy's bathroom. For one thing, depending on who might be in there, it could be potentially dangerous. When I would sneak into the girl's bathroom, sometimes I could get away with it, but there were other times that some girl would rat me out, and I would end up sitting across from the principal's desk, yet again.

My arguments that I was not a boy had never flown before, and they were not about to lift off the runway at that time. The principal, Mr. Slater, had long been frustrated with me. It was apparent he didn't like me, and I assumed that, had he been fifteen or sixteen, he might have been like one of the boys abusing me. In his late fifties, with graying hair and melancholy eyes, it was evident, at least to me, that he also longed for retirement, and I was not making his job easy.

"Steven, I don't have a clue what to do with you," he scolded after I had been caught again in the girl's restroom.

"My name is Stephanie," I replied with a determined scowl. "It is my legal name now. Miss Mattie adopted me and had my name legally changed. You have to address me by my legal name, Stephanie Christine Laroquette."

"I don't have to do any such thing," he snapped. "Now, you're about to leave me with no choice but to expel you. You have violated school policy over and over, and no form of punishment seems to have any effect on you."

"Oh please, Mr. Fox … don't throw me in the briar patch," I sassed with a quote from Uncle Remus.

His sullen look was an indication that he was not amused.

"I have straight A's," I argued. "I don't get into any other trouble except when I fight back because I'm bullied or go into the girl's bathroom, where I should be allowed to go because I am a girl. I also should be allowed to go there because I don't want to get cornered in the boy's bathroom by some of the thugs who attend school here."

By then, midway through ninth grade, I had also begun to look like a girl. The outside was starting to match the inside.

Miss Amanda had found an endocrinologist willing to prescribe my hormone replacement. That further enhanced my breast development. I had grown my hair very long and always wore makeup and earrings. They had stopped trying to make me wash off the makeup. I would reapply it if they didn't confiscate it, or I returned the next day wearing it again. On the makeup front, I had won. They decided the battle wasn't worth fighting, especially when Miss Mattie frequently marched into the school with our attorney. Miss Mattie had taken me to the makeup counters at the high-end stores, where I learned to apply makeup appropriately and tastefully. I wasn't garish with it, and I could afford more if they took what I had.

"Young man!" he scolded. "As long as you have a penis, you are NOT a girl. You were born a boy. Your birth certificate says 'boy,' and you are most assuredly a boy. It doesn't make any difference what you do to yourself or what you have your name changed to. You can wear a dress your whole life, shoot yourself up with women's hormones or whatever, and it will not make you female. You were born a male. So, a male—is what—you are!"

"I am going to have surgery," I responded.

"I don't care!" he snapped again. "You can cut your penis off, cut your testicles off. "Then, you will be a boy without a penis and testicles. You still won't be a girl, and I am telling you right now. This is absolutely the last straw and your last chance. You will be expelled if you set foot in the girl's bathroom one more time! Is that clear?"

"But I am a girl," I pleaded.

He slammed his fist on his desk with the veins bulging in his neck. "YOU ARE NOT A GIRL, AND YOU WILL NOT SET FOOT IN THE GIRL'S BATHROOM ONE MORE TIME! IS THAT CLEAR!"

I winced back in my chair when he hit the desk, feeling intimidated and threatened as I had once felt when Jake raged. My heart pounded, and my mind returned to Jake beating my head on the floor, telling me he would kill me.

I did not respond.

"IS THAT CLEAR!" he shouted again and beat his fist onto his desk again.

"Yes … ss … sir," I softly replied.

"GET OUT!" he commanded.

I quietly picked up my things and left. By that time, I had begun carrying a purse. I pulled it to my chest as though hugging a Teddy bear and walked quietly out of his office.

I could never understand why so many of them hated me, why they appointed themselves judge and jury to convict me of the crime of being myself—nothing I ever did caused any harm to them. I didn't even attack anyone unless I was defending myself. Honestly, in my entire life, I had never really attacked anyone except in self-defense or at least my perceived need for self-defense when I felt violated.

Thankfully, most of the time, I got only verbal insults or attempts to intimidate and berate me, and the physical attacks were simple things like a shove in the hallway or a quick punch to my arm. I tried to ignore it. I had gotten past trying to out-prank them or insult them back. It wasn't worth it. Rarely would I even say anything when they started something. Miss Mattie had taught me that a person's judgment and behavior are about what is happening inside them and had nothing to do with me. Still, I couldn't understand why they did it. Maybe I might have understood if I deserved punishment for doing something horrible. Still, I wasn't bullied because I had committed some atrocity or perpetrated some evil act that caused overt or irreparable harm. I had even stopped stealing after Miss Mattie got custody of me. I was doing nothing illegal, immoral, or unfair, except perhaps according to their self-righteous judgment. They attacked me simply for being different because they hated me for failing to form into the mold that society had prescribed for me. I was a square peg, and society was a round hole. I did not fit; I was never going to fit, yet a cruel and bombastic punishment was executed on me almost daily. My makeup caused no lacerations to their skin. My earrings cut no one. My purse was not a weapon. My feminine walk took nothing from anyone. My only crime for which I was brutally, unfairly, and regularly punished was for being different and refusing to act out a role for them.

The irony is that, as much as the church and many of these church-going people despised me, the church had saved me from the hell of Pruitt Igoe. One of their ministers gave me the Trust and made it possible to escape the moralistic oppression that the McNeils and their church had forced on me. At least the McNeils had never overtly abused me as others had. Perhaps I had been ungrateful. Maybe I was supposed to have given up telling anyone I was a girl, started acting like a boy, given up attraction to males, and played the role of a heterosexual boy. The problem is that I would have been performing. I would have had to be on that stage every moment of every day and put in the energy and effort to pretend to be something and someone that I wasn't. Maybe I was being punished because the church had saved me, but I had not conformed to the expectations of the church. There had been wonderful gifts I had received at the McNeil home: reading, certain manners, structure, and stability. I was not ungrateful for that. I had the feeling, however, that the same bullying and rejection would have occurred if it had not been the church that saved me from Pruitt Igoe. Regardless, I was doomed to be despised simply for being myself.

Joan had also gotten in trouble on that last day that I was called into Slater's office. She had been the lookout for me when I used the girl's restroom. The stupid girl who turned me in knew what was going on when she saw Joan at the bathroom door and, of course, made sure to implicate Joan in her rant to the authorities. She had pushed past Joan and specifically looked for my feet under the stall.

"Get out, Stephen!" she commanded. "I know you're in here! You are not a girl! You are not supposed to be in the girl's bathroom!"

Then, I made the mistake of defying her. I came out of the stall and went to the sink to wash my hands and check my makeup in the mirror. She stood there repeatedly, screaming, "GET OUT!" I ignored her, said nothing, and went on as if she wasn't there, but a teacher heard it; she ranted to the teacher about it, and the next thing I knew, I was sitting in Mr. Slater's office.

Most of the time, Joan could get some girl to wait a minute to let me finish. Some girls didn't care and would come in anyway, and some would wait, but this particular girl and some of her friends had assigned themselves as the bathroom police with the determination to keep me from using the girl's restroom. The truth is, I didn't feel comfortable in either restroom, but at least, in the girl's restroom, I felt a little more relaxed and a little safer. I never used the urinals in the boy's bathroom, but apparently, it was a crime to sit down to pee. When I was in the boy's restroom, some boys had been known to dump trash over the stall door, if not the whole trash can. That was the least of it. I usually stayed in the stall until the bell rang, and I figured they had left for class. I had learned to squat on the edge of the commode so no one could see my feet below the stall door. This often worked as long as no one had seen me go into the stall, and if I waited until there was enough quietness to be sure the bathroom had emptied, but if I happened to sneeze or something, they would be onto me and would start their shit. Sometimes, they would go from stall to stall, checking to see if I was in one. Like some girls, some of the boys didn't care, but there was a faction in each bathroom that had assigned themselves as the bathroom militia, and regardless of whether I was in the girl's or boy's bathroom, they thought I had committed a crime against them.

Many kids just ignored me. They didn't hurt me, but they never befriended me, either. I could handle the indifferent kids. As much as I wanted to be liked and accepted like any other kid, indifference was better than bullying. Knowing I was in there, the girls who would come in to use the girl's restroom didn't seem to care. Some of them would even talk to me. They would go on about their business as they would if there had been any other girl in the stall next to them. I never saw any of their junk, and they never saw mine. Any undressing or exposure of flesh occurred inside a stall, and we were back in full dress when we came out. Some boys cared less, as well. It meant nothing to them if I sat down to pee or stood at the urinal. They would come in, use the urinal, and go about their business without feeling like they had to hunt me down and harass me. Yet, there were the few who took it upon themselves to make me as miserable as possible.

Of course, everyone knew about the latest incident and that I had been called into Slater's office, yet again, for daring to pee in the girl's restroom stall. It seemed like every time I got in trouble for something like that, the bullying got worse. If the administration didn't punish me, the bullies would. Most often, I got it from both.

Before that particular day was over, I was to be punished as I had never been punished before. The tattle tale bitch had made sure that it was all over school that I had gotten caught, yet again, using the girl's restroom. I suppose that had been the straw that broke the self-righteous camel's back. That afternoon, I had been walking past the bathrooms on my way to class when about six boys grabbed me and dragged me into the girl's bathroom. Joan had been walking with me and ran to get help, but the deed had been done by the time anyone with authority got there.

I was tackled like a quarterback in the football playoffs, dragged into the girl's bathroom, and given the punishment they thought I deserved.

"So, you want to use the girl's room, MOTHER FUCKER!" One boy snapped. "Here's your fucking chance!"

They picked me up and dunked my face down into an open commode. I was screaming like a banshee, but it did nothing but egg them on. I was dragged out of the stall and slammed against the wall. Just as my back hit the wall, I was able to nail one guy in the nuts with a foot between his legs, and he went down, folded into a fetal position on the floor, screaming and groaning.

Then, a couple held me while others took turns punching me. When the guy I had kicked finally got back to his feet, He yelled, "HOLD HIS MOTHER FUCKING LEGS APART!" The others complied, then he slammed his fist repeatedly into my crotch, stood back, and kicked me in the crotch as brutally and as often as his strength would allow. "YOU WANT TO BE A GIRL, YOU STUPID FAGGOT MOTHER FUCKER? HERE! I'LL KICK YOUR FUCKING NUTS OFF!"

The pain was shattering. It took my breath and my will to fight. I knew I was fucked. I knew there was nothing I could do, and it did not escape my mind that they would probably kill me. I could only feel pain and terror as I struggled helplessly to get free.

Even though it felt like it would never stop, it was likely only a few minutes. As they beat me, the pain began to disappear into a numb malaise with barely an echo of the event calling from some vast corner of my mind where such things go to hide from consciousness. I knew I was bleeding. I tasted salty blood in my mouth, but I could barely feel my mouth, and I reached a point where I could barely feel my body itself, as though each punch and each kick were dealt to a sandbag with no flesh or nerve remaining. Then I felt a hand behind my head that grabbed a fist full of hair. A second later, I saw my face plummeting toward the sink. There was an instant crack of pain as my skull hit the porcelain; a flash of light split through my brain and then blank, dark nothing.

CHAPTER 12

ONE DOOR CLOSES

I felt a tightness on my hand, something squeezing, pushing a little, and squeezing again. Then, I began to feel pain. My head hurt like spears with jagged glass points that had been thrust into it from every direction. My whole body ached with a numb soreness, making any movement feel like a Herculean effort. I opened my eyes, struggled to see through a fog, and recognized Miss Mattie sitting by my bed, but it wasn't my bed. It was a different bed, and the room was white and stark. She was rhythmically and nervously squeezing my hand.

"Dere's my girl," she sweetly commented as her hand softly and subconsciously crunched over mine. Her voice sounded almost as though it were an echo.

I was confused. At first, I almost didn't recognize her as fear and foreboding permeated my mind. My eyes moved around the room, seeking evidence of threat or danger lurking anywhere. Everything was white, including a white man in a white lab coat standing opposite the bed from Miss Mattie. I pulled my hand away from Miss Mattie's and moved it to my forehead, where I felt wires.

The man said, "Careful there," as he gently pulled my hand back down. I winced when he touched me but allowed him to move my hand.

I wasn't thinking as much as reacting. Tubes were going into taped places at the crook of my elbow. I felt like I needed to pee, reached down, and realized a catheter was in my penis.

The man in the white lab coat said, "I'm glad you're awake, but try not to touch anything. Now, can I ask you to tell me your name?"

I looked at him. His face was blurred; a dark gray fuzzy oval obscured his face and faded into the scenery around his head. I could not see his eyes and had no idea who he was.

He asked again, "Can you tell me your name?"

"Ste-phan-e," I moaned while aching with pain.

The man in the lab coat looked over at Miss Mattie.

"Dat's her legal name," she said. "Should be on de chart."

"Yes, I see it on the medical record," the man said. "Stephanie, I am Dr. Willis. It's good to see that you are awake. It looks like everything is going along fine. I need to listen to your chest and do some checks on you. Is that okay?"

I nodded slightly, but sore discomfort allowed no more than that. He put a stethoscope against the palm of his hand and held it for a moment. Then, he placed it on my chest and moved it around. "Good," he said as he lifted my eyelids and shone super bright light into my eyes. After a couple of quick flashes in each eye, he stood upright. "I'm going to have the nurse come in and take your vitals, blood pressure, and the like, and then I will come back and talk to you again when you have had a little more time for your head to clear. We had to put you into an induced coma for a while to ensure your brain had a better chance to heal. Do you need any pain medication?"

I nodded.

He turned and walked out of the room. I could barely turn my head back in the direction of Miss Mattie. My head especially hurt, but I did manage to turn to look at her and moved my hand back to hers. "Where ... am ... I?"

"You in Barnes-Jewish Hospital," she replied. "Trauma unit."

I sucked in my breath but didn't speak. I noticed Joan had pulled a chair up to the other side of the bed after the doctor left.

"What ... happ ... ened?" I groaned.

"Do you remember any of it?" Joan questioned.

"Bunch ... of ... shits ... jumped me. Not ... much ... else."

"You got beaten pretty badly," she went on. "By the time I got some teachers there, they had taken off. There were six of them. I recognized four of them, but it all happened so fast that I didn't see who the others were. When you get better, a detective will come to talk to you about assault and battery charges, maybe even attempted murder."

"No," I slurred.

"The state is pressing charges," she replied. "I have already told the detective what I know. The four I recognized have already been arrested. They ratted out the other guys. They have all been expelled, and there are warrants for the other two."

"No," I slurred a little more firmly. "No de-tect-ive. No char-ges."

"We gonna do what's right," Miss Mattie interjected. "Hold dem accountable."

"No," I groaned again. "Let … it … go."

"Well, we leave it alone fo now an talks bout it later." Miss Mattie smiled and squeezed my hand again. She knew I was getting upset.

"Was … Glen … one of them?" I asked.

"No," Joan replied. "Not that I could tell."

"Surprised," I said.

"You need to pursue this," she insisted. "Those bastards need to go to prison!"

"No," I moaned one more time.

I was in the hospital for almost two more months, in pain and even more pain when they poked, prodded, and ran tests. By the third day, after coming out of the coma, I was pretty coherent and pissed off that they had shaved my head to attach electrodes so they could get EEG readings. Thankfully, the injury to my head healed better than they initially expected, but I had a mild traumatic brain injury that caused me problems for a while. The doctor noted that the younger you are when you sustain an injury, the more likely you will fully heal from it.

Still, I had been knocked unconscious, and there were precautions that I and Miss Mattie would have to take when I got home, but it could have been a lot worse. They had placed me in an induced coma to keep my blood pressure low and let my brain rest. I had been in the coma for several days before they woke me. Joan's Mom and Dad visited a couple of times, but Miss Mattie and Joan pretty much sat by my side the whole time. I had no memory of a lot of it.

When I had developed some coherency again, Dr. Willis returned to discuss further treatments and recommendations.

"Unfortunately, your head was not the only thing injured," he informed. "You have a couple of broken ribs and were beaten around your testicles so much that both are ruptured. I can save the left testicle, maybe, but the right one will have to be removed."

"Take them both," I said without hesitation. "I don't want them."

He explained all the reasons, boy reasons, why I should keep at least one testicle. Maybe I might want to have a child someday. It could interrupt my sexual functioning. I would need to be on male hormones without it, etc., but to me, that part of the beating had done me a favor. I told him, "I am female. I don't want to be in a male body anymore. I don't want kids. I don't care if I never have sex. It just isn't that important to me." He knew that I had been on hormone replacement therapy. It was documented in my chart, and there was evidence in my body.

Dr. Willis protested about taking both testicles, and Miss Mattie interjected. "If dat what she want, I will sign de papas."

"Well," he acquiesced. "There is a risk he could lose the other one anyway. Both testicles were severely damaged. This means he will never be able to have children, though."

"I don't care!" I affirmed. "What do I need to do to make that clear to you? I've never wanted children. I would just fuck them up like my so-called mother fucked me up, even if I tried to do better than her. If I could have the change surgery right now, I would. Let's do it! The sooner, the better."

"I can't do that," Dr. Willis said. "But I know that Johns Hopkins Hospital has been doing those types of surgeries. They may not want to do it for someone so young, but I can discuss a referral with your endocrinologist, and we'll see. In the meantime, with your guardian's approval, I will have you prepped for surgery, and we'll remove both testicles tomorrow morning."

"She's my Mom," I replied. "She adopted me. She is not my guardian. She is the only real mother I ever had."

"Very well," Dr. Willis replied without taking note of my protest. "I'll get things started, and Ms. Laroquette can sign the paperwork later today."

The next day, they took me in and removed my testicles. The only way I could have been happier would have been to have the complete transition surgery. They left the scrotum. Dr. Willis knew that I would need that for the process of transition surgery later. In a couple of more weeks, I was discharged to go home. Still, I had to go back a couple of times a week to be checked and also see if my behavior had changed from having the head injury. I had to have some physical therapy to get my body functioning again, and psychotherapy was also insisted upon, but I had been seeing a therapist ever since Miss Mattie got custody, and had been with a different therapist appointed by the state when I was with the McNeils.

By the time I left the hospital, summer vacation from school had begun, and I was supposed to enter my tenth-grade year in the fall. The teachers had allowed me to do make-up work for the classes I missed, and I was moved on to the tenth grade, but I didn't want to go back to school. I didn't want to endure any more of the bullshit, the taunting, and bullying, and I damn sure didn't want any more beatings. So, in the fall, Miss Mattie hired a private tutor to home-school me. I wouldn't have to be around the assholes anymore, and I could use my own bathroom whenever I wanted, but I didn't get to see Joan as much. I am not sure I could have walked back into that school anyway, not knowing who my enemy was or who wasn't. I had already gotten to the point that I would jump like a scared cat every time there was a sudden noise. I had also become very irritable and would start screaming over the littlest thing. My therapist questioned whether my behavior meant something was wrong with my brain, if it was due to the hormone replacement, or if it was because I had been tortured and abused my whole life. Maybe it was all the above, but I was emotionally miserable.

Thankfully, the scandal of the beating and the shock went through the school and the community. Because of it, Joan had some minor taunting when she returned to school, but the incident seemed to have calmed things down quite a bit. Now, they were afraid of carrying it too far. The teachers and administration looked after Joan more carefully than they had previously. Maybe they feared a potential lawsuit, and Mr. Riggs raised the option of a lawsuit, but Miss Mattie declined. She knew I just wanted to let it go and put it behind me as soon as possible.

I'm not sure what it might have been like for Joan if I had returned to school. The assholes who had done it were prosecuted. I was shocked that Glen Tucker had not been one of them since he had probably picked on me more than anyone there. I didn't remember all of them, and the whole thing was a total blur, but Glen was never identified. They were prosecuted as adults for assault, battery, and several other charges, but because I refused to testify, or maybe because they were rich white kids, they got very light sentences. I did a deposition for the prosecuting attorney, but there was only so much I could remember, and I was not about to get on the stand before any of them. Still, they all got very little punishment for what they did to me. I didn't care. I wanted to forget about it and move on.

I had to see a psychiatrist who wanted to shove pills at me. That would have been fine except for the crap they put me on. Mellaril zonked me like a zombie, and I had to quit taking it. When I took it, I was among the Walking Dead for about two weeks and could barely function. I was sent to a neuropsychologist who did a crap load of testing on me and concluded that my brain function was only slightly impaired and that I had a good chance of healing over time. So, the symptoms of irritability, nightmares, and getting startled at a fly whizzing by were not from the brain injury but probably due to all the crap I had experienced for most of my life, and that beating at school was the straw that broke the vindictive camel's back. I would eventually come out of most of it, but it took time and therapy. As soon as she had gotten custody, Miss Mattie found a therapist who was trying to understand and help me instead of trying to convince me that I could not be a girl or that I shouldn't be attracted to men. We saw each other at least twice a week after the beating occurred.

After the Mellaril, they stuck me on this stuff called Elavil. I was also not fond of that because it wasn't much better. Finally, they took me off that and let me go without psychiatric medications. Still, I knew I needed something, but I didn't get on a good anti-depressant until the 1990s. In the meantime, I stayed in therapy and struggled with bouts of depression that varied in severity. Sometimes, I could feel pretty good. Sometimes, I could function like a normal person, but other times, I didn't want to leave the house, and I would lay in my bed simply staring at the ceiling. In the 90s, I got on Prozac, and that seemed to help more than anything. One doctor stuck me on Valium, and that shit made me crave it like my so-called mother craved dope. I told him to take me off it, and the corresponding withdrawal put me through two weeks of hell before I was halfway back to normal.

Dr. Willis consulted with my endocrinologist, who referred me to Johns Hopkins Hospital and a doctor there doing transition surgeries. Then, a few months later, Miss Mattie and I flew to Baltimore. She paid for the tutor to come with us, and he stayed in a room down the hall at our hotel. We were there for several weeks. I went through another battery of testing with another psychologist. This time, it was personality testing, and I was given the MMPI, which was supposed to tell them what made my personality tick. The psychologist wanted to make sure that I was emotionally stable and that I really did want the surgery. I don't think I was emotionally stable, but I was willing to do whatever it took to get that surgery. The surgeon, Dr. Leeto, talked with me about the surgery and the steps I would have to take. Ultimately, all the parties involved decided that I would have to wait until I was eighteen to have the surgery, and I had to remain in therapy the whole time. Dr. Leeto consulted with the endocrinologist back in St. Louis. They agreed to continue my previously prescribed hormones, and I would continue to live as a girl. That was all fine with me because I had dressed in girl's clothes as much as I could get away with for most of my life. By the time I had the surgery, I had been on the hormones for two years. The surgery occurred in 1978, after my eighteenth birthday.

I continued to see my psychologist in St. Louis for two more years before the surgery, and I went back to see her after the surgery. She was great and did more to help me recover from all the trauma than to help me adjust to my life as a woman, but she accepted me and didn't try to change me. That did more to endear my trust in her than anything else. She taught me things I could do to calm myself, like meditation. She taught me how to work on reducing my startle reactions. Most of all, she taught me that I didn't have to be afraid of the future because of my past.

I was afraid because, even though I might have been able to handle myself with one or two asshole boys when I was younger, I was no match for a bunch of assholes ganging up on me. The psychologist taught me that the rest of my life didn't have to be like my beating at school or any other experience of trauma and that I could begin to let it go. Most assuredly, that took a while, and I continued to struggle with it into my adult years, but without the therapy, I'm sure I would have been lost. Miss Mattie had been my rock through it all. She kept me from going any crazier than I would have without her. Having her in my life allowed me to realize that some people could be trusted and others would have my back, even if some mistreated or abused me. The psychologist got me to recognize that since I could always trust Miss Mattie, then maybe others could also be trusted. I trusted that psychologist, Dr. Martha Peters, and kept seeing her off and on well into my adult years.

When I turned seventeen in January of 1977, I did so with baited anticipation of my surgery, which would take place just after my birthday the following year. I could hardly wait to go, and that year, I would endure the torture of anticipation. I had grown some decent-sized breasts by then and had a closet full of tasteful clothes. Even though I wanted to dress a little slutty, Miss Mattie admonished me to keep things somewhat conservative. She said when I got older, if I wanted to go out on a date and show a little cleavage, that would be fine, but I also needed to know how to make myself as presentable as a lady for church. She insisted on going to church and goaded me into going with her, even if I didn't want to. What I did not want to do was dress in some of the flashy outfits she chose to wear to church. She looked beautiful but like an old lady beautiful. I had other clothes in mind.

"Those people hate me and want to change me," I pleaded. "They think I would be better off dead than to be the way I am."

"Dey may hates ya," she argued back, "but God don't, and it be de good Lord dat matters. Jest cause somebody go ta church and don't live da word don't mean you can't. Sides, if you listen, you will learn somethin' every time you go. Dey's truth in de Good Book, no matta 'bout people's garbage. You gots ta dig fo da truth and de love."

I went, and I dressed tastefully. I learned that it was also better to dress tastefully outside of church. I listened for the truth under the garbage, and I found it. My favorite lesson was when Jesus was asked about the greatest commandment and told them that we are all supposed to love God with all our hearts and neighbors, meaning other people, as ourselves, and that this is the greatest commandment of all. So, love is supposed to be the bottom line. Treat others as you would want to be treated. I took that to heart and tried to do better about controlling my temper. Over time, I developed a spirituality separate from the church. I took spiritual lessons from other sources besides Christianity, but I remembered that beneath everything else, the greatest commandment of Jesus was for us to love each other.

Miss Mattie said, "Cause dey do wrong, don't mean you gotta do wrong. You ain't livin' dere life, dey ain't livin' yours. Respect yoself and live by de word da best way ya know how, and de word is love."

I realized that I can't change other people, and they can't change me. I realized that life flows more smoothly when we stop trying to interfere in the lives of others and try to live our own lives with love for ourselves and others. Yet, it was going to take a while before I'd be able to conquer that one. Despite all my therapy, Miss Mattie's guidance, and developing spirituality, I could never shake the deeply indwelling hatred I had for Jake Carter. Any reminder brought astringent bitterness and malice into my heart. That was my most vicious demon, the most difficult to face and conquer.

Dressing tastefully for church notwithstanding, I would still alter the package a little here and there and show off a small glimpse of my female parts if I could. I loved my breasts, and I loved it when I caught some guy looking at them. I loved being physically admired. I had learned to put on makeup tastefully and had a collection of lovely jewelry. Since I did not have testicles competing with the female hormones and had started the hormones early enough, my voice had not masculinized that much, and I sounded like a woman. I loved sounding like a woman just as much as looking like a woman. I reveled in my femininity.

Joan and I had remained close friends and spent the remainder of my teen years doing things teens do. We spent the night with one another, talked about cute boys and sometimes cute girls, and went to movies. Even though she was primarily lesbian and liked to wear boy's clothes, she was still very much a girl. She would fix my hair, help me do makeup, and go shopping with me. She wore a little makeup and kept a hint of her feminine side even though she enjoyed wearing things like men's slacks and a button-down men's dress shirt with the sleeves rolled up. She usually wore that with a woman's belt, high heels, and earrings. She always looked stunning.

Joan and I got our driver's licenses when we were sixteen, and parents on both sides, for the most part, let us come and go as we pleased. We were not getting in trouble like other kids. Plenty of drugs were around in those days, and I wanted no part of it. I wouldn't even try pot, even though I knew kids who used it and seemed to have no problem. I had seen what drugs did to my so-called mother, pot, and alcohol among them, and that was something I definitely didn't want to repeat. Most of the time, if Joan and I were out, it would be going to the movies or sharing ice cream on a park bench. She had made other friends at school, including a girl named Sarah Gilmore. She was stuck on Sarah, and Sarah was obviously into her too. It got to the point that wherever Joan and I went, Sarah went. Miss Mattie let me take the car anytime I wanted to go out as long as it didn't interfere with something she had planned, and I followed her stipulations about what I was and was not allowed to do.

In the autumn of my seventeenth year, only a couple of months before I would turn eighteen and go to Baltimore for my surgery, Joan and I came home from a movie on a Saturday night at about 10:30 p.m. We had dropped Sarah off at home, and Joan planned to spend the night with me. After we parked the car in the garage, we came in through the back door. As we went past the kitchen into the living room, we noticed Miss Mattie slumped over to the side in her chair. The television was still on, and *Saturday Night Live* was playing.

"Oh, look," I said. "She must have fallen asleep watching TV again. She does that sometimes."

"Well, let's not wake her," Joan commented. "We can go upstairs and visit for a little while before bed. Nobody has to get up early."

There was a sense of trepidation, a feeling deep in my soul that seemed ominous and wrong.

"She told me always to wake her when she does that so she can get up and go to bed," I countered to Joan. "She said she gets a crook in her neck when she sleeps in the chair."

I went over to Miss Mattie's chair and nudged her arm. "Miss Mattie?"

She didn't move. She had always been easy to wake. Her eyes would pop open. Then, she would smile at me and say, "Whoops! I done did it again."

This time, she was silent—unresponsive.

I nudged her again, a little harder, and she still didn't move.

"Miss Mattie?" I called again—nothing.

When I reached down to take her hand, I realized it felt cold and stiff.

"Oh, God, Joan," I cried. "Something's wrong."

Joan had been standing right beside me. "You want me to call my Mom?" she asked.

"No!" I almost shouted. "We need some help quick!"

I ran to the phone and dialed the operator, who took my information and then sent an ambulance, but it seemed like they would never get there. In truth, it must have been less than fifteen minutes, but I felt like time had become a slow drift of lava burning languidly into my consciousness. I cried, tried to revive her again, pleaded with her to wake up, and paced while Joan did her best to comfort me. I was desperate, but time was not. When I saw the lights out front, I ran to the door and shouted to the EMTs, "Here! Here! Hurry! Please hurry!" Yet, I already knew what they would tell me. I just didn't want to accept it.

They were with her immediately, feeling for a pulse, checking this and that, when one of them turned and asked, "How long has she been like this?"

"I don't know," I cried. "We came back from a movie about twenty minutes ago, and she was like this when we came in."

"I think she has been gone for a while," the medic said as he got to his feet. "There is really nothing we can do for her."

"What do you mean, gone?" I screamed as cruel tears streaked my makeup. "She can't be gone!"

I fell to my knees beside her chair and begged, "Miss Mattie, please! Please wake up! PLEASE WAKE UP!"

I felt Joan's hand on my shoulder, and she knelt beside me to gently speak into my ear. "I'm sorry, Steph, I'm so sorry." It was obvious that she was crying, too.

"Do you know the lady's age?" the medic asked.

"She turned eighty-four this summer," I mumbled through my runny nose.

Joan ran to grab more tissues from the dispenser on our coffee table.

Over my shoulder, I heard the medic, apparently talking to the hospital. He affirmed, "Yes, we have an eighty-four-year-old black female for transport, likely D.O.A."

After he finished that conversation, he turned around and asked, "Who is the next of kin?"

"I am," I replied with my face against Miss Mattie's hand. "She's my Mom."

"How old are you?" the medic requested.

"I'm seventeen."

"I thought you looked young. There's no other kin, perhaps an adult?" he continued.

"There is no one else," I responded. "We only had each other. If there is any other family she has, they are in Louisiana."

"Are you in contact with her other relatives?" He asked.

"I don't know of any other relatives!" I snapped back. "She came here a long time ago, and I don't know of her even being in touch with anyone back there."

The truth is, I knew very little about Miss Mattie or her background. I didn't even know how she had gotten to Pruitt Igoe from New Orleans. She told me once that she had run away for her safety and because of shame to her family, but she didn't give me any details, and I hesitated to ask because it seemed very painful for her. I had no recollection of anyone from Louisiana ever having contacted her or that she contacted any of them. I knew of no letters or phone calls—nothing. She said her family rejected her. I didn't know why. Apparently, she had left everything and everyone previously known to her and just ran away. I had no idea where she had been before coming to St. Louis, and suddenly, I wished I had asked more questions.

"Do you know someone to call to help with this, some adult?" the EMT pressed.

"I'll call my Mom and Dad," Joan interjected.

She got up and went immediately to the phone. I heard her dialing and the faint jabber over the line when someone picked up. She explained what had happened, and just as she hung up, the EMT said, "We will be taking her to St. Mary's unless you prefer another hospital. From there, the doctor will have to be the one to pronounce her deceased and determine the cause of death. We need to go ahead and load her into the ambulance. Do you have any identification for her?"

I went to Miss Mattie's bedroom, found her purse, and returned with her driver's license.

"Do you mind if I take this for identification at the hospital?" he asked.

"Can you wait till my parents get here?" Joan inquired.

"They can meet us at St. Mary's emergency department," the medic replied. He looked over at me. "You can also meet us there or ride in the ambulance with her."

"I'll wait on her parents," I replied quietly, feeling numb like a balloon stretched over my head as though my heart was encased in wax.

The medics loaded Miss Mattie onto a stretcher and took her out the front door. I saw no reason to follow them. I sat on the sofa, and Joan held my hand beside me.

"I don't know what I'm going to do?" I heard myself cry. Tears began to flow again, rolling in little rivers off my cheeks and onto my blouse.

Joan moved her hand from mine to put her arm around me and pulled me close. I sobbed.

We heard a knock at the front door in a few minutes, which had remained unlocked. Joan knew it was her Mom and Dad. "Come in," she called.

Soon, Miss Amanda sat opposite Joan on my other side, and her dad stood nearby. "Baby, I am so sorry," she said as she held my hand. "You are going to come stay with us for a while, okay? We will get through this."

"I don't know what to do," I continued to cry. "I just feel completely lost. I have lost the one person I loved most and the one who loved me most."

"Honey, you are not lost, and I know what to do," Miss Amanda returned. "I know what to do, and I'll help you through this."

"Should we go to the hospital?" I asked.

"We don't have to," she replied. "But if you want to, we can. I don't really see much use in it. They will identify her, determine a cause of death, and move her to the morgue. We can deal with whatever else we need to deal with tomorrow."

"Why did she die?" I whimpered.

"Honey, I don't know," Miss Amanda replied. "At her age, there could be any number of reasons. She might have had a heart attack or a stroke. It depends."

"Why did she leave me?" I continued. "Now I don't have anyone."

I heard Joan saying, "Yes, you do. Of course, you do. You know you always have me."

Miss Amanda gripped my hand. "You have us." She glanced up at her husband and back to me. "We will be here for you. We will get you through this."

I spent the night with the Wilsons but didn't sleep. Darkness was parted by the gray light of a street lamp filtering into the room from Joan's bedroom window. I was in bed with Joan, and although I felt more like pacing than sleeping, I didn't want to disturb her. She had fallen asleep while holding me. So, I lay there and stared into the gray darkness while she slept. I watched the shadows of the ceiling fan twirling in the dim darkness for the rest of the night.

The next day, we got up early to follow up. The doctor determined that Miss Mattie had died of an undiagnosed heart defect and most likely had fallen asleep before her heart stopped. Given her heart condition, he said it was a miracle she had lived as long as she did. I was thankful that she had died in her sleep. I didn't want to think she might have been in agony, crying out with no one there to help her.

The Wilsons helped me to make funeral arrangements, and we had a tiny gathering a few days later. Our maid Symone and my tutor came, and one neighbor Miss Mattie had finally befriended came. Other than that, there was no one there except for me and the Wilson family. I thought it was a shame that more people did not know what a wonderful person she was. Her name would never go down in history. She would never be remembered or honored the way some famous people are, but I would always honor her in my heart and remember her for all she did for me during the brief time I knew her. I was thankful and will eternally be grateful for that time.

It was October 17th when she was buried, the following Monday after she died. The temperature was in the upper 50s and required jackets, but the sun was shining and felt warm on our skin. I watched as hired pallbearers lowered her coffin slowly into the ground. By then, I had become a little less frightened about how I would survive without her, but I knew there was a void in my heart that only she could have filled. There was a space where she should have been. It took time to realize that she would always be with me and that only her body was gone. Her spirit lived in me. Her love and wisdom were gifts she had given me that time, nor any person could ever take away.

The week after she died, I had discussions with Mr. Riggs. He ensured I had the funds I needed for all the burial expenses. I sat down with him to discover that the TV preacher's Trust fund for me was far more extensive than I had realized. Mr. Riggs was supposed to maintain management of the Trust until I turned twenty-one. Still, given the circumstances, he suggested that the Trust be turned over to me at eighteen, which would occur in only a couple of months. He made it very clear that it was entirely possible to spend the whole Trust and have nothing left. Although it seemed like more than I could ever spend in a lifetime, he endorsed that I could manage it responsibly and live in comfort for the rest of my life or squander it and have no more than anyone else. Miss Mattie had already talked with him about using a portion of the funds to pay for my transition surgery, so that would go as planned. I had no idea what I would do after that or what life would be like as an adult. I had no idea what life would be like without Miss Mattie or how I would ever cope without her, but my therapist helped.

After the funeral, I stayed with the Wilsons but had to make some trips home to get clothes and toiletries. I couldn't stand to stay in our house anymore. Whenever I walked through the living room, images of Miss Mattie's body slumped in that chair plagued my mind. Every time I saw that chair, I started to cry. I didn't want to be in that room ever again, but I had to be. I had no idea how much it would take to resolve all that needed to be resolved after someone's death, but it required more than I wanted to experience.

Mr. Riggs managed the bills for a few months before I turned eighteen and taught me how to manage the money. I told him I didn't want the house and asked if we could sell it. He found a realtor and put the house on the market, but it didn't sell until May. Over November and December of that year, I went through all of Miss Mattie's and my own things and cleaned the house of everything except the furniture. Joan went with me, and sometimes her little brother would help. What I didn't want or couldn't use was sent to thrift stores or charities. The rest was packed and placed in storage. Sometimes, I would come across something, such as the pillow Miss Mattie gave me when my so-called mother was killed. That pillow had been on my bed the whole time, and I had gotten to the point that I paid it little attention while I went about my daily activities, but when it came to retrieving things from the house, that same pillow caused me to sit on the bed and cry while I held it to my chest. When I was in foster care, it had been the closest thing I had to a hug from Miss Mattie, and I held it to my chest every night as I fell asleep. After she died, it became the only thing I would ever have again that was even close to receiving a hug from her, and it would remain on my bed wherever I lived for as long as I lived.

Thanksgiving and Christmas were tough that year, and I longed for Miss Mattie more than ever. The Wilson family did their best to include me in their family celebrations. Even though I loved them, I couldn't make myself feel like they were my real family or that I had ever had a real family, except Miss Mattie, and I couldn't help wishing that Miss Mattie could have been there. Until she died, Miss Mattie was the only person I had ever considered to be my family. I never counted my so-called mother or anyone related to her as any real family. Holidays with her might have been like any other day. Most of the time, she paid no attention to holidays. Usually, there was nothing. There was never a tree, festivity, or gifts unless she would toss some cheap little trinket at me and say, "Merry fucking Christmas. Merry—kiss—my—ass!" Miss Mattie never had a tree when we lived at Pruitt Igoe, but she would always bake something extraordinary, hang some decorations, and have at least one present wrapped for me.

The McNeil family did Christmas up like a fucking display at the mall. Mrs. McNeil would have a designer come in to decorate a massive tree in the living room that looked like some gaudy spectacle, and every last corner of the room would be decked with wide ribbons and garland. She did something different every year. None of the kids were allowed in that room, especially at Christmas. There was a small tree in the back kid's lounge, usually decorated with hand-made ornaments we had made at school, and Mrs. McNeil would brandish it with candy canes and tinsel. There would be gifts for the foster kids under that tree. Often, the gifts were new clothes, but there was always at least one toy. The McNeil family, at least, had a Christmas, but they were never my family, and I never felt included as though I was wanted.

The first Christmas I spent with Miss Mattie in our new home was the best Christmas I ever had, even though it was just the two of us. Miss Mattie bought a tree and had some guy come to set it up near the fireplace. She bought decorations to go over the fireplace and a wreath for the front door. She went to Hallmark and bought practically every keepsake ornament they had in those days. Then, she went to the garage and brought back a box of ornaments she had saved from back home in Louisiana. She also began to unwrap those and place them on the tree.

"First time dat I had a tree ta put dez on since I left Nawlens." She smiled as she opened the box and unfolded antique ornaments from their paper wrapping. She told me stories about the ornaments as she unwrapped them, how one had belonged to her grandmother and had been given to her when her grandmother died, how one had been bought for her by a close friend she had in school, and how she purchased one from an antique store when she got her first apartment. In particular, there was an ornament of Santa Claus driving an old firetruck that she admired most. Every ornament seemed to have a story, and after that first Christmas, the keepsake ornaments also had a story. They were our ornaments from our first Christmas in our new house.

On that first Christmas, Miss Mattie presented me with an ornament in addition to all the other gifts she bought for me. "Dis here yo ornament fo ya to remember ole Miss Mattie." It was a purple glass gorilla wearing a pink tutu. "Dat's cause you is strong like a gorilla, but you is girly an frilly like a ballerina." She grinned from ear to ear as she watched me unwrap it while she explained her meaning. I immediately hung it on the tree and looked at it every day until we took the tree down a few days after Christmas. It meant pure love to me. I found out later that she had it made specifically for me by a local artisan, but it didn't have to be extravagant or expensive for me to love it. If it had been something cheap from the dime store, it came straight from her heart and meant the world to me. Every year, for the few years that we remained in that house, Miss Mattie gave me a different ornament for Christmas and would buy the latest Hallmark keepsake ornament.

Of course, I kept all those decorations when everything was being cleared from the house. I would never part with them. I had them in storage with a few other things I wanted to keep. I didn't want any furniture and told the realtor she could sell it furnished if she wanted to. Otherwise, as far as I was concerned, the furniture could go to charity stores. Then, shortly after my eighteenth birthday, I rented an apartment over a storefront at Fells Point near Johns Hopkins Hospital and temporarily moved to Baltimore.

CHAPTER 13

ANOTHER DOOR OPENS

When you lose someone you love, there is an emptiness that can't be explained, a void within your heart that only they could have filled. I had lost Miss Mattie for the second time, and this time, permanently. There would be no hope of having her returned to me, no promise that Pastor Dennison could ever make that would bring her back. The tears would stalk and pounce on me like a carnivore on prey when I least expected it. Some word or phrase, some memory triggered by an object or an encounter, could cause them to rip at my emotional flesh. When this happened, I couldn't collect myself for a while. Numb existence and vacuous detachment seemed to be my experience whenever I wasn't in tears, and those tears continued relentlessly for a long time. Eventually, acceptance set in, and the tears became less frequent, but even years later, a triggered memory could make my eyes release them.

Joan's family allowed me to move in. So, Joan and I shared a room at her house after Miss Mattie died. The last thing I wanted to do was to stay alone in our house. I felt empty enough without sitting in that place with the essence of Miss Mattie all around me but finding her presence nowhere. When I had to go back there for some post-burial obligation, I couldn't walk through the living room without anguish and heartache as though her lifeless body still lay in that chair, leaving no trace of the beautiful and miraculous spirit it had once contained. Without her, I would have been completely lost. Without her, I would never have been able to find my way, and I know that I would have drowned in the sewer of Pruitt Igoe. I owed her my life. I owed her my commitment to live up to the principles and truths she taught me.

I determined that I would one day fully possess the wisdom and loving heart that had been her gift to me, but fear remained my constant companion for a duration, and I could not deny that I was angry about losing her.

When I moved in with the Wilsons, it meant nothing for Joan and me to sleep in the same bed, at least not to us. Her father disapproved of it but acquiesced after Joan and her mother pleaded their case that we were not lovers, not interested in sex with one another, just girlfriends. I was not allowed to hear this conversation, but Joan told him, "Look, Daddy, first, she's attracted to boys. I don't qualify, and I'm not attracted to her. Second, she *is* a girl. She doesn't have testicles anymore, and I don't care how she was born. She is *still* a girl."

Joan and I had been having sleepovers ever since we met, but Joan's dad usually required that I sleep on the couch during those times and not be in her room overnight. After I temporarily moved in with them, he finally realized that we were a couple of girlfriends sharing a room, and that's all. It was not an easy thing for him to wrap his mind around. It is not easy for most men to wrap their minds around. They can understand men dressing as women, to a point. They may disapprove, but they get cross-dressing as long as it is for some heterosexual fetish. They cannot seem to comprehend what they see as a man, in their mind, wanting to be a woman. They especially don't seem to understand that it is not a man wanting to be a woman. It is someone already a woman who was born with the wrong equipment. So, the idea that I was already female, but I just happened to be born in a male body, was something that Joan's Dad, like so many men, had difficulty comprehending. If he didn't completely understand it, at least he was willing to trust that Joan and I were just friends, and her mom did her best to explain gender dysphoria to him. Even if he didn't understand, at the very least, he was kind.

Joan was wonderful and so accommodating about letting me move in. She made room in her closet for my clothes and let me have a couple of drawers in her vanity. After a short while, we settled in together, and the family seemed to adjust to my being there even though it was only a little over two months. What Joan and her mom did not want was for me to have to be alone after Miss Mattie died. They did their best to treat me like a member of the family. They did their best to comfort me during the most overwhelming grief I had ever experienced. However, it was difficult for them to understand how I could freak out and practically cower in a corner with some of the triggers I experienced, such as anything that reminded me of the attack at school, Jake, or Pruitt Igoe. To them, it was like a violent scene in a TV show, and I know Joan's dad thought that I was overreacting, being a drama queen, and maybe just trying to get more of their attention, but it took me weeks to force myself to use the sink again. Miss Mattie's death seemed to have brought it all back, and I struggled again with memories of the beating at school. Maybe it was because I felt so vulnerable when Miss Mattie died, completely helpless again, like when I had been tortured and abused. If I couldn't deal with the sink, I would kneel and wash my hands or brush my teeth in the bathtub. After a while, even though the memories of having my head bashed would happen every time I had to use it, I could make myself use the sink without having a panic attack. We finally visited together with my therapist, and I was grateful she explained post-traumatic stress to them. Before that, I fought the urge to isolate and sit in my car, formerly Miss Mattie's, where I somehow felt safe. I stared into blank space as the engine kept the heater going and did my best to block the pain from my mind. Nonetheless, I got through it. I forced myself to rejoin the family, especially with their encouragement and my therapist's encouragement.

On the 11th of January, 1978, my eighteenth birthday, Joan said she wanted to take me shopping to buy my birthday present. I hesitated. It had not been that long since Miss Mattie died, and there was a sense of guilt about celebrating without her. I had felt the same over Christmas but managed to trudge through it. Until I lived with the McNeil family, Miss Mattie had been the only one who recognized my birthdays, the only one who ever made a cake or lit candles, and I had never really felt any joy without her when I was with the McNeils. Mike would stuff a five-dollar bill in my pocket, but he never gave me a card or a gift, and he made sure that Mable-bitch never saw him do that. I had only a couple of birthdays with him before he was gone, but at least I knew he remembered and made a gesture. Often, my birthdays were just between me and Miss Mattie with some simple box cake she had made form a mix. She once gave me a doll when I was about seven or eight years old and insisted I take it home. I hid it, but Mable-bitch caught me with it and threw one of her tantrums, screaming, "YOU ARE NOT A FUCKING GIRL," as she decapitated it and threw it off the fire escape.

My first Christmas without Miss Mattie left me with repeated bouts of tears. The Wilson family let me put my tutu gorilla ornament on the tree and gave me gifts, but nothing could fill the void in my heart where Miss Mattie had been, and I could not see that ornament without crying. Sometimes, I would take it from the tree, sneak into the bathroom, sit on the floor, hold it to my heart, and weep. Then, I would remember that Miss Mattie told me that the gorilla meant I was strong. So, I would gather my strength and return it to the tree.

I ordered Christmas gifts for the Wilsons from a catalog because I still could not force myself to go anywhere. I still didn't want to go anywhere, but Joan was insistent.

Had it not been for Joan and her family, I would have been completely lost, afloat like a castaway in the middle of the ocean, not even knowing which way was east, west, north, or south. For my entire life, I had felt like a castaway, trying to find my bearings, trying to find someplace solid where I could set my feet. Even with the Wilsons, I found it challenging to feel I had a place in the world. I can't say that thoughts of suicide never crossed my mind. I wanted to be with Miss Mattie. I wanted to die because I couldn't imagine my life without her, and I couldn't imagine any other way to be with her, but even though she was not physically present, I could hear her voice echoing in my mind, "You gots ta be strong, child. You better dan dis. You needs ta hold yo head up proud 'o who ya are and walk on down de path of life like you da queen dat everybody loves, even if dae don't act like it. You gots ta start by loving yoself first. If you don't love and respect who ya are, you can't expect nobody else to. You gots ta show dem how ta treat ya, how to love ya. Don't let dem treat you, jest any way dey want. Dey don't treat you right, den you move on an you put dem out cha life."

"But I'm a freak," I heard myself responding to her in that memory from years before. "Nobody wants me."

"I wants ya." She replied, "An' you, not a freak. You is different, jes different, dats all, an' de ain't nothin' wrong wid bein' different. Dey don't treat you right; den dae don't gets ta treat you at all. You don't has ta be 'round peoples dat don't treat ya right."

Joan's words snapped me out of my daze of memories, "Oh, come on. It will be fun," she goaded. "We will stroll through the stores. When you see something you really want, I will buy it. Happy birthday!"

"That's sweet, Joan, honestly, but I just don't feel that much like celebrating, and I don't want to be around a bunch of people."

Joan stood there staring at me for a while, and then she said, "Okay, but what would Miss Mattie tell you? Just a thought. Maybe would she'd tell you, 'don't stop living just because I'm gone?'"

I knew she was right. I didn't want to go, but I knew I needed to. My birthday fell on a Wednesday that year, and not exactly the time of the week that I think about going shopping. However, fewer people would be at the mall, and Joan wouldn't let it go.

"Damn it," I said. "That's exactly what she would say." So, I reluctantly pulled myself out of my doldrums and went.

We got to the mall about four o'clock after Joan left school. We walked through a couple of stores, did some window shopping, and hung out in an arcade for a while, but I didn't feel like playing games. As uncomfortable as I felt with my grief, I tried to live up to the celebration. Still, a pretend smile doesn't feel the same as a real one.

At least I was becoming increasingly comfortable with my body. By that time, the hormone therapy was giving me a pair of Goldilocks titties almost as attractive as Joan's, and I loved that I could walk around with her without anyone realizing that I still had a penis between my legs. I was female. I was feminine. The penis was irrelevant. However, I was careful to tuck it away, still avoided wearing pants for fear of a bulge, and wore loose skirts or dresses. Before Miss Mattie died, I loved dressing up and going out. However, I wasn't into being there that day. I picked out a nice blouse at a specialty store, then told her I wanted to go home.

"But we haven't had dinner yet," she insisted. "Let's go have dinner before we go home, my treat for your birthday. What kind of food would you like?"

"I'm not really hungry. Besides, won't your maid have something prepared when we get home?"

"Mom gave her the night off," Joan replied. "I'll just call Mom and let her know we'll have dinner before we come home."

I couldn't help noticing the shit-eating grin on her face. She was having a good time trying to cheer me up, and even though I didn't feel like being cheered up, I went along with it.

"Okay," I said. "How about something quick? Let's just stop at the food court."

"Surely we can do better than that?"

"Okay," I said, feeling a little frustrated. "How about Chinese food? A buffet would be fairly quick."

"Why are you in such a hurry to get home?" she prodded. "It's your birthday! Let's have a good time."

"I don't feel like having a good time."

"But you have to eat."

"True." My appetite did not agree with what I said, but I knew I hadn't eaten all day and should probably make myself eat something.

"Chinese?" She grinned.

"Sure."

"Done!" she exclaimed. "Let's go to Mr. Foo. Just give me a moment to call Mom on a payphone."

So, we went to eat Chinese food. Joan stopped at a phone booth on the way and called Miss Amanda. I waited in the car. Then, by the time we finished eating, it was about eight o'clock. Joan insisted on stopping to call her mom again. We drove home, and when we entered the kitchen from the garage, the rest of the Wilson family and her friend Sarah were all standing in a kitchen full of balloons, shouting, "SURPRISE!"

My startle made me yelp like an injured dog. My heart pounded, not from joy but from the anxiety of being startled. For a moment, I panted, trying to catch my breath, but kept telling myself, "It's okay. I'm safe." It took me a moment to collect myself, but I had been practicing reorienting myself to the moment and situation, just as my therapist had taught me. I was surprised that, given my past reactions, they didn't realize that would trigger me.

My birthdays had gotten significantly better after I was placed in foster care. The McNeils always did a little party for each foster kid's birthday, but I had never had a surprise party before and certainly had not expected one.

Joan's Dad came and put his arm around my shoulder. "Are you okay there? You look a little rattled for the guest of honor.

"I'm sorry, I—I'm a little shocked … Wow!" I exclaimed, catching myself and trying to hide my anxiety. "You guys didn't have to do all this."

Jeremy stepped up and said, "Okay, we will return everything to the store then." He moved to the counter where a cake full of candles was sitting and pretended like he was going to pick it up.

"Hold on there," I teased him, faking a smile and playing along with the expectations. "Maybe I might like to have a little piece of cake." The truth is, I didn't want it, but I knew that they had gone to a lot of trouble and that refusing them would have been rude.

They all gathered around me, closer than I wanted, wishing me *happy birthday*, but at least consciously, I knew and affirmed that I was safe. Miss. Amanda went to the freezer to bring out a carton of ice cream. She instructed Jeremy, who had only recently turned thirteen, to light the candles on the cake. He complied, and the next thing I knew, I was blowing out candles while they sang happy birthday to me.

After blowing out the candles, I turned to Joan, "So, shopping was only a ruse to get me out of the house for them to set up a party?"

"Well, that and Mom had to work late today, and I hadn't gotten you anything until you picked out that blouse."

"And Chinese food?" I asked.

"I had to throw that in to give Mom enough time to get home. I didn't think you were going to pick something so quickly."

"Speaking of presents," Miss Amanda interjected. "We got you something ourselves."

"You guys didn't have to do that," I said again. "I'm not used to having big birthday bashes. Really, you didn't need to do anything."

"Okay, then, we will take it back to the store," Jeremy teased again as he headed for a box sitting on the counter.

"No, wait!" I pretended to laugh. "I had better check that out first." Truthfully, I still felt rattled and unsettled, having walked into a shout of *SURPRISE!* I fought anxiety with every breath and did my best to be a good actor.

The wrapping paper on the box was a very girly pink with a giant pink ribbon. I opened it to find pink crepe paper stuffed everywhere. Amid the paper I found a small velvet box containing a butterfly necklace with matching earrings. Both had multicolored stones creating the wings of the butterfly. There was also a box that said Polaroid on the side.

"The jewelry is beautiful, you guys," I said as I pulled the necklace from the container, held it in my palm, and admired it.

"Butterflies because that is what you are becoming," Joan interjected.

"Oh, you guys!" A tear rolled off my cheek. "The gift is even sweeter now."

"That's a Polaroid One Step," Jeremy interjected, pointing to the box I had set aside. "It's a camera that takes instant pictures. That was my idea."

"Oh, thank you, Jeremy," I responded. "That's really cool."

"Maybe you can send us some pictures from Baltimore when you get there," he continued.

"Maybe," I replied. "Maybe I can take some here today to remember you guys and this beautiful event."

"Here, I'll get it ready for you." Jeremy volunteered as he began opening the camera box. "We got some film for it, too."

"Have you heard anything back from that realtor in Baltimore?" Mr. Wilson asked.

"Not yet."

"You need to find a place pretty soon, don't you?" he continued. "You have the surgery in February, right?"

"Actually, I have to be there for a while before they do the surgery. They have to do some standard checks, and I think I have to go off the hormones a few weeks before the surgery."

"All sounds pretty complicated," he commented.

"It is pretty complicated," Miss Amanda interjected. "We are not talking about a small surgery here; we may actually be talking about multiple surgeries." She turned to me. "I don't want to scare you, but Stephanie, it will not be easy. I hate for you to be up there facing it all that by yourself."

"I'm tough," I grinned, unsure if I believed what I was telling her. My mind wandered to Pruitt Igo, living with my so-called mother, and how tough I had to be just to survive. I figured I could take about anything if I could handle that shit when I was just a little kid. That did not mean that I didn't feel squeamish about it.

"I could go up and stay with her," Joan offered.

"You have the school year to finish," Miss Amanda told her. "You can't just be away for months out of your last semester."

"Yeah, and what about me?" Sarah interjected. "I would miss you so much if you were gone that long."

Joan hugged her.

"I'll be fine," I defended. "If I can survive Pruitt Igoe, I can handle this."

Having finished early with my tutor and having passed my GED, I didn't have to worry about things like school. College might have been an option, and maybe I should have considered it, but I didn't want to put off my transition any longer than I had to. Unlike other girls who had to scrimp and save for the surgery if they could afford it at all, I was damn lucky to have the finances to deal with it.

Miss Amanda glared at me for a moment, not with negativity but concern.

"Let's have some cake." She suddenly smiled and changed the subject.

Everyone immediately gravitated back toward the cake. Miss Amanda began cutting pieces for everyone while Jeremy piled ice cream on it. They had just handed me the first piece when the phone rang in the living room.

"Joan, would you get that?" Miss Amanda pleaded over her shoulder as she licked some icing off the end of her thumb.

Joan ran to the living room and called back, "Stephanie, it's for you."

I hadn't wanted the cake anyway. It was a formality. I played along and would have taken only two or three bites. I set it on the counter and went to the living room.

"Hello?" I spoke to the receiver.

"Is this Stephanie Laroquette?" the phone voice asked.

"Yes, Ma'am," I replied courteously.

"This is Donna Nowakowski," the voice said, "Your realtor from Baltimore."

Her voice elevated at the end of each sentence, almost like she was asking a question when she was making a statement.

"Yes, Ma'am," I politely returned.

"Miss Laroquette, I think I have found an apartment for you," she informed. "It's a little expensive at $350, but it is in Fells Point, a decent area near Johns Hopkins. It is a one-bedroom flat above a community grocery, and it's furnished."

"That sounds fine," I replied, having no more information than that. All I knew was that I had to get there. I had to have the surgery. I couldn't bear the thought of being incomplete anymore. I felt so incomplete because my true nature, my internal self, did not match my exterior. To be complete, I had to have the surgery. For my body to match how I felt and who I knew I was inside, I had to have the surgery.

"If you can wire the first month's rent plus a $150.00 deposit. I will secure it for you," she went on.

"Yes, Ma'am. I will go to Western Union tomorrow," I replied. "Let me write down your information for the transfer." I grabbed a pen and a notepad near the phone and wrote where to wire the money. I got the address and instructions to contact the landlord who owned the grocery store when I arrived. Then, I came back into the kitchen with a wide grin. "I have an apartment!" I gleamed, this time with some sincere happiness.

"That's wonderful!" Miss Amanda exclaimed. "But I'm still worried about you going all the way to Baltimore and going through this alone. I hope you will hire a nurse to help you at home because this will probably not be as easy as you think."

"I'll be fine," I replied, and "I'll hire someone if I need to. I'm sure the hospital has recommendations."

"I can go. Mom, let me go. Maybe even Sarah can go," Joan pleaded.

Miss Amanda looked at her momentarily, pausing as if she might be considering it. Then she said, "No. Neither of you is a nurse, and you have to finish this school year. Stephanie needs a professional attendant, and I also seriously doubt that Sarah's parents would let her go."

"Mom, can I at least ride up with her and take a plane back?" Joan asked.

"How much school would you have to miss?" Miss Amanda questioned.

I replied for her. "If we leave on Friday the 27th and drive up over the weekend, she should be able to return the following Monday. I'll pay for everything." I wanted to offer to have my tutor work with her so she could stay with me, but I knew the surgery would be very expensive, especially if I went on to do cosmetic surgeries. I did not want to use up too much of the money Pastor Dennison had left for me, and at that point, I didn't know how much it might cost for additional surgeries.

"I don't know," Miss Amanda continued. "You never know what the weather will be like around here at this time of year, especially for a drive to the northeast coast."

"We can always play it by ear," I responded. It might take a little longer if there are weather problems. We might have to pull over and stay an extra night in a hotel, but if the weather is terrible here, they will probably close the schools anyway."

"Stephanie," Miss Amanda went on. "As much as I don't want you having to drive up there by yourself, neither of you are experienced drivers, especially when it comes to snow and ice."

"Mom, please?" Joan pleaded.

Miss Amanda glanced over at Mr. Wilson. He shrugged his shoulders. "Ah … " he stammered. "Maybe I could take some time off work and drive up with her, but that is awfully short notice."

"Mom, we will be fine," Joan continued to beg. "We will use our best judgment."

Her Mom smirked. "That's exactly what I'm afraid of. I still don't trust your best judgment." She paused, took a deep breath, and stared at Mr. Wilson. He shrugged again and put his palms up.

"Okay," she finally gave in. "but you have to call me every day till you get back."

"Please call me too," Sarah interjected.

"I will! I promise." Joan ran to her mom and threw her arms around her. Then Joan ran to Sarah and hugged her again. "It will only be for a little while. I'll be back soon."

"All right, all right," Miss Amanda exclaimed. "Let's have some cake and ice cream."

As it turned out, we couldn't leave on the 27th because a massive blizzard blew across the north eastern United States on January 24th. It covered our entire route to Baltimore. Nothing fell on St. Louis, but everything between us and Baltimore was covered with snow and ice. We argued that the roads had surely been cleared by the 27th. Nonetheless, Miss Amanda made us wait until February 3, 1978, the following weekend. She was still obviously worried, but she allowed us to go.

We got up earlier than usual on that Friday morning so the family could see us off before Mr. and Mrs. Wilson had to go to work, and Jeremy had to go to school. He had begged to go with us, but Miss Amanda had thankfully determined that to be out of the question. We loved him, but we certainly didn't want him tagging along.

We had packed the night before and had everything ready to go early the next morning. After breakfast, we had to shower, get in the car and go. Mr. Wilson and Jeremy put our luggage in the trunk of Miss Mattie's Lincoln. She had left everything to me, even a savings account she had built up in addition to all the money from the Trust fund. I guess she didn't feel assured that Pastor Dennison might not take the money back, or she thought I would need more. Maybe she didn't have anyone else to leave it to. She had stuffed away almost thirty thousand dollars before she died, a hefty sum in those days. That would pay for surgery and maybe leave enough left over for my apartment in Baltimore. I wouldn't even have to dip into the Trust. Later, the house sale would give me a little over three times that amount. I might not even have to dip into the trust for a while. I debated with myself over whether to hire a tutor for Joan if her parents would even allow it, but a part of me wanted to do this by myself. A part of me felt very private about it, even with Joan, and I wanted to prove to myself that I could stand on my own two feet, even if I had to hire a nurse. I knew it would be difficult, but almost my whole fucking life had been difficult, and if there was nothing else I learned about myself, I knew I was brave. Even with my damned anxiety attacks, I was still brave.

Joan's dad had come out to warm up the car while we were showering. So we wouldn't have to get into a cold car and shiver before we could get some heat. We got hugs from everyone before leaving. Then, I backed the Lincoln out of the drive and headed toward Interstate 70. The wonderful thing was that I-70 would take us all the way to Baltimore. When we got to the first stop light, Joan slapped her hands on the dash like she was playing the drums, laughed, and said, "Whooo Hooo, we are going to Baltimore!"

I turned, gave her a stern look, and said, "Girl, you better calm your panties." Then I slapped the steering wheel and shouted the same thing. After a round of roaring laughter, we began to calm down.

It wasn't long before we were on I-70. Soon, we could see vestiges of the blizzard from the week before. Even though the interstate was clear, we could see snow almost everywhere. We had been warned to watch for black ice and be careful over bridges, but we didn't have a problem. We hit one patch where the car slid for a few seconds and then caught traction. It gave us both a startle but passed quickly, and Mr. Wilson had given us instructions on how best to deal with it. Even though we could have made the whole trip in one day and would have arrived in Baltimore at about 9:00 p.m., we decided to get a hotel in Columbus, Ohio, and finish the journey on Saturday morning.

We made it to Columbus about 1:30 p.m., got a room in a little roadside motel, and had lunch at a nearby café that was a brief walking distance from our room. When we got to our room, Joan called and left a message with her mom's clinic receptionist. Then, we spent the rest of the afternoon lounging around the hotel room and watching television. Watching soap operas and afternoon game shows was boring as hell, but I didn't want to have to find a hotel in Baltimore late at night. Also, I knew I was supposed to meet the guy who owned the community grocery to get into my room, and the grocery would be closed by the time we got there. We could have left St. Louis later in the day, but I was chomping at the bit to go.

We went back to the same little café for dinner, and not long after ordering, I noticed a guy sitting at a nearby table who kept looking at me. He must have been in his mid-twenties, and there was a pretty brunette with him who was about the same age. Then, as he glanced back toward me, I heard him lean over to the woman and say, "You notice something odd about that girl's neck?"

"What girl?" she asked as she whipped around.

I felt myself flush with embarrassment. My hypervigilance from years of abuse made me notice practically everything, and I could hear a gnat fart from across the room. The ghetto in me wanted to stand up and shout, "What the fuck are you looking at, mother-fucker? You want to see a fucking show?" However, the training I had received from Miss Mattie and the McNeils told me to handle it gracefully. I said nothing but looked at Joan and smiled a timid, Mona Lisa fake smile.

"Are you okay?" Joan asked.

"Sure," I lied.

The brunette turned back to the guy and said, "You mean that olive-skinned girl with the curly blondish red hair?

"Yeah," he whispered. "Look at her neck."

"It looks like an Adam's apple," she responded as she twisted to look at me again. "Do you think that's really a guy?"

Through all the clatter and bee hive mix of restaurant discussion, I heard what they said. Maybe I heard it because I knew they were star-ing at me, talking about me. Perhaps I heard it because my vigilance caused me to notice the slightest nuance of a threat.

I felt a mix of sadness and anger. I had put a great deal of energy into stealthily hiding the male aspects of my body, and most of the time, I thought I had gotten away with it, but I had not given much thought to my Adam's apple showing. At once, I wanted to burst into tears with embarrassment, but I was also pissed off that they were star-ing at me and talking about me. A part of me wanted to go into a screaming rage and take out pent-up anger. I saw myself breaking a catsup bottle against the edge of their table and threatening to slit their throats with the jagged glass. I pulled myself back from the imaginary impulse and scratched a fork around the food on my plate.

"Can we go soon?" I asked.

"I'm not finished eating," Joan replied, then caught that I was upset. "Steph, are you sure you're okay?"

"I would just like to get back to the room," I replied. "Maybe we could take something back."

I was half-way afraid this guy might start some trouble or, God forbid, follow us when we left. I had lived with so much male hostility that I dared never fail to suspect that any man would question my right to simply be allowed to live my life. So many of them seemed to want to punish me for their hatred of women. So many men appeared to hate any female they couldn't control, and if they thought someone was a guy acting like a woman, that was the worst offense of all.

Joan took the hint. "They have some pie at the counter," she commented. "Maybe we could take a couple of pieces of pie back to the room, or we can order to go, and I'll come back and get it later."

"Maybe," I tried to smile and remain calm, "but I'm not really hungry, anyway." She heard my voice trembling and saw the tears hiding beneath my lashes. "Okay, let's go," she encouraged. "Come on."

"Let me waive the waitress over for the check," I said as I glanced around the room looking for her.

"We'll get it at the counter," Joan said and got to her feet. "Come on."

We grabbed our coats. I dropped a cash tip on the table and followed her toward the counter at the cash register.

I felt that couple's eyes on me as I walked past their table. I wore a V-neck blouse with ruffles around the V-line, a jean skirt, and high heel boots. The blouse showed a bit of my cleavage and the outline of my breasts that were, by that time, as large as or larger than the average woman.

"That can't be a guy," the man whispered. "Look at those tits."

The shock went through me, a jolt of lightening to my heart, almost worse than being taunted at school. There they were, summing me up like a display at a freak show.

The woman shushed him.

I kept walking, acting like I didn't hear any of it.

"That's not a woman's ass," I heard her say, knowing she had twisted around to look at me again.

I reached into my purse and handed Joan a twenty-dollar bill. "I'll wait for you outside," I said.

I put on my coat and walked directly out the door. I stood outside in the cold, pulling my coat around my collar more to hide the Adam's apple than to brace against the chill. Joan paid the bill and met me on the sidewalk carrying a paper bag. As we walked back to the motel, she asked, "What was that all about?"

"You didn't hear what those people said?" I asked.

"I wasn't paying attention."

"You had your back to him, but that guy kept staring at me," I went on. "He asked that woman if something was wrong with my neck."

"What?"

"She said it looked like an Adam's apple."

I never had anyone notice that before. At least no one ever said that they noticed it. I guess I was living under the illusion that no obvious vestiges of a male body were left after hormone treatment and that people saw me as a woman.

"I'm sorry," she comforted and put her hand in the crook of my arm as we walked. She leaned her head briefly on my shoulder.

"You know that I love you, right?"

"Right," I whispered, halfway unsure if I was telling the truth or if anyone other than Miss Mattie had ever really loved me. "I love you too."

"And I got some pie!" Joan lifted the brown paper bag and nudged me.

"I just know what I have to do now," I said, ignoring her attempt to cheer me up. "This is only going to be the first surgery. I will have to do something about the structure of my body. I won't feel complete until no one, who doesn't already know me, can tell I was born with a dick. I don't want any male left. I don't want it! I don't want to look any fucking thing like a man! I hate looking anything like a man!"

"Well, there are plastic surgeons," she affirmed. "They can surly do something about all that. I know women can get their tits made bigger, and people have nose jobs and other facial adjustments. I mean, they are literally going to give you a woman's genitalia, aren't they? If they can do that, surely … "

"Yes, but that's not enough," I countered. If I still look like a man in the face, neck, and ass, I don't know. It's just weird. I want people to look at me, look closely at me, and see nothing but a woman and who I really am. At least my tits won't need any work."

"Well, there is that," she teased. "You do have really nice titties."

We were nearing the door of our room. Joan handed me the paper bag and fumbled for the door key. "We can ask my mom. Maybe she knows some plastic surgeons or how to find someone to do that for you."

"Maybe," I replied.

We spent the rest of the evening lying in our beds, eating pie, and watching TV. To me, eating pie or any sweet was no more than three bites and only one bite of a donut or a very rich dessert. Even then, I felt like I was over indulging. I had determined years before that I would never let myself put on too much weight. Sometimes, I had people look at me and tell me I was too skinny, but I tried not to let myself get too thin, either. That night, I indulged and ate the whole piece of pecan pie and loved it! However, whenever I went to the bathroom that evening, I pulled my head up to look at my neck in the mirror. The thought crossed my mind that no one could see the Adam's apple if I put on enough weight. Then, I could eat all the pie, cakes, and donuts I wanted, but big did not fit with the image I had for myself. If someone else was big, that didn't matter to me, but I wanted a different figure. After running all that through my head, I lifted my neck and stared into the mirror again. My Adam's apple might not be as prominent as some, but it was there nonetheless, and I knew, after that evening, that it was too noticeable, and I knew I had to get rid of it.

CHAPTER 14

TEAMWORK

Alarm clocks suck! They are the work of the devil! They suck like a vacuum cleaner! They suck more than anything could possibly suck, and motel wake-up calls are no better. I hated having to climb out of bed, but we needed to get up to finish our drive. I had no idea how late we stayed up, but it was past "The Tonight Show" with Johnny Carson, and I had been drifting in and out before Joan finally turned the TV off. The fucking phone began ringing with our wake-up call at 5:30 a.m., and it hit my dreams like a warning bell in a prison riot. I jerked awake and fumbled for the receiver. When finally bringing it to my ear, the sweet and cheerful voice said, "This is Brianna at the front desk with your wake-up reminder call."

"Thank you," I mumbled, barely able to speak. I would have slammed the receiver back onto the phone, but I didn't have the energy. Instead, it fell to the floor, and I went fishing for it, pulling on the cord until I could trawl it up from the depths and hang it up.

"Oh, God!" I heard Joan dribble from the other bed. "Let's reset it and sleep two more hours."

"Aaaaaaaahhhhh!" I exclaimed. "Why do I do this to myself?"

"Cause you're wicked, and you want to torment me too," Joan teased through the blanket she had pulled over her head.

"Who's first in the shower?" I asked.

"You!" she huffed. "Call room service and get us some breakfast."

"What do you want?"

"Anything with meat, eggs, bread, and coffee."

"Ah, so hog slices, chicken ovums, baked white powder, and drippings of brown granules."

"Exactly!" she exclaimed, rolling her face into the pillow.

I took a deep breath and threw the cover off me, kicked my feet in the air, and shouted, "FUCK!"

Joan giggled.

I picked up the phone to order room service only to discover that there was no room service in that cheap little motel. We would have to go back to the café or come up with something else if we wanted breakfast. I convinced Joan to shower first, and while she was in the shower, I threw on sweatpants, kept my pajama top, and buttoned my coat to cover my neck. I walked over to the café and ordered some muffins and coffee to go. My hair looked worse than the Wicked Witch, but I didn't care. Sorry, no hog slices, no chicken ovums. They could have made breakfast to go, but I would have had to wait for that, and I didn't feel like sitting around being gawked at by early-morning customers. So, I got coffee and muffins and headed back to the room.

We sat on the edge of our beds and ate after showering and finishing dressing. Then we had an after-meal tooth brushing and finished our packing. We hit the road again by 7:30 a.m. for the remainder of the trip to Baltimore and arrived there at almost 3:00 p.m. We pulled over at a gas station to check the map for more details to find my apartment. After getting lost twice, asking for directions, and finally finding the street, we pulled up in front of *Arron's Community Grocery* at approximately 4:15 p.m. We got out and walked into the grocery, where we noticed a slightly chubby, grumpy-sounding man, probably in his late fifties, calling from a glass booth in the back of the store, "Make it quick. I close at five."

"Hello?" I said as I walked toward the back. Joan stayed at the front of the store.

"Yeah, What?" he half snapped.

"I'm Stephanie Laroquette," I informed. "I'm here about the upstairs apartment?"

"Oh, you must be that girl from St. Louis," he said as he stepped down from the booth and started up the aisle.

"Yes, sir." I smiled back at him.

I had made sure to wear a turtleneck that day. I hoped that nothing of an Adam's apple would show. I didn't need a possibly bigoted landlord casting me out on the street before I could even get into my apartment. It was better that he not know why I was there.

"Come on to the back. I'll get the lease," he said and turned after quickly shaking my hand.

When he had come out into the florescent light that lit the aisleways, I could finally get a good look at him. He was probably quite handsome in his younger days before fading metabolism wrapped a tire around his middle and age creased his face with indented lines. It looked like he might have colored his hair jet black. That only accentuated the wrinkles that were, perhaps, premature. Still, the contours of his face were handsome.

"I'm Arron Nowak," he said while wobbling back toward the booth as though he had hip problems. He motioned for me to follow. "I'm here every day except Sunday if you happen to need anything, and of course, groceries are convenient, but I close every day at five on the dot, no exceptions. Open at eight, close at five, Monday through Saturday." He continued to talk over his shoulder as he shuffled ahead of me. "There are two apartments upstairs. Mrs. Zajek has lived in the one on the east side for eighteen years since her husband died, and the two of them lived there for about ten years before that. Mrs. Reynolds rented the other one on the west side until her family shipped her to a nursing home a few months ago. I understand that you want this temporarily."

"Yes, sir," I replied politely. "But I don't know for how long, exactly."

"That's why it costs more," he grunted. "I have to charge extra because I don't usually rent temporarily. As you just heard, my tenants tend to stay for years, and I keep their rent reasonable for that, but short-term costs more."

"Yes, sir." I glanced back at the front of the store to see Joan milling around, picking up products to look at them and then putting them back on the shelf. I couldn't see much more than her silhouette against the light coming through the broad front windows.

"Six months is my absolute minimum, and I don't like doing that," he said. "I'm used to having renters stay for a while. If you decide to say long-term, I could cut you some slack on the rent."

"Yes, sir," I replied. "I expect to be here for probably six months, and if I should leave before that time, I will pay you for the full length of the lease."

"Damn right you will!" he exclaimed. "That's why you are signing a lease."

"Joan, come on!" I shouted to the front of the store where she was examining some can of something. She put it back on the shelf and came jogging after us.

"Would you like me to pay you the full six months up front?" I asked.

He paused and looked at me strangely for a moment. I saw the thought process rolling round his face and doubted he ever had such an offer. In a moment, he said, "Nah, why break tradition? Month by month will be fine. If you need to stay longer than six months, we'll keep it month to month till you tell me you are ready to move out." He motioned to the booth at the back of the store, and we followed.

His office was a tiny, cluttered cubicle elevated above the aisles with a window overlooking the store from his desk. He plodded about six steps into it, plopped down in a wooden chair with rollers, and scooted up to his desk.

We followed into the booth.

"I got the lease right here," he explained as he ruffled through piles of paper and didn't look exactly sure he had it.

Eventually, he pulled out the lease and shoved it in my direction.

"Here, take a look. Make sure you read it. Let me know if you have any questions."

I sat in an adjacent chair and mulled over the paperwork with precious little idea of what I was looking at, but I figured I probably wasn't signing away the deed to the farm. So, I said, "Okay," and reached for a pen on his desk.

"Don't you have any questions?" he queried, noticing how quickly I had scanned the paperwork.

"I figure I will learn as I go," I replied, leaning over his desk to scrawl my illegible signature onto the space marked for me to sign. I didn't miss the glimpse he gave at my tits outlined by my sweater as I leaned over. I loved the idea of being desired that way. He said nothing, but I knew what his eyes were doing. It didn't matter that he was old enough to be my grandfather; I found it flattering to be desired as a woman, and I felt safe when it was merely a glance of ardor rather than a come-on.

"Water and utilities included," he instructed. "Trash pick-up is on Thursday mornings. Have your trash in the bins on the west side of the street no later than 7:00 a.m., or it won't get picked up, and no trash on the landing. If I catch trash, trash cans, or bags of trash out there, I will fine you a half month's rent. No loud parties and no pets in the building." He gave me a stern look. "And no men visitors sneaking out in the middle of the night disturbing my other renter. Is that clear?"

"Yes, sir," I responded politely. "I am not going to have time for that. I am here for some treatments at Johns Hopkins. I'm not going to have time for, or maybe even feel up to, much of anything else."

"Treatments?" One eyebrow shot up above the other. "Pretty young girl like you sick or something?"

"It's a genetic condition," I nervously replied. "I'm here to get treatment for it. They have specialists at Johns Hopkins."

"Oh. Too bad. Too bad for you. Well, I hope everything goes okay. You wanna see your place?"

"Sure," I replied, grateful that he didn't ask questions.

"Come on then." He grabbed a ring of keys from the edge of his desk, pulled a thick coat off the rack, motioned for me to follow, and began sliding his arms into the coat as he wobbled back down the steps from his office. As he rounded a corner, through a door, into a room stacked with unopened boxes that led further back, he shouted over his shoulder, "Marlene! Be right back."

I had not known anyone else had been in the store, but his wife apparently helped him run the place.

Joan stood around quietly during this process and dutifully followed while remaining silent.

Arron stopped to look her over. "You aren't planning on her living with you, are you? Rent goes up with a roommate."

"Oh, no, sir. This is my friend Joan. She just came along to give me some company on the trip. She'll fly back to St. Louis in a few days."

Arron took his stare away from her, turned, and put his shoulder to a door at the back of the storage room. The door popped open onto an alley leading to a perpendicular street with a large parking lot on the opposite side. Fading sunlight cast shadows around street lamps and a telephone booth, but only a few cars were in the parking lot across the street. There was a small parking area behind the store on our side of the alley, and to the left was an external flight of stairs leading up to an open second-floor landing with a paint-chipped wooden rail around the edge. There were a couple of chairs and a café table on the landing at the top of the stairs, but even if the weather had been nice enough to sit out, the only view was over the end of the alley, to the street and parking lot. A few other old buildings were on the opposite side of that. At the top of the stairs, directly across from the café table, was a single door with a couple of clay flower pots on either side holding crinkled dead flowers, obviously killed by the cold. Arron turned to his left at the top of the stairs, and there was another door on a small walkway that jutted off the landing. He fumbled at the door with one of the keys.

When he was able to jiggle the lock, the door opened, revealing a long room that cut across the building, exposing windows that appeared to have been there since the 1920s or 30s. Each of the three had a brick transom across the top and a brick sill at the bottom. They were each about three feet wide, about a foot apart, and about eight feet high. The apartment ceilings were at least twelve feet. There were no curtains or blinds, and since my apartment was on the west side of the building, the windows faced south toward the front of Aaron's store. Through the windows, I could see other old buildings across the street. The apartment floors were an unpolished dark hardwood with no rugs. The walls and door facings were all painted egg shell white. A floral, Early American-style sofa sat on one side of the room with mismatched end tables and lamps on either side. The coffee table, a modern 1970s-style maple wood with four glass pieces fitting into the top, also did not match. A couple of shell-back metal patio chairs were on either side of the sofa. Each was painted lime green, and a console TV sat across from the couch with a rabbit ear antenna perched on top.

To the right, from the front door, was a large wooden door standing open to reveal a relatively large bedroom with no windows. The full-size bed had a 1940s-style wooden headboard that backed up to a brick wall. There appeared to be no closet space except for a couple of ancient-looking dark wood wardrobe cabinets against one wall. To the right of the bedroom door was a small bathroom with a pedestal sink and a clawfoot tub with a shower rail installed around it. A clear plastic shower curtain hung from the rail, which was more to keep shower water from escaping the tub than for privacy. Pipes came up from the back to create a shower over the tub. The commode had a fill tank about six feet up the wall with a large pipe running down to the bowl. A pull chain with a wooden ball attached on the end brought it to flush. There were also no windows in the bathroom, but the lighting was ample since theater makeup lights were installed over the mirror behind the pedestal sink. Opposite the tub was a large old free-standing cabinet with white paint chipped with age.

A door led to a small kitchen on the opposite side of the living room. A wooden dining table with four miss matched chairs sat in the living room beside the kitchen door. The kitchen was furnished adequately, with an avocado-colored stove just to the inside right of the door. A white porcelain sink was directly across from the stove, and a small refrigerator was to the right. The countertops were worn linoleum with a chrome metal border tacked around them. To the left, on the west side of the kitchen, was a window over a fire escape.

After seeing it all, I stepped back into the living room and looked around again. It wasn't exactly the Taj Mahal but a mansion compared to Pruitt Igoe. It was furnished, and there were intriguing architectural elements that I loved. Over time, I became enamored with architectural attributes from yesteryear and developed an appreciation for restoring old buildings.

Joan had followed me around through the whole tour without saying a word. Often, I could feel her standing close enough at the doorways to have body contact, and she would occasionally nudge me like she was trying to get my attention, but she wouldn't say anything. She said no word but looked over everything with an obsessive thoroughness. She leaned toward my shoulder when we finished the tour and whispered, "This place is a dump."

Instead of responding, I turned to Mr. Nowak with a courteous handshake and said, "Thank you, Mr. Nowak. This looks like a wonderful place to live. Where might I find the sheets and towels?"

A strange look came across his face as though I had just asked him to shit a gold brick. "No, those do not come with the apartment." he groaned. "Renters supply their own basics."

"Well, a girl can't think of everything for her first apartment," I said with a smile. "When the realtor said it was furnished, I assumed that meant everything."

"No, furnished means furniture," he responded.

"Is there any place, this time of night, where we might buy sheets, towels, or blankets? We will need some covers for sleep tonight in case it gets cold, and we will want to bathe after a long trip." By then, time had already passed 5:00 p.m. and closing time for most stores.

Again, he looked like I had just told him aliens had landed. "We agreed. The price goes higher if you have a roommate."

"Sir," I tried to be courteous. "She is not going to be my roommate. As I said earlier, she just came along to help me with the trip and get settled. She is flying back to St. Louis in a couple of days."

"I suppose we could impose on Mrs. Zajek to see if she might loan you something for the evening," he responded. "But I don't like to disturb her. She is very quiet and stays to herself most of the time."

"Well, I could at least meet her, and if she says no, then I may have to see about getting a hotel for one more night. Does everything close at five in Baltimore?"

"The malls might be open till 9:00 p.m.," he interjected, "but that is a haul from here. Come on. I'll take you next door to meet Mrs. Zajek."

We followed him back onto the landing, and he knocked on the door between the two pots full of dead flowers. We heard the latch in a moment and saw an elderly eye peek out before releasing the burglar chain.

"Is something wrong?" she questioned as she opened the door and glanced back and forth between the three of us.

"No, Ma'am," Mr. Nowak said and gestured toward us while we stood slightly to the side. "This is Stephanie Laroquette and her friend. Stephanie drove up from Missouri to rent the apartment next door and didn't think to bring sheets or towels. She was wondering if you might have extras and could loan her a set for this evening."

Mrs. Zajek flashed a dramatic look of shock, which might be seen on the face of a bad actor in a community play. Gray hair was pinned behind her head, and she clutched a pink bathrobe around her neck to brace against the cold drifting through her door. I could tell that her eyes must have been a brilliant blue in the past but had faded into a slight bluish gray. She was a thin woman with high cheekbones like Katherine Hepburn and had a kind of elegance and poise.

"Oh, for heaven's sake." She smiled. "Of course, you can."

She pulled the door further open and looked directly at me. "How do you do, Stephanie? My name is Thelma Zajek. It is very nice to meet you."

She extended a thin, wrinkled hand through the frigid cold to shake mine.

"How do you do," I replied, feeling her chilling fingers across my palm. "This is my friend, Joan."

"Nice to meet you, sweetheart." She smiled at Joan. "You go back to your apartment and get out of this cold. I will be over in just a moment to bring you some supplies." She gently closed the door.

Mr. Nowak turned, handed me the apartment key, and said, "Well, I guess you can take it from here. I'm going home. I'm sure the Mrs. is ready to go home and have dinner, too."

As he began carefully stepping down the stairs, hand firmly gripping the rail for each step, he continued speaking, "You can park your car here under the landing. Keep it out of the alley. You can't park in the alley or in that lot over there. If you park in that lot, they will charge you for it. If you park even six inches into the alley, the city will tow the car and fine you. Oh, and don't block my back door when you park down there. There needs to be at least enough room for trucks to pull up for deliveries, and you might want to go ahead and get your car off the street out front."

"Yes, sir," I replied, watching him wobbling carefully down the stairs. "What about Mrs. Zajek's car?"

"Doesn't have one," he popped back over his shoulders. "I don't even think she knows how to drive."

"Give me the car keys," Joan commanded. "You go on back inside and wait for Mrs. Zajek. I'll move the car."

I did as she commanded, and while I was examining everything in the apartment again, there came a light tapping at the door. I opened it to find Mrs. Zajek standing there in her pink bathrobe and thick, pink, fuzzy slippers with an arm full of linens and blankets.

"May I come in, dear?" She croaked. "It's a bit chilly out here."

"Of course. Let me get those for you." I lifted the linens from her hand, carried them to the bedroom, and tossed them onto the bed. When I returned to the living room, I found her staring around the room.

"I miss her," She said quietly. "Mrs. Reynolds and I were next-door neighbors for many years before she had to go. We spent many cool summer nights sitting at the table on the landing, having a glass of wine and talking about all kinds of things." She motioned toward the dining table by the kitchen door. "Who knows how often we shared tea and cookies at that table?"

"I'm sorry you lost your friend," I almost whispered, not knowing what to say.

At that point, Joan rattled the knob at the front door and opened it. She came in, obviously shaken from the cold, and appeared happy to be back in a warm space.

"Is your friend going to be staying with you?" Mrs. Zajek asked when she glanced back toward Joan, who had begun dragging suitcases behind her.

"No, unfortunately not," I replied. "I wish she could, but she has to fly back to St. Louis in a couple of days."

I rushed over to help Joan pull the suitcases inside and get the door closed. "You didn't have to carry them up alone," I said. "We could have gotten them later."

"At least it's done," Joan replied, obviously winded by the experience.

"Oh, I'm so sorry you can't stay, dear," Mrs. Zajek told Joan and then returned her attention to me. "Are you planning on staying for long?"

There was almost a wishing in her voice, a hint of the loneliness that elderly people experience when they have outlived most of their friends and family or have lost connection through the years.

"No, Ma'am," I smiled politely. "I will be going back home in a few months after I have had some treatments at Johns Hopkins.

"Oh … forgive me for being forward, but are you one of those girl-boys I've heard about? Are you changing from a boy to a girl? I've heard they are doing those surgeries at Johns Hopkins—I think it's exciting!"

Her forwardness completely took me aback. I never expected such a question, and I immediately began wondering whether there could be any hint of maleness about me. My Adam's apple was covered by my turtleneck sweater, or at least I thought it was. I was wearing feminine, flattering, tasteful clothes from high-end stores. I thought, *How could she know?* Being taken aback, I did not feel threatened, for her voice had no hint of hostility. It appeared curiosity rather than animosity had prodded the question. On one hand, I resented curiosity. On the other, I could understand it. I hesitated with my answer and tried to concoct some lie quickly. Then, I heard unexpected honesty coming out of my mouth, perhaps because I was also curious.

"Yes," I said, finally. "How could you know that?"

I had been frightened that people might pick up on it, like the couple back at the Café. After what I had been through with the beating in high school, rather than flaunting it, I had tried to be very subtle and discrete. I didn't want any other group of assholes to decide they needed to punish me for being myself.

"Oh, my goodness," Mrs. Zajek grinned without answering my question. "We have a lot to talk about. I want you to tell me all about it, and when we get a chance to converse, I will tell you a secret of my own."

My mind popped with unsaid words: *A secret of her own? Damn! Okay?*

This little old lady certainly did not hesitate to get to the point. She didn't appear to have the morbid, judgmental curiosity that many people had in which they saw me as some anomaly of humanity to be perused with grotesque wonder. She seemed to genuinely want to get to know me.

"Okay?" I confirmed.

"Oh!" she chirped. "Have you girls had dinner?"

"No," I replied.

"Do you have food?"

"We didn't think about it," I said.

"I have already had dinner," she continued, "but I will bring you some leftovers and snacks in a few minutes. I will leave them at the door and knock." She seemed to be continually smiling. "Oh, and would the two of you like to join me for breakfast in the morning? I would be happy to prepare a breakfast for you. I have to go now. We can talk later."

"Okay," I said after glancing at Joan.

"How about nine o'clock?" she invited. "You must be tired from your trip, and I'm sure you will want to sleep in, at least a little."

Joan and I looked at each other again. In brief, I spoke. "That sounds wonderful, Mrs. Zajek. Thank you so much for all your help and your hospitality."

"I'm glad you are here, dear," she commented as she shuffled toward the door. "Come knock around nine o'clock in the morning. I will have breakfast ready. I'm sure you will want to know about the area, the city. I can tell you more about that in the morning. Goodnight, now."

She disappeared through the front door, closing it gingerly behind her.

Joan and I had breakfast with Mrs. Zajek the following morning: bacon, eggs, English muffins, grapefruit halves, and coffee. She was charming and didn't pry into the usual stupid questions that people often ask, such as, "How do you hide your junk?" She agreed she would not tell Mr. Nowak why I had come to Baltimore. As far as I was concerned, he only needed to know that I was having treatments for a genetic condition, which was still the truth. I had no idea how he might react or what he might do if he were to know the whole truth.

After breakfast, Joan and I spent some time driving around, getting to know the city, and trying to locate things I might need. I bought pillows, sheets, and a lovely coverlet for the bed. Thankfully, pots, pans, dishes, and utensils had been sparingly furnished. When we returned and made the bed, I placed Miss Mattie's embroidered pillow at the head for decoration. Since I first got it from Miss Mattie, that pillow had always gone with me. In years to come, I would occasionally have it dry cleaned and have to be apart from it temporarily, but I intended never to let it go.

I discovered that Mrs. Zajek, who had long since become incapable of lugging laundry up and down the stairs, had a service that would pick up her laundry, complete it for her, and deliver it back, neatly folded or on hangers. I began using the same service. Groceries, of course, were right downstairs, and we located a nearby department store where I bought more supplies.

Before Joan left for home, we were strolling through a local mall when I stopped and gazed at a toy store display where Barbie dolls were perfectly posed in their boxes. I stood there staring, and tears began to drift down my cheeks.

Joan, who had kept walking, turned to see me and returned to my side. "Are you okay?" she gently asked.

"I never had a whole Barbie," I replied. "Mable-bitch would find any doll I had and tear it up."

"Get one," she urged.

"The McNeils damn sure were not going to let me play with dolls," I confessed, "and after Miss Mattie came to get me, I don't know, I guess I was over it. Why bother? I never asked for one, never bought one, never had one. It was part of being a little girl that was stolen from me."

"Get one," she urged again. "It can be your fuck Mable-bitch doll."

I smiled a little, and more tears drifted. I reached into my purse for a tissue and began tapping my face, tucking it under my eyes and trying not to smudge my eyeliner. Then, I said, "Maybe I don't want to say 'fuck Mable-bitch' anymore. She was my mom. She was horrible, and I hated her, but she was still my mom. I guess, maybe, I loved her more than I thought I did. I wish we could have had the kind of relationship you and your mom have. I wish I had a real mom and dad, a normal childhood."

Joan stepped in front of me and hugged me. "You know I love you, right? You know that we all love you."

"Yes," I sighed.

"Then get the fucking doll!" She commanded as she pushed me back, hands firm on my shoulders and looking at me straight. "So, you didn't have a happy childhood, a normal childhood. Now what? It doesn't have to be a 'fuck Mable-bitch' doll. It doesn't have to be a making-up for a shitty childhood doll. It can be your celebration of becoming a complete woman doll. It can be your celebration of breaking free from your chrysalises and becoming a beautiful butterfly. You came to Baltimore to complete yourself, and you will go home from Baltimore restored. A complete doll, a complete woman—you!" She grabbed my hand and tugged, "Come on! I have a better idea. I will get the doll for you. A girl shouldn't have to buy her own dolls. All a little girl's dolls should be gifted to them. Have you ever heard of a Quintanilla?"

"A what?" I proclaimed.

"A Quintanilla," she explained. It is a celebration in Hispanic cultures celebrating a girl becoming a woman. They have a huge party, and she is gifted her last doll because she has now become a woman. Let's make this your Quintanilla! Let me buy you your first complete doll to celebrate becoming a complete woman."

"Okay?" I said sheepishly and let her pull me into the store. Still, I was half tugging back, not wanting to go, judging myself for being a grown woman looking at dolls. Still, the other half recognized that, in my emancipation as an adult, I could do any fucking thing I wanted to do as long as it was legal. We looked around a bit, with Joan pulling out boxes of accessories and dresses. Some of the fashion packages had several dresses in a container. I selected a doll dressed all in yellow with a cute yellow hat. Then, of course, I had to get something for her to wear in addition to the yellow dress that came with the package. So, I chose several extra boxes of dresses and accessories.

"Joan," I insisted. "I don't mind paying for this. It's a little expensive."

"Nonsense!" she replied. "To have meaning, the doll has to be a gift."

Before we left the store, Joan had me laughing again. Something that should have been common for a little girl had finally come to me. I felt a little girl's cheer, almost an innocence that had been confiscated from me before I could experience it.

That afternoon, I bought groceries from downstairs and made us a nice dinner. One of the most important things I learned from Miss Mattie was how to cook food so good your eyes would roll back in your head. It didn't occur to me to invite Mrs. Zajek over as a thank-you for her hospitality, but I wanted the time just between Joan and me. We had purchased tickets for Joan's flight before we left St. Louis, and we had only one more night together before she had to go home. The following morning, I would have to take her to the airport, and after dropping her off, I would have to go to my first appointment at Johns Hopkins at 1:00 p.m.

After dinner, we carefully took Barbie out of her box, dressed, and accessorized her. We laughed and talked about dolls from our past as we contemplated different outfits to dress her in. Joan had played with Barbie dolls for as long as she could remember, but she had never had the kind of doll experience I had. She laughed her ass off when I told her about sticking naked, partially decapitated Barbie down my pants so Mable-bitch wouldn't catch me with her. Decapitated Barbie started slipping down my leg, and I began grabbing my crotch, trying to prevent the doll from sliding down my pants leg.

"What the hell you doin'?" Mable-bitch had exclaimed. "Grabbin' your crotch like some of these damn thugs out here."

"I am a damn thug," I replied. "Look here how I grab my stuff!"

"Baby, you barely got any stuff to grab," she laughed and wandered off in her usual disorientation, fooled by my accidental ruse.

After playing with my first complete Barbie, I ensured she was dressed just as she had been when Joan bought her in the store. Then, I put her back neatly into her box. I leaned her against the window sill to keep watch over my apartment, and we went to bed.

The following day, after a tearful goodbye at the airport, I drove to my doctor's office and had difficulty finding it, even though I had been there two years earlier with Miss Mattie. I was finally able to locate it, and when I walked into Dr. Leeto's lobby, I looked around and didn't see anyone who looked remotely like me. I had forgotten that Dr. Leeto also did other types of surgeries. It looked like the office of any other doctor. I signed in with the receptionist and waited with my purse by my feet while I thumbed through a magazine.

When I was a third of the way through reading an article in an old Vogue, the nurse called me to the door. After stopping at the scale to check my weight, she led me down the hall to an examination room, checked my blood pressure and temperature, and then handed me a hospital gown. "Please get completely undressed and put on the gown," she instructed. "Dr. Leeto will see you in a few minutes."

I did as I had been instructed and then sat for a while staring at different things around the office: a glass jar with a chrome lid filled with cotton balls, brown-colored liquid soap in a dispenser by the single stainless-steel sink, and a goofy-looking picture of a puppy with extra-large eyes hanging slightly crooked on the wall.

After a tapping at the door, Dr. Leeto entered the room. He was taller than I remembered and was a little grayer around his temples. In his late forties, he sported reading glasses atop his nose with a little silver chain secured around his neck.

"Ms. Larouquette," He spouted as he entered the room and shoved his hand out for me to shake. "It's been a long time."

"Yes, sir," I responded as I lightly touched my fingers to the palm of his hand in a lady-like gesture that I had seen Mrs. McNeil teach the girls in foster care.

"Let's see what is going on." He flipped through paper files that he held in his hand. "Dr. Willis has sent me your records. It looks like you have been remaining healthy. I was very sorry to hear about your mother's passing. So, are you here on your own this time? Eighteen now, able to sign your own forms? Looks like you have done pretty well on the hormones, and you stopped those as instructed about a week ago?"

He didn't even give me a chance to respond to his questions or his condolences before he moved on. There were too many questions, and I almost felt like I had been called into the principal's office. I sat on the edge of the examination table, wondering what he was going to do.

"So, we have the first stage of your surgery scheduled in about two weeks. Is there anything I can do, between now and then, to talk you out of it?"

"Why would I want you to talk me out of it?" I asked.

"Deep breath," he commanded as he placed the cold stethoscope below my shoulder. "Research has shown that some folks are not any better adjusted after the surgery than before and, honestly, Johns Hopkins is thinking about halting the program." He moved the stethoscope to another place on my chest and then went to my back. I'm unsure how he thought he could hear anything while we talked, but he continued.

"It doesn't matter if I am better adjusted after the surgery," I insisted. "I have had plenty of things to deal with that get in the way of feeling well-adjusted, and they have nothing to do with having this surgery. At least I'll feel like my true self. I will finally have a chance to feel like a complete person."

"You have been through a lot," he commented. "This is not going to make your life any easier necessarily. You realize that."

"Yes, it will," I argued. "I will be able to feel complete. I won't look down every time I pee and see something that isn't supposed to be there. I know it will not take my problems or past away, but at least it will allow me to feel like a whole person, a whole woman."

"That's not what I'm talking about," he continued. "I mean with society, with people. General society still doesn't accept transsexuals just because they have had surgery. Just because you look more like a woman doesn't mean society will suddenly become accepting. You will pass better than most because you started the hormones young, but there will still be problems."

"I don't care," I found myself becoming irritated. "I have had problems my entire life. What's new? I grew up in the slums with a drug whore mother who got murdered. I got bullied, ridiculed, and beaten at school. I've been raped and beaten since I was little, for as long as I can remember. I can deal with fucking problems. The very least this will do is let me feel like my body matches who I am, and if I can't get it here, I will get it somewhere else. I will fucking go overseas to get it if I have to. I'm not worried about problems. Right now, my biggest problem is this dick between my legs."

"Okay, then," he calmly responded. "Let's finish your physical and get started with the process. So, two weeks with no hormones. Looks like Dr. Willis already got you started with that. So, you will check into the hospital on February 14th. How's that for a Valentine's Day gift?"

"I can't think of any better gift," I replied.

In the next couple of weeks, I spent quite a bit of time visiting with Mrs. Zajek. It was too cold to sit out on the landing, but we would sit at her dining table or mine and sip tea while we talked. I learned that English tea with a bit of cream and sugar was quite good but delicious when combined with an oatmeal cookie. I would still never have more than one and often eat only half.

I had never had the kind of relationship that we were building. She told me stories about growing up in Baltimore as the daughter of a factory worker, joining the Army, becoming a nurse, getting married, and having one stillborn child and one son who was killed in an auto accident at the age of nineteen leaving her with no children or grandchildren.

One evening, after a sip of tea, she said, "You know you are not the first transsexual I have ever met. Transsexual—that's what they called them back in the day. Do they still call it that?"

"I don't know," I replied, "but I think the term isn't very accurate. I think it's not really about sex. It's about gender. I'm female regardless of my body and sexual desires."

"So, here's the secret I told you I would share," She went on. "I had a friend when I was young who was a transsexual, not a girl-boy, like you, but a boy-girl. We met when I was serving as a nurse in the Army back in the early 1930s, before World War II. He was also a nurse, and we served together. Nobody said 'he' though, definitely not in those days, except that I began using 'he' because he asked me to when we were away from others. He was not attracted to women but sexually attracted to men. Yet, he felt like a man even though he was born a woman. So, he was a man, attracted to men, but born physically female. I always thought it rather odd that he would not be attracted to women when he felt like a man, but the whole thing was a lot for me to wrap my head around in those days. Still, there was no sexual attraction between us, and we became terrific friends, but it took me a while."

"That's why the term is wrong, maybe," and pondered as I spoke, "because it isn't about sex or sexual attraction. It has nothing to do with attractions. I'm sexually attracted to men, but I don't suppose you have to be attracted to one or the other, both or neither, just because you feel like a woman or a man. Honestly, I don't know. I have actually never met anyone else like me."

"At first, it was difficult to accept," Mrs. Zajek continued, barely noticing what I said. "In those days, who had ever heard of such a thing? We hit it off right away, but I had difficulty accepting the confession that he was really a man. He looked everything like a woman and had feminine mannerisms. In those days, such things were almost completely unknown and would surely have been despised by society. His birth name was Gina, but he liked to be called George. Of course, he kept all that a secret. He dared not let that get out, especially in the military, especially then. I was surprised he ever told me, except we both had a little too much to drink one night, and the discussion became intimate. I never knew what happened to him. We lost touch after the service. I heard he married and went on living as a woman even though that was not how he wanted his life to be. I don't suppose he could have done anything else. This stuff that Johns Hopkins is doing simply wasn't much of an option back then."

"Probably most of us live our assigned role for our whole lives and never let anyone know," I speculated aloud. "I'll bet there are people who have lived their entire lives keeping the secret strictly to themselves, never telling their families or friends, living that private torture their whole life. I'm lucky that there have at least been a few people who have accepted me all along. I'm lucky to have the money for a very expensive surgery. I wonder about all those people who can't afford surgery. Except for my mother being killed and a stroke of blind luck, that would have been me having to live my life as a constant actor, playing a role, maybe having no options. I don't know exactly what gave me the fire to claim my gender and stand up for myself, but I did. I feel so sorry for those people who go through their entire lives never telling anyone how they really feel, living a lie, day in and day out, in a body that doesn't feel like it is their own, like it doesn't belong to them. Probably, most never have surgery. Maybe some don't even want it."

"Back in the day," she reflected, "there was no such thing as surgery for something like that, not that I ever knew of, and I still don't know of any surgeries where they can convert a female body into a male; not yet."

"What made you so accepting?" I questioned.

"Humpf," She grunted. "Maybe it helped to have nursing training, but who doesn't have a skeleton in their closet? I haven't lived the perfect life, and I don't expect anyone has—or has to. Besides, I learned a long time ago that we are all different, but we are all the same— human. Who am I to say someone must think, feel, or be like me? We are what we are, and unless it's harming me, the life that someone else is living isn't any of my business."

"That's a good philosophy," I commented.

"It has kept me out of many people's way and them out of my way," she replied. "Why should we spend our lives getting in one another's way? So, what's going to happen with this surgery of yours?"

"I'm going to get a vagina," I replied.

"No, that is not what I mean. How long are you going to have to be in the hospital? What kind of recoup time are you going to have? When will you be able to come home, and what will you need when you get home?"

"Oh, I try not to think about it," I replied.

"Well, you need to think about it. You don't just pop back up when you have surgery, especially a major surgery, and I expect that one will be challenging."

"I'm supposed to go in on the 14th, and I guess I will have the surgery on the 15th. Then, I'll be in the hospital for a few days while they make sure everything works right, and I will come home and wait a few weeks before the second phase of the surgery."

"Don't you have any help or support?" she pried. "You are going to need help. You can't just come home from the hospital after major surgery and expect to do business as usual."

"I'm doing this on my own," I replied. "I suppose I could hire someone if I needed to, but I don't really have any family or friends who could be here."

"Well, while you are here," she insisted. "I will be your family. What happened to your family? You told me your mother was killed, but what about the rest?"

I heard the sigh come from deep inside me after a breath that I very much needed. It was a discussion I hated almost more than talking about transition surgery.

"I never had a father," I said. "At least, I don't know who he is. My biological mother said she slept with a lot of men, so she didn't know.

Yes, she was murdered when I was ten. I was placed in foster care for a couple of years, and my friend, who used to take care of me in the projects, got custody of me and adopted me. She was the only one who ever acted like a real mother, and she died last October. I never claimed my biological mother as a real mother or any of her family."

"What about your friend who was here?" she continued.

"She is still in high school," I replied. "One more semester. She can't be here because she has to be in class, and I don't know that she would know how to help me anyway. Her mother is a doctor with a busy practice, and her father is an executive with the Busch Brewery in St. Louis. They all have other obligations, and there has never been anyone else."

She reached over and softly patted the back of my hand. "Well, while you are here," she promised. "I will be your family. If you need anything, call me, and I assure you I will come check on you anyway."

She went to her kitchen and returned with a number written on a torn piece of paper.

"That's my number," She said. "Use it, and don't forget that I'm a retired nurse. Oh, and don't forget to put me on the visitor's list when you are in the hospital."

I was touched by such unexpected kindness. As much as there were terrible people in the world like Jake Carter and my so-called mother, there were also good people who seemed to have no ulterior motive, people who just cared about you because caring is what they do.

It would be another couple of days before I would have a phone installed, a yellow one, which I had placed beside my bed. The first thing I did was call Joan. We had a long conversation, and then I called Mrs. Zajek to let her know my phone number.

Several days later, I went into the hospital for my first surgery.

CHAPTER 15

A NEW LIFE

I went from totally unconscious to screaming. The last time I had come from nothingness to sudden awareness was on the day that I came out of my daze in the McNeil van when Mrs. McNeil had slapped me on the leg, except this time, I wasn't screaming with anger; I was screaming with horrible pain. I had been in pain when I woke up in the hospital after being beaten in high school, but it was a different kind of pain, a severe pain, but subdued and manageable, more of a sore pain, and I woke gradually. This was sudden, excruciating torment.

I was on a gurney wheeled down a hallway with lights flashing overhead as I rolled beneath them. On either side of me were nurses wearing surgical masks and surgery head coverings. I began writhing on the gurney because the pain was so intense.

"Sush, sweetie," One of the nurses muttered. "Hold still. We are almost at the recovery area and will give you a little morphine when we get there. Try not to move too much, honey."

I couldn't shush. The last damn thing in the world I wanted to do was shush. I couldn't hold still when I felt as though my insides were being ripped out between my legs. I had not had pain even close to that since they removed my testicles back in St. Louis, but I didn't suddenly pop out of anesthesia. This hurt worse than any damn thing I had ever experienced, but morphine, oh God, morphine, maybe that would kill the pain. My mind latched onto the morphine and getting some relief.

Soon, we turned a corner into recovery, and I was left on the gurney while the nurse pulled out a vile of morphine. They had hooked the IV bag to a stainless-steel pole above the gurney. Then, the nurse broke the top off the glass vile, drew up the morphine, and injected it into the IV port in my arm. "Ms. Laroquette," she apologized as she injected the substance. "You woke up sooner than we were expecting. I am so sorry."

Soon, the relief of the medication began to filter through my body, and I began to feel drowsy.

Later, I found myself in my hospital room, in my bed, and I began to wake after the sweet solace of nothingness, no existence, just quiet darkness and no awareness of anything. I had come to love being unconscious and briefly escaping hell. Dr. Leeto was standing over my bed; apparently, it was early the next morning.

"How are you doing this morning?" he questioned.

My mouth was dry, and I still felt a bit groggy. "I hurt like hell," I mumbled, but not as bad as it was."

"Understandable," he proclaimed in a matter-of-fact tone.

"*Under ... stand ... able!*" I sassed with a twist in my lips as I shot him a dirty look.

He chuckled. "You did well. The surgery went smoothly, and we are not expecting any significant complications. You are going to be here at least another week for aftercare, longer if we need to. We will need to make sure all your physical equipment works right before you go home. The catheter will come out in a few days, and you will need to void and defecate normally before we send you home."

"Speak English, please," I muttered.

"You will need to urinate without the catheter and have normal bowel movements. In the meantime, you will eat a lot of soup and the nurses will do bandage care for a while before you go home. If you can keep it down, we will let you start having solid food in a few days. In the meantime, if you need to go number two, use your call button, and the nurses will put you on a bedpan."

"That sounds disgusting," I retorted.

"Depends on your perspective," he countered. "Anyone who has bowels must move them. It's just a natural thing. So, we have things tucked away down there, and I will periodically check everything to ensure there are no complications."

"That explains everything," I sassed slightly. "What about my vagina? I have a vagina, now?"

"You do—of sorts."

"Of sorts? What the fuck does that mean, of sorts?" I had not given him time to complete his statement.

"I mean," he calmly countered, "that you have the beginning stages of having a vagina, and we will complete that process with a couple more surgeries. First things first. Now relax, watch TV, and read some of these cards on your flowers over there. I'll be back to see you again tomorrow morning."

"But I have questions?"

"There will be plenty of time for questions as we go through the process. You and I will see each other regularly, and I don't plan to let you walk out of here without knowing what is what. Now, just relax and try to stay as comfortable as possible." He patted my arm and strolled out of the room.

I had not even noticed three sets of flowers on nearby tables. They were beautiful, but I couldn't reach the cards, and he was gone. With frustration, I pressed the call button.

A few minutes later, a pretty blond nurse stuck her head through the door.

"Can I get you something?" she politely asked.

Then she walked up to the bed and began checking the drip on my IV before I could tell her what I wanted.

"Can you hand me those cards from the flowers so I can read them?" I asked.

"Sure thing!"

I loved the sweet little ring of her northeast accent. I didn't know if it was a Baltimore accent, a New York accent, or what. My ears couldn't tell one from the other. I could only discern it was an accent from north and east of St. Louis.

She retrieved each of the three cards and handed them to me as she pointed out which set of flowers they had been attached to.

"You want a little breakfast? Let me get you a tray and see if you can eat a little something."

I barely paid attention as I pulled the cards up to read. The first card was from Mr. and Mrs. Wilson and Jeremy. It was short and sweet, "*Thinking about you and praying for you. Wishing you all the best and that you will be up and at it soon.*"

The next card was from Mrs. Zajek, and she had sent the largest and most beautiful bouquet. "*I noticed that you like yellow,*" it said. "*So, I got you some yellow roses.*"

She had probably noticed my yellow phone or maybe Barbie in her yellow dress sitting on my window sill. The note continued, "*I will see you as soon as they allow visitors. I am looking forward to talking to you.*"

The last card was from Joan, which was more of a letter than a card. It had been mailed and had come separately from the flowers. She had filled up the inside of a fancy embossed *get-well* greeting card to the point that the actual published sentiment was barely noticeable, and she had continued writing onto the back side of the card.

Steph,

I miss you so much. I wonder and worry about you every day. I wish I could have been there with you through all this. I know there is no way it can be easy. I look forward to seeing you again as soon as possible, and Mom and Dad said I can fly up over Spring Break next month if you are up to having a visitor. We might not do anything but sit around your apartment unless you have to be in the hospital during that time. Then, I will sit with you in your room, but that is definitely okay with me. If you are in the hospital, I will spend time with you there, and the rest of the time, I can take care of myself back at your apartment. It will be good to see you and spend time with you.

Everybody here is doing well. Same old, same old, except Jeremy has met a girl and is having his first crush. Well, except for his crush on his seventh-grade math teacher, maybe that wasn't really a crush, just lust. Do you remember that day that he jizzed in his pants while he was fantasizing about her instead of paying attention in class? Hilarious! No wonder he sucked at math. Anyway, his girlfriend is over here half the time, and he is over at her place the other half. It is so funny to watch. They stay curled up on the couch together. Dad, of course, will not let him take her to his room, but it wouldn't surprise me if they haven't already had sex. Whatever, the kid has got to grow up.

I am so going to look forward to seeing you over Spring Break. I just want you to know that you mean so much to me. You are like the sister I never had, and whatever goes on up there, keep me in your mind and know that I love you."

Always,

Joan

I laid the cards over my chest and closed my eyes.

The next thing I knew, the nurse came in with some milky gruel that did not look appealing. It tasted almost as bad as it looked, and it tasted even worse when it came back up about five minutes after I ate it.

It would be a couple more days before I could eat or keep anything down other than clear bullion or water. I didn't care. It was worth it. It meant I could finally have the type of body I should have been born with. I comforted myself through the nausea that if I were to drop a pound or two, it would just make me look sexier.

In about five days, I was mainly eating solid food again. They took the catheter out and had me walking to the bathroom to pee and poop. That was a significant ordeal because everything was still sore as hell, and I had laid in bed for a week, getting stiff muscles. They had come and moved my arms and legs around and had me sit on the edge of the bed, but that wasn't the same as actually walking, and that first time in the bathroom, I realized that I was going to have to learn how to pee without a hose. I accomplished it, though, even if it hurt a little bit and felt different. The bowel movement was another story. Pain medications and lying around had caused me to be constipated. Dr. Leeto had to order a laxative for that to happen.

Mrs. Zajeck came by almost every night during visiting hours and sat by my bed to chat. She had to take a cab, and I offered to pay for it, but she refused. She had more stories—Lord, the woman had more stories than a library, but I loved it and began to feel close to her. Her stories were fascinating, and the kinds of things she had done and experienced were amazing. When I got ready to go home, she took a cab to the hospital and then drove me home. My car had been in hospital parking the whole time.

"I haven't had a driver's license in about thirty years," she said, "but what the cops don't know won't hurt anything. I still know how to drive." She got us safely back to our apartments, which mattered to me.

When we got home, she was careful to help me up the steps to my apartment. Although, I think if I had fallen, she would not have been able to prevent both of us from tumbling down the steps. Walking up those steps was not the easiest thing to accomplish, but it was probably good for me, and it was good to be back in my own space again.

Mrs. Zajek took my grocery list and a handful of cash to grocery shop downstairs for my first week back in the apartment. I told her that if there was anything she wanted for herself, to go ahead and get it, and I would pay for it, but as far as I know, she never took me up on that. Whatever cash was left over, she would tuck beneath my telephone by the bed. Half the time, she would come to my place to cook for me or bring a cooked meal over from her place and eat with me.

"Now you have to walk, dear," she encouraged. "Get things moving again. Don't just lay around all day."

She insisted I get out of bed and eat at the dining table. When I showered, she stood nearby to ensure I could step into and out of the tub. On one hand, I thought she had to be a fantastic person to be so generous and giving, but on the other hand, I thought that taking care of me also did something for her. She had been lonely in her apartment when her friend went to the nursing home, and she seemed to enjoy caring for others. Since she had been a nurse, maybe it gave her a renewed sense of purpose.

As the weeks passed, I became more comfortable and began to get my sea legs back. The week of March 12th was Spring Break, and the week before, I was to have my next surgery. Joan flew in, and I picked her up at the airport on the afternoon of Monday, March 13th. She stayed until the 18th when I put her on a plane for home. While there, she wanted to go and do things that I couldn't bring myself to do. I tried going to the mall with her, but I couldn't do all that walking yet. We ended up having to leave the mall early and spent most of our time sitting around my apartment, although we ate out a couple of times and took in a movie.

The good news about laying around at home was that I had gotten permission from Mr. Nowak to install cable services on the apartment television, and I bought a VCR. So I could record movies and shows to watch later. I had recorded ten or fifteen movies and shows by the time Joan arrived. So, sitting around the apartment was not as difficult as it might have been. At least there was ample TV to watch. As far as I was concerned, local channels were mostly for news, weather, and the occasional sitcom. In those days, The *All in the Family* sitcom had reached its peak in popularity. Miss Mattie and I had watched it religiously, mainly to laugh at the bigot *Archie Bunker* being shown up repeatedly, but also realizing that beneath his stupidity was a tender heart. There had even been a transsexual character on the show once.

Mrs. Zajek had gotten into the habit of checking on me every day and was often in my apartment. I enjoyed her company and was delighted in all that she could talk about, from the history of Baltimore to going to New York for Broadway shows and meeting Broadway stars. She actually had dinner with Carol Channing once because one of her friends knew her, and that story, alone, was fascinating.

During the week that Joan was there, I noticed that Joan would get antsy when Mrs. Zajek came over. She would try to come up with something else for us to do and would interject something that had absolutely nothing to do with conversations I was having with Mrs. Zajeck, "Hey, let's go to the movies and see what is showing tonight?" or "You know, I heard there is a Japanese restaurant around here somewhere. Have you ever had Japanese food?" Other times, she would sit on the sofa playing solitaire, flipping the cards onto the coffee table, and completely ignoring us.

It got so bad that one day, after Mrs. Zajek returned to her appointment, I sat on the sofa next to her as she flipped cards onto the coffee table and said, "Let's talk."

"Something wrong?" she questioned, knowing something was wrong.

"Just put the cards down," I said again, patting her on the knee.

When she turned to me, I said, "Girl … what the hell is the matter with you?"

"What?" She questioned like she hadn't noticed a thing."

"What have you been doing every time Mrs. Zajek has come over here by cutting into her conversation, trying to get me to leave my visitor and go somewhere else, sitting here flipping cards and pretending there is no one else in the room? What is that all about?"

"I just want to spend some time with you," she replied. "I haven't seen you in two months, then I get one week for a visit, and you want to spend it sitting around jabbering boring crap with that old lady."

"That old lady is my friend."

"Oh, so I'm not your friend?"

"Did you hear me say that?"

"But you don't care that I came all the way up here to see you, and you want to ignore me?"

"Joan, how am I ignoring you? You can visit with Mrs. Zajek at the same time that I do, and … we have done stuff together."

"I don't want to listen to all that boring, old fart crap."

"I happen to think that it is fascinating. Mrs. Zajek has had a fascinating life and she's lonely."

"But her being a lonely old woman is more important than our friendship. She was a lonely old woman when you got here, and she will be a lonely old woman when you leave, and I only have a week to spend with you while she is taking up *our* time."

"When I get back to St. Louis, we will have the rest of our lives to spend time together, but I'm only going to be here a few months, and at least I can give Mrs. Zajek a little company while I'm here. Besides, she has done so much for me and taken care of me after surgery."

"I offered to stay and help you, but you said you didn't want me to. In the meantime, you act like you don't even care that I'm here."

"No … " I reflected. "I didn't say that I didn't want you to. Your mom told you *she* didn't want you to stay with me and wanted you to finish your last semester in school, and I don't think I have been acting like I don't care that you're here. Joan, you know I love you, and our friendship is not going to go anywhere."

"Well, it feels like you don't even notice me."

"You know, I kind of felt like that when you met Sarah," I replied, "but I tried to be friends with Sarah instead of shutting her out. Besides, have I not spent a huge amount of my time with you this week? Have we not gone to the mall? Did we not just see *Return from Witch Mountain* at the movies the day before yesterday? Isn't that noticing that you are here? And … when Mrs. Zajek is here, you are welcome to participate in the conversations instead of boycotting. That's up to you."

"I'm getting a little weird, aren't I?"

"Yes, girl, you are."

"Maybe I'm jealous, afraid that you will decide to stay in Baltimore and won't come home."

"Honey, I have to come home."

"Why?"

"Because you are there."

A smile crossed her face. She relaxed and hugged me.

"I'm sorry," she said.

"Don't worry about it. Listen, we have one more day together before you return to St. Louis. What do you want to do with it?"

"Why don't we go to a spa, get a massage, and get our hair and nails done?"

"Are you sure that's what you want to do?" I questioned.

She grinned. "We both like girly things and being pampered. Maybe we can get a cute guy to give us a massage."

"You want a cute guy to massage you?"

"Okay, maybe a cute girl. Either way. I like both, and it will be fun."

"Sure, why not?" Then, I hesitated. "But … maybe I should call the clinic and ask if it is okay to do something like get a massage."

"Why wouldn't it be okay?" she pondered.

"I don't know," I replied. "But I better ask."

At the time of the conversation, it was about 4:30 in the afternoon. I was afraid I wouldn't be able to get hold of anyone when I went to the bedroom to make the call. Still, I spoke to a nurse who gave me some precautions: lower legs only, no abdominal massage, no deep tissue massage, and be careful around the buttocks. When I hung up the phone, I told Joan, who had followed me into the bedroom. "Let's get the yellow pages and see what we can find."

We spent about thirty minutes flipping through the yellow pages trying to discern the difference between a legitimate spa with a massage therapist and a whore house listing massage. We found a legitimate service a short distance away and called the next morning to ask about it.

We went to be pampered the following afternoon. She had a complete massage and got a somewhat matronly-looking middle-aged woman, which we laughed about for the remainder of the afternoon and evening. I got a pedicure, a manicure, and a facial, but I skipped the massage. It was good just to be touched in a non-threatening and gentle way. What I loved the most was when my hands and feet were massaged. I had gotten hooked on pampering myself, which I had surprisingly never deeply explored. Once I finished my surgeries and moved home, I got a regular massage therapist and found a lovely salon for manicures and pedicures. After that, a one or two-hour weekly pampering became my obsession.

We relaxed at home for the remainder of the evening, ordered a pizza, and watched a movie on my VCR. Joan even suggested that we invite Mrs. Zajek over to join us.

I said, "You know what? This is our last day before you go home, and we don't have to invite Mrs. Zajek over."

Joan got up, went to the bedroom, and called Mrs. Zajek herself. Mrs. Zajek made an excuse that she had her own television programming that she wanted to watch, and I wondered if she might not have picked up on what had been going on with Joan. Nonetheless, it was just the two of us for the evening.

After the movie, we played with my Barbie for a while, dressed her in different outfits, and decided that she should go on a date. Joan got an ink pen and pretended it was a Ken doll, a one-legged Ken. I laughed because her Ken was more put together than most of my Barbies after Mable-bitch had gotten hold of them. When I realized I was laughing about it, I wondered if I could finally forgive my mother. Maybe I was finally having a childhood; playing like a little girl should be allowed to play. I also wondered if I might finally be able to accept that Miss Mattie was gone. That, however, would not come for quite some time.

The following day, I put Joan on a flight back to St. Louis with hugs and goodbyes, all the usual stuff, and a little tinge of worry about the plane's safety. Then I meandered alone through the terminal back to my car, feeling disconnected when hundreds of people surrounded me. I watched people conversing, fiddling with luggage, and eating at food courts. Somehow, I felt separated from everyone, as though I was not a part of society. That was on a Saturday, and the following Sunday, I couldn't help noticing how empty my apartment felt. Even though I had grown up as an only child, I had never actually been alone. At least I had never lived alone. For some reason, I felt terribly alone that day.

On Monday, I entered the hospital again for my second round of surgeries. It was not as bad as the first round. They must have learned their lesson about my anesthesia because I woke up in my hospital bed instead of on the gurney. There was pain, of course, but it meant something to me. I thought about the pain that biological women must feel when they give birth and decided this pain meant that I was giving birth to a new me. This was the caterpillar emerging from the chrysalis as a butterfly.

After a week to recoup from the last round of surgery, hopefully, the last round, I was instructed in dilation and the importance of keeping my vagina dilated for the rest of my life unless I was regularly sexually active with a man. All that was well and good, but I had something else I wanted to talk to Dr. Leeto about. When we had our conference before I was to go home, he told me again that I had done better than many, that my healing process should be smooth, and that I would need to follow up with my doctors when I got back to St. Louis.

I told him, "That's not enough."

"What do you mean that's not enough?" he asked.

"I need more than this," I commented. "I still look too much like a man."

"What do you mean, you still look too much like a man?" he argued. "You are one of the prettiest girls we have had here. You started hormones young, and that is almost unheard of. That gave you a more feminine body, and your voice sounds exactly like any other woman's. I would say the surgery has been a magnificent success."

"Yes, it has been," I continued. "But it's not enough."

"What more do you need?" he asked.

"For starters, I need this damn lump in my neck removed. Being skinny, and I plan to stay skinny, makes it appear even more evident." I tapped my forefinger at the Adam's apple.

"You know you could stand to put on a few pounds. No law says you have to keep yourself that skinny. It might, in fact, be a bit unhealthy skinny."

"That's not the point," I pressured. "I'll manage my health and weight and put a few pounds back on when I get home, but this has to be gone so my neck doesn't look like a man's neck. I don't want anybody noticing it or having any questions about it, and while we are at it, I need my cheekbones raised a little."

"You already have high, beautiful cheekbones," he argued. "You can thank your genetics for that. Like I said, you are beautiful, and a little rouge would accent the beautiful cheekbones you already have. You don't need to change that, and your lips are perfect."

"The only thing about my face that is beautiful are my eyes and my lips, but I might need my nose trimmed a little, too."

He sighed deeply. "Have you ever heard of body dysmorphic disorder? You have to be very careful about it, especially if you have had a lot of shaming about your body. It's kind of like becoming addicted to having plastic surgery, and a person who does it can make themselves look grotesque in the long run by having too many surgeries."

"It is not my intent to look grotesque," I replied. "Okay, maybe the cheekbones are fine. Maybe I don't need a nose job, but I do need something done about this Adam's apple, and I need to have hips that look like a woman's. Obviously, my tits are fine."

He acquiesced. "Okay, so that you know, I don't do those surgeries. I'm willing to make a referral for a consult with a plastic surgeon, but you may have to go somewhere else to have that done."

"Fine," I replied. "Give me some options. Please put me in contact with doctors who can do this for me. I want to know who the best plastic surgeons are."

I spent the next several weeks recovering from my second and, thankfully, final surgery, at least for a while. Still, I had to deal with the painful first dilations and spend an hour or more a day doing it. I had to leave the insert in for ten minutes three or four times daily and thoroughly clean everything afterward. After a few months, this would become my daily routine, but at least I could cut it down to once a day and about twenty minutes for completion.

I spent as much time with Mrs. Zajek as possible, and she was utterly fascinated with the whole process I was going through. It was not a morbid curiosity she had but a medical curiosity. She was fascinated with the medical techniques and asked more about technical procedures and follow-up than anything else.

Before I left Baltimore, I spent a lot of time researching plastic surgeons and reviewing the resumes and stats of some of the ones Dr. Leeto recommended. I logged several names into my address book to follow up for the other surgeries when I got home.

Then, the time came that I had to go. I had become very fond of Mrs. Zajek. She had become a good friend. We remained friends for several years after I moved back to St. Louis, and on my trips back to Baltimore, of which there were several, I would always stop to visit with her. We were alike in so many ways. Neither of us had family, and I wondered if, when looking at her, I was seeing my own future, alone, with no family or friends around to care about me.

I was so happy, about a year on when Mrs. Zajek met a widowed and recently retired man in his early seventies. They met downstairs in the grocery. At first, he moved into the apartment next door, just as I had done, and they also became good friends. His name was Frank Thompson. Of course, I met him. He was a lovely and charming man. They married about a year after meeting, and he moved into her apartment. About five years later, Mr. Nowak sold the grocery and the building. The new owners planned to tear it down and had no sympathy for an elderly couple, so they had to move.

Mrs. Zajek, now Mrs. Thompson, moved into a little house with her husband near his daughter in the suburbs. They seemed to be blissfully happy together, and I was extremely happy for her, delighted more than anything, that she could spend her waning days with people who loved her. She never told Mr. Thompson my secret. I'm not sure how he would have handled it, but it wasn't necessary for him to know. Just Like Mr. Nowak, he was told that we met when I came to Baltimore for some treatments for my genetic condition. He did not ask questions. I had my life in St. Louis, and they had their lives in Baltimore. Some cards and letters went back and forth, and she always sent a box of candy at Christmas. I didn't forget about her, but my life went on without her. In the spring of 1994, I received a tearful phone call from Mr. Thompson telling me my friend had passed away. I didn't cry. I simply went through everything I had that reminded me of her, remembered the stories she told me, and was happy that I had known her.

Over the first two years after moving back to St. Louis, I had multiple surgeries, about four. I could have gone back to Baltimore for other plastic surgery, but I found a surgeon in Las Angeles who was also known to do work with celebrities. It was pricy, but I would rather have had less money in the Trust and have to work than not look the way I wanted.

I didn't meet anyone like Mrs. Zajek on my trips to LA, although there were a few notable encounters. I hired any help I needed to recoup from surgery and stayed at a spa hotel when I wasn't in the hospital. I got my nose trimmed only slightly, my jaw tapered just a little, my Adam's apple shaved to reduce the size, and I had implants that widened and enlarged my hips, but not too much. The last thing I wanted was for my body to look exaggerated. I left the titties alone. Why bother with perfection? Hormones had been enough to give me Goldilocks titties, just like Joan. Otherwise, I made sure that the changes were subtle. I did not need any appearance of exaggerated femininity. After all, I was a woman, not a drag queen.

While I was going through all this and spending a sizeable amount of money, Mr. Riggs became concerned about my use of the Trust. "Why don't you take some of these funds and go to college?" he pleaded. "Get a degree in finance. Learn how all this works so you can build on what you have. You could end up rich instead of just comfortable relying on the Trust."

"Honey, me and math don't get along," I smiled as I consulted with him that day. I spent a fair amount of time sitting in his office and being lectured on what I should or could be doing when all I was asking was, "Do I have the money to cover this?"

I didn't need his permission, but I asked it anyway. I had been emancipated and given charge of my Trust early when Miss. Mattie died. Technically, I was not supposed to get it until I turned twenty-one, but the papers indicated that I would get it as an emancipated adult if something happened to Miss Mattie before that time. I might have had charge of it and could have spent every penny if I wanted to, but I knew that I knew nothing about finance and needed to make it last. So, I continued to consult with Mr. Riggs. He kept me in check, so I didn't drop the principle too much and could still have a nice annual check from the interest. I started leaving ten percent of that in the principle, and then he decided to hook me up with an Edward Jones agent. If I didn't know how to invest, they did. So, they began to make additional investments for me, and I had more money than I needed to survive, but I decided to work anyway. I bought a nice little one-bedroom condo in downtown St. Louis, and my new life began.

By 1981, I was done with all the surgeries and only needed periodic follow-up. I was twenty-one, looked hotter than Cleopatra, and I loved it! I could stroll down the street, hips swinging, tick-tock, and feel men's eyes on me. Sometimes, I would deliberately walk by a construction zone just to see if I could get a cat call or a whistle. What many women considered to be sexist and offensive, I considered a compliment, proof that I had made it, that I was finally the woman I was always meant to be. Men like Jake Carter and Ronza had lusted for me when I was a little boy, but that was sick shit, and it certainly didn't count. That wasn't desire. That was a perversion. The desire I came to know as an adult was not like perverted lust from a rapist or a child molester but came from an ordinary man's libido and his appreciation of my femininity. That was the kind of desire that I loved to experience. It didn't matter that I never had sex with any of them. It only mattered that they thought I was attractive.

Maybe I should have gone to college as Mr. Riggs suggested, but after completing the surgeries, I wanted to live what I hoped would be a kind of ordinary life. I wanted to work, but getting up to go to a job at 8:00 a.m. was not appealing to me. Maybe that part of Mable's behavior rubbed off on me. As I said, I have always hated alarm clocks. After being hired as a bar back in a little bar near my condo and getting to know a collection of regular patrons, I discovered that I enjoyed the bar scene, at least that bar scene. I learned to bartend from the bartenders there, and what time I wasn't washing dishes and racking them back up for the bartenders, I was watching them make drinks and asking questions.

The condo I purchased was in a renovated historic building in downtown St. Louis a couple of blocks from Willard's Pub where I went to work. Before I turned twenty-two, I worked there full-time as a bartender and loved it. It was a sports bar, and more often than not, all I served was beer to men who would sit around and watch ball games on the TVs mounted on either end of the bar. The occasional glass of wine would be ordered, and occasionally, a mixed drink. I never got into drinking much, myself. I damn sure didn't want to become anything like my so-called mother, but I could serve up a dynamite Margherita, Martini, or Old Fashioned. I enjoyed the fact that most of the patrons were men, most of them local businessmen, I assumed. They loved to leave excellent tips for a pretty bartender, and I didn't mind flirting with them. As far as they were concerned, I was the same as any other woman. I had my invitations, but I didn't date. I didn't want to. Even though I was attracted to men and found several of them desirable, the idea of sleeping with a man frightened me. At that time, I was technically still a virgin. I had never had sex since my surgery, or for that matter, before. Being molested as a child did not take my virginity because that certainly wasn't making love. It took my choice, innocence, sense of safety, and what should have been my childhood joy. That was not real sex, not lovemaking, and I, therefore, considered myself a virgin regardless of what happened to me. That was not me surrendering my body to someone I desired, so it didn't count. As far as I was concerned, I was a virgin and was fine with always remaining a virgin.

Everything seemed perfect to me except for not dating or having a life mate. I had a comfortable, enjoyable life. I had all the money I needed and more. I could take trips, eat out with friends, go to the movies, or go shopping, and I thought I was happy. I could live my life my way, make my own decisions, and do whatever I wanted. For all I knew, all I had to do was get on with it and enjoy all my blessings. However, I was wrong.

CHAPTER 16

OLD FRIEND, NEW FRIEND

The only problem with my little one-bedroom condo was that both the bedroom and living room windows faced east. This was great during the day because I was on the fifth floor and had a great view, but after working late at the bar, streams of sunlight crossing directly over my face in the morning were almost as tormenting as an alarm clock. So, I hired a designer to install blackout drapes that would still look attractive but block the morning sun, which made a vast difference in the quality of my sleep. With the drapes pulled back, the views at night were beautiful, and also beautiful in the afternoons, but I damn sure didn't like any view that would wake me up when I wasn't ready to get up.

Otherwise, I loved my condo. There were hardwood floors throughout and an exposed brick wall behind the headboard of my bed, just like there had been at the apartment in Baltimore. However, the difference was that my condo was freshly renovated and tastefully done. It had a walk-in closet, great for a girl who likes to dress up, and an en-suite by my bedroom. The designer's touch had caressed my condo, and I had loved it from the moment I first walked in with the realtor. The kitchen was small but well-appointed, opening into the living room with a small bar. The stovetop was installed in the bar, so I could stand there while I cooked and look across the living room at the view of St. Louis. There was a coat closet and a small half bath by the door. I put my TV set on another exposed brick wall across from my sofa, perpendicular to the living room window. My tan leather sofa backed to the bedroom wall across from the TV and had a large, beautiful picture of white horses hanging behind it. I even tried keeping a couple of potted plants and managed to get a six-foot-tall variegated Ficus tree to survive in the corner of the living room by the window so it didn't block the view. I could have hired someone to come in and clean, but it was small, and Miss Mattie had instilled within me the need to keep my home presentable. So, I picked up after myself every day and maintained a regular cleaning schedule. My adult life was the polar opposite of the life I had been born into.

I settled into a routine, working at Willard's Pub Friday through Tuesday evenings and having Wednesday and Thursday off. The only problem with bartending is that you usually have to work weekends, which is also when most of your friends want to get together. However, my shifts could rotate depending on the needs of other bartenders, and we could trade shifts if one of us needed to be off on a specific day. While working there, I made new, but not close friends, and remained close friends with Joan and Sarah. After graduating high school, she started spending much more time with Sarah. They got an apartment together, and it looked like they were becoming a couple. Joan enrolled in the pre-med program at Washington University and was determined to follow in her mother's footsteps. Given her school schedule and my work schedule, we visited as often as possible, had dinners here and there, and parties with her gay friends. Other than the gay people I had met through Joan, I had deliberately kept myself separate from the gay community, but I enjoyed visiting with and teasing her gay male and lesbian friends. None of them became close personal friends, but we enjoyed seeing each other at parties. Still, I didn't let anyone know that I was transsexual and admonished Joan and Sarah to please keep my secret. I didn't want to be known as a transsexual. I wanted to be known as a woman, just like any other woman, and I didn't want any rumors of it going around. St. Louis might have been a big town, but it was a small town in many ways.

Sometimes, my visits with Joan, Sarah, or other friends had to be after I got off work, early mornings on a Friday or Saturday as the bar closed at 2:00 a.m., but my afternoons were available, and meeting for lunch wasn't out of the question. There were times when Joan and Sarah would meet me at the bar at closing time, and we would have a late-night breakfast at a twenty-four-hour breakfast joint a few blocks from there. She and Sarah had become involved with the local gay and lesbian community, including related politics, and she had been introducing me to their gay and lesbian friends as soon as I moved home. There was a movement afoot for Gay Rights, and it was just beginning to get a foothold in the early 1980s, only a little more than ten years after the Stonewall Riots in June of 1969. That is also when tragedy struck.

On Thursday, June 17, 1982, I had just made myself a turkey sandwich for dinner and was sitting in my living room watching the evening news on NBC when Tom Brokaw announced a new disease among gay men that had the CDC baffled. It appeared to be sexually transmitted, was becoming an epidemic, and was deadly. My heart sank. Even though I had not gotten to know them well, my mind immediately began to call up the faces of gay men that Joan and Sarah had introduced me to. As soon as the broadcast was over, I picked up the phone and called Joan.

"Hey, what's up?" Joan chirped when she answered the phone.

"Got a minute?" I questioned.

"Sarah is in the middle of cooking dinner, and I am nursing a glass of wine at the counter. You got something you need to say?"

"Did you happen to catch the news this evening—NBC?"

"Nope, missed it. I just walked in the door a few minutes ago after being at the library all afternoon. My microbiology class is kicking my ass."

"Speaking of microbiology, there was a report that disturbed me."

"Really, what about?"

"There is this disease that has been going around with gay men causing things like Kaposi's sarcoma, unexplained pneumonia, and stuff. Apparently, a lot of gay guys are dying from it, and the CDC doesn't know what's going on."

"I had heard a little buzz about it at school, but I didn't know it had made the news."

"They think it is sexually transmitted and becoming epidemic."

"Jeez, and this just came out?"

"Yeah, the CDC is investigating. Apparently, it is lethal and breaks down a person's immune system."

"What the fuck?" she exclaimed, and there was a silence that followed.

"Are you there?" I asked after a moment.

"Yes. My mind is trying to wrap around how the hell an infectious disease can cause the immune system to shut down. Then I wonder how many of my friends may have already contracted it. Some of them fuck a lot."

"Yeah, I started thinking about some of the guys you introduced me to. I hope nothing happens to them."

"I know, right?"

"I mean, we are safe, aren't we? I don't have sex at all. The last time I had any sort of sexual contact was when I was being molested back at Pruitt Igoe, but they don't know that much about this yet. You and Sarah should be safe, shouldn't you? There's no reason you should get it? I mean, they don't know how it spreads, really, and we have all been around gay guys."

She sighed, and I could have sworn I heard her gulp the rest of her wine. "All I know," she said, "is that there is a lot more I need to know. I'm going to bring this up in my microbiology class and see what I can find out from recent publications in medical journals. I'm also going to ask Mom about it."

I took a tenuous breath. "It's just scary, that's all."

"Yeah."

"How is Sarah?"

"She's good. She almost has dinner ready. Can we chat more tomorrow or this weekend?"

"I'll be working, but sure. Whenever we can find the time."

That was only the beginning of the insidious and nocuous effect that AIDS had on America and the world. No one went unaffected by the tentacles of that hideous monster that cloaked itself beneath the surface of our collective psyche. Whether you had it or not, you probably knew someone who had it or was at risk of getting it. Whether you had it or not, you had an opinion about it, and any progress made toward a more tolerant and accepting world deteriorated into the politics of repudiation. It got much worse over the coming years, and the 1980s was certainly no picnic, at least not in the gay community. In the early days, they really didn't know for sure how it could be transmitted, if it was just sexually transmitted like gonorrhea or syphilis, or if there could be other routes of transmission. The more they learned, the more frightening it became. Gay people became the new lepers, and gay rights were set back another decade or more. There were also groups like ACT UP that started protesting the government's sluggish response to the pandemic. It seemed they thought it was just a gay disease, and the easier thing to do was let them die. Then news came out that it was rampant in Africa, that drug addicts were getting it by sharing needles, and that it was also spread through heterosexual contact. Had it happened in the sixties, I was certain that my mother would have contracted it.

One of Joan and Sarah's friends contracted AIDS in 1985 and died in 1987. At least 1985 was when they discovered it. Joan said he had been showing initial symptoms as far back as 1978 that had confused his doctors. Who knows how many other men could have been infected during that time? Apparently, it could take years before the full impact of the disease set in. That alone was frightening. I went with them to visit him at his apartment one day and felt like I was looking at a holocaust victim. He was so emaciated and weak that it appeared to be a chore for him to even walk across the room; he was only twenty-four. Despite all the assurances that we couldn't get it by visiting with him, my implausible fear would accept no assuagement. What if I had touched something that he had touched? Since he had a dog, what if a flea had bitten him, and what if it bit me? After all, the Bubonic Plague had been spread by fleas. On that day and long after, my apprehension became overwhelming, but I wasn't the only one suffering. It became so prevalent in society that it became known as AFRAIDS. Far more people had AFRAIDS than ever contracted AIDS, and I'm sorry to say that I had an unrelenting case. Since they said that the incubation period for AIDS could be ten or twelve years, my mind went back to Jake and Ronza and whether they might have infected me when they molested me. There certainly was no such thing as *protection* with what they did.

It didn't matter that I had no sexual contact with anyone since becoming an adult. I had been around Joan's gay friends. I knew there were times when someone handed me a drink, "Here, taste this," and I took a sip without giving it a second thought. There were times I had sat across the dinner table from gay men, shared appetizers, and dipped in the same dip bowl. My mind tormented me with the idea that I would die, just like they were dying, even though I had done nothing that could have been determined as high-risk behavior. I had finally reached a point when things were going well, and I felt reasonably safe and comfortable with life, but AFRAIDS brought that to a screeching halt. I didn't even want to work at the bar anymore. AFRAIDS, combined with my general distrust of strangers, became almost overwhelming. Even though it wasn't a gay bar, my job meant milling around in close contact with all kinds of people. My mind regressed into torment.

I got to the point where I had to talk myself into going to work. I could have quit. It wasn't like I needed the money, but I also needed to get out of the house and do something besides vegetate. I did my best to go on as usual. I acted like everything was okay, but my mind constantly tormented me about AIDS. I had hesitated about having sex since my surgery. Not only was I unsure of and had trepidatious about what it might be like physically, I didn't know how a man might react if he found out that I wasn't born female or if I even wanted to let a man get that close to me, especially a stranger. I damn sure was not going to sleep with anyone after that horrible disease started going around. The last thing I needed was another reason to be afraid. Yet, life gives us reasons.

I returned to my therapist; we had a new issue to discuss this time. I continued to ruminate wildly about contracting AIDS and dying. Then, one day, after a few months of biweekly therapy sessions, I was walking to work with my mind barely paying attention to my surroundings as it wallowed in dreadful agitation when a different thought popped into my awareness: *What difference does it make what you die of or when? Everybody has to do it.* For some reason, that allowed me to relax and brought my mind off AFRAIDS into mindfulness and awareness of the present. I noticed colorful flowers with delicate petals blooming in concrete pots that the city had positioned along the streets. I felt and heard my feet clumping against the sidewalk as each step became a rhythm. I noticed the faces of passing strangers, the colors and patterns of their clothing, their expressions, and their reactions to the world around them, and I began to smile. After a few minutes, another thought came to me: *It is not until we accept—not just admit—but fully accept that we are going to die that we truly begin to live. Life is in this moment, and this moment deserves my living it.* AFRAIDS was over.

In the autumn of 1986, I turned around one day, early in my shift, when no one was in the bar yet, and saw Glen Tucker sitting there. He was older, of course, more filled out in the face, more mature in his appearance, but there was no mistaking him. It was odd to suddenly see the adult man where the boy had once been. Since my only emotional reference was the boy who tormented me in high school, my face flushed as anger and anxiety permeated my body.

"*Shit!*" I heard myself exclaim under my breath. The last thing I wanted to do was wait on Glen Tucker. Yet, there the mother fucker sat at my bar. A flashback of high school torture excelerated my heart, and I was teetering on a panic attack when I told myself, *Keep your shit together, Steph! You can do this! Maybe he won't recognize you.* After all, I had surgical changes since the last time he had seen me, and he had never seen me since I had matured into my Goldilocks titties. I quickly decided to pretend like I didn't know him.

"What'll you have, buddy?" I snapped as I slapped a paper napkin in front of him."

"Budlight, if you have it." He replied.

"Of course we have it," I returned as I pulled a Budlight out of the chiller, snapped the lid off, and set it on the napkin before him. "You gonna want another; want to run a tab?"

"I'll run a tab," he replied.

Shit! I found myself thinking. *Mother fucker is going to be here all night.*

Then he asked the question that I least wanted to answer.

"Hey, you look familiar. Do I know you?"

"I don't think so," I sternly replied. "And don't get any ideas. I don't sleep around."

"Oh, No! No! I didn't mean to give you the impression I was coming onto you. I—I'm not coming onto you—really. It's just that your face looks familiar to me for some reason."

"Well, you don't look like anyone I want to know," I said as I turned away from him and tried to find something to keep myself busy. What I told him was the truth. He was not someone I ever wanted to know.

He called from behind me as I was straightening glasses on the rack. "Hey, I thought bartenders were supposed to be friendly. You don't seem very friendly."

"I'm as friendly as I have to be," I flatly announced without turning around.

Then, something else happened that I absolutely did not want to happen. Someone else came in. One of our regulars, Mark Cushman, was planting himself at the bar and called out, "Hey Stephanie, the usual please."

I felt myself trembling. I should not have been trembling. I had faced much worse, but I felt like my life was on the line. I was terrified that I was about to be exposed, outed by the same bastard who had tormented me in high school. What if he put two and two together? What if the house of cards I had built was about to come tumbling down?

"Sure, Mark," my voice cracked. "Whisky sour coming right up."

I turned to make the drink without looking at Glen, hoping he wouldn't get it, but the wheels in his pathetic brain had already started turning. Initially, softly, he said, "Stephanie?" Then he got louder, "Stephanie … Oh my God! You're Stephanie Laroquette! I do know you!"

I ignored him and placed the whisky sour in front of Mark, who was sitting about three stools down from Glen.

"Yeah, Stephanie's a great gal and a great bartender," Mark affirmed.

"I'm sure," Glen tipped his beer toward Mark.

The term, *Mother fucker* jolted through my mind, and I felt my teeth clench as I continued trying to ignore Glen.

Then, he turned his attention to me—just where I didn't want it. Not only did I not want to deal with him, but I didn't want any of my customers to know anything about my past, and there sat the potential to destroy everything I had built for myself since I came back to St. Louis. "So, Stephanie, how have you been? How have things been going? You look really different."

Fuck! I wanted to snatch the beer out of his hand and tell him to get out. I wanted to dash back into the alley, scream and run. I wanted to punch him in the face, but the last fucking thing I wanted was a conversation with him. I continued to ignore him, and his demeanor began to change.

"Look, Stephanie, can I talk to you?"

"No," I flatly replied.

"Damn!" Mark chimed in. "You two ex-lovers or something? Looks like somebody trying to make up for a bad breakup."

"It was a bad break up," Glen replied to him, "A very bad break up, and Stephanie … " He turned back to me. "I'm sorry. I am really, really, sorry for everything I did to you and for what happened to you."

"Sounds like this needs to be a private conversation," Mark announced as he got up and carried his drink to the nearby pool room, where he began rounding the pool table to pick a cue.

Glen sat looking at me. A sadness had come over him. He said nothing else until Mark had left the area.

"What I did to you in high school was horribly immature," he began, "but more than that, it was appallingly wrong. For years, I have wished I could apologize to you, but you disappeared after that incident—you know. I didn't know what happened to you after that. Some kids started spreading a rumor that you had died. I didn't know what was true and what wasn't, but I prayed for you to be okay."

"Okay, Glen … Well, you clocked me, but enough was enough," I replied. "I have had more than enough hell for more than one lifetime. I don't need to be reminded of any of the hell I've been through."

"I just want you to know that I'm sorry, and I didn't have anything to do with what happened, those guys beating you up," he confessed in almost a whisper, "but I knew it was going to go down. They tried to get me to join in, but I told them no way. Still, I never told anyone. I should have gone to the principal or maybe the police. I knew what they were going to do, and I didn't do anything to stop it. I didn't know it was going to be that bad, but I figure, by standing back and letting it happen, instead of trying to stop it, I am as guilty as they are."

A tear rolled slowly over his cheek.

I said nothing but stood there watching him, trying to discern if he was sincere.

"I've lived with that guilt ever since high school, for years," he went on. "I suffer with that regret every day, and not just because I tormented you, but because I let the worst possible thing happen and didn't try to stop it. Nobody should ever have to go through what you went through."

More tears came, and he wiped them with the back of his sleeve. "Do you think … that you could ever find a way to forgive me? I mean … I have hoped for this day, prayed for a day when I could see you again, tell you that I'm sorry, and ask for your forgiveness. I thank God that I just happened to choose this bar today. I'm not usually downtown, but I met with a client and happened to wander in here."

I felt tears beginning to drift and grabbed a napkin to try to blot back my mascara. What was I supposed to say? I had every reason to hate him, especially knowing he had let the beating happen and didn't try to stop it. I had tried to forget about that. I had tried to forget all the hatred dumped onto me for most of my life. I had never been able to understand it or why it happened. It had made no sense to me that people would try to hurt or kill me just for being who I am. Then, it was almost as though he read my mind.

"I don't hate you, Stephanie," he continued. "I never did. I know I acted like I hated you in high school, but I think what I really hated was what you represented. You didn't follow the rules, what we were always taught, how we are supposed to be as guys, you know? You were the opposite of that. I bought into the macho bullshit. I guess we don't realize how much "*be a man*" is brainwashed into us, like you can't be anything else, like you have to live up to some stupid standard that nobody fits, as though there aren't other ways of being a man besides some regulated warmongering bullshit that somebody came up with thousands of years ago. I think I hated that you didn't follow the rules when I had to and felt like I had no choice but to follow the rules. You were changing the fucking rules. Now, I admire that."

"What do you want from me, Glen?" I asked.

"Nothing," he replied. "You don't owe me a damn thing, not even your forgiveness."

"You know, forgiveness is not something I can just pull out of my ass," I scoffed.

"Speaking of which," he smiled. "Have you ever figured out how to watch your ass without rearview mirrors?"

A quick burst of humor parted my lips. I couldn't help it. "It's a much nicer ass to watch than it used to be," I commented and smiled.

"Indeed, agreed," he affirmed.

"Another beer?" I questioned when I noticed he was nearing the bottom of his first bottle.

"Sure."

I pulled another Budlight out and served it to him.

"Cheers," he said as he raised the bottle toward me and sipped.

"So, what about you?" I asked and turned the discussion away from me. "What have you been up to? Married, got kids?"

"Gay," he quietly replied. "I'm gay."

"What the fuck!" I heard myself exclaim.

"I guess that's one of the reasons I tormented you so much," he continued. "Maybe I hated myself for being like you. Maybe I hated that you openly displayed what I was trying so desperately to hide. I felt threatened by you. Who the fuck would care about me if they knew I was gay? I saw what you were going through, not just with me, and I damn sure didn't want that. I knew if they found out, I would be fucked over just as much as you were. Maybe jumping on you served to throw the sent off my trail. Anyway, I finally got real with myself, at least partially real. I finally admitted who I am."

"Jeez … " My tone changed to compassion. "You safe?"

"Not really."

"What do you mean, 'not really,'" I asked.

"HIV positive."

"Oh my God, Glen. I'm sorry." A mix of emotions rolled over me. I saw the wash of anxiety rush over him. That was hard to confess, even to someone else who was gay. You never knew who would reject you, even among your own. In the days of the AIDS epidemic, nobody really knew who was safe or who wasn't unless they confessed to having HIV. Some gay guys who had their own case of AFRAIDS went overboard trying to protect themselves from getting it. Some guys stuck their heads in the sand and fucked like the virus didn't exist.

Some could walk around looking perfectly healthy and spread the virus because they hadn't started showing symptoms and hadn't been tested. In those days, about the only connection gay men had to each other were bars, bathhouses, and hook ups. Society despised and drove gay people into the shadows and punished them for being there. Not only were you not allowed to be a part of society, but how dare you *not* be the way that society demanded? As long as you kept your mouth shut and pretended that you weren't gay, some people would look the other way, but what you damn sure did not want to do was openly display what they didn't want to look at and wanted to pretend didn't exist.

The medical field had only recently come out with a test for HIV at that time. There was precious little in the way of treatment, and who knew who had slept with whom. Bathhouses continued to offer the option of indiscriminate and often anonymous sex. Also, there was a phenomenon for many young gay men when they first came out during that time of repression: they could feel like a kid in a candy store filled with delicious men. When they realized that there were lots of men who would sleep with them, they slept with lots of men. Society didn't allow gay people to marry or have legitimate relationships anyway. So, why not just fuck around? In the seventies and eighties, almost all gay society was like that. Stonewall had only occurred in 1969, and acceptance in mainstream society was nowhere near getting started when AIDS came along, and it set the clock back almost to the beginning.

Unlike gay men, I had a way out. I was different, or at least thought I was, and I had options. I had the money to have surgery, hormone treatments, and pretend like I wasn't really a part of the gay community, but the gay community always seemed to find me. I wasn't even around other transsexual women except for a couple whom I met while going through medical procedures, and I had no exposure to things like Ballrooms and scenes in places like New York or San Francisco. Who knows? I might have been in the same predicament as Glen if I had been more closely associated with gay culture or on the streets fighting for my life instead of being set up with money. As much as I had hoped to fit into life as a heterosexual woman and pretend that I wasn't a part of gay culture, I was part of it. I could pass as a biological woman, but it didn't matter. I had to accept that I was a part of gay culture. The fact that I had never slept with anyone gave me a sense of separation, not only from being part of the gay rights movement or gay society but from AIDS. It was at least some comfort to know that I had never been with any man, much less a gay man.

"No need to be sorry," Glen replied, pulling me out of my doldrums. "It's the cards that life dealt me, karma, I guess, for how I treated you."

My heart sank, and I reached across the bar to place my hand over his. "Nobody should suffer like that and die for being a stupid kid. Please don't think of it that way."

"Who knew that having sex with two or three guys could give you AIDS," he continued. "I didn't even sleep around, but I never asked or even thought of asking how many they had slept with."

"Hopefully, there will be a cure soon," I commented.

"Time will tell, I guess, but I don't have a lot of hope in that," he replied. "So, I either have to be celibate or only practice safe sex, if you can call anything safe with this shit. If I tell a guy who I like that I have it, he may just walk away. I guess that's the safest sex of all."

"No steady lover?" I asked.

"You know there is a joke going around," he said. "What does a lesbian bring to a second date? —*A moving truck.* What does a gay guy bring to a second date? —*What second date?* There seem to be precious few gay men who are even remotely interested in settling down and trying to create a family. It is easier to fuck around than have meaningful connections. It's easier to go out late at night and try to fly under the radar; easier to hide that way. Maybe it was just easier for me. Besides, America doesn't really want to let us be seen in the daylight. They try every day to suppress our right even to exist, much less have equal rights like marriage or protection from getting fired if your bigot boss happens to find out. If you live with someone, your neighbors and your family ask questions. It's easier, safer, to remain stealth at the edge of the faint glimmer of streetlights in the darkness than to let them see us in broad daylight."

"You haven't told your family?" I asked.

"Shit! My dad? My fucking, macho by the book, slap the Bible and rant, dad? Why the fuck would I tell him? I would be blocked from coming home from seeing other family. I would be cut out of the will, which would be the least of what I would have to put up with if he knew. I guess HIV will force me to tell him sooner or later, and he will find out anyway. Then, I will not only have to deal with dying, but I will also have to deal with being hated by my own father while I'm dying."

"Maybe your dad will come around." I tried to comfort him. "Maybe he would surprise you and love you anyway."

"Not likely," he sighed. "I was more his project than his son."

"I'm sorry," I said. "I guess I'm lucky that I don't have to worry about that, at least not anymore."

"That old black lady that adopted you. She's cool about it, right?"

"She died when I was seventeen, but yes, she was cool about it."

I still had difficulty admitting to myself that Miss Mattie had died. I had never stopped missing her, and even though I had slept with her pillow clutched to my chest every night since I left Pruitt Igo, sometimes I would forget the grief lurking beneath the surface.

"I'm sorry," he quietly remarked.

"I'm okay," I replied. "At least I'm getting okay. I'm sorry you can't have a good relationship with your father. It sucks when your own family won't accept you."

A quick rush of air came up from his lungs. "It is what it is, I guess. Since I'm HIV positive, who knows how long I'll have? Who knows how long till I have to face him with it? In the meantime, when I'm with him, I pretend I am what he expects me to be."

He had finished his second beer and set the empty bottle on the bar.

"Look, Stephanie," he faintly smiled. "I've got to go. If I give you my number, would you call me sometime?"

"What for?" I asked.

"Maybe spend some time. Maybe let me try to make up for the shit I did to you in high school. Maybe … I hope … be friends?"

My ambivalence was evident in my expression.

"Look, it's okay." He plopped a wad of cash onto the bar and got up. "I get it. I don't blame you. I probably wouldn't want anything to do with me either if I were you."

"Sure," I heard myself saying, and I reached next to the cash register to get a little notepad and a pen. I handed him the pen and paper, and he scribbled his name and number. "You want my number?" I asked.

"No," he said as he pushed the notepad back across the bar. "If you call me, I'll know it is because you are open to more talks. If you don't, I will understand. I don't want you to feel any obligation, and I don't want you concerning yourself that I might call you up if you are not sure yet."

He reached his open hand across the bar as a gesture to shake mine. I reached across and shook his hand.

"Bye now," he said. Then, he turned to walk through the door at the front of the bar and stepped onto the sidewalk into a cold Missouri drizzle.

CHAPTER 17

NO ACCOUNTING FOR FATE

A few weeks after I saw him in the bar, I called Glen and left a voicemail that only said, "Hi, this is Stephanie. I just want you to know that I forgive you. I hope nobody ever keeps resenting me for the stupid shit I did in high school. We were both young and stupid. I want you to know that I've thought about it, and I forgive you. I'm not going to call you again, but you are welcome to stop in at the Pub if you ever want to talk to me. I'll be happy for you to stop by any time. I work every Friday through Tuesday evening."

He never stopped by the pub again, and I never saw him again. I never knew if he lived or died or whatever happened to him. I only knew that I honestly did forgive him. Having him come into the bar caused me to think a lot, though. I thought about people I had known in school, the McNeils, and many different people who influenced and impacted my life. Most I would probably never see again. One of them was Mike Foster.

Over the years, I had thought a lot about Mike, but that's all I had done, think about him. I often wondered how he was doing or whether he had even survived prison. Now and then, I had heard stories about men being murdered in prison, but there was no way I could find out how Mike was doing, or at least that's what I thought. I wished I could see him, but I knew there was likely no way they would ever let me in as a visitor. I hoped I could know something, but I had no idea how.

In mid-October of 1986, I had sat down with a TV dinner. I started watching the local news when the news anchor said, "Convicted murderer Mike Foster was in court again today on his third appeal to overturn his 1972 conviction for the murder of Mable Saunders at Pruitt Igoe."

The television image switched from the news anchor to a courtroom where Mike stood handcuffed in a prison uniform before a judge. He was standing next to a well-dressed man who, I assumed, must have been his attorney. I gasped at the sight of Mike on the TV with the obvious stenciling of age. Perhaps he had aged quicker by being in prison, but I had remembered him as young and handsome. I set my TV dinner on the end table by my sofa, got up, and walked across the room to my television to get a better look. It had been sixteen years since I had seen even an image of him. Prison had obviously taken a toll on him. He looked gaunt, and his hair had become a salt-and-pepper gray. Yet, it was evident that I was looking at the image of the man I loved.

The announcer continued speaking as the camera panned the almost empty courtroom. The appeals court, however, was having nothing of it or the new type of evidence from DNA that Mike's attorney sought to introduce. The judge ruled that evidence of alternative DNA found at the scene was insufficient to establish reasonable doubt but noted that the fact that Mable's blood was found on Mike's clothing and his blood and DNA was found under her fingernails was an indication that he was at the murder scene with a sufficient motive to kill her. Nothing was mentioned of the long-disputed evidence that neither Mike's shoes nor his shoe size matched adult footprints found in the blood at the murder scene. They assumed he had an accomplice who was never located, even though Mike denied an accomplice and always proclaimed his innocence.

My heart sank into a pool of sadness. Memories of Pruitt Igoe and images of Mike when I had known him began to flood my vision. I wondered if he had felt forgotten after all that. I was sure that he must have lost his family and probably lost contact with his children, but I didn't know. His kids would have been adults then, and perhaps he even had grandchildren he had never seen. Who knew? What I did know was his innocence. I had always known it. I knew that my so-called mother's blood on his shirt and jacket was from the fight the day before she was killed and that he would never kill her. He just wasn't the kind of person to murder someone. I felt it in my heart even though I couldn't be confident that my heart knew the truth. The more I thought about it, the sadder I became, and for the first time, it occurred to me that I could write him a letter.

On October 21, 1986, I sat down and wrote to him. I told him I would like to visit but assumed the prison authorities wouldn't let me do that. I explained my experiences and changes since he last saw me and told him about having been molested by Jake. I affirmed knowing that he didn't kill Mable, that he didn't deserve to go to prison, and that I prayed he was well. Before I mailed it, I had Joan take a picture of me with my old Polaroid, and I placed it in the envelope. I put on one of my prettiest dresses and smiled at the camera while standing at the wall between my living room and bedroom. I looked up the address for the penitentiary and mailed the letter in care of the Warden. I could not know if the letter would ever reach Mike, but I had to try. Even if he got the letter, I didn't know if I would ever receive any correspondence back. I had no idea how he might react to my letter or what he might think about my transition and confessions, but to be sure he knew who the letter was from, I wrote *Stephen Saunders* above the return address.

Months went by. Thanksgiving and Christmas passed, and I spent the holidays with Joan and her family as usual. Even though I loved them and loved spending time with them, it was not lost on me that I didn't have a family of my own. The only semblance of a real family I had ever had was during the few short years with Miss Mattie. I had a loneliness that had nothing to do with the Wilsons. I knew they loved me, and I also loved them. Having no doubt of their love, I knew they weren't my real family. They were just extremely good friends. I resolved myself to the fact that I would likely never have a real family, and I determined that I was okay with always being alone. It took me a while to realize, like Kurt Vonnegut said, "A purpose of human life, no matter who is controlling it, is to love whoever is around to be loved." I finally came to understand the real meaning of family. My mother and grandmother were blood, but they were horrible people. Miss Mattie had no kin to me but was absolutely my true mother. Years later, I understood that bonds of spirit are much more important than bonds of flesh.

Christmas came and went, and I didn't hear back from Mike. So, I assumed that either my letter never reached him or that he chose not to respond. The weeks passed, and I finally began letting go of hope that he would ever write back to me. I stopped pulling my mail out of the box daily, looking through it for a letter from Mike. I assumed I would never hear from him, so I went back to only checking my mail every two or three days.

New Year's Eve came around, and of course, I had to work at the pub. The weather didn't look promising, and there was a forecast for snow and freezing rain. The weather may have stopped some people from coming out, but bad weather or not, every bar was crowded on New Year's Eve, and Willard's was no exception. There were several of our usual customers there. Some had brought relatives who had not yet gone home after their Christmas visit. Some people, who weren't regulars, just stumbled in off the street. We had three bartenders and two barbacks working that night, and every damn one of us was busy as hell. There may not have been as many people in the bar as there might have been had the weather not turned dreadful, but there were significantly more than usual. The bar was packed beyond what the fire marshal would have legally allowed, but hell, it was New Year's Eve, and nobody was checking.

I was working my ass off, just like the other two bartenders, when one of the regulars started motioning me over to the end of the bar. His name was Dennis Walker, and he was a nice man about the same age as Mike, in his late forties or early fifties. He worked downtown, and I had waited on him almost every weekday evening that I was on the job for a couple of years. He would stop in after the workday, about ten minutes after 5:00 p.m., and order scotch on the rocks. He would drink just one, tip me twice as much as most people would have, and before he got off the bar stool to go home, he would always tell me to "be a good girl." He was a joyful, friendly kind of guy with thinning hair, thick dark glasses, and the beginnings of middle age spread.

"Hey, Stephanie! Stephanie!" I could barely hear him over the roar in the pub. He was motioning, hand above the crowd, for me to come to the end of the bar. I assumed he wanted a drink and immediately pulled the scotch off the shelf to pour his usual. I took it to him and realized that he was already quite tipsy.

"Oh, thanks, sweetheart," He grinned. "You didn't have to do that. I just wanted to introduce you to someone."

We had to yell to be heard. I looked over to see his arm around a very handsome young man with pale red hair and blue eyes that gleamed like a swimming pool on a sunny day. He had a hint of freckles and stood probably a couple of inches over six feet tall.

"This is my nephew, Jordan Walker, my brother's oldest son."

"Hi, how do you do?" I shouted over the roar and reached to shake hands with him.

"Hi!" Jordan reached around his uncle, over the end of the bar, to shake my hand. "Very nice to meet you."

"This is Stephanie Laroquette," Dennis shouted to Jordan through the slurred words of intoxication. "Isn't she about the prettiest girl you ever saw?"

"Indeed!" Jordan smiled back at him. Then he turned back to me, looked me straight in the eye, and said again, "Indeed, definitely."

"Oh shit," I thought to myself. "Dennis is trying to set me up with his nephew."

I was suddenly nervous feeling timid. Never in my life had anything like that happened. I was overwhelmed, flattered, but also frightened. I didn't know what the hell to do.

"It's very nice to meet you," I shouted with a smile, "but I have to get back to work. Can I get you anything?"

"Sure," Jordan replied, "Budweiser, please."

"Draft or bottle?" I shouted back.

"Draft, please," he shouted.

His eyes were stunning. I couldn't stop looking at his eyes; he was obviously looking at me. Each glance seemed to increase the magnetism between us. There is a sense one gets when the attraction is more than sexual and when there is a hope of more than just some physical tryst. I had that sense with him. I wasn't seeing lust in his eyes. I was seeing something else. He was polite, not pushy at all, and I felt a tingling in my heart when I looked at him. Still, in the back of my mind, the question always loomed, as it did with any man who showed even a remote interest in me, "What would he do if he knew?" No matter how nice a man might be, I always feared that there might be a misogynistic core that wouldn't accept me and could be abusive.

I poured him a draft, brought it back to the end of the bar, and Dennis pushed a wad of cash into my hand. "I've got it! I've got it!" he shouted at Jordan.

I looked down at the wad of bills in my palm. "Dennis, this is too much," I shouted back. There were two twenties and a ten in my palm.

"Nah! Nah! Nah!" he shouted back at me as he began to turn back into the crowd. "You keep the change. You're worth it, darlin'."

I looked at Jordan with a look of exasperation. He merely shrugged his shoulders and smiled. Then he disappeared into the crowd.

Things continued to be a little rowdy, but by the time everyone shouted the countdown at the New York ball drop showing on our TVs, more than a third of the crowd cleared out, perhaps trying to beat the weather. Then there was the countdown to Midnight in St. Louis, and when it came an hour later, several people stepped out onto the street to watch the fireworks over the Gateway Arch. Then, the bar thinned out earlier than usual.

Willard, the pub owner, who had been there assisting all evening, came around and announced that we would close an hour early because of the weather and announced the last call at a quarter to 1:00 a.m. I noticed that Jordan was still in the bar but couldn't see any sign of Dennis. Jordan had never come to order another drink, but when the last call was given, he came and planted himself at the bar.

"What can I get you?" I asked him.

"Another Bud would be nice, thank you," he smiled.

When I brought the beer, he said, "So, tell me more about Stephanie Laroquette."

"She's pretty much a closed book," I replied. "People can look at the cover, but very few ever get to read what's inside."

"I hope I get to read what's inside," he smiled.

I felt myself blush, and heat rushed into my face. I was flat out, fucking scared to death. Should I give him the cold shoulder, and try to get him off my trail, or should I be friendly and take a considerable chance? Because Dennis was a regular, I didn't want to be unfriendly to his nephew.

"Where's Dennis?" I asked, looking around the bar. "I haven't seen him in a while."

"Oh, my dad took him home almost two hours ago. He was getting sauced, and they also wanted to try to beat the weather."

"Is he okay?" I asked.

"Yeah, he's fine," Jordan smiled as he sipped on his draft. "He just got a little drunk, that's all."

"Your dad was here?"

"Yeah, Sorry I didn't introduce you, but we were kind of occupied trying to contain Uncle Dennis. Then Dad decided that he should probably take him home."

"Why didn't you go with them?" I asked.

"Didn't want to," was his quick and brief reply.

The other staff and I were cleaning up the bar at the end of the shift. I was wiping down the bar and going into the main room to pick up the glasses off the tables. The barbacks were busy at the sinks, try-ing to get everything cleaned up before closing.

"You should probably be heading home, yourself," I suggested, "before it gets so bad you can't."

"Don't have a car," He flatly replied. "We all rode together, and Dad used the car to take Uncle Dennis home."

"What the hell do you think you are going to do?" I asked.

"I told Dad there are hotels around, and I can always get a room, or maybe I could take a cab home."

I rolled my eyes, assuming he hoped he would get invited to my place. My previous thoughts about him genuinely liking me flipped into feeling like a piece of meat that he was trying to pursue so he could get his rocks off. "That is if all the hotels aren't already booked for New Year's," I said.

"So, what do you normally do after work, Stephanie Laroquette?" he asked.

I thought, *Shit! Here we go, the lead-in for an expected score.* Then, I was terse with him, "I go home, to bed—alone."

At that point, he had the perfect opportunity for some hokey come-on, such as offering to keep me company so I didn't have to sleep alone on a cold night, but he was a perfect gentleman.

"Breakfast sure sounds good after a night like this," he commented. "You have worked pretty hard. I'll bet you are hungry. Is there any kind of all-night breakfast place around here? Either breakfast or a burger sounds good to me."

"Yeah, I guess," I replied, my faith in him only slightly renewed. "There is an all-night breakfast joint a few blocks away."

"Can I take you to breakfast?" he asked. "Will the breakfast joint be open on New Year's morning?"

I hesitated. My mind reeled. He noticed me hesitating.

"Can I?" he questioned again with those gleaming blue eyes fixed on me as he watched me roll around in my ambivalence.

"I think the proper grammar is 'may I,'" I replied.

A huge grin crossed his face. "May I take you to breakfast, Stephanie Laroquette?"

"You seem to like the sound of my name," I said.

"I do, indeed, love the sound of your name," His face beamed like a neon sign. "It is definitely a very beautiful name."

"Thank you."

"So, *may* I take you to breakfast?"

"You know that we will not be done here for about another hour, right?" I was very matter-of-fact with him. "By the time we walk over there, especially in this weather, and have breakfast, it will be at least 4:00 a.m. or after, and I don't know where you are staying. You haven't booked a hotel room?"

"Not yet," he replied, but I'm sure it can't be that difficult, especially in the morning when rooms start to clear out. There are several hotels downtown."

"You assume they aren't fully booked for New Year's Eve," I cautioned. "A lot of people come into town to see the fireworks and celebrate."

"I might just have to get myself arrested." He grinned.

"That's not funny." I flatlined him.

"Sorry, maybe I could bribe a concierge into letting me sleep in the lobby of one of these places, or maybe I could just spend the night at the breakfast joint. I'll figure something out, but I would like nothing more than to have a conversation with you over breakfast, face to face, with no distractions."

"Oh, there are distractions in a breakfast joint, honey," I explained. "You've heard that the freaks come out and night? Lord only knows what we might see in there on New Year's Eve."

"Well, it will be entertaining either way. So, what do you say, Stephanie Laroquette?" He propped his chin on the backs of his hands, elbows to the bar, and fluttered his eyelashes at me. I couldn't help laughing.

"Okay, okay," I surrendered, "but you don't know what you are getting yourself into."

He looked up at me with the most beautiful smile. "I can't wait," he said. "I want to read the book cover to cover."

Not once had he made any suggestion about staying at my place. Maybe he really was a gentleman, and maybe I was overreacting.

"Anything I can do to help you guys close up?" he asked.

Willard, the owner, had been watching this whole process between Jordan and me while he continued darting around helping with the clean-up.

"Steph, go on," Willard said. "We've got this."

"Are you sure?" I asked. "I don't want to leave you stuck with cleanup."

"Absolutely sure," he responded. "I hired extra help tonight. You and Romeo, there, go have a bite to eat. Have a little fun. Happy New Year's."

"Thanks, Willard," I said. I tossed the glasses I was holding into the sink and patted him on the arm as I walked from behind the bar, "I owe you one."

"No, you don't, kid," he replied. "You've earned more than an hour off. Now, go on."

Jordan stood up to meet me when I came around the bar.

"Come on, Romeo," I said. "Daddy Willard said to go have a bite to eat."

I went to the store room behind the bar and got my coat, galoshes, and umbrella. I came out, sat at one of the tables, and put the fur-lined galoshes over my flats that I wore to tend bar. Jordan grabbed his overcoat from the back of a nearby chair and sat across from me as I bundled up.

When we stepped out of the bar onto the icy street, he came up beside me and asked, "May I hold your arm? It's kind of slippery out here."

I gave him a questioning look. I had never been on a date before. This seemed like a date. I had no idea what was supposed to happen except for what I may have seen in romantic comedies, and this was surely different from the average date. Was it even a date at all?

"I guess," I hesitantly replied.

Jordan reached over and took my arm. He held my umbrella over us, but it didn't help much, and we slid and laughed more than walked four blocks to the breakfast place in the crisp and biting freezing rain. To my amazement, it was open, but only one other table had customers. Some guy at the bar looked like he might have been homeless. He was talking to himself over his cup of coffee.

"Let's sit at the bar," I suggested. "It will be nice to be on this side for a change."

We initially ordered at the bar and started to eat there, but decided to move to a booth when the homeless guy appeared to get a little too rowdy, shaking his fist at the ceiling and apparently having a heated conversation with God. We carried our plates to a booth by the window and listened to sleet and freezing rain pelting the glass and crusting itself atop the fallen snow.

"Have you lived in St. Louis all your life?" he asked.

"Yes," I replied as I sopped a piece of toast into the yolk of my eggs over easy. I most assuredly was not about to tell him about my six months in Baltimore.

"So, where did you go to school?" he continued.

"You know," I said and flipped the conversation. "I already told you that Stephanie Laroquette is a closed book, and most people never get to read her. Are you a closed book? Why don't you tell me where you grew up and went to school?"

He smiled broadly. "I grew up in Jefferson City," he replied, "and I attended school there till we moved to Columbia when I was sixteen, not that far away. I finished high school in Columbia. My favorite color is blue—more of a sky blue, not that dark stuff. My favorite food is pizza, and my favorite music is anything that doesn't scream at me. My favorite movie is "Amadeus." I go to the gym four or five times a week—more because I want to stay in shape than to become a muscleman. I believe that all religions have validity and that we all go to heaven. If God truly does love all of us, then no one will be left out. I have a degree in architectural engineering from Missouri S & T. I have a younger sister named Shawna and two younger brothers, Pete and Danny. I love to travel. I love eating out. I love football. I love watching people, and now I work for an architectural firm in St. Louis."

"How long have you lived here?" I asked.

"I just moved here about four months ago when I got a job with the company here." He never stopped smiling.

"Where do you live?" I asked.

"Ladue," he replied.

"Oh, holy shit!" I exclaimed, suddenly feeling terrified for no good reason.

"What?" He looked baffled.

"Nothing," I replied.

"Have I said something wrong?" he asked.

My mind was suddenly in the girl's bathroom in high school. I was a terrified teenager again and getting the living shit beaten out of me. What if he had neighbors who knew about that? What if there were still stories going around the community about it? I looked up at him, suddenly feeling extremely anxious. "I need to go to the restroom," I said as I dropped my fork onto my plate and slid out of the booth.

I rushed across the restaurant to the women's room, locked the door behind me, and stood with my back to the wall, panting like a dog, heart pounding, tears rolling down my cheeks.

"Shit! Shit!" I exclaimed aloud. "I shouldn't be feeling like this. I shouldn't be reacting like this! Why is this happening now? All he did was say 'Ladue,' and now I feel like I'm going fucking nuts!"

The mere mention of Ladue had thrown me into a full-blown panic attack with memories I didn't want flashing through my mind. I thought I was over that shit! I don't know why it triggered me, except that it felt like he had gotten too close to my past.

"It's only the name of a community," I told myself. "It's not like I haven't heard it before. What the fuck! Stop it, Stephanie!"

I pulled my dress up, dropped my pantyhose, and sat on the commode. I continued to cry and yanked wads of toilet paper off the roll to wipe the smeared makeup on my face. I didn't understand how specific thoughts could still overwhelm me all these years after the fact, but sometimes, something out of nowhere would set me up and level me. This time was worse than most. I had talked about Ladue before, and it didn't bother me. I asked myself, "Why now? What made this different? Maybe the very reason that I liked him made it different. Maybe knowing that he was kin to Dennis made it different. It was too close, too intimate."

I urinated, pulled out more toilet paper, and collected myself. I got up, flushed, and looked into the mirror to see that my makeup was an absolute fucking mess, and I didn't have my purse with me. I had left it on the booth. I wet some paper towels and attempted to wipe off the smeared makeup.

"Goddamn, it!" I heard myself exclaim. "What the hell am I going to tell him when I go back out there?"

Maybe he'll be gone, I thought as I cleaned my face the best I could. I hoped that he might have left. Then I startled and yelped when I heard a tapping at the door behind me. Jordan's voice came from the other side.

"Are you okay in there?" he asked. "I have been getting worried about you. I didn't mean to upset you. I'm sorry."

He had to have heard my outcry when he tapped at the door. I didn't know what the fuck to do. I was scared of what he might think.

"I'm fine," I lied. "I just had a little stomach upset. That's all. Maybe you should see if you can get a cab home or try to find a hotel."

"I want to know that you're okay," he comforted with a gentle and soothing voice.

"I'm fine. Really—I am," I continued to lie and felt my heart pounding again. "You go on. I can walk home from here. It isn't far."

"Stephanie," he sighed loud enough for me to hear it through the door. "I know you are not okay. I don't know what is wrong, but I know something is wrong, and it's not just your stomach. Please let me help."

"You can't help," I called back.

"I can at least give you a hug and let you know somebody cares," He reassured.

"I don't think that would help." I turned toward the mirror and wiped a cold, wet paper towel across my face. The cool water helped to calm me.

"Well, let me walk you home, at least, and make sure you are safe," He pleaded.

"I walk these streets five or six nights a week," I replied. "I'll be fine."

"That doesn't mean you'll be safe or have been safe when doing that. This is downtown St. Louis, for God's sake. It's not exactly a safe place at night."

Flabbergasted, I turned and opened the bathroom door to see him standing right there with my coat draped over his arm and purse in his hand.

"Okay! Here it is!" I exclaimed. "Now, you see me in my true form, a total fucking mess, an emotional mess, and a mess with makeup smeared across my fucking face like a horror movie freak!"

He raised a gentle hand and wiped a tear from my cheek with his thumb. "I still like you," He softly responded, "and you don't look anything like a horror freak to me."

When he did that, I broke down into sobs. He immediately took me into his arms and hugged me while I cried. He didn't say a word. He just let me cry. I had not felt that loved and comforted in years. I had not let anyone see the hurt inside me in years, and no one had gotten that close to me since Miss Mattie died, not even Joan. I didn't know what triggered it except that he said he lived in Ladue, and my mind went rushing back to all the cruelty and torment I had experienced there, including losing Miss Mattie. When it felt like I was finished crying, I began to pull back, but he had held me the entire time and only let go when I pulled back.

"I'm sorry," I said.

"Nobody ever needs to be sorry for crying," he reassured. "It's a beautiful thing if you stop to think about it. It cleanses the soul and lets the anguish out."

"Thank you," responded.

"Can I walk you home now?" he asked.

I wiped my cheeks with the palms of my hands. "I think the proper grammar is 'may I?'" I replied

He smiled and looked straight into my eyes with his beautiful blues and said, "May I walk you home now?"

"Sure," I replied, even then feeling uncertain about my response.

He helped me put on my coat. I gathered the rest of my things and the umbrella he had left at the table. I reached in my purse for my wallet and headed toward the cash register.

"I already paid," he said. "I assumed you probably didn't feel like finishing your meal."

I turned to meet him at the door, and we stepped back out into the cold Missouri winter just as dawn was peeping first light over the Gateway Arch. We walked to my building with him carefully holding me, so I didn't fall. When we arrived, I realized I had not checked my mail since the day after Christmas.

"Do you mind?" I asked. "I haven't checked my mail in a few days."

I stepped into the mail room just off the main lobby, placed my key into my mailbox, pulled out a small wad of envelopes, and returned to the lobby where he had waited for me. As I was flipping through them to see what junk mail I needed to toss into the trash before going upstairs, I came across an envelope with a return address from the penitentiary, and Mike's name was written above it. My heart pounded again, and Jordan saw the shock across my face.

"Is everything okay?" he asked.

I looked up at him with tears, once again, drizzling down my face. "It's a letter from an old friend," I said. "I haven't heard from him since I was little … I'll be okay."

"May I come up to your condo with you?" he asked.

I looked at him with a mix of distrust and longing, fighting for precedence in my head.

"Do you plan to stay?" I asked.

"Only if you want me to," he replied, "and if I stay, I will sleep on the couch. No questions asked, no expectations … Okay?"

"You assume I have a couch?" I half smiled. Trust and longing defeated distrust at that moment. I took his hand and led him to the elevator.

We took the elevator to my floor, and I led him down the hall to my condo. As we walked in, I set the letters on a side table by the front door and took hangers from the entry closet to hang up our coats.

"Aren't you going to read the letter from your friend?" he asked.

"Not now," I replied. "I'm drained. I need to go to bed."

He walked over to stand in front of the large window overlooking downtown St. Louis. "Very nice view," he commented.

I went to the linen closet to get him some sheets and blankets, took an extra pillow from my bed, and made a place on the sofa for him to sleep.

He sat down on the sofa and began removing his shoes. "Thanks," he said.

"No problem," was my reply.

I pointed to where the half bath was located in case he needed it before morning, closed the drapes, and went to my bedroom door. "I think I'm glad I met you, Jordan Walker," I said. "I'm not exactly sure yet, but I think I'm glad I met you."

"I definitely know that I am glad I met you, Stephanie Laroquette," he replied, looking up at me from the sofa where he had already laid down, clothes still on, shoes on the floor, and the blanket pulled up to his chest.

"Well, you have seen more of the inside of this closed book tonight than anyone has seen in many years," I said. "If that didn't scare you away, I don't know what would. What do you think?"

"I think it's a book I definitely want to read," He replied.

"Then, you must be as screwed up as I am."

"I don't think you're screwed up," he said. "I think you're hurt. There's a difference."

I looked into my room and felt torn whether I should offer to let him sleep in my bed, and then said. "Good night."

"Good night, Stephanie Laroquette," he smiled and snuggled into his pillow.

CHAPTER 18

LURKING SHADOWS

The morning did not exist on New Year's Day. Time passed in complete darkness and unconsciousness. The world outside was mostly silenced by people sleeping off a night of partying, and like being under sedation, I slept soundly, unaware until about 3:00 p.m. Finally, consciousness tugged my eyes open into the darkness of my bedroom, with the blackout blinds doing exactly what they were designed to do. I rolled over and flipped on my bedside lamp in a sleepy daze. Then, I got up and rummaged through my closet for my bathrobe, which was stuck in the back. I never had cause to wear it because I had never had overnight guests. However, if I was going to step into the living room and greet Jordan, I needed to be at least decent, if not entirely presentable.

When I opened the door to my living room, the blankets and sheets were neatly folded and on top of the pillow. He was gone. A note was scribbled onto a paper towel that lay atop the blankets.

Stephanie,

I had such a wonderful time with you last night. Thank you for letting me be there with you and allowing me to park on your couch. I hope we can see each other again and that you won't mind if I stop by Willard's now and then to chat with you. I wrote my number below in case you ever want to give me a call. I hope that you will. I really like you, and I want to know you better.

With deepest regards,

Jordan

I stood there staring at the note momentarily, torn between multiple feelings. On the one hand, I liked him too. He was cute, sweet, gentlemanly, and compassionate. I couldn't think of anything more that anyone would want in a man. However, the chances of him finding out about my past were pretty high, and would he be the same person if he were to find out that I had come from the slums, had a murdered drug whore mother, and started life in a male body? What I never wanted again was the kind of abuse, taunting, and disgust thrown at me when I was growing up. I had considered moving out of St. Louis, going somewhere that no one knew me, where some of the episodes of my past had not been broadcast on local news stations, where I could make up a story and live my life as someone else, maybe never having to reveal to anyone about my surgery, but I had stayed. I stayed for the town where I had been raised. I stayed for Joan and our friendship. I stayed because I had no assurance that any other place would be any better.

I determined that I would not call Jordan. I decided that I did not want to put bait in that possible trap. Although, I had no idea how I would react when he showed up at Willard's. I would cross that bridge when I got to it.

I left the sheets and pillows on the sofa, reached over to the coffee table, and grabbed the remote to turn on the TV. I flipped through the cable channels until I got to HBO and started watching a movie about halfway into the feature. I let the TV babble, went to the kitchen, started the coffee, and tossed half a bagel in the toaster. When I had my cream cheese-smeared bagel folded in a paper towel and a cup of black coffee in hand, I stopped by the side table to pick up the letters that I had brought up the night before. I sat on the sofa, staring at Mike's letter, and the TV suddenly went from background noise to annoying. Maybe my anxiety made me more sensitive, but the sound became so irritating that I had to pick up the remote and turn it off.

I took one bite of my bagel, chewed it slowly, and stared at the letter, wondering if I could even bring myself to open it. What would he say after getting a photo of me as a grown woman? The letter was addressed to Stephanie Laroquette. So, he, at least, used my real name, not the name I determined had died with Mabel. After arguing with myself for a while, I took a sip of coffee, set my mug on the coffee table, and began tearing into the back of the letter. I stopped briefly before getting to the last bit of flap, took a deep breath, and ripped it open. Then I read the letter in silence.

December 22, 1986

Dear Stephanie,

First, let me apologize for taking so long to write you back. I almost didn't, thinking that it is best to let sleeping dogs lie, but I have read your letter several times over the past couple of months and decided that you deserve at least my acknowledgment.

Next, let me say that I am so sorry for everything that happened to you as a child, that you were molested, that you had the mother you had, that you went through having her murdered, but I am also sorry for how I treated you. You said that I didn't deserve to go to prison, but yes, I did. You are right that I did not kill your mom, but I did plenty of other things that I just hadn't been caught for. I purchased illegal drugs. I used your mother as a prostitute, betrayed my wife and kids, and betrayed you by ignoring what you were going through. I had a problem. It wasn't drugs, but it was an addiction, nonetheless. I was addicted to excitement, getting away with things, secrecy, and lies. So, yes, I did deserve to go to prison. I just didn't deserve to go to prison for your mom's murder. I hope they find who did it someday, but I think they are more interested in having someone behind bars who didn't do it so they can say the case is solved than they are in finding out who really did it. Nonetheless, here I sit with appeal after appeal denied. If this will always be my fate, then I have to accept it.

You certainly have grown into a beautiful young woman. The photo you sent me is shocking to me. I remember you as a little boy. I can tell that it is you. I can tell by the structure of your face, even if you might have had surgery to change it. You may not like this, but you also look very much like your mom, except that you have obviously taken much better care of yourself. I don't know what it must be like for you to live your life that way. It is always difficult for others to comprehend what they have never experienced. All I know is that it is your life, and you have a right to live it. How you live it is none of my business, nor is it the business of anyone else.

If you want to write me again, I guess that would be okay.

Yours,

Mike Foster

I sat there holding the letter, feeling anxious and unfulfilled. I don't know what I hoped or expected from Mike, but I felt like I didn't get it. Maybe I hoped he would say, "Oh, you're a woman now. When I get out of prison, let's get married." Even though my adult self knew it was immature and unreasonable, that childhood fantasy persisted. I knew he was right that he deserved to go to prison for other things, but I hated that he had to be there and had a life sentence. I appreciated his honesty and that he didn't shame me for having transition surgery, but I don't know what I expected. All I knew was that I still felt like something was missing. I didn't know if I would write him back. There was a part of me that said, "Why bother?" I wasn't sure what else, if anything, I had to say. I couldn't save him, and he had to live out what life had dealt to him. I couldn't see how I could turn it into a friendship with him in prison, and even though I wanted to write back, I also felt like I should let it go.

I set the letter on the coffee table, flipped the TV back on, leaned over onto the folded sheets Jordan had slept on, and went back to watching

TV. The lingering scent of Jordan's cologne had found its way to the sheets and pillow. I threw the sheets over myself, nuzzled my head into the pillow, and repeatedly pulled the sheet to my nose to savor his seductive aroma as I watched TV or napped for the rest of the evening.

I enjoyed my New Year's Day off and did nothing but watch television. The following night was a Friday, and I had to work. The bar was not nearly as crowded as it had been on New Year's Eve, and the temperature had risen slightly above freezing, just enough to turn the left-over ice and snow into a dirty slush. I wondered if I would see Jordan enter the door, but he didn't. Instead, I came in to find a bouquet of yellow roses and a box of donuts with a note from Jordan saying, *I noticed the Barbie dressed in yellow above your TV and assumed that you must like yellow. Enjoy the flowers for as long as they last, and share some donuts with your coworkers. –Yours, Jordan.*

"That's it?" I heard myself mumble under my breath. In a way, it was romantic. In a way, it was weird. I didn't eat a donut, of course. I had stopped eating them years before when I discovered that each one had over half the daily fat recommendations, and the rest was just starch and sugar. The other bartender enjoyed a couple, and Willard had several. The rest I threw out at the end of the shift.

The following weekend, Jordan came in early in my shift, walked straight up to the bar, plopped himself on the stool, and said, "Hey, Stephanie Laroquette, I'll have a draft Budweiser, please." The grin on his face left minimal territory for anything else.

I didn't say a word but brought the beer. "You want to run a tab?" I asked.

"Sure," he replied, reaching for the mug handle and taking a swig of his beer.

There was practically no one else in the bar at that time, a couple of guys playing pool back in the pool area and one older man with the flush look of an alcoholic at the opposite end of the bar from Jordan.

"So, did you get the flowers and donuts?" he asked.

"Yes, that was very sweet of you," I replied.

"Did you like the donuts?" he continued. "They come from a little specialty bakery called Domingo's."

"Thank you. I don't eat donuts."

"What do you mean you don't eat donuts," he smirked. "Everybody eats donuts."

"I don't eat them." I smiled while I did some preparations for things to get busier later in the evening.

"Don't you like donuts?" he persisted.

"Of course I do. I love them, and that's the problem."

"Well, you can give yourself a little treat now and then," he teased again, with that gleaming grin that was almost impossible to resist.

"What is it with you and donuts?" I returned.

"You mean besides the fact that they are exceedingly delicious and Domingo's makes the best I've ever had?" He leaned forward onto the bar as though revealing some government secret to a spy. "When I was a kid, some of my fondest memories are of donuts. On Saturday, instead of my mom fixing breakfast, Dad would load us all into the car and take us to the donut shop. We could get any kind we wanted, and it was the one time we were allowed to have as much as we wanted. It was beautiful."

"And that's why you sent me donuts?" I mused.

"Not entirely," he replied. "When we were out on New Year's Eve, I noticed that you kept eyeing the donuts on the display counter at the breakfast joint."

"Oh, was I doing that?" I countered and lied. "I didn't really notice the donuts. I was thinking about how they display them and what they do to try to make them look appealing."

"Okay. No more donuts for you, Stephanie Laroquette." He took the last swallow of his beer and returned the mug to the counter. "How did you like the flowers?"

"They were beautiful," Thank you. "I took them home and set them on the counter between the kitchen and the living room. They lasted over a week."

"You never called me," he said flatly. "Did you lose my number?"

"No, I didn't lose it."

"Then why didn't you call me?"

I felt a rush of pressure in my chest, a sudden longing to know what to say or do. I really liked him and didn't want to hurt his feelings, but I just couldn't see myself engaging with him any further, not when it would be too easy to track down my history, not when he would be asking questions about it. What was I going to tell him? As cute as he was, as much as I liked him, I was terrified of letting the relationship go any further. I contemplated that if I told him anything and he told Dennis, Dennis might tell Willard, and I could potentially lose my job. I didn't need the money but had become attached to the experience. Willard's was my second home.

"You know," I said after he watched me squirming for an answer. "I just don't think I am into dating. I am kind of a loner."

"So, you're rejecting me," He sighed but tried to keep his composure. "That's okay, I guess. I have been rejected before, especially by pretty girls like yourself. I get it."

"Jordan," I pleaded. "I'm not rejecting you. I think you are wonderful. I'm rejecting dating. I'm rejecting getting into each other."

"Someone must have really hurt you badly," he consoled. "Some guy must have torn your heart apart."

"Yeah, I guess you could say that," I returned. "I've had my heart broken too many times. I just don't trust men, especially cute ones." He had no idea that all my broken hearts had come from abuse or loving someone I couldn't have.

"You like me," he pressed, "and you think I'm cute, but you don't trust me because I'm cute."

"I do like you. I think you are a wonderful guy, and some girl is going to be very lucky to have you, but that girl can't be me."

"So, what if we don't … *date*?" he pondered. "What if we just become friends? No strings attached, no should or shouldn't, no demands, just buddies?"

"I told you, I'm not into dating. I'm a loaner."

"I didn't say date. Don't you have friends?" he interrogated. "You don't date me or anyone, ever, but friends are kind of nice to have around."

"I have a couple of friends but I think I have all I need."

"What's one more?" he pressed.

I threw up my hands in exasperation, "Oh, Jesus! Jordan! ... You want another beer?"

"Sure, I'll have another," he said, smiling his Cheshire Cat ear-to-ear smile.

He knew I liked him. Damn it! He knew I was attracted to him. Despite all my poker face attempts, he could tell something was there. I was not about to be mean to him or hurt his feelings. I had no idea what I was going to do. It came down to having to be mean to him to get rid of him or letting him go on trying to win me over. If I was mean to him, I could potentially offend Dennis. *Maybe he'll get tired and give up*, I thought to myself.

I poured him another Bud and plopped it down in front of him. By this time, some other people had bellied up to the bar, and I had to take care of their needs instead of devoting my attention to Jordan.

He watched me, not in a sleazy way but more in an admiring kind of way. I knew he was watching me, which made me highly uncomfortable for various reasons. I had had men indicate their attraction to me before, and a couple of times, I had to set a man straight when he was coming on with some cheap ass come on that was cheesier than a block of cheddar, but that was easy. I could joke with the customers and let them know that I was not up for grabs, and if anyone did think I was up for grabs, the cops could grab their ass and escort them out. This was different, very different.

When I walked back by him after serving the other customers, he said, "So, if I hang out here all night and wait for closing, will you go to the breakfast joint with me again?"

"I'm not in charge of whether you hang out here all night. That's up to you as long as you don't break any of the rules, but I'm going home *alone* when I get off, and you are not invited."

"Okay," he said as he stood up and slapped a wad of cash onto the counter. "Keep the change."

Then he turned and walked directly to the door, but just before he walked out, he turned around and said, "See you next Friday. If that's okay?"

I threw my hands up in a shrug.

Jordan kept coming back like clockwork every Friday night just as the bar was opening. He would never have more than two beers, and he would never be intrusive. He began to engage me in conversations about movies and musical groups and tried to engage me in a discussion about football, but that one fell flat. Not only did I know nothing about football, but I had no interest in it whatsoever.

"Shhhhh," He said one night, leaning into the bar toward me. "Don't tell anyone around here, but I'm a Kansas City Chiefs fan."

"Good for you," I giggled. "I'm sure the Chiefs will honor you someday at one of their games."

"Speaking of games, when football season starts next year, we should take in a Chiefs game."

"No, I don't think so."

"Come on. It'll be fun."

"I don't do football."

"Or donuts." He smiled.

"I don't do football. I don't do donuts."

"Is it okay if I like football?"

"You can like anything you want. I'm not in charge of you. I'm not the judge of you."

"I like you."

"Oh, Jesus! Here we go again."

He laughed and changed the subject.

"So, Stephanie, why won't you tell me anything about yourself besides your favorite movies or music?"

"It's nobody's business," I popped back.

"Okay," he said and swigged down the last of his beer. Again, he stood, plopped a wad of bills on the counter, as he did every time he hit a dead end with me, and turned for the door. As always, when he got to the door, he looked over his shoulder and said, "See you next Friday. If that's okay?"

This went on for months.

The whole time this had been going on, Willard, whom the employees often called Daddy Willard, had been observing. One day before we opened, he came behind the bar and asked, "Stephanie, why won't you go out with this Jordan boy? You can see how much he is into you."

"I just can't. That's all."

"How old are you now?" Willard queried.

"Twenty-six. I'll be twenty-seven in January," I replied.

"And you have been working here since you were twenty-two? In all that time, I have never known of you going out with anyone, and I have watched you turn down multiple offers." He leaned back against the bar. "I hate to ask this, and maybe it is inappropriate of me to ask this, but if this is the case, maybe you just need to be up front with the guy … Are you a lesbian? I mean, I see those lesbian friends of yours meet you after work some nights. It's okay—if you are. None of my business … but … "

I thought, *Oh my God!* I hated it when people questioned me. I hated having to answer prying questions. I didn't want anyone to know my past. I wanted to forget about it.

"No," I calmly replied. "I am not a lesbian. I'm attracted to guys."

"Then why won't you give this kid the time of day?" He pondered.

"I just can't. That's all."

"At least go out with the boy," he pressed. "What do you have to lose? Go to dinner, see a movie, have fun, and enjoy your life a little—Hmmm?"

He cocked his head to one side and gave me a look that I knew meant he cared.

"Yeah, I don't know," I replied.

On the following Friday evening, July by that time, Jordan asked, "So, Stephanie, do you ever get a Friday or Saturday off?"

Willard overheard it and answered, "Yes. She can have any Friday or Saturday off that she wants. When would you like for her to have a Friday or Saturday off? Tomorrow, maybe? Saturday night? That's a great night to go out."

"Jesus, Willard!" I interjected.

"Tomorrow would be great!" Jordan replied as he gleamed adoringly at me with his incredible smile.

"Tomorrow it is!" Willard replied.

"Can I pick you up at your place at about 6:00 p.m.?" Jordan questioned.

"Oh, my God!" I blurted with exasperation. "Did the two of you conspire to back me into a corner."

"No," Jordan smiled. "It's fate, just fate. It was meant to be."

"All right! Okay!" I surrendered.

"I'll be there promptly at six," Jordan grinned. "Wear something a little formal."

"What?" I asked.

"I'm taking you to a nice place," he said. "You can wear sweatpants if you want. Whatever you want to wear is okay, but I will take you someplace very nice."

"Where?" I begged.

"It's a surprise."

Then he plopped a wad of cash onto the bar and turned toward the door. Just before he walked out, over his shoulder, he said, "See you at 6:00 p.m. tomorrow, your place Stephanie Laroquette. If that's okay?"

After Jordan left, I asked Willard, "Why the hell did you do that to me?"

"Because you need it, sweetheart," He replied. "You need to get out of yourself. You need to experience more than this bar, your apartment, or some all-night dive. Give yourself a treat. That boy is into you more than I have ever seen any man be into any woman. He is smitten. Just relax and allow what is going to happen."

"I don't want anything to happen," I protested.

"Yes, you do," He continued. "You are smitten, too. It is written all over you. It is written in the way you look at that boy, how you perk up when he walks in the door. I don't know why you are resisting because it sure as hell looks to me like something that was meant to be."

"Jesus! Daddy Willard! —Okay! Tomorrow night. I'm going out."

He smiled. "Let it be, child. Just let it be."

Jordan buzzed from the building's street door at 5:59 p.m., and I pressed the intercom to answer him. "Yes?"

"This is Jordan Walker calling for Ms. Stephanie Laroquette," He said. "Is Ms. Laroquette prepared for the evening?"

"Jesus!" I muttered under my breath. Then, I pressed the door button to let him in and said, "Yes, come on up."

A few minutes later, there was a knock at the front door. When I opened it, I found him facing my door in spit-polished black shoes practically on my threshold. He wore a dark gray suit with a baby blue shirt and navy blue, gray, and white striped tie. He was holding a bouquet of white and yellow roses.

"Holy shit!" I exclaimed.

"You look stunning," he admired.

I had chosen a figure-fitting, simple black dress with a string of pearls around my neck and short dangling pearl earrings. I stood slightly taller in my four-inch spiked heels but wasn't as tall as Jordan. I was so grateful that I had not gotten very tall, but at five foot eight inches, I was still taller than many girls. The heels brought me up, closer to Jordan's height.

"Thank you," I said as he handed the roses to me. "These are gorgeous. I love them. Yellow is my favorite color."

"I know," he smiled. "You may not recall, but that is one of the few pieces of personal information I have managed to pry out of you over the last six months."

"Don't let it spoil you," I said, carrying the roses in their beautiful vase to the living room to set them on the coffee table.

I turned to find him still standing at the threshold of the door. "Why are you still standing in the hall?"

"You didn't invite me in," he said.

"Oh, Jesus! Come in!" I sputtered. "I'm not used to formalities."

He came in and stood between the kitchen and the living room.

"Give me just one second to double-check my makeup," I pleaded. "I'll be right out."

I darted through my bedroom to my en suite bathroom and quickly checked things in the mirror. Then, I joined him back in the living room.

"Wow!" he commented. "You meant it when you said you would be right out. Most girls would leave me sitting another thirty minutes, at least."

"I'm not most girls," I said. "So, where are we going?"

"It's a surprise."

"Again, with the surprise," I chided. "You can't tell me where we are going for dinner?"

"Nope," he smiled.

"So, are we ready to go?" I asked.

"Nope." he smiled again. "The reservations are at seven."

"Seven? Then, why did you tell me you would pick me up at six?"

"Because, as I said, most girls would keep me waiting for at least thirty minutes. I have learned to come early."

"Well, why don't you just say you'll pick them up at six thirty if you have reservations at seven?"

"My experience has taught me that when I do that, they are not ready till seven, anyway, and we still miss our reservation. One girl I went out with insisted on vacuuming her apartment in addition to spending almost an hour getting ready after I got there. Needless to say, we missed the movie."

"You have done a lot of dating?" I asked.

"Enough to learn a few things," he said. "Haven't you learned a few things from dating?"

"No," I said flatly.

"Why not?"

"Can we just go?" I said rather tersely.

"Well, we may be a little early. We could stop at Willard's for a drink before we go."

"Have you thought about what it would be like for me," I questioned, "sitting on the opposite side of the bar with almost everyone there knowing me?"

"Okay," he continued. "Maybe we could just drive around for a little while, or heck, we could go to a different bar for a drink, visit here for a while, or maybe see if the restaurant will take us a little early.

"Okay, whatever," I said, trying not to be annoyed.

"Do you want to stay here and visit for a while?"

"No," I snapped again. "Let's go, whatever." I didn't want him to have any more opportunity to question me than I could possibly give him.

"Come on, then," he said and took my hand. "I managed to find a parking spot on the street, just around the corner."

I grabbed my purse off the side table on our way out the door, and he continued to hold my hand, except for letting go long enough to let me get my keys out and lock my door. Then, he retook my hand, held it while we waited for the elevator, held it in the elevator, and held it as we crossed through the lobby and onto the street. When we turned the corner, he approached a brand-new silver-gray Mercedes.

"You must make a lot of money at the Architecture firm," I said.

"What makes you say that?"

"That is not a cheap car—ergo."

"I do okay," he said as he opened the passenger-side door for me.

I slipped into the leather seats and made myself comfortable. He got in on the driver's side, started the car, and we were on our way.

"This is a very nice car," I complimented.

"I like it," he said. "What do you drive?"

I still had Miss Mattie's 1973 Lincoln. I didn't drive it much since I could walk to work. Over the years, I had mechanics working on it several times to keep it road-worthy and probably paid a lot more to get it fixed than the car was worth.

"I drive a 1973 Lincoln Continental," I replied, "kind of an olive green."

"Cool!" he commented. "Are you into classic cars?"

"I don't know what you mean by classic cars," I said. "It was my mother's car. I got it when she passed and have never been able to bring myself to part with it."

"I am so sorry you lost your mother," he said. "You must have been young."

"I was seventeen," I replied, already thinking that I had said too much. I could have lied. I could have told him anything, that I bought the car at an auction, that an old boyfriend gave it to me. Instead, I told him the truth.

"Oh, man!" he pried. "Is your father still alive?"

"Can we talk about something else?" I said, and gazed out the window at the sidewalks reflecting sepia tone in the yellow streetlights. He had to have known that I had some dark shit in my past simply from my reaction at that breakfast dive the first time we went out. I had no idea why that and my constant rufusal to talk about myself had not scared him off.

"Okay, sure," he responded. "What would you like to talk about?"

"How about those Chiefs?" I said, forcing a smile back at him.

"Seriously? You want to talk about football?"

"Well, not really, but it gets the subject off of me."

He reached over and placed his hand on mine while he steered with the opposite hand. "I think I'm beginning to figure out why you are so secretive," he said. "It's okay. I promise I will try not to pry.

Obviously, you have a lot of pain about losing your mom, maybe about a lot of other stuff."

He had no idea.

"You know what?" He said. "Let's just take a quick drive by the Arch and then head to the restaurant. If we get there a little early, we can wait."

With that, he made a turn, crossed over to Chestnut Street, and headed east. On Chestnut, you can see the Arch all the way down the street, and when you get close, it feels like you will drive right through it. On the way down Chestnut, he began talking about the architectural design of the Arch, how he had studied it, and how it was an amazing accomplishment. We cruised around near the Arch for maybe an extra fifteen minutes. Then he made a turn on 4th Street and then onto Broadway. I had no idea where he was taking me until we pulled up in front of Antonio's Italian restaurant. It was upscale, more expensive than most, and they served dishes that the typical Italian restaurant wouldn't serve.

"Antonio's? Seriously? Antonio's?" I questioned.

"You don't like Italian food?" he asked.

"I love Italian food, but this is expensive, highbrow Italian food. I'm not used to dining out like this."

He laughed. "Didn't I tell you I was taking you to a nice place?"

"Are you fucking serious?" I asked. "Do you know how much it will cost for us to eat at a place like this?"

"I can afford it, and you are worth it," he replied. "Haven't you ever eaten in a nice restaurant before?"

"Well, no. Actually, I haven't. Not one like this." I responded. "Are they going to make me hold my pinky out and make sure I don't eat dessert with the damn salad fork?"

Even though I had more than enough money to eat in the most excellent restaurants, I maintained the conservative edge that poverty had created. I rarely spent more money than was absolutely necessary. Usually, the most upscale place I ate was at some national chain.

He laughed again. "You can put your pinky anywhere you want to. You can eat dessert with any damn utensil you want. You can pick the plate up, mash it in your face, and go, NAUM, NAUM, NAUM, NAUM."

"Oh, stop it!" I shoved him gently on the arm and giggled. "Okay, let's eat at Antonio's."

Jordan had the valet take his car for parking and slipped his hand into the crook of my elbow to escort me into the building. I felt like I had never felt before. This must have been what I had missed in high school, the pomp and circumstance that other kids had taken for granted on prom night. This must have been what it felt like to walk into prom with your date by your side. My first ever legitimate date would be at Antonio's at the age of twenty-six. Maybe we could have counted New Year's morning at the breakfast joint as a date, but that didn't seem to make the cut.

Suddenly, my heart began to pound as I thought about something that had not previously occurred to me. The McNeils were rich. What if I ran into Mr. or Mrs. McNeil in there or maybe some of their friends from church? What would I do? How would I act? Would they spot me, recognize me, come up, and ruin something for me before I ever had a chance to have it? I fought the urge to turn around and run, and my breath quickened. I consoled myself with the awareness that none of them had ever seen me as a woman.

"Are you all right?" Jordan questioned when he spotted me getting a bit shaky.

"I'm fine," I said, drawing in as much air as possible and trying on fake resolve.

Inside, the maître d greeted us, and Jordan told him we had reservations. By that time, it was 7:00 pm.

"Indeed, Mr. Walker," he said. "Right this way."

We were led to a corner table, which I appreciated since I could sit with my back to the wall and watch the remainder of the room, and I immediately scanned the walls for exit signs. Each table was covered with white linen cloths and appointed with fine china. The walls were paneled with very dark wood, and white sconces lit the room from the sides.

The waiter, in his white shirt, black slacks, and red waistcoat, came, handed the menus to us, and introduced himself. "My name is Joseph and I will be your server this evening. Would you like to start with something to drink?" I was about to tell him that water would be fine when Jordan said, "I think I would like to have some wine this evening. Stephanie, would you like a glass of wine? They have a very nice selection here."

"Wine?" I couldn't say that I knew nothing about it. Willard's had a small collection, and I had to learn a little about it, so I had at least tasted the six selections available at work. I knew there were some that I hated. "Ah, okay. I'll have a Chardonnay."

The waiter then began to call off several different brands of Chardonnay, and I had no idea which to pick because I didn't know one brand from the other. What we sold at Willard's was not high-end.

"Chardonnay sounds good," Jordan interjected. "Bring us a bottle of Chardonnay Jermann, please."

"Very well, sir. Excellent choice," the waiter said with a smile and continued his duties.

In a little while, the waiter returned with the wine, opened it at the table, and poured a little into a glass, which Joran then sniffed, swirled around, and tasted. Upon Jordan's approval, the waiter poured it into our glasses and set the bottle in an ice bucket at the table.

"Are you ready to order, or would you prefer a little more time?" the waiter asked.

"Give us a moment," Jordan said. Then, he perused the menu as the waiter left the table. "Do you like seafood?" he asked.

"Yes, I love it," I replied.

"You like salmon, lobster, shrimp, scallops, snapper, other types of fish."

"Yes," I replied with a smile. "There isn't much that I don't like."

"Then, I suggest the grilled scampi and lobster tail. I've had it, and it was delicious."

"Okay, sold," I said.

When the waiter returned, Jordan ordered that for me and the Lobster Albarello for himself. Then we sat, sipping wine and nibbling on bread while waiting for our meals.

"How do you like the wine?" Jordan asked.

I was already feeling tipsy when I had finished maybe half of the first glass. I rarely ever drank.

"It's good," I replied. "I'm not much of a drinker."

"Now that's fresh," he commented. "A bartender who is not a drinker."

"I have tried to make sure that I didn't make a habit of it," I replied.

We continued small talk, commented about the ambiance, and chatted about things that didn't matter. By the time the meals came, I had finished my glass of wine and was poured another.

I began to eat and commented that the food was delicious.

"It always is," Jordan returned as he forked into his lobster.

I smiled and felt uncomfortable and out of place.

"So, when do I get to read more of the Stephanie Laroquette book?" he asked.

"Never," I replied.

"Why not?" he pressed. "It's not a horror story, is it?"

"It kind of is," I replied. "I wouldn't want it to frighten you."

"Really?" he went on. "You know I don't scare easy, don't you?"

"If you were scared easily, you would have dumped me after that first night at the breakfast joint," I replied.

"See," he said. "I can handle a complex story."

"Well, I'm scared to tell that story," I replied. "I don't want to remember any more than I absolutely have to."

He stopped eating, reached over, and gently touched my arm. "Stephanie," he said. "I have already read enough to know that some terrible hurt must have happened to you. That hasn't stopped me from caring about you and wanting to get to know you. No matter what may have happened, I can see that you have come out of it as a good person with great strength. If it's too painful to talk about, I get that, but I hope you will trust me enough to tell me one day."

"I don't think you can handle it," I replied. "You came from a normal family and a middle-class upbringing. I—I—" My fork was trembling in my hand, and I put it down. "Can we talk about something else?"

"So," he pleaded, "if you were to tell me and it was too much for me to handle, if it made me freak out and break off any contact with you, would you be any worse off than you were before I met you?"

"Yes," I replied.

"How."

"Because … you have changed me, Jordan. I'm not the same person I was when I met you. I like you, I really do, but I don't want to hurt you, and I don't want to lose you either. I'm just as afraid of losing you as I am of letting you in."

"Try me," He said with compassion in his gaze.

I felt my breath quicken as it was prone to do. I felt tears lingering at the edge of my lashes, and I felt myself trembling with anxiety and grief.

"I can't tell you here," I said. "Please. I'm not sure I can handle it either."

"It's okay," He comforted. "This is not the time or place, but could we have a heart-to-heart talk sometime, maybe later this evening?"

"Jordan, I'm terrified."

"Of what?

"If I tell you here, I'm probably going to break down and cause a scene like I did back at that breakfast joint. If I tell you when we're alone … I'm … I'm afraid you'll hurt me."

He was taken aback and sat back in his chair.

"Stephanie, I don't make a habit of hurting people, not anyone— ever. I absolutely never would deliberately hurt anyone I'm close to. If I were ever to hurt you, it would never be because I intended to."

"I need time." I tried to smile.

"I think you also realize I am a very patient man," He responded. "I just … I just want to be inside you—and I don't mean that sexually, although I think you know I'm attracted to you. I just want to be included in your life, and I want you to be included in mine."

He reached over, patted my arm, and said, "Let's talk about the movies, our jobs, music, where you got that dress, and anything else, okay? I'm sorry I spoiled the evening by digging too deep. I don't want to upset you. I don't want to hurt you, and I don't want you to hurt. If I could heal you right now, I would. If I could make all that pain disappear, I would, but I understand. You've carried it so long that you don't feel like you can let go of it."

"Thank you," I said. "But you don't know how messed up I am. You just don't know."

"So, seen any good movies lately?"

He sat back and stuck his fork into his dinner again.

I half smiled my acknowledgment and did the same.

CHAPTER 19

THE FIRST TIME

Jordan didn't press me again for a long time, and I began relaxing with him. He gave me time and started coming by Wednesday and Thursday evenings to hang out and watch TV. He would stay until about 9:00 p.m. and then go home to prepare for work the next day. I allowed the relationship to continue with the ongoing underlying trepidation that it was doomed from the beginning. He would lounge on my sofa with me while we watched cable movies. He had me over to his house and gave me a key so I could meet him there when he got off work. Then, we could have a little more time together, and I would go home about ten or ten-thirty. He had one of the smaller houses in Ladue, but it was still a charming three-bedroom, two-bath home, and he had it all to himself. He had put a guest bed in one of the bedrooms and used the other as an office. His home had obviously been decorated by a man, and not a gay man who would have, in most cases, had better taste. He had minimal furniture, no dining table, and Kansas City Chiefs memorabilia stuck all over the house. I didn't care. I was not a stickler about décor, although I loved the designer touches in my condo. There were family photos of his mom and dad, siblings, and friends he had gone to school with. There were pics of him posing with some guy friends from school, his high school football team, and a couple of pics of extended family, including his uncle Dennis and aunt Marlene. The photos were all in stand-up frames and scattered haphazardly about the house, on shelves, tables, and some on the fireplace mantle. Here and there, he had big floor pillows and a couple of mismatched pillows thrown onto his overstuffed couch. He also had two cats named

Thisone and *Thatone*. Thisone was a fat furry gray thing with a flat nose, and Thatone was a regular-sized yellow tabby.

"This is interesting," I said, walking through his front door the first time.

"Interesting?" he replied. "It's just a house. What does 'interesting' mean? You don't like it?"

"Why do you think it means I don't like it?" I asked.

He snickered. "I used to have a friend who would say, 'It's interesting' when he didn't like something but didn't want to hurt someone's feelings by telling them the truth. So, what does interesting mean to you?"

"Maybe I should have said this is a surprise instead of interesting," I returned.

"What's the surprise?"

"Well … " I hesitated. "You're an architect. I thought architecture and design went hand in hand. I'm surprised it doesn't have a designer's touch."

About that time, *Thisone* came angling around my leg. "And you have a cat?"

"Two cats, to be exact," he replied. "*Thisone* is this one, and *Thatone* is a yellow tabby who will hide until he gets to know you."

"What are their names?" I asked.

"*Thisone* and *Thatone*," He replied.

"What?" I responded, confused.

"That's their names," he said while grinning. "*Thisone* is this one, and *Thatone* is the one you haven't met yet. I call them *Thisey* and *Thatsey*."

"That's their names? Ugh!" I slapped my palm to my forehead and laughed. "You're a nut, and that's something else I never expected. Cats? You have cats! I assumed there would be a golden retriever bouncing around here if you had any pets at all."

He came out with a belly laugh and kissed me on the cheek. "I can understand how you might evaluate me that way. I was an average high school jock before I became an architect," he replied. "Besides, I do industrial architecture, high rises, and things like that. My firm gets contracts from all over the world. I'm not an interior decorator, and since I am pretty much comfortable with whatever, I never sought to hire one. I've always liked cats, not that I don't like dogs, but cats are low maintenance. Give them food and a litter box, and they are good to go. Dogs, you have to get up and let out."

"Oh, lazy too," I giggled.

"A bit," he replied. "So, what do you actually think of the house?"

"It's cool," I said. "It feels nice; feels homey and relaxing." Then, I went over, plopped myself on a sofa pillow, and held out my arms for him to join me.

I became comfortable in his home, and he seemed comfortable in mine. We became comfortable with each other, and for the longest time, we did nothing but hang out and cuddle with maybe a little kissing. We enjoyed cuddling together and watching TV, and I tolerated sitting through a football game. We had gone out to dinner, went to the movies, and did average dating things, but sexually, we hadn't done any more than a little light petting. Then, one night at his house, he leaned into me and kissed me passionately. He had kissed me before, but never like that. It was urgent, and it seemed like he wanted more than cuddling and petting. I was immediately terrified. I had known that time was coming eventually and had ruminated over how I would handle it when it happened. Still, I wasn't ready.

"I can't," I said and gently pushed him back.

"Why not," he asked. "Aren't you attracted to me? We have been dating for months. Shouldn't we be ready now?"

"I'm very attracted to you, but I can't."

"Stephanie," he said, "I'm in love with you."

That was even more frightening. I said nothing. I knew I was in love with him, too, but I didn't want to admit it, and I was scared that our lives could never really fit together regardless of love.

He sat back and looked at me for a moment. Then he got up, went into his kitchen, and got a beer. He popped it open, came back to sit near, but not beside me, and began silently sipping his beer."

"I'm sorry," I said.

"For what?" he asked. "I get saving yourself for marriage. I get wanting to remain a virgin."

"That's not it," I said, feeling exasperated. I knew something had to give. I knew I couldn't continue the relationship and keep putting him off like that.

"You are not a virgin?" he asked.

"It's complicated," I replied, feeling my breath quicken. I fought my usual panic attack. "Actually … I am sort of a virgin, but not really. I have never—It's complicated." I looked away.

"Oh, God," he exclaimed. "Stephanie, I'm so sorry." He paused for a long time before asking, "Have you been raped?"

"Shit!" I heard myself exclaim before I could catch myself. I got up and began pacing around his living room.

He immediately got up to come to my side, but I waved him back. "It's okay. I'm okay—please."

"I'm so sorry," He almost whispered as he stood a couple of feet from me. "This explains everything. Have you ever had any therapy, gotten any help?"

"It doesn't explain everything," I replied. I continued to pace and felt the anxiety building. I realized that I could not continue to go down a path with him with a life that was so completely different, and it would be unfair not to tell him the truth. Finally, I turned back to him and said, "Sit down, please."

He sat quietly back on the sofa and leaned over, his hands gripped in front of him.

I came and sat beside him with tears streaming down my face. I snatched a couple of tissues from the dispenser on his coffee table and began dabbing at the tears. "Jordan, you have wanted to read this book ever since I met you, and I have never really let you read more than the misleading description on the cover. You don't really know anything about me, but I know a lot about you. I know that you came from a conservative, midwestern, middle-class family. You've told me about your mom, dad, sister, and two brothers. You have told me about college, college buddies, and high school friends, but I have told you nothing about me. I have been scared to tell you, but I know it is unfair to you or us to continue down this path if you don't know the truth." I got up again and looked back at him. "Yes ... I have been raped, but not how you think, and that's not the whole story. Yes, I've been in therapy since I was eleven."

My heart pounded like fierce native drums, and tears continued to trickle from my eyes. Should I tell him everything? I still had fears that I would lose him if he knew. Was I prepared for that? Even though he swore that he would never intentionally hurt me, I still had fear that he might. If there was a hidden misogyny behind his kindness and compassion, would he freak out knowing that he had been kissing and petting someone born in a boy's body, someone he might consider a man? I knew that men freak out over things like that. I knew the additional backlash that the gay community had gotten since the onset of AIDS. Even though he had never voiced any AFRAIDS or homophobia, I pondered how much I could tell him.

He looked up at me and remained silent, waiting.

"Jordan, you have no idea how hard this is for me," I pleaded, hoping that he might step back and let me change the subject and continue to keep my secrets.

He said nothing but silently waited.

I mustered my courage and trembled as I said, "Yes, I have been raped, but not as an adult. I was repeatedly molested by one of my mother's friends and one of his friends when I was little."

"Oh Jesus, Steph—"

I threw my hand up before he could finish his sentence.

"Please don't ask any questions," I admonished. "Please don't express sympathy. I don't like sympathy for this. It saps my strength. Just let me tell you, and then if you want to end our relationship, I understand."

"I don't want—" he started.

Again, I threw up my hand.

"How long have you lived in St. Louis?" I asked.

"I guess about two years at this point," he replied.

"Something terrible went down before you moved here," I said, "and I was a part of it. The person you think was my mother was not my birth mother, but she was the only real mother I ever had. She adopted me. Before that, I was growing up in the slums of Pruitt Igo. I'm not sure if you have heard of that. Pruitt Igoe was demolished several years ago—Good riddance! It was a horrible place."

I returned to the couch and turned my knee into the back cushion to face him. He leaned back into the arm of the couch.

"My mother was a drug whore, a heroin addict. She would send me to the house of one of her friends and as far back as maybe four years old and whored me out to him. He molested me almost every week, and a teenage boy who buddied with him also molested me. My mother didn't care. All she cared about was her next fix. She fucked for money or drugs, and she sold me for it. She got paid to pimp me out to pedophiles.

Jordan's eyes were stretched wide as his astonishment was evident. Yet, he remained silent and listened, and there was still discernable compassion.

"This guy started coming by to sleep with my mother, maybe when I was about six years old, and he became regular. None of the others were regular. He kind of befriended me, and he was good to me. He was the only man who was ever good to me, but they had a big fight, and he left. Anyway, the day after their fight, when I was ten, I walked in to find my mother stabbed to death."

"Jesus Christ!" he uttered and leaned forward, but when He saw me wince, he said, "I'm sorry … I'm listening."

"The guy, the regular guy, who had befriended me, was charged with my mother's murder, and he is serving life in prison. I was taken into Christian foster care by a family here in Ladue and stayed there for two years until I met the televangelist Ronald Dennison."

"I've heard of him," he commented.

"Pastor Dennison felt sorry for me and left me a Trust Fund. That got me out of foster care and allowed Miss Mattie Laroquette, my real mother, to adopt and care for me. She had looked out for me when I was at Pruitt Igo. When she adopted me, I took her last name. We got a house in Ladue, she kept me in the same school, and she raised me till she died a few months before my eighteenth birthday."

I was silent for a little while, staring down at my fingers as I fiddled with the tissues in my hand. Jordan was also quiet. When I looked up, I could see the turmoil on his face. Finally, he said, "No wonder you are a closed book. I don't think I have ever known anyone who has been through even a fraction of what you have been through, but Stephanie, that doesn't mean I don't love you. It doesn't mean that I want to end our relationship. Clearly, you have come a long way since then."

"I have come a long way, and it has been tough, but I'm not finished," I said. "You don't know everything and need to know everything before deciding to be with me. Love doesn't fix everything; loving someone doesn't mean they are right for you. I've never told you my name before Mattie Laroquette adopted me?"

He sat there puzzled. Finally, he said, "Okay?"

I turned, put my forehead down into my palms, and leaned on my knees. I didn't want to look at him. I didn't say anything for a while, and he patiently waited for me to speak. I looked up, faced him, and said, "My birth name is Stephen Christian Saunders."

Again, he was puzzled. "What does that have to do with anything?"

"Stephen," I reiterated. "Not Stephanie Christine—Stephen Christian."

He continued to look puzzled. Then, the shock on his face meant he was beginning to understand.

"I was born a boy," I quietly affirmed.

His eyes darted from side to side as he tried to process what he had just heard.

"But you're a woman," he affirmed nervously. "You have breasts and a woman's hips and the face and figure of a woman. Your voice is a woman's voice. Are you saying you have a dick?"

"No, I have a vagina," I confirmed, "but I used to have a penis. I've had surgery and female hormones to change into what you see."

A wash of emotions filled his face. He stood up, hand to forehead, thinking. He sat back down. "So, this is why you didn't want to have sex with me? This is … This is … This is a lot."

"I know," I affirmed. "I should have told you sooner. I'm sorry that I let it go this long. I should have told you in the first place. This is why I tried not to get involved with you. I don't want anyone to know. Only my closest friends know. I don't know how others might react, especially straight men who I'm around almost every day at the bar. This is why I thought you might hurt me."

"Stephanie!" he scolded. "I am not going to hurt you. No matter what, I'm not going to hurt you. I wish I had known sooner. No—maybe I don't wish I had known sooner. If I had known sooner, maybe I wouldn't have gotten to know you, and I'm glad I got to know you. My feelings are all over the place. This is a lot to process. I don't know. It's kind of beyond me. Explain it to me."

"I was physically born as a boy," I replied, "but I have never been a boy. I have never felt like a boy. I grew up as a boy until I was thirteen. Then, Miss Mattie allowed me to change my name when she adopted me. It's a long story."

I fiddled with a ceramic football on his coffee table.

"I want to hear it," he said. "Let me finish reading the book."

"Are you sure?" I asked.

"I'm sure I want to know everything," he responded.

"Okay." I hesitated. "I may have been born as a boy, but I felt like I had been put in the wrong body. I've always been female, but society doesn't like it very much when those they perceive as male express themselves as feminine. They have no real place for people like me, you know. So, people like me are supposed to stay in the place that they define for us instead of being who we are. Everybody is expected to follow specific rules whether you have a penis or a vagina, and most people don't much like it when somebody breaks the rules, even if they feel like there is no way to keep from breaking the rules. Even if living up to the expectations doesn't fit who you are, you are still supposed to play the role they assign. You get labeled as a freak and an outcast if you don't play that role. You get hurt and abused.

"At thirteen, with Miss Mattie's blessing, I began to dress as a girl, sometimes. Usually, she would only want me to do it at home, but sometimes, she would let me dress as a girl and take me to the movies or out to eat on the other side of town where we weren't likely to be recognized. In junior high school, I was bullied, and I didn't feel comfortable in the boy's bathroom, more because I was afraid of being cornered and bullied than anything else. I started using the girl's bathroom, but you can probably guess that it didn't go over very well. Then, a group of high school thugs did me an unintentional favor. They beat me so badly that I ended up in the hospital in an induced coma after they slammed my head into the counter, but it wasn't the head injury that was the favor. My testicles had been bruised so badly that they had to be removed. For the first time, I felt like I was beginning to have the body I was supposed to have. After that, Miss Mattie took me out of school and hired a tutor to home-school me. Because of the Trust Fund, we had enough money to afford it. So, I started hormone therapy and went to Johns Hopkins when I was eighteen to have transition surgery. All my parts are female, but I have to be on hormone therapy for the rest of my life, and I have to dilate my vagina regularly unless I have a sexual partner."

He sat back down in a chair away from me. His distance didn't surprise me. He said, "I've never met anyone like you. I'm not sure if I have even heard of anyone like you. I've never heard of anyone who has been tormented as much as you have, much less, born in a boy's body."

"I'm sure you haven't," I commented. "I don't think there are very many like me. At least, the only place I have met one or two other transexuals has been a brief encounter when I was in for one of my surgeries."

"Do you have to have any more surgeries?" he asked.

"Not unless something goes wrong," I replied.

He sat there staring at his fireplace.

"I'm angry," he said, keeping his gaze on the fireplace. "I don't want to be angry, but I'm angry. I feel deceived, but you warned me, and I wouldn't listen. I'm angry that I have feelings for you and didn't know this sooner. I feel betrayed, but I don't know if I'm angrier with you or myself. I pushed you when you tried to keep me away."

"So, what do we do now?" I questioned.

"I need some time," he responded. "I need some time to think. I don't know if I can deal with this. I don't know if we can continue. I'm feeling confused and overwhelmed right now."

"So, do you want me to go now?" I asked.

"Yes, please."

"I understand," I said quietly.

I got up to walk to the door, but before I could leave, he asked, "You said that you are kind of a virgin. What does that mean?"

I turned around. "I've had no sexual contact with anyone since I was molested," I replied. "I've never had any kind of sexual contact with a man since my surgery until you kissed me. I've never had intercourse."

He turned back to stare at his fireplace. I waited a moment and left.

I didn't hear anything from Jordan. He didn't come into the bar. He didn't call, and I didn't call him. After about a month, I assumed it was over. At first, I spent a lot of time crying, wandering around my condo as though it were a jail cell, bored by everything and unable to make myself do much of anything except get up and go to work. There, I plastered on a fake smile to cover my grief. What I had considered my one opportunity for love had been taken from me, as I knew it would be. Everything was always taken from me, and I knew in the long run that Jordan would be unable to deal with the truth. He had done better than I expected, but in the end, he had done exactly what I had expected. Although he remained a gentleman and didn't go into some homophobic freak fest where he took out his unresolved masculine insecurity on me, as most men probably would, he ended our relationship.

I felt destined to be alone without any genuine or lasting companionship.

I knew I could pick up men in bars and probably fuck all I wanted to without any one of them knowing that I was born as an assigned male, but I didn't want to. That wouldn't be real. Ultimately, all it amounted to was an illusion and an orgasm. I had masturbated to orgasm a few times since my surgery, more to prove that I could have an orgasm than anything else, but where sex was concerned, it was just a pleasurable spasm of certain muscle groups. So what? I didn't want just sex. I didn't want frivolous, no account, carnal knowledge. I wanted a genuine and sincere relationship with a man I loved who also loved me. I assumed that would be something I could never have, and I told myself I had to accept being alone long before I met Jordan.

About two months after my talk with Jordan, the phone rang early Wednesday evening. I picked up the receiver and said, "Hello."

"May I come over?" It was Jordan's voice.

"Why would you want to come over?" I asked.

"Because, now, I have a confession to make."

"Jordan, we might as well admit it's over."

"I have a confession," he said. "I need to tell you something."

"Can't you just tell me over the phone, now?"

"No, I need to see you, Stephanie," he pleaded. "I need to be able to look into your eyes when I say this."

"Okay," I hesitantly responded. "What time?"

"I'm on a payphone by Willard's," he said. "I can be there in five or ten minutes."

"What's so pressing?" I asked.

"I just … I need to see you."

"Okay,"

Click went his receiver, and the dial tone resumed.

In short, he was ringing the buzzer for my condo at the front of the building. I let him in the building, and next, there was a tapping at my door. When I opened it, Jordan stood with a bouquet of yellow roses and a box of donuts.

"What the hell?" I said while watching his face. "This is not how we left it."

"May I come in?

"So, what's going on, Jordan?"

"I need to talk," he replied. "These are for you." He shoved the roses and donuts toward me.

"The roses are beautiful," I said, "but I told you I don't do donuts."

"You should," he said. "Especially when you have something to celebrate."

"I don't have anything to celebrate?"

"I hope that you do," he continued. "I pray that you do."

I put the roses in a vase and set them and the donut box on my kitchen bar. I returned to find Jordan standing by the door, waiting for me. The door was left open. I walked over, closed the door, and motioned him toward the sofa. He sat on the east end of the sofa, and I sat opposite.

"Okay, what?" I asked.

"I've been doing a lot of thinking," he began. "I've had a lot of shit running through my head, and I finally had to ask myself if it was my thinking or thinking that had been programmed into me. Like those role expectations you were talking about, you know how men are supposed to act and how women are supposed to act. I've been thinking a lot about that, like am I being who I am, or am I trying to live up to ingrained expectations? I don't have to tell you that I was very uncomfortable when you finally told me about your change."

"It wasn't a change, Jordan," I countered. "I wasn't changed. I have always been female. I didn't change who I was; I simply adjusted my body to be congruent with who I was."

"Okay—right," he stammered. "This fucks with a man's head. You know that it does. I think that's why you didn't want to tell me. All kinds of shit ran through my head, like, does it mean I'm gay because I kissed you? All the things that guys grow up with, you know? Like you have to be macho and manly all the time. You have to work your ass off to be a real man. It isn't okay to have any attractions that aren't to women. Problems need to be solved with force and domination. Why isn't it okay for a man to be attracted to another man or a woman to be attracted to another woman or both? What difference does it make, and why is that the business of anybody else but them? Some guys like big boobs; some guys don't. Some women like tall guys, and some don't. Is that really any different than being attracted to someone for other reasons? My mind went on and on! It worked my nerves, Stephanie."

I sat quietly listening, and he paused.

"Stephanie, I was miserable without you. I couldn't sleep or eat. Every day, I missed you, and I fought with all the shit in my head daily. I questioned my manhood. I questioned what kind of future I could ever have with you. I fought with myself over the things I've heard guys say in locker rooms. I cried, and I wrestled with my upbringing, what the church says about being a man or a woman, or being homosexual, and I thought about what it must be like for you to have to keep that secret for fear of how people would react if they knew. I thought about what it might be like if I had to keep a secret like that. It must be miserable to have to live with that kind of fear. Nobody should have to live with that kind of fear. Nobody should worry about being hurt, shunned, or abused just for being who they are. Then, I thought about everything that made me love you: your smile, your wit, your character, and how you always try to do the right thing. I thought about what originally attracted me to you and what kept me attracted to you. I'm a straight guy. I'm attracted to women, but you *are* a woman, beautiful, sexy, sweet, affectionate, and tender. It might have been different if I hadn't been in love with you. Maybe I could have brushed it off and moved on, continued with my indoctrination about gender roles, and passed it off as a mistake, but my feelings were all mixed up. I had to ask myself, what's really important?"

I leaned forward. "That's why I had to tell you," I reflected. "It wouldn't have been fair to think that you could have the kind of life that you want with me. You can't have that kind of life with me, and it's not just about me being a transsexual. It's about coming from where I came from compared to where you came from. It's about all the mental and emotional shit I'm still dealing with because of how I grew up. You've seen me have panic attacks. Jordan, I have to fight my trauma daily; sometimes, it wins. I'm no walk in the park."

"What kind of life do you think I want?" he asked.

"Jordan, it only took walking around your house to see the kind of life you want; your family photos include vacations with friends, moms and dads, aunts and uncles." I leaned in. "You want the kind of life that I can't give you. You want a family like the rest of your family. You want kids and a normal home life, football games with old buddies, and maybe a wife who attends the PTA and drops the kids off at school. You want the middle-class mold that I can never fit. I can never give you that."

He sighed and turned to the front of the sofa. He leaned forward, then turned his head toward me. "That's what I thought I wanted," he said. "That's what we are supposed to want, right? I can't say that I don't want kids, but you know what? I will be thirty-one soon, and I have never been married. I don't have any kids. What the hell? Most guys my age are married and have two or three kids by now. What's different about me?"

"I don't know," I replied. "You tell me."

"I've dated girls before you," he went on. "I've dated several girls, but it never felt right. It never felt like I had met someone I could spend the rest of my life with. It just always felt off, like I would be committing myself to someone without really loving them just because that's what I'm supposed to do. I actually had one friend ask me if I was gay because I had never married, but I wasn't going to marry someone who wasn't right for me so that I could have a family. I knew it had to feel right. Then, I met you … and felt something I had never felt before, almost like I already knew who you were deep down inside like I knew the real story even if I hadn't read the book. It felt like there was a beautiful story within your story, a beautiful soul buried in there somewhere. Maybe something like a story about a beautiful princess kept in a dungeon. I knew there was more to you and that it was beautiful, even if you hid the truth. Then, when you told me about being born a boy … it fucked with my head. Stephanie. I can't lie. It really did, but I've done a lot of soul-searching over the past couple of months and have come to some conclusions. I don't have to want something just because my family, the church, or society says I'm supposed to want it. Maybe I don't want a middle-class home with an average of 2.5 children. Maybe I don't want a lot of things I'm supposed to want. Maybe what I really want is you."

I sat back and momentarily stared up at the ceiling. "What about your college buddies, your mom and dad, your brothers and sister, Uncle Dennis, and Aunt Marlene?" I challenged. "What about them?"

"I still love my family," he replied.

"You know I don't fit your family," I challenged again. "I'm not the middle-class housewife type. I've never met any of your family besides Dennis, and what if they find out about my background? Do you think they will want you to be with a transsexual from the slums of Pruitt Igoe who had a drug whore mother? Your family is important to you. I understand that, and I accept that."

"They are important to me," he confessed. "but you are as important, and they don't ever have to know you are transexual. As far as your childhood … well … we can work around that."

"Jordan, the truth is easier to find than you think. Don't you think your family will ever put two and two together? 'Here is the child of that woman who was murdered in 1971 in the slums.' Mike, the guy who went to prison for her murder, was on the local TV news just two months before I met you. His attorney filed another appeal to the courts. How do you think you and I can have a life where you won't have your family finding out about me and hating me? They always hate us. Transexuals, especially colored transexuals, are at the absolute bottom of the rung. We get looked down on by everybody, even some gay people. One of the reasons I want to keep it secret is that people like me get murdered just for being who we are."

"I don't care that you are transexual, not anymore," he replied.

"Yes, you do," I confronted. "You care a whole lot more than you might admit to yourself. Family was never anything to me. I never had a family except for Miss Mattie, which didn't last long. She died, and she had no family. Where foster care was concerned, I wasn't really a family member; I was just a charity project, and where Miss Mattie was concerned … well, it was just the two of us, and most of the time, it felt like us against the world. I had an old bitch grandma from down in the Ozarks, and I expect she is dead by now. I couldn't care less. She was less family than my so-called mother, but you have had and still have a real family, something I have never had and will never have. I don't even know what it's like to be in your kind of family."

"What if you could have it?" he asked. "What if you were to meet my family? Give them a chance; let them give you a chance? It's not what you have been through that matters. It's not who you were in the past that matters. It's who you are now, and Stephanie, I *know* you are a good person."

"How will you feel the first time your mom asks me when I'm going to give her a grandbaby?" I asked.

"Lots of couples can't conceive children." He replied and leaned back. "If you want children, we could adopt children. If you don't want children, I don't care. I'm already older than most men when they have their kids. I don't care."

"What will you do if your whole family finds out I'm a transsexual?"

"All I know," he sighed, "is that I want to spend my life with you, and I've concluded, after all that soul-searching, that you are the only one I want."

"You are talking like we are going to get married," I glared at him.

"I know," he replied. "I've thought about that too. I've thought about what kind of life I could have with you, and I don't want to lose that. I don't want to lose our relationship."

"So, what would we say when your mom or your dad asks me about my family?" I asked. "You know they will. Dennis only knows me from the bar. All he knows is that I serve him drinks and chat with him. I know he likes me, but he doesn't really know me."

"Except for telling them that you are a transsexual, which they never have to know as far as I'm concerned," he continued, "we tell them the truth, and the truth is that you have pulled yourself up from the pits of hell. You have become a good person despite all that shit. Who doesn't love an overcomer, someone who built themselves up despite their past? They will respect you for that. I don't think they will ask too many details about your upbringing. They don't have to know you were born into a male body. I didn't know all this time, and I am very close to you. They don't have to know that, and as far as your background, I believe they will give you a chance, Stephanie. I really do."

"And if they don't?" I asked.

"Then, I will love you anyway."

"Jordan, I could never ask you to give up your family, and you know the chances of them figuring out that I am transsexual are eventually high. I don't want to come between you and them."

He scooted closer to me and took my hands in his. "Stephanie, no family is perfect. Every family has skeletons. No family exists where everyone gets along with everyone else. There can be disagreements about politics, religion, or which fucking football team to root for. There can be judgments of one another, personality clashes, and family members who are fucked up. Families fight. Families disagree, but if the love is real, they get over it and love each other anyway. Uncle Dennis drinks too much. I know he only has one drink when he comes in after work, but Jesus, you should see him on the weekends sometimes. When we met, do you remember that my dad had to take him home on New Year's? He drinks like that often. My dad is a Republican, but I'm a Democrat, and sometimes, we get into heated arguments over politics to the point that Mom has to intervene and tell us to calm down. I don't know if anyone in our family is gay or transsexual, but if one of my little brothers or some cousin, niece, or nephew were to be, I would love them anyway, and I think most of my family would love them anyway. They might struggle with it, but they would probably come around. You don't have to ask me to give up my family because I think my family will love you just like I do."

I took a huge breath. "You know I've never been through anything like this."

"I know," he said. "Neither have I, but I've never been through anything that might happen in the next five minutes. Who knows what might happen? A bird could fly into the window. Mt. Vesuvius might erupt. All I know is that I have decided—I have firmly decided—that I want to be with you. I want you in my life, no matter what."

"Jordan, with my mental health issues alone, you are taking a risk."

"Everything is a risk. Life is a risk. Getting up in the morning is a risk. Are you still in therapy?" he asked.

"Not right now," I replied, "but I've been in therapy off and on since my mother was killed."

"If you needed to go back, would you?"

"Of course, I would. It has played a huge role in getting me through this, and I'm on medication."

"Then the risk may not be as big as you think," he responded. "Heck, I might even go to therapy with you. Maybe we should do that, continue to iron out these fears, both yours and mine, and solidify our relationship."

"How do you know this is what you really want?" I asked.

"I know," he replied. "I have fought that demon over the past couple of months, and love has won. I love you. I have admitted to myself that I truly do love you, which is more important than your background, mental health problems, or being transexual. If you weren't taking care of your mental health, that would make it a lot more difficult, but you are taking care of yourself. Life is full of challenges, Stephanie. Everyone's lives are full of challenges. I want to face life's challenges with you. I think we make a great, winning team, and we're going to make it."

"You've never even had sex with me," I said. "You don't even know what it would be like to have sex with me, but you want to make that kind of a commitment?"

"You don't know what it would be like to have sex with me either," he countered. "Besides, lots of couples, at least according to the church, get married without ever having sex. We don't have to. Is it really about the sex, Stephanie? I don't think so. I think it's about two people who love each other and want to make a life together. A relationship is like cake. Sex is just the icing on the cake. If one bakes a good cake and goes through all the processes, the cake is still good, even without the icing. The icing makes it taste better, but icing, alone with no cake, can get overwhelming and feel unsatisfying."

"What makes you think I love you?" I asked.

"You wouldn't have told me your truth if you didn't love me," he replied. "You would have just used me and wouldn't have cared how I felt about it. You wouldn't have worried if I knew about your past or not. You wanted to give me that choice. That's love, Stephanie. You wanted to let me make my own choice, to have what I needed to make an informed choice. You were willing to let me go if that was my choice. That's what people do when they love each other. They don't take advantage. They don't go on some selfish agenda where they don't care how it affects the other. I know you love me, and now I have made that choice. I don't care if you were born a boy. You're a woman now, prettier and sweeter than most women I've known. I don't care if you came from the slums or any of that. I care that you were molested only because I know it still affects you, but it doesn't make any difference in how I feel about you, and I will do whatever I can to support you in your recovery. Please give me a chance."

"What if I never really recover?" I asked.

"Then, I will support you in working your journey, keeping your head above water, and try my best to help you have the most peaceful and enjoyable life possible." He scooted closer to me, gazed into my eyes, reached out his hand, and touched my cheek. "Please," he pleaded. "I truly love you and want to be with you."

I felt an urge to push him away. I felt a fear of letting him get any closer. I knew that I couldn't have him without his whole family. I knew he couldn't have me without my history and emotional baggage. I gazed back at him. Then he leaned in and kissed me gently. He pulled back and looked into my eyes again, searching, it seemed, for my consent or denial. I looked back at him, and he leaned in to kiss me again.

"What are we doing here?" I asked.

"I hope," he said, "that you will allow me to make love to you for the first time. I hope you will allow me to be your first, last, and only. I want to share my life with you. I want to commune my body with yours and make love to you."

Despite my anxiety, I began to surrender to him. He kissed me gently and touched me tenderly. It felt so strange, so mixed with desire and trepidation. He got up, reached out to me, and when I took his hand, he led me to my bed, where he softly and sensually undressed me. Afterward, he undressed himself and lay down beside me.

"Are you sure you want this?" I asked.

"Are you sure *you* want this?" he asked.

"I'm scared," I replied. "I've never been sexual with anyone when it wasn't forced on me. I've never had real sex, and you're big."

He glanced down at his erection and smiled. "It's only seven inches."

I giggled, "You've measured it?"

"Sure," he said. "Every guy measures his dick. We want to know how we compare."

"It's big," I said again.

"We can stop if you want," he comforted. "We can stop any time you want, or I can be very gentle, and we can take our time. I don't want you to feel rushed or forced. I want you to feel safe and comfortable."

"Okay," I said, reaching for the lube in my bedside drawer that I used to dilate. "Remember, I told you I have to dilate daily with this if I don't have a sexual partner." I pulled my dilater out of the drawer and showed it to him. "This is the only thing that has ever been in there, except maybe the doctor's fingers and tools."

"It looks like a dildo," he said.

"Well, sort of, but maybe a little different."

He smiled and took the dilater, held it up, and turned in the air. "I wonder if I can compare," he teased. "You still up for this?"

"We'll see," I replied. "You will stop if I ask you to, right?"

"Absolutely."

He put the dilater on the bedside table and began kissing me again. He ran his hands over my body and down to my vagina. He put his mouth over my nipples, moved along the torso of my belly, and put his mouth over my vagina. I gasped at the sensation so different from anything I had ever experienced. It was both frightening and pleasurable at the same time. For the first time in my life, someone was being sexual without hurting me. For the first time, someone was with me without forcing me.

It was difficult to keep my mind off Jake, having my head pounded into the floor while he did what he did. Yet, I was determined that Jake had no place here. This was my time with Jordan, and I began working on kicking Jake out of my mind. I used the mindfulness techniques that my therapist had taught me to bring my attention back to the moment, back to Jordan, his tenderness and gentleness, the sensation of his skin against my skin, the smell of his cologne, and the softness and passion of his kiss.

Jordan would periodically stop and gaze into my eyes for permission to continue, but he also seemed to enjoy looking into my eyes. No one had ever looked at me that way. No one had ever made love to me; this was a million miles away from the abuse I had experienced. I felt tears drifting from my eyes, and Jordan noticed I was crying.

"Are you okay?" he asked. "What's wrong?"

"Nothing is wrong," I replied. "I'm just overwhelmed. No one has ever touched me like this. No one has ever been tender and caring. It feels so beautiful, and I don't want anything to ruin it."

He propped himself up on his elbow and wiped tears from my eyes. Then, he kissed very softly and tenderly.

"Let me know when you are ready," he said.

I smiled. I was so ready. All that I was experiencing was long overdue. "I'm ready," I said.

"Is it okay if I don't have a condom?" he asked. "I've been safe before I met you and haven't been with anyone else since I met you. Before that, I would get tested, and it was negative. I won't do anything if you don't want me to."

"It's okay," I whispered. "I trust you."

He took the lube and applied it generously to himself and me. Then he positioned himself on top of me and slowly pushed into me. I felt a gasp rise as he gradually entered, and I drew in a deep breath.

"Are you okay?" he asked.

"I'm very okay," I replied. "It hurts a little, but it's a good hurt. I'm fine."

Then, he gradually and slowly began to rock with me, taking his time, stopping to kiss me, waiting a moment to check on me before he started again. Gradually, he moved a little faster. I had my hands on his back, feeling the movement of his body as he made love to me. I tried to mindfully focus my full attention on Jordan, the warmth and sensation of his entire body as he moved with me. Then, I began to feel an orgasm building. He noticed the change and stopped to ask again if I was okay.

"Don't stop," I gasped. "Please don't stop."

He began moving again, and soon, I was climaxing, unlike any I had ever experienced. Masturbation, either before or after my transition, could not hold a candle to the waves of pleasure surging through my body. Not long after, I heard Jordan's breath quicken and felt his movements become more rapid. The next thing I knew, he was climaxing. It lasted several seconds, longer than I expected it would. A deep grunting came from his mouth, and then he relaxed atop me. He lay there for a moment, caressing my face and kissing me. Then, he rolled over to my side, looked at me, and smiled. I smiled back.

"Well, Stephanie Laroquette," He taunted, "how was your first time?"

"I've never experienced anything like that." I began to cry again.

He immediately leaned over and began trying to comfort me, "Baby, don't cry."

"No, it's beautiful," I said. "Very few men have ever touched me lovingly, and that was only a pat or a hug. The only orgasms I've ever had were from masturbating. The only time anyone ever touched me sexually was abusive, and there were no orgasms with that, only pain. Maybe I enjoyed fooling around with a couple of guys when I was a kid, but that was probably a side effect of abuse. This was totally different. You were so sweet, tender, and patient. I wasn't even sure if I could orgasm from sex, but it was wonderful. I'm just overwhelmed. Happy—but overwhelmed."

He pulled me to him and kissed me. "Well, it's about time someone made love to you instead of taking advantage of you, and I'm so glad I could share that with you. I'm so glad I could be the one to show you what lovemaking feels like. This is the icing on our cake." He smiled and pulled my head over onto his chest.

"How was it for you?" I asked. "How did it compare?"

"To what?"

"To other women," I responded. "You've had experiences I've never had."

"It was the first time I ever made love to someone I am in love with." He comforted. "There is no comparison."

I relaxed and felt comforted. Then, we lay there, lingering in each other's arms, and fell asleep. I awoke at about 9:00 p.m., and he woke when I did.

"Do you want to stay?" I asked.

"I would love to stay, but I have to work tomorrow."

"Okay," I said, "want a little dinner before you go home?"

"You know what, fuck it," he said. "I rarely take a day off work. I can call in and pretend to be sick tomorrow. What's for dinner?"

CHAPTER 20

TIME TO KILL

My trepidation faded, although much remained. I began spending more time with Jordan. Either he was spending the night at my place, or I was at his. Having him make love to me became like taking a treat from a box of chocolates, and he seemed to love it as much as I did. I longed for him to touch me. I longed to feel his skin's soft electric tingle and his lips' velvet touch when brought gently to my own. My entire concept of sex changed. I yearned for it and looked forward to it, but only with Jordan. I couldn't imagine ever wanting any other man. This was what I had been missing for my entire life. This was the treasure hidden beneath the feculent venality of sex that abuse had trained into my consciousness. No wonder I thought I didn't want sex. All it did was remind me of terrible things that had been done to me. An orgasm wasn't worth subjecting myself to the intrusion of obnoxious memories. I had been brave that first time with Jordan, and finally, in my late twenties, I began to understand the difference between making love and being raped. It wasn't really about the orgasm. That was just the icing on the cake and a delicious culmination of sensual communion with one another in both spirit and flesh. Still, I had to practice mindfulness and focus on the experience with Jordan, or the moment could be lost. I had to make him stop a few times because something triggered a memory I never wanted to have associated with him. Given my general opinion of men, he was so patient and understanding, which I realized might be rare.

We did a lot more than have sex. We talked, and I opened up to him for the first time, not just telling him what I had been through or how and why I had been through it, but telling him about myself, letting him see the fears and cautions behind my tears, but also allowing him to see the freedom I felt with him. For the first time, I was genuinely laughing, not pretending to laugh because I thought I was supposed to in a situation, but feeling safe to let go, to feel comfortable with his teasing, which was never dismissive or cruel. I loved him and felt his love for me the way I had always known that Miss Mattie loved me. I felt him connect with me, value me, and care for me. We went to movies, ate out, went to dinner with friends when possible, and curled up on the couch to watch TV together. I even attended a few local high school football games with him, but I still couldn't be sure. My lingering fear of abandonment kept me suspicious that I would lose him just like I had lost everyone else.

I picked up the remote one afternoon and paused the movie we had been watching.

"So, is this what normal feels like?" I asked.

He smiled and turned his attention from the television to me.

"Are you assuming that there is such a thing as normal?" he asked.

"A house, picket fence, kids and pets?" I replied. "Isn't that what most people consider normal? No, I'm talking about just feeling safe, being with someone you love, laying around the house, doing chores, fixing dinner for one another, being courteous, listening to more than what is being said, listening for the emotion beneath the words, cuddling next to each other and falling asleep together. That's what we're doing. Is that what normal feels like?"

"Well, since about half of all marriages end in divorce," he replied, "I don't know if this is normal, but it gives a better chance of not becoming the half that doesn't make it. Maybe it is the kind of thing that people do for each other when they love each other. It's the kind of thing my mom and dad do for each other, and they have been married for thirty-nine years now. Uncle Dennis and Aunt Marlene have had some troubles, but they always manage to get through it, and I think every couple fights sometimes. When you love each other, you try to see through the anger and respect each other even if you're angry. I think, most of the time, it's selfishness and expectations that destroy a relationship. If two people come together without selfishness and expectation, in my opinion, they have a good shot at making it. What's normal? I don't know."

"I've never experienced anything like this," I commented. "I don't know what we are doing, but I like it."

"I do, too," he replied.

"Which half do you think we might be?" I asked.

He smiled and leaned over to kiss me. He placed his hands on my cheeks and brought his lips to mine. Then he leaned back and said, "I can't predict the future, but I think you already know which half we are likely to be. I can tell you that I will commit myself to loving you."

"What about the fact that I was born in a boy's body?" I questioned. "Does that bother you anymore?"

He sighed. "I think that's something you need to stop worrying about. I'm attracted to women, and you are as beautiful and as womanly as any woman I have ever met. I love who you are now. I wasn't in your past. It's not for me to judge your past, but I'm here, now, and this is our normal."

I took his hand, leaned back into the sofa beside him, and picked up the remote to continue the movie.

Soon, Thanksgiving of 1988 was rolling around. Jordan propped himself on one elbow after making love to me a few days before Thanksgiving and said, "You know, Thanksgiving is coming. My parents usually have Thanksgiving dinner at their house or go to my mom's parents there in Columbia, and then come down here for Christmas to spend Christmas and New Year's with Uncle Dennis and Aunt Marlene. They are reversing it this year because my grandma, Dad's mom, has had to move into a little mother-in-law suite at Uncle Dennis's house, and she is getting to the point where it is difficult for her to travel."

"What about your grandpa?" I asked.

"He passed about three years ago, and Grandma finally had to have some assistance. Mom and Dad didn't have room for her back in Columbia, but Uncle Dennis had his garage converted into a little apartment for Grandma Walker. So, she is living in St. Louis now. Want to have Thanksgiving with the family?"

"I've never even met anyone in your family except Dennis," I replied. "Is this the kind of thing where you make introductions like that, bring the girlfriend to Thanksgiving when no one has met her?"

"I think it is as good a time as any," he returned. "Besides, if we are truly a couple now, then the time will come when we meet one another's family. I've met the Wilsons, and they are kind of like your side of the family. I want you to meet my side of the family."

"I don't know, Jordan. I don't know what to expect," I said. "The only time I've had any Thanksgiving celebration with family was when I was in foster care or with the Wilsons, and I think foster care doesn't count. It was more like an orphanage than a home; none of them were my family. The Wilsons didn't have a lot of other relatives in. It was usually just them and me."

"Well, you have experienced a lot of firsts with me, and I have experienced a lot of firsts with you," he replied. "If you think about it, every day we live is a first. We have never experienced this day before."

"But what are they going to think of me? What are they going to think of my background, my color, and what if they ask questions?"

"They are going to love you because I love you," he responded. "My family is not the kind to try to rule over their children's lives like some parents do. They know we're adults and have a right to our choices. I don't think they will ask too many questions, and we don't have to tell them anything until we are ready to tell them, but we will cross that bridge when we get to it. For now, it's just a celebration of Thanksgiving with my family."

"What about my color, Jordan?" I pressed. "I'm biracial. That's not something I can hide. Has anyone in your family ever dated a black girl? How do they feel about things like that?"

"What I know," he said, "is that my life is mine to live, not theirs, and they know that too. I can't promise that there isn't a racist in the family, even a closeted racist, but you know Uncle Dennis loves you, and it made no difference to him to introduce me to you or that I've been dating you. My mom and dad will be the same. I'm sure my siblings will. As far as anyone else, fuck them! It's my life, and I will live it the way I want, and I want to live it with you."

"But they will ask questions," I continued. "I don't like questions. How am I supposed to answer their questions? They are going to ask where I'm from and all kinds of shit like that."

He reached over and placed two fingers under my chin to bring my eyes to his. "You don't like questions because you are ashamed of where you came from and think others are going to shame you for it, but Stephanie, you don't have to be ashamed about anything. Where you have been is not where you are now, and if others shame you about it, that's their own bullshit. It's not about you. You don't have to feel ashamed just because somebody thinks you should."

"But you know people shame me, right? They always have."

"That doesn't mean they always will." He smiled. "My family is not like those thugs in school who tormented you, and as far as those assholes are concerned, fuck them too! Most of them were probably bullied themselves. It's like a pecking order trying to prove you are tough when you don't know shit about anything."

"What am I supposed to say if they ask questions?" I went on. "What am I supposed to say when they ask where I'm from, where I went to school or any of that shit."

"Tell them the truth, but maybe not the whole truth," he replied. "Tell them you are from St. Louis, that you grew up in Ladue, that your mother passed away when you were seventeen, and you have been on your own ever since. Tell them you are a bartender. Uncle Dennis already knows that. Tell them we met at the bar on New Year's Eve. That's all the truth. If they push beyond that, change the subject. Say, 'Why don't you tell me a little about yourself?' Talk about the food, the weather, the ball games, and the Macy's Parade. There is so much to talk about other than yourself. Flatter them by showing interest in them. Ask them questions. You can do this."

"Okay," I said. "How am I supposed to prepare for this?"

"Well," he continued. "Aunt Marlene will prepare the turkey, and Mom will likely be in the kitchen helping her with side dishes and desserts. So, all we have to do is show up and have a meal with the family."

"Who's going to be there?" I asked.

"Mom, Dad, Aunt Marlene, Uncle Dennis, Grandma, Shawna, her husband Bill and their two kids, Pete, his wife Michelle and their baby, Danny who isn't married yet, but he might bring his girlfriend, my cousin Cathy, her husband Gary, their two kids, you and me. Oh, and my cousin, Cheri, will probably be there. Her mom is Dad's little sister. Her dad is in the Navy and is retiring. They are moving everything from Virginia Beach to Corpus Christi, and Cheri has put up some resistance. So, Uncle Dennis suggested she stay with them for a few days. I think she is finishing the first half of her senior year in Virginia Beach and should start the spring semester in Corpus Christi. That's tough for a kid having to split her senior year."

"Oh, my God!" I chirped. "Nineteen or twenty people in the same house?"

"Well, five of them are little people," he reasoned, "and one is very little. Pete's baby is only six months old."

"Still," I pleaded. "I don't know if I've ever been around that many people in one closed-in place in my life. I get shaky about things like that, especially when I don't know people."

"You're around that many people at the bar several nights a week. You know some of those customers, but not all of them."

"That's different," I argued. "I'm on my turf there, and I know the rules. I don't know the rules at your house."

"The rules are just come and enjoy yourself," he reasoned. "You know me, and you know Uncle Dennis. We both like you. He and Aunt Marlene have a big house. So, it's not like we will all be cramped in a little room, and they will do their best to make you feel comfortable."

"I have usually spent Thanksgiving with the Wilsons since Miss Mattie died," I commented. "I'm sure they will be expecting me."

"Well, we can stop by there if you want," he reasoned. "We can at least say hello, but I want you to meet my family."

"Jordan, this feels like sink or swim," I countered. "Couldn't I just start with meeting your mom and dad?"

"Okay … well," he reasoned. "Could we at least stop by for a quick hello with my family, maybe have dessert?"

"This is really important to you, isn't it?"

"Kind of."

I gave in. "Okay, Aren't we supposed to bring a pie or something?"

"You can bring a pie if you want, or we can just take a bottle of wine, or just show up," he replied. "It's all okay."

"I guess I can make a pie," I said. "I like to cook."

"Done deal," he replied.

That evening, I thumbed through magazines for recipes and found a somewhat exotic-looking apple mango pie recipe. I never was much for traditional things, and I thought it sounded like a nice twist on tradition. The next day, I went to a grocery I usually wouldn't go to because it was bigger, a little further from downtown, and had more options. I wanted to make sure I had all the ingredients and mangoes were not to be found in my usual grocery. I wasn't sure if I could even find mangos. I knew there was a specialty grocery near the mall and thought I might be able to find mangoes there.

I got up the following day and drove to the store near the mall. I was standing in the produce aisle, looking at apples and searching for mangos, when I glanced up to see a man standing on the opposite side of the bins. He looked familiar, and a chill of anxiety ran through me. I quickly put my head down and turned the other way. My mind was chattering like several TV stations going at the same time. I began to see images I never wanted to see again: a man over me, drooling in my face, screaming, and beating my head onto the floor. I glanced back to be sure, and it was him, older and uglier, but it was Jake Carter. My heart hammered the inside of my chest, and I fought terror. I fought to breathe and practice the self-calming techniques I had been taught. Then, my logic kicked in, and I had a mental conversation with myself. *Stephanie! The last time he saw you, you were a ten-year-old boy, not a grown woman. It's not the same as Glen Tucker, who knew you were a transsexual, or Mike, who noticed features after you sent him a picture. It's totally different. Jake knew you only as a little boy. He would never suspect you would ever grow up as a woman. There is a snowball's chance in hell that he will recognize you. Get a grip!*

Then, I thought about my pledge to kill him if I ever saw him again. An ancient and festering hatred began to rise out of the mire of my memories, and my anxiety converted to anger. What had once terrified and blindsided me with any unexpected sound or encounter had become a vicious and tormenting anger. The rage of a child who could not fight back, fury that could not be expressed, reanimated from a place hidden within the recesses of my heart, and a scheme began rising in my mind. A temptation began to rise from stagnant and fermenting anger, a need to kill, a seething desire to kill. I *could* kill him if I could get him alone. The question would be how to get him alone. I remembered his fetishes, his sick, perverted corruption of sex, and I began to surmise a way that I could use it against him. Mustering all the courage I could, I decided to approach him.

I threw my coat over the shopping cart and unbuttoned my blouse to show some cleavage but hesitated. I knew that killing him would be wrong. I knew that it was something that Miss Mattie, Mike, Jordan, and the Wilsons would all forbid, regardless of my excuse. I battled with myself and heard my mind chanting, *If there is any man who deserves to die, it's that mother fucker, and if he dies a horrible death, much better, and if I'm the one who makes him die, that atrocious death, better still!* I gritted my teeth, amassed my courage, and marched right up to him.

"You look like a man who knows his potatoes," I said with a sultry smile, still trying to control my trembling at the very sight of him.

He did exactly what I expected him to do. He turned, glanced at my face, and immediately eyed my tits. A grin came across his face, showing some of his missing teeth. I knew I was flirting with the devil, but this was a devil that I was determined to eliminate. Despite all the things that had gone well for me, despite therapy and Miss Mattie's guidance, the festering loathing of Jake had never gone away. My heart became a noxious emotional boil festering with the rotting purulence of contempt. It needed to be lanced for it to heal, and the only way I knew to lance it was to kill him. The desire for revenge stalked my mind like a prowling panther, and I determined that I could never find peace until I killed him slowly and painfully.

He looked at my face after eying my tits and said, "Dang, if you don't look familiar. Have we met?"

My heart pounded like tympani drums, and I felt my face go flush and red. I had to catch myself quickly, but he noticed.

"Oh hey, ain't nothing to be embarrassed about," he flirted. "I get round a bit and meet lots of folks. Who knows where I've seen ya?"

I convinced myself that I could act the part. After all, I had been acting my whole life, always putting on a show for someone. I often played the role they wanted me to, even though I didn't want to. It was part of how I survived. *What's another role to play?* I heard hate appealing in my thoughts. *Don't let this opportunity pass. This is a role that will get you what you have always wanted.*

"Oh, I get that a lot. Somebody is always telling me I look like someone they know, but I don't think we have met." I tried to convince myself to keep it going. "I don't usually get over to this side of town, and I would surely have remembered meeting a man like you. No, I just noticed that you were picking around the potatoes, and I like potatoes, but—I'm not the best cook. So, I don't know."

"Well, what's the matter, little lady," he groaned. "Ain't nobody taught you how to pick out a good tater?"

A smile of confidence crossed my face, and I knew I had him. He would overlook the initial embarrassment if he thought there was the slightest chance he could get laid. "Mmm," I moaned as I ran my polished nails lightly across my cleavage. "Can you give me any pointers?"

At that moment, my mind dismissed thoughts about Jordan. I thought about how much I loved him and how much he loved me, but I had a long overdue job. I convinced myself I would do the world a favor by getting rid of Jake. A deep wickedness possessed me, and thoughts of murder waged a coup in my mind. The question of exactly how I would do it escaped me for the moment, but I had already concocted a plan to make him think I was interested in him, at least the beginnings of a plan to get him alone. I knew that putting the whole scheme together might take time, but luring him was a start.

He picked up a potato, "Well, you see them little spots right there?" He pointed to the potato eyes. "Now, you want to try to find one that an't got many of them unless you plan on plantin' some. If there's green around them little spots it means the tater is old and about to sprout. If you're gonna eat 'em and not plant 'em, cut out them little spots, 'cause if you cook 'em that way, it'll make ya sick."

"Fascinating," I said. "I've never cooked potatoes before. Do you cook potatoes?"

"I like 'em fried," he said as he eyed my cleavage.

"So, you like *hot* potatoes," I teased. "Would you like to heat up my potato sometime?"

His eyebrows raised, and he eyed me like a dog held back from a raw steak. I could see the lustful intrigue all over him. I knew what he liked and that he was stupid and easy.

He grinned again and stopped making any pretense that he wasn't looking at my tits. He looked around the store as though he was afraid to get caught, as though other customers could read his thoughts. Then, his eyes went straight back to my tits.

"You think you might like ta get a little friction on your tater?" He asked, and half snickered with his twisted lust.

I could see his excitement at having a pretty young girl coming onto him, and of course, he had no clue who I was. Realizing that gave me an extra boost of confidence. I don't know what I would have done if there had been a hint of recognition. Maybe I would have run from the store or flown at him with all the pent-up rage of an abused child. I was thankful he didn't see through my veil into our past.

"By the way, my name is Jenny," I lied to him, not wanting him to have the slightest hint of my actual identity.

"Hey, Jake here," he returned.

The mere sound of that name sent a chill through me, but it also confirmed that I had the right man in my sights. I covered my anxiety and went on. "You know, I have a pen and paper in my purse. Maybe you could give me your number, and I could call you up sometime; maybe get together and have a little fun."

He looked around again and whispered, "How much are you gonna be chargin' for this?"

He assumed correctly that no pretty girl would be coming on to him except a prostitute. If he thought I was a whore, it gave me a corridor of opportunity to implement my intent. I played along as wicked ideas filtered through my mind. I began to recognize that I could use the ruse to get him right where I wanted him—at my mercy.

"Wait a minute," I said. "You have to tell me. Are you a cop?"

"Hell, no, I'm not a cop," He snapped back. "Are you?"

"Of course not," I replied. "But I have to ask. A girl has got to make a living, and cops don't seem to understand that, but I know they are legally required to tell me if I ask."

"So, how much?" He grinned and eyed me up and down.

I teased. "I like older men, so I'll cut you a deal. Thirty bucks for a blow job and seventy-five to get in my pussy. A hundred for a little extra; maybe you like sticks and stones?" I grinned as I eyed him up and down. I already knew he liked it kinky.

A wide grin crossed his face. "I do kind of like sticks and stones," he teased. "Okay, gimme your phone number."

"Oh no," I replied. "You can't call me. You'll have to give me your number, and I'll give you a call. I might be … occupied … if you know what I mean. So, when I get some free time, I'll see if you're available."

"I can make myself available," he affirmed while making no pretense of his intentions. "I gotta watch my schedule, though."

"Oh, busy man, are you?" I teased.

"I can be at times. Sometimes, I got somethin' planned." He continued to eye the room as though someone might notice his sick intentions.

"Well, we'll work around schedules," I replied. "So, want to give me your number?"

"Why ain't you got a pager?"

"Oh, I do." I continued the deceit. "I just don't give out the number until I know someone will be a regular customer. I don't want just anybody blowing up my pager and running bullshit on me."

"Makes sense," he agreed. "Let's get together. I just might be a regular."

He could have picked up whores off the street, but I presented as quite a bit more sophisticated and better dressed. Like I said, he was stupid. I started to respond to him but had to give it a moment because someone else was approaching the produce section. When they passed by, I continued. "So, what are you into?" I asked. "You like kinky stuff, leather? Whips? Like to give a girl a spanking, or would you prefer an ordinary boring fuck?"

I saw his eyes light up. I knew he was a cruel bastard, and he liked for it to hurt. I just had to figure out how to get him vulnerable.

"Now, you are talking my language, baby," he cooed. "I told you I like sticks and stones. I wanna see what you can throw at me."

I reached into my purse, pulled out a small pad and pen, and handed them to him. He scribbled his name and phone number on the pad and returned it to me. I looked down, just for more confirmation. There was no last name, but he had written *Jake C. from the grocery* and a phone number. I needed no more evidence. I only needed to figure out exactly how to get him alone and kill him.

"Gotta go now, honey," I said as I pursed my lips toward him in an air kiss. "It might be a few days, but I'll call you."

I ripped the paper from the pad and deliberately tucked it between my tits for him to see and rolled the grocery cart away.

I ended up not making a pie after all. I couldn't find any mangos, but that was not the cause of my lost interest. Instead, I couldn't get my mind off plotting how to kill that ugly bastard. I knew that he had also done to other kids what he did to me. Who knew how many? I knew he had taken pictures of me and other kids and had to have those somewhere. I remembered the room upstairs where he would pose us for photographs. I decided to find those pictures and confront him with them before I slit his throat. In the meantime, I had Thanksgiving to attend with Jordan's family.

Jordan picked me up early on Thanksgiving to drive me to Dennis and Marlene's house. It was a classic house, two-story, almost as big as and similarly styled as the McNeils house. Cars were lining the block. My nerves were showing, and I was almost trembling with anxiety, not just from meeting Jordan's family but from the war of conscience that had begun when I ran into Jake. The part of me that had determined to kill Jake battled with the part that was in love with Jordan and knew I would give up everything if I got caught. I also battled with the morals and ethics that Miss Mattie instilled in me. Even if I never got caught, I knew a certain guilt would forever haunt me. Still, the war raged on, and the determination to kill Jake grew stronger every minute.

When Jordan pulled the car to the curb, he took my hand. "You okay?" he asked.

I looked up at him with trepidation while combating anxiety and moral discord within myself. He had no idea that more than half of my mood was due to obsessing about killing Jake.

"It will be okay," he promised. "Look, if it gets to be too much, let's come up with a sign you can give me, and I will make an excuse to leave."

"You would do that for me?" I asked.

"Of course, I would, honey," he reassured. "Let's see. What would be a good signal you and I would recognize but others would not pick up on? How about, If it is getting to be too much, you act like you are brushing something off your hair?"

"Okay," I replied. "I guess that would work. I'll handle it as long as possible and try to make it through the day."

"So, we are expected at Wilsons at about 5:00? Let me know if you need to leave before then."

I patted the back of his hand. He leaned over and gave me a quick peck on the lips, and I reached to open the door. He came around the car, took my hand, and walked hand in hand with me into the house. There was no knocking and waiting at the door. Jordan lightly tapped it, then opened it, and we walked in.

Inside the foyer, the dining room was to our left, and a large dark wood table was set with ten matching chairs. People were milling around everywhere, and children were playing in what appeared to be an office set up as a playroom across from the dining room. A hall led to what seemed to be a family room in the back.

"Hey, everybody," Jordan shouted as we came in.

"Jordan!" several people responded. One of them was a tall woman with hair almost the same color as Jordan's, and I could immediately tell that she must be his mother and where he had inherited his height and looks. His father followed right behind her. He was a little shorter than her, with graying hair that was slightly receding and a rugged, handsome face gleaming with a smile.

"Mom, Dad," Jordan said after a quick hug from his mother and a pat on his dad's shoulder. "This is Stephanie."

His mom eyed me like a prize cow at the state fair and cooed, "Oh, sweetheart! Look at you! Do you hug? Can I have a hug?"

My anxiety didn't want me to be touched, but I allowed her to hug me. Then Jordan's father hugged me without asking. If Mrs. Walker had permission, he assumed he did too.

"Nice to meet you, Stephanie," he said as he pulled back from the hug. "It's good to meet the girl Jordan has been dating."

"Jordan," his mom commanded, "why don't you go sit down with the guys and watch some TV while Stephanie and I get to know each other."

"I'll get around to everyone," he stated. "Besides, I would like to hang out with Stephanie." He had committed to helping me through this and would not leave my side, at least not initially.

"Okay, then, let's go say hello to folks in the kitchen," his mom commented as she placed her arm around my shoulder to guide me toward the kitchen. I wasn't used to that much physical contact, especially from someone who was still essentially a stranger, but I accepted it without protest.

"I'll see you guys later," Jordan's dad said, returning down the hall beside the stairs in the foyer.

Various women were milling about in the kitchen, and the smells of the season were wafting through the oven-warmed air. It was in the low sixties that day, and there had been a bit of a cloud cover. Someone had opened a couple of the kitchen windows to let some heat out and get a breeze into the house.

"Shawna!" Jordan's mother exclaimed. "Come over and say hi."

A woman with Jordan's family features placed a dish on the counter and came to stand before us.

"Shawna," Mrs. Walker announced. "This is Stephanie Laroquette, Jordan's girlfriend."

"Hi," Shawna responded with a beautiful smile and a sweet demeanor. "Welcome to Thanksgiving with the Walkers." She turned her gaze to Jordan. "You didn't tell me she was so pretty."

I felt my face blush with embarrassment. Obviously, Jordan had been telling his family about me. Who knew how much? I felt hesitant about having someone talk about me, a residue from my time at Pruitt Igoe. It was never a good thing to have someone talking behind your back, and because of that environment and abuse, privacy was a huge trust issue for me. I decided it must not be a big deal in the real world, that Jordan would not betray my trust, and tried to relax. Jordan had also told me things about his family. Still, I felt as though I was at a disadvantage as far as information was concerned.

"She is much more than pretty," Jordan responded as he took my hand. "She's a wonderful person."

His mom must have noticed my blush and evident anxiety. "You know, it is a lot to take in when you are the new kid on the block," she said. "Stephanie, I know this can be a little overwhelming, meeting the whole family at once. Why don't you and Jordan grab some snacks off the snack table over here and sit in the family room? There are extra chairs. Jordan can do any further introductions."

"Would you like help in the kitchen?" I asked.

"No, sweetheart," she responded. "We have too many cooks as it is. Go sit down and relax."

"Come on," Jordan coached. He led me to the snack table, where we picked up a few things and poured ourselves a soft drink. Then we went into the living room, where chairs had been arranged to face the TV. In one corner, a young woman sat in an overstuffed recliner. She had a baby wrapped in blankets, suckling a bottle. A young man sat on the arm of the chair next to her.

"Come on," Jordan coaxed as he approached the young man and woman. "Stephanie, this is my little brother Pete and his wife Michelle, and that little bundle in Michelle's arms is Cassy. Guys, this is Stephanie."

Pete stood to greet me and reached out to shake my hand. He was a little shorter than Jordan and perhaps had more of his father's looks. Michelle, a dark-haired, pretty woman, was preoccupied with the baby and didn't get up but nodded in my direction. "Good to meet you," she said.

Their friendliness felt intimidating. I was not used to social gatherings other than with the Wilsons or some of Joan's friends, but that started with Joan's introductions when I was still a kid, and I was used to being around them. It was also usually not a house full of strangers. I didn't know what to do or how I was supposed to act with people who were all strangers to me except Jordan. So, I didn't say much at all, but I affirmed that it was nice to meet them, too.

I was introduced to others. Then we sat down and made small talk, or at least Jordan did. I only listened with quiet embarrassment. Most of us barely noticed what was on the television. Time passed, but the war in my mind raged on. I looked around and realized that probably no one there had a clue what it might be like to grow up in Pruitt Igoe. I wondered what, if anything, we could ever find in common. My fears of rejection and ridicule returned when I started thinking about having little or nothing in common. What would they do if they knew how I had grown up, that I had been in foster care? What would they do if they ever discovered that I was a transsexual? Would they be so accepting, then?

I felt suddenly overwhelmed, suffocating in a room full of people. The chatter of conversation and background noise became almost deafening. I leaned over and asked Jordan, "Where's the bathroom?"

"Oh, there's one at the top of the stairs," He replied.

Beside the hall from the foyer to the living room was a set of stairs that descended into the living room. I rounded the corner, climbed the stairs to the second floor, and found a bathroom across from the landing. I couldn't wait to get into that room, close and lock the door, have some silence, and breathe. I flipped on the vent fan to have a little white noise to drown the chatter, which the climb to the second floor had already partially muffled. After I finished, I continued to sit on the commode for a while, simply staring at the room. The bathroom had peach tiles, matching towels, a brown granite countertop, and a matching porcelain sink with an ornate brass faucet. I sat there for quite a while, savoring the silence. Eventually, I came out, sat on the top step, and buried my face in my hands. Soon, I felt the presence of another person, who came to the steps and sat beside me. I was initially startled and looked up to see a teenage girl in blue jeans and a t-shirt sitting beside me. Her bare feet rested on the next step down.

"Sucks, doesn't it?" she said, looking straight ahead.

"What sucks?" I asked.

"All these people." She replied. "Even if they are my family, they overwhelm me sometimes with all this false congeniality and shit."

"You don't think they are sincere?" I asked.

"Oh, I guess maybe in their way they are," she replied. "Aunt Marlene and Aunt Sarah seem to get off on it. Otherwise, I think most people do holidays just because they think they are supposed to."

I gave her a closer look. She was pretty but had not fixed herself for the occasion as the others had. She had dawned no makeup, her hair was frizzed, and she looked like she had just pulled on her jeans after she got out of bed. On the other hand, I had spent the entire morning fussing over my looks, makeup, and hair. I had tried on at least four different dresses before I told myself, *Fuck it, just pick one!*

"So, you're not saying they are not sincere people?" I questioned. "You're saying all this is just a put-on for the holiday."

"Isn't that what people do?" she said. "They put on a show for the holiday. They might be good people, and don't get me wrong, I love my family, but I'm just not into pretending we're having a good time just because it's some holiday."

"I take it that you are not having a good time," I responded. "By the way, my name is Stephanie."

"Cheri," she said as she extended a hand for a brief shake.

"Oh, you're Jordan's niece," I commented. "He said you might be here."

"Yeah, I'm stuck with it, and, no, I'm not having a good time, and neither are you."

"You clocked me." I smiled and asked, "Why aren't you having a good time?"

"I'm only here because my mom and dad are moving to Corpus Christi, and I just don't want to deal with that shit anymore." She continued to stare forward. "Besides, I had to leave all my friends in the middle of my senior year, and I had barely made friends over the last two years in Virginia."

"You don't want to move to Texas?" I asked.

"No, that's not it, exactly. I don't really like Texas, but you know? No, I'm leaving my friends—AGAIN! My dad is career Navy, and we have had to move so damned often. I suppose this will be the last one—God, please!—since my dad is *finally* retiring." She folded her hands as though in prayer and lifted them into the air. "We have had to move so often that every time I made friends, I've had to move away. Why even bother? So, here we go again, and I will have to finish the last half of my senior year of high school with kids I have no history with. At least I'll graduate in May and start having some control over my life."

"I'm sorry that has frustrated you," I commented. "Maybe you can create some history with the kids in Texas." Her complaint seemed trivial compared to what I had been through, but I knew it was significant to her, and I was not about to start comparing who had it worse.

"So, what's your gig?" She changed the subject. "What got you here?"

"I've been dating Jordan," I replied.

"Thought so when you said he told you about me, but he's my cousin, not my uncle. He's a good guy."

"Yes, he's wonderful," I commented with a smile.

"My mom is Jordan's dad's little sister," she explained. "She was the baby of the family. That's why I'm so much younger than Jordan." She paused and turned toward me briefly. "So, I know why I'm hiding out and staying upstairs. What about you? Why are you sitting up here instead of down there with Jordan and the family?"

"Crowds can be a little overwhelming for me," I replied. "Jordan and Dennis are the only people I know here."

"And now me … You'll get to know them if you and Jordan stay together," she assured. "They're all good people—really. I mean, what family doesn't have its faults, but they will probably be good to you."

"Thanks," I replied. "I don't know if Jordan and I will make it. I don't know if his family will like me."

"Why not?" she asked.

"It's complicated," I replied.

"Too complicated to talk about," she asked.

"Especially with a teenage girl," I continued.

"You're not much older than I am," she pressed. "Come on—spill it. I spilled to you."

A hefty sigh came out at that point, and I debated whether to tell her anything. "I'm just not from this kind of family," I said, finally.

"Because you're African American?" she asked flatly.

I was shocked at her question, and she saw it on my face.

"Does that question bother you?" she asked.

I was nonplussed. I almost wanted to take offense, but I knew she meant well. I hadn't yet stopped to think how much I might have internalized racism. I knew it was all around me, but I hadn't stopped to consider that I had it within me. For a moment, I was taken aback as I tried to figure out how to respond to her. I suppose a part of me wanted to pass as white, and sometimes, it seemed that I did. I had not thought, until that moment, that I was almost as scared of being outed for being black as a transsexual. As much as I loved Miss Mattie, as dark as she was, as much as she fit the stereotype of some old black woman from the South, I had never judged her and dearly loved her, but I knew she had been judged. My mind went back to seeing her manhandled by a white cop just for sitting in her car in front of a house in a white neighborhood. Then, there I was, in a house full of white people, dating a white man, not knowing how I would be received or whether I would be accepted. I wanted his family to like me, but I was terrified they wouldn't. Maybe I had fooled myself into believing that my African part didn't show anymore. Maybe I wished that it didn't show.

Finally, I replied, "I guess I do worry about being the only black person in an all-white family, but that's not really it."

"If you were the color of charcoal and Jared loves you, the whole family would love you. Believe me. There might be a bigot in the family, here or there, but not in close family, and they know to keep their mouth shut and treat you with respect even if they have some racism going on. Growing up in the military, you are around all kinds of people from all walks of life. You learn early that people are just people no matter what they look like." She grinned. "Besides, Jordan would kick their asses if they disrespected you. So, if that's not it, what is?"

"It's a long and complicated story," I said. "Maybe I'll tell you someday, but for now, let's just leave it as our secret that I grew up in the slums, and I'm not used to all this. I don't know how to act around all this."

"I like you," she said.

I smiled. "I like you too." Then I asked, "What's wrong with moving to Texas?"

She rolled her eyes. "I don't know," she replied. "My Dad was stationed in Corpus Christi for a little while when I was in elementary school. I barely remember it. Maybe it is because the military is so prominent there, with a Navy base in Corpus Christi, a base in Kingsville, the Army Depot in Corpus, and, of course, a commasary. I've been around the military my whole life; I practically don't know anything else, and I would like to experience something else for a change. Even though I know with my dad retiring, Corpus will probably be our forever home; I'm afraid I won't really be able to get close to anyone. I've never been close to anyone but my family."

"I guess we have some similarities," I said. "We're both afraid of letting people in, of letting others get close to us."

"Oh, my God! You're right!" she affirmed. "I'm scared that if I let anyone get close, I'll lose them, like I've always lost friends when we moved."

"I guess we both need to open our hearts a little," I commented as I reached over and took her hand.

She squeezed my hand and smiled.

About that time, Jordan came up the stairs. "Oh, hey," he called. "There you are. I was beginning to think you got lost or left or something. Hi, Cheri."

"Hi, Jordan," she responded.

Jordan leaned over and whispered, "Would you like to see the deck and get some fresh air?"

"Yes, that would be nice," I said, half smiling.

I stood up, waved at Cheri, and said, "Nice to meet you."

"Nice to meet you too," she replied without getting up. "Can we maybe call and have some more chats?"

"Sure," I replied. "You can reach me through Jordan. I'll look forward to talking to you again." I later discovered that we would become friends.

Then Jordan took my hand, and we walked downstairs, out onto a large covered deck at the back of the house, and into the cool, refreshing air. A young man was sitting in one of the deck chairs smoking a cigarette.

"This is Gary Johnson, my cousin Cathy's husband," Jordan introduced.

"Hi, how're you doing?" he said, grabbing a can of beer from a nearby table and taking a swig.

"Gets a little crowded in there, hmmm?" Jordan said, and Gary responded, "Yup."

"Come on, let's take a walk," Jordan said, reaching for my hand.

"Where are we walking?" I asked.

"Eh, just up the street and back, maybe around the block."

He led me off the deck, down a walk to a gate. Passing through the gate, we stepped onto a small sidewalk that led out from the driveway. All the time, he held my hand.

"How are you doing with this?" he asked.

"It's kind of nerve-wracking for me," I replied. "It's not just that there are so many people, but they're people I've never met. They seem to know things about me, but I don't know much about them."

"You'll get to know them in time," he said. "You're probably not going to see most of them except for the occasional visit and the holidays anyway. You would be amazed how many people in a family don't know much about other members of the family, especially those who have married in."

"Where's your grandmother?" I asked.

"Probably in her apartment," he replied. "She is not much for the company, either." She'll come out for the meal and then go back when everybody settles down in the afternoon to watch football."

"So, is this what normal families are like?" I asked.

"Pretty much, I guess," he replied. "Not everybody in a family likes each other. Some of us are close, but sometimes, we just tolerate each other with congeniality for the holidays. It's all okay. Just the way things are done, I guess—bonding."

"Do you like to do this?" I questioned. "Cheri was telling me she thinks it's kind of all fake just for the holiday, just because people think they are supposed to."

"Yeah, it could be a little, I guess, but I like the food, and it's nice to catch up with family members I haven't seen in a while." He laughed and pulled me into a side hug. "I know you are not used to things like this, but you've had some practice with the Wilsons, and why don't we just go ahead and leave right after the meal and spend some time with them? You've met my close family. So, that's enough for today."

"Okay." I felt relieved. "Are they going to do the thing of going around and everybody saying what they are grateful for?" I asked. "I don't want to do that shit."

"Yeah, that's not something we force on people," he said. Just a prayer of thanksgiving that Uncle Dennis will probably give and then dig into the meal. We won't even all sit together. Too much family and not enough table."

The walk helped, and I felt relieved. When we got back, the meal was being served. Dennis prayed in the kitchen before the process started, and we lined up to serve ourselves. Jordan and I went to a little breakfast nook off the kitchen where Jordan's grandmother and his little brother Danny sat. Cheri quietly came down the stairs in her bare feet t-shirt and jeans, filled a plate, got a drink, and went back upstairs. Ultimately, it ended up being just the four of us at that little breakfast nook, and that was a lot easier to handle. Jordan introduced me to his grandmother and little brother, who had not brought his girlfriend. His grandmother smiled with a sweet "Hello," and most of the discussion was between Jordan and Danny.

After the food, Jordan announced that we needed to stop by and spend some time with "Stephanie's family" and didn't bother to tell them that the Wilsons were more my adopted family than anything else. We spent a little time with the Wilsons, and on the way home, I was reticent.

"You okay?" Jordan asked after an extended silence.

Truthfully, my mind was on Jake and how I could accomplish what my contempt was calling me to do. I had begun to realize that I would have to set Jordan aside for a while if I was going to do it. I knew I was risking the loss of Jordan's love to appease an ancient abhorrence, but the hate was winning at that point. I was obsessed with the idea of killing Jake. I had fantasized about it since I was a tiny child. Then, after running into him at the grocery, that fantasy had become an obsession about a plan to eliminate him.

"I'm okay," I lied. I was anything but okay. I was preoccupied with murderous thoughts, malice aforethought, plotting, and premeditation.

"Was today a little too much for you?" he asked.

"A little," I replied, "but I got through it. So, now I know that I can do it. I really like your mom and your sister. They are very sweet, and I like Chri. She's a sweet kid."

"Yeah, my mom is wonderful," he replied. "She likes everybody until someone gives her a reason not to. That's why I said you will be okay with my family. I know you are not going to give them a reason not to like you."

"You don't know," I responded. "How do I even know if I won't give them a reason not to like me? People have not liked me for my whole life for all kinds of reasons. People have not liked me just because I wasn't like them. I don't place much faith in people liking me, but still, I want to be liked."

"I know it's been rough," he replied. "I know enough about you at this point to realize that it is never easy to meet someone new and that it is a rare event when you trust anyone. Hell, you had fallen in love with me before you ever trusted me. But, Stephanie, my mom has a good system. In the long run, in most situations, unless there are overt red flags, it is better to trust people until they prove they can't be trusted than to trust no one until they prove they can be trusted. Granted, some people absolutely can't be trusted, but I'll bet that if you trust yourself, you can spot the red flags that let you know to back away from those kinds of people."

"Maybe you're right," I said. "I just need some time to process. Jordan, please drop me off at my condo today. I need some time to think and some time to be alone."

"What do you need to think about?" he asked.

"Us," I replied.

"Us?" he questioned. "Haven't we crossed that bridge already? I know it was tough for me when you told me everything, but I'm over that now. Really, I am. What's left that we need to process."

"Not we, Jordan," I said. "We don't need to process anything. I need to process. Right now, there's nothing we need to discuss. I need time to think and sort things out in my head. I'm fighting a battle within myself, not with you, and I need time to process that. I might call my therapist and go in for a few sessions."

"Okay? So, this is something you can't discuss with me?"

"Not yet," I responded. "Maybe someday, but not yet."

"I'm confused," he stated, "and I'm uncomfortable with this."

"Jordan, I gave you time. I thought I had lost you after finally confessing what I had been through. Don't you think you could do the same for me?"

"You're right," he replied. "If you need space, I need to give you space—okay." He sighed very deeply. "Can I call you during this time? Can we at least talk on the phone?"

I smiled. "I think the proper grammar is 'May I call you?'" I responded.

"Dang!" he exclaimed and laughed. "I wish I had had an English teacher like you when I was in high school. So, may I call you during this time?"

"No," I replied. "I think it would complicate things and make it difficult for both of us. It's just best that we have no contact for a while."

I could see the disappointment wash over him. A sadness filled his face.

"Jordan, I will call you when I'm ready, okay? I promise that I will. Until then, I need to straighten some shit out in my head."

He didn't know why I needed time away from him, and I knew I might have to take a considerable amount of time, depending on how complicated my plans might become. I hoped it wouldn't take long to dispose of Jake and return to my life, but I needed privacy to accomplish my goals. The battle still raged within me between my conscience and my hatred, but it felt as though malice had made a nest to hatch a brood of revenge. I had to kill Jake. I felt like I had no other choice. I had to keep him from continuing to hurt children. If I was going to go through with it, there were things I needed to buy, and there was research I needed to do to set a trap for Jake that he could not weasel out of. I knew I was taking the most significant risk of my life and could face the death penalty or life in prison if caught. I was going to be very careful that I didn't get caught. Still, I knew I could be losing the best things that ever happened to me. I didn't know what I would do or how I would feel after I killed Jake, but I had it wedged in my mind that killing him must give me a release and a satisfaction that I wouldn't be able to find any other way. I told myself that I wasn't just doing it for myself alone but for all the other children he had hurt for who knows how many years, kids that he could still be hurting.

Jordan dropped me off downstairs on the street in front of my condo. "May I come up?" he asked before I got out of the car.

"No," I replied, seeing the puddles of tears forming at the base of his eyes. "I have to be alone. I can't tell you why, but I have some things to sort out." I reached over to kiss him on the cheek and hug him. "Jordan," I continued. "I want you to know this. No matter what happens, whether we stay together or break apart, I love you down to the depths of my soul and will always love you, no matter what. I've never known anything like this before, and it terrifies me more than you know, but no matter what happens, I want you to know that this has meant the world to me."

The tears flowed for both of us.

"Stephanie," he pleaded. "You are the best thing that has ever happened to me. I don't care about your past. I don't care! I love you and will also love you forever, no matter what, but dear God! I pray fervently that this will not cause me to lose you."

"I have to go now," I said.

"I'll be waiting for your call," he implored. "I will look for and long for your call. When you have sorted out whatever you need to sort out, I will be waiting."

"I know," I softly replied, kissing him quickly. Then, I opened the door and crossed the walk to my building. I turned at the front entrance to give him a brief wave and proceeded to the elevator.

CHAPTER 21

RAT IN A TRAP

After returning to my condo on Thanksgiving, I went to bed and cried for most of the evening. I felt like I had already lost Jordan like I had sacrificed him to my seething hostility for Jake. I found myself torn between the risk of sacrificing any future I might have with Jordan and finally living out the revenge I had contemplated since I was a small child. I had an obsession with killing Jake. I thought that getting rid of him would be doing the world a favor, and I had convinced myself that the world would be better without him. I hated what I was doing to Jordan and spent several days crying about it, but my need to get back at Jake seemed to outweigh everything at that time. I knew I could be sacrificing the rest of my life, but I solaced myself by thinking that, even if I got caught, I would be getting a child predator off the streets.

A few days after Thanksgiving, I called Willard and asked for an extended leave.

"Are you okay? Not sick or something?" he asked.

"I'm fine, Daddy Willard," I replied. "I just need some time. I haven't had a vacation since I started there. I just need to be on this side of the bar for a while. I plan to come back if you'll have me."

"You and Jordan aren't having any problems, are you?" he continued.

"No, we're fine," I lied. Any problem I had with Jordan was of my own creation due to my fervor for revenge. I had a solicitous craving to see Jake squirm just before I took his life. I could put a bullet through his brain, but that would be too quick and easy. I didn't want him to die quickly and easily. I wanted him to suffer like I and other children had suffered because of his brutal perversion.

"Okay," he replied. "How much time do you need?"

"Can I have off till New Year's Eve," I asked. "I'll be happy to work the big night for you. I might need a little time again after that."

"Yeah, sure," he affirmed. "Let me talk to the other bartenders and see if we can shift the schedule for the next few weeks, and I can work the bar if I need to.

He knew I didn't have to work. He knew I had enough to live on with my Trust and that I worked because I wanted to work. I don't know what he thought might happen if Jordan and I got married, whether I would quit at that point or continue working. Of course, we could not legally marry then, and the state had remanded that despite my name change and transition surgery, my birth certificate and driver's license would continue to state that I was a male. A couple of states allowed transsexuals who had completed surgery to marry, but Missouri wasn't one of them. Willard didn't know any of that. I wasn't required to show him my birth certificate or driver's license when he hired me, only my social security card.

The whole issue of the world not accepting me as female and preventing me from legally marrying the man I loved was also part of what I needed to work out. No matter how much we loved each other, my papers said I was male. Even though I was a woman in every respect except bearing children, we still could not have the marital privileges others took for granted. I could not be considered Jordan's next of kin, nor he mine. No matter how much we loved each other and committed our lives together or how long we lived together, we were separated by law and by the demands of social norms that didn't fit who we were. I debated if it would be unfair to Jordan to be with someone like me when we could not have the legal protections others took for granted. We could perhaps go to a different state to get married, but no matter how much he said he loved me and wanted to be with me, we would always have obstacles. I worried that those obstacles could prove insurmountable despite loving each other.

"I'll give you a call after Christmas," I said. "Okay, Daddy Willard? Maybe I'll call you before."

"Sure," he replied. "Enjoy your time off."

After I had secured everything with Jordan and my job, and I knew that I would have my way clear, I had some shopping to do. I went to some of the local sex shops and looked for some murder paraphernalia. That included black leather dominatrix outfits and accessories. That included a skin-tight corset and thong and a tit-boosting leather braw that showed more of my tits than it didn't. There were holes at the tips of the braw where the nipples fit through, and I bought leather pasties with tassels to hang over the nipples. The outfit had metal loops and grommets. I purchased a rider's crop, a cat of nine tails, knee-length high-heel boots, and tight, thin leather gloves that pulled up to my elbows, but I was not finished shopping. Afterward, I went to a knife store and looked for switchblade knives. The legal limit was a five-and-a-half-inch blade. I knew that would be enough to slit his throat, but I needed more because I wanted to scare him as much as I wanted to kill him.

I went to a weapons store and goaded the sales clerk. He showed me one of the knives, and I asked, "How sharp is it?"

"Let's just say you could shave with it," he said.

"Got anything bigger?" I asked.

"Five and a half is the legal limit," he replied.

"Surely, there is a little wiggle room, maybe with a few extra bucks," I replied, sliding five hundred dollars across the glass counter.

No one else was in the store, but he looked around like someone could walk in at any moment.

"You got any more?" he asked.

I laid another five hundred on the counter.

Again, he looked around nervously. "I might have an eight-inch in the back," he said.

"How sharp is it?" I asked.

"Lady, what are you planning to do with this?" he questioned.

I smiled. "Maybe I need some protection. I'm a bartender and walk home at about 3:00 a.m. downtown. How safe do you think that is?"

"Maybe you just need some mace," he said.

"Got that," I replied. "I need something more."

Truthfully, I didn't have that far to walk, but he didn't have to know that. I also trusted the skills I had learned at Pruitt Igoe to keep me safe; he didn't need to know that either.

"So, how sharp is it?" I asked again.

"Sharp enough to shave with," he said. Then he went to the back and came out with the knife in a nice leather case. He opened the case to show me the knife.

"Beautiful," I said. How much is it?

"Another thousand," he replied, assuming I was willing to pay it.

He was right. I had brought plenty of cash. Since I didn't need it, I had stowed thousands of dollars of tips from the bar and would occasionally take bits of it to the bank to trade ones for larger bills. I kept most of it hidden at home. At Pruitt Igoe, you never knew when you might need some extra cash, and I had been hiding money ever since I was old enough to think.

I reached into my purse and handed him two five-hundred-dollar bills. He snatched the remaining bills from the counter, pocketed them, and said, "You better go now."

I closed the case on the knife, put it into my purse, and walked out. I only had a couple of more things to do for my plan. I went to a uniform store and bought a gray zip-up coverall. After that, I came home and stashed everything in my condo. Then, I took a cab to a car rental company and rented a white van.

A couple of days later, I tried to talk myself into calling the bastard. After trembling and trepidation that evening, I picked up the phone receiver several times, put it down again, and decided that getting dressed in my murder outfit might boost my courage a little. So, I put on the black leather dominatrix outfit and slapped the ridding crop around on nearby furniture. I had also purchased a Santa hat since it was getting close to Christmas. I dawned the hat and glared at Santa-bitch in my full-length mirror. Courage restored, I got out the paper with Jake's number and called.

"Hello," I heard his disgusting voice.

"Hello," I said sweetly and seductively. "Is this Jake?"

"Yeah, what ya want?"

"This is Jenny, the girl you met at the grocery store last week. You ready to have a little fun?"

"Oh, Hey, baby," he growled in what he thought was a sexy voice. You ready for me to come over?"

"Let's talk a little," I replied. "Give me some details about what you're into."

"Humph … you already know I like me some sticks and stones," he teased. "What you got in mind?"

"Yeah, you like the kinky stuff, don't you, big boy?" My gut was wrenched at what I was having to subject myself to. "What kind of kinky stuff do you like?" I asked. "Do you like to whip a girl? Make her behave? You might need a spanking if you're a bad boy, like a domina-trix to order you around?"

"I just might be a bad boy," he whispered.

I knew that was true, but 'bad boy' was an understatement. I knew precisely how evil he was. At least, I thought I did.

"I thought so," I moaned. "If you need to be disciplined, I am the hot mamma for the job. Want to hear what I'm wearing right now?"

In my mind, I could see him salivating through that ugly mouth. "Oh, yeah, baby," he growled. "Give it to me. Tell me all about it."

"Mmmm, I am wearing black leather everything," I teased. "I have a black leather corset and a thong that runs across my pussy straight up the crack of my ass. I have a black leather push-up bra with my nipples sticking out the front and leather pasties on each one. Yeah, do you like a woman masked? I have a cat woman mask, and I'm sitting here with a riding crop, flicking it across my bare legs."

"Oh fuck yeah!" he groaned. "When are we gettin' together?"

"First, I need to know where you live," I growled seductively. "Then, I have some stipulations and surprises."

"Why do you need to know where I live?" His suspiciousness was evident. Of course, he was suspicious. God knows how many years he had been hiding his malevolent bullshit.

"Because I have to come to your house if we are going to do this,"

"I thought we would be doin' this at your place," he protested. "I don't much like having people at my house."

"I'm not people, baby," I crooned. "I'm your sexiest nightmare, and that's part of my stipulations."

"What kind of stipulations?"

"I come to your house and set up the whole scenario in whatever room you want."

"I thought you maybe had one of them S & M torture rooms or somethin'," he disclosed. "I figured I would come to your place."

"Oh, we can't do that, baby," I crooned.

"Why the fuck not?" He sounded irritated.

"Because I care for my grandmother, and she doesn't know I'm hooking," I lied the quickest and best lie I could come up with. "The kind of thing I do would upset her, and I don't want her knowing about it. Since it's how I support us and she wouldn't like it, I have to keep that from her. I tried waiting tables, but I can make a lot more money and have a lot more fun making sure my men are pleased."

"Well, I don't like nobody at my house," he continued to resist.

"You got a wife or something?" I knew better.

"No."

"You live alone?" I asked.

"Yeah, but that don't matter."

"What's the hold-up, baby?" I continued trying to weasel in.

"What kind of scene-nar-io are you plannin' to set up?" He asked.

"If you live alone, I need to set some things up first, okay? I'm a professional and have a protocol to ensure my customers get the abso-lute pleasure they deserve."

"What are you talking about?"

"I need to set up the atmosphere a little. You know what I mean? I want to ensure you get the titillation you deserve, emphasizing tit and the elation. You like my tits, don't you? Wouldn't you like to have some tit-illation? I need time in the house to set everything up while you're out. Then I can give you a big surprise when you get back." I knew there would be an issue of trust. Those who can't be trusted are the ones who trust the least. I banked on his intrigue and sick lust, outweighing his lack of confidence.

"I told ya. I don't care for nobody in my house, especially if I ain't there," he countered.

"I know, baby," I moaned. "I get that, but you're really going to like this. I bring all my equipment, set everything up for my little pleasure palace, and then I'll give you the best time you ever dreamed of. I try to make sure the first time is fabulous because I like my regular customers, and it only gets better from there. Besides, you seem like the kind of guy who will want me back for another show. After this first little taste of ecstasy, you'll know I'm worth it. Tell you what. I'll cut the price a little for the first time—twenty-five percent off. If you don't like it, no harm done. If you do like it, I go back up to my regular price."

"How do I know you ain't gonna rob me or something?"

"You don't," I replied, "but that would be stupid of me. Don't you think? If I want a regular customer, I need to keep the customer happy. I'll bet you wouldn't be happy if I robbed you. Besides, that isn't my profession. I operate with class and can make much more money building up a safe but kinky experience for my regulars. Well … as safe as you want it to be, but having a regular clientele is safer for me and for my clients. I won't walk in with my dominatrix outfit on. We don't want the neighbors getting suspicious and asking questions. I wear a jumpsuit uniform and drive a van to your house. I look like I'm making a delivery. Then, once inside, I set it up so you will have the time of your life."

"Okay," he said hesitantly.

"First, some questions." I continued.

"Okay."

"Do you have a good sturdy dining chair?" I asked.

"Well, yeah."

"Any kind of mood lighting? If you don't, I can bring some things to set the mood."

"Okay," he replied. "You can bring yer lights. All I got is lamps and overheads."

"Ever had hot wax dripped on your nipples?" I crooned.

"Oh, baby, you are talking my language," he groaned, "Can I drip some on yours?"

"Absolutely," I responded. "I'm going to enjoy this as much as you will."

"Anything else you need to do?" he summoned.

"Yes," I replied. "I need you to leave a key for me, like under your doormat, and I need you to be out of the house for at least an hour."

"Why the hell do you need to do that?" he questioned.

"I told you, baby," I purred. "I need to set the mood, get everything ready for our lovemaking. I've got some tricks up my sleeve like you ain't never seen. I have a few gadgets that I need to bring, and I want to get everything just right for you."

"I don't like the idea of just goin' away and havin' somebody in my house without me being here," he chided, "and I don't like leavin' my key for nobody."

"How bad do you want to fuck me?" I asked. "How much of a build-up do you want before you get there?"

There was a silence on the line, and for a moment, I thought I might have lost him. Then he said, "Real bad. I want to fuck you real bad, but I don't want to leave a key out for just anybody who might come along."

"All right, baby," I agreed. "What do you want then?"

"I'll meet you here," he said, "and then I'll leave after I see some of what yer bringin' in."

"Give me the address," I submitted. "Let's set up a date and time, and I need at least an hour to set up after I get there, but I don't want you seeing *everything*. I want to give you a nice surprise."

"Why can't I be here while you are settin' up?" he asked.

"Oh, now that would spoil the surprise, wouldn't it, baby?" I teased again. "You do want a nice big surprise, don't you?"

"Yeah, I wanna have a little fun," he answered.

"Sometime tomorrow, good for you?" I asked.

"Yeah, what time?" he replied.

"You want daytime or evening?" I asked.

"How about afternoon? Maybe about one o'clock."

"You got it, hun," I replied. "I'll see you tomorrow."

He gave me an address on North 20th Street, and I knew the area was run down. I didn't know where he had taken me as a child. I didn't know to look at the addresses or the streets, but I remembered what the house looked like. I hoped he was in the same house because I knew my way around that house and planned on snooping.

"What does your house look like?" I asked.

"It's brick, got white trim and a big fancy front porch with white columns and shit. The damn thing is about a hundred years old, but I got it cheap."

"So, you own your own house?"

"Yep," he reflected. "I need me a little privacy. I don't like that rentin' shit. I'd rather live in a dump that belongs to me than live in a fancy apartment with everybody all up in my business."

I thought to myself, *I'll bet you would, scumbag.* His description matched the house I remembered. So, I knew where things were and put together my plan's remaining touches. That included taking about fifteen minutes to set up and the rest to see what I could find.

"Okay," I replied. "I'll meet you there about 1:00 p.m. tomorrow. Then you can go have a drink somewhere while I get us all set up."

"Yeah, I might just do that," he replied. "Havin' a drink or two first sounds good. I'll see you then."

"I can't wait, baby," I said, feeling like I would choke on every word. My heart was pounding, and I was scared, but I was also determined. I decided to push through the fear. I wasn't going to let anything stop me.

The next day, I got into the leather outfit and stashed the switchblade in a pocket on the side of my boot. It fit snugly but was easy to retrieve and wasn't overtly noticeable. I put some candles in a brown cardboard box with some black lights I had also purchased. I placed handcuffs, a small rubber ball, a gag, and cotton ropes into the box. I had a specific plan for the rope. I didn't want him to get away, and if I could trick him into letting me tie him up, well, "Come into my parlor said the spider to the fly." Either I would kill him, or he would kill me, but I made a pact with myself that I would make sure he didn't hurt anyone else. I put the coveralls over the regalia, picked up the box, and carried everything to the rental van.

I arrived at his place about five minutes before one. I recognized the house, a brick Victorian with squared columns wrapped around the front porch at intervals. The house had been sufficient for an upper-middle-class family of its time but had certainly seen better days. The white paint was peeling from the columns and trim, and the bricks had the muffled color of age. I parked the van and carried the box up the steps to the front porch with a throbbing heart, feeling more like I was going to faint than kill someone. When I knocked on the door, I heard, "Just a minute."

He opened the door and eyed me like a piece of candy. "Baby, you're even more beautiful than when I saw you the other day."

I had been generous with the makeup because I knew he was more into sleazy than anything else.

"Well, thank you, sugar." I smiled and teased. "You ready for some excitement?"

"Mmm... baby, I can't wait," he groaned. "Why don't you gimme a little sample?"

I unzipped the coveralls to my sternum and showed him the outfit. Before I knew what was happening, he leaned over and licked between my tits up to my neck. I fought nausea but quickly caught myself. I stepped back and forced a smile.

"Ah—ah—ah," I teased while choking on what I had to do, but it would be worth it if it got him dead. "You'll get a lot more than that if you are a patient boy. You want to be patient for momma, don't you?" I pulled the riding crop from inside the coveralls and slapped it across my palm.

He looked at the riding crop and grinned. "Okay, I'll be a good boy—for now. Maybe I'll be a bad boy later." Then, his demeanor changed. "My car's parked in the back. Come on in, do what ya gotta do, and I'll be back by two."

"Now, that's a good boy," I taunted. As he stepped back inside the house, I popped him on the ass with the riding crop.

"Hooo Hooo," he chimed. "Gettin' frisky already!"

"Go on, lover boy," I moaned. "I'll have it all ready for you when you get back."

"Bathroom's that way if you need it," he instructed and pointed. "I brought the dining chair out here in the living room. You got something special you want to do with it?"

"You bet I do," I replied teasingly. "Now, go on. I want this to be a surprise."

He wiggled and danced toward the back door as though I actually wanted to look at his ass. A little later, I heard his car start. I went to the front window to peek through the curtain at the front driveway and be sure he had driven away. Then, I put on my leather gloves. I didn't want any fingerprints left around the house. I locked the back door and wedged a chair under the door knob. I found another chair to wedge under the knob of the front door after I locked it. If he wanted to cheat on the time, I wanted to be ahead of him so he couldn't get in the house until I was ready.

I began to set up the living room. I plugged in the black lights and set the candles out. I would light them later. I got out of the coveralls and draped them over the arm of his grungy couch. I moved his coffee table to one side and laid out my paraphernalia, the rope, the crop, the cat of nine tails, and handcuffs across the sofa. Next, I tested the designated dining chair to see how sturdy it was. Satisfied, I placed it in the center of the room, facing away from the sofa, and decorated it with leather strips that I tied about the chair. None of that took long, and I already knew what to do next. I knew exactly where I was going to go.

Narrow steps descended into the living room from the second floor. Up the steps and to the right was the room where he took his pictures and where he had molested me and several other kids. I climbed the stairs slowly, still unsure if I wanted to see what I was sure would be in that room. I came to the door and found it locked. Jiggling the handle and jostling the door around did no good, and I knew I had to get into that room somehow. I considered trying to break it down, but I was finally able to pick the lock with a paper clip that I found on the floor. All of that wasted precious time.

When I managed to open the door, I stepped in quietly with stilted breath and flashbacks of what had been done to me. The cruelty of what I had experienced in that room assaulted my mind. I flipped on the wall switch as I came in and gagged when I saw it. I bent over, feeling nauseous and jittery, but I clenched my teeth, caught my breath, and slammed my fist against the wall. "You sick mother fucker!" I screamed.

It was still set up as it had been when I was a child. The cameras had been updated to modern versions, but it was obvious that he was still doing the same shit. He had set up the lights and a camera on tripods, with his viewing area on an opposite wall. That's where he made us pose. I began to see images of Ronza doing things to me while Jake flashed pictures. The windows had been covered with plywood from the inside, so the room was dark except for the overhead light. I remembered when the tripod lights glared down on us like a bright sun in the burning hell that had been my childhood.

I stepped back and leaned against the wall, looked up at the ceiling, and said aloud, "Breathe, Stephanie! Breathe! Get control of yourself!"

My mind flashed with the bullshit he had done to me. I felt myself crying and heard myself talking. "Stop it! You are stronger than this! Get it together, Girl! Get it together!"

I drew the air as deeply into my lungs as possible and returned my attention to the room. There were bulletin boards tacked with photos of little kids doing awful things that no child should ever be exposed to. He had built out a corner of the room into what looked like a closet, but when I opened the door, I could see it was his dark room where he could process the film himself. He certainly would never risk dropping it off at a pharmacy or photo shop where he could be found out.

There were shelves around the room, and on one of those shelves was a pair of men's shoes. I spotted them and moved closer. They appeared to have dried blood around the soles and splattered on them. Beside them was a butcher knife with dried blood still on the blade and handle. I recognized the knife as one that Mable had kept in our kitchen. Behind that leaned a photo of me at about eight years old, and Mable stood smiling beside me with her arm wrapped around my shoulder. We were standing in the doorway of her bedroom at Pruitt Igoe. I didn't even recall ever making the picture, but there it was. My heart pounded again, and a new rage began to build.

"It was him!" I said aloud. "He fucking murdered her!"

I threw my palm to my forehead and paced around the room, hearing myself exclaim, "Holy fuck—holy fuck—holy fuck!"

That was something that I had not expected to find. I knew I would see the photos of kids. I intended to confront him with those, but now I had something else to confront him with. I quickly pulled some of the photos of kids from the bulletin boards and found one that he had taken with Ronza doing awful things to me.

Where is Ronza? I thought. I wondered if Jake was still in contact with Ronza and if maybe Ronza had set up his own place like this. I didn't know, but God forbid.

I continued to look around and found envelopes with names and addresses. Then, I realized why Jake had taken all those pictures. He had been selling the photos to sick mother fuckers like himself.

"Jesus Christ!" I said as I trembled while looking at everything. I wanted to kill him more than ever. However, discovering those shoes and that butcher knife made me realize he was more dangerous than I thought, capable of murder. I knew I would have to be extremely careful and wondered if I could fight him off if I had to.

"Stephanie!" I scolded myself aloud. "You have got to pull it together! You have to snap out of this! You have a job to do! You have a job that you *must* do!"

"Yes," I answered myself. "I have a job to do, and I had better not fuck it up."

I took the knife, the shoes, several photos of the kids, and the photo of me with Mable and carried them back down the stairs. I hid them between his sofa and his end table where he could not see them.

I took the chairs from under the doors and unlocked them. Then, I sat and waited with knee-bouncing anxiety. Yet, I also planned how to get him into that chair, tied up and vulnerable. I had to be very careful. I had brought a cheap bottle of wine and two glasses, but I knew that wouldn't be enough to get him drunk, even if I could get him to drink it. Still, I opened it and set it on the coffee table with a wine glass on either side.

Shortly, I heard his car pull in behind the house. I got up, entered the kitchen, and posed for him. Then, I heard a tapping on the back door and saw it slowly open.

"Knock, Knock," He teased. "Daddy's home. How's my little girl?"

When he stepped into the kitchen, I ran my gloved hand between my breasts and down to my thong. Holding the riding crop in my other hand, I slapped it into my palm.

"Daddy," I crooned. "Your little girl has been so lonely. I've been waiting for you to come home. You've been such a bad boy to go away and leave me here all alone." It took everything I could muster to hide my disgust and apprehension. The truth is, I was scared as fuck, and I only hoped that I could pull off what I intended.

He walked straight to me, threw his hand to my neck, and gripped it tightly. Then, he snarled through gritted rotten teeth, "Why don't I just *fuck* you right now and then kill you?"

My heart rattled my ribs, shaking the chains of imprisonment. *Think fast!* I told myself. I could knee him in the nuts and try to overpower him, or I could try to outsmart him. All the terrors of my childhood bludgeoned me as I tried to fight those internal demons for some clarity of thought. He seemed superhuman. There was a terror inside me that said I couldn't beat him. Finally, I squeaked out, "Now, that wouldn't be much fun, would it? You would miss all the surprises I have in store for you."

His demonic eyes glared at me while he continued to hold his grip. Then, he released me and laughed, "Awe, shit! I'm just fucking with ya. Let's have some fun!"

Immediately, I slapped him across the face with the riding crop that I had still gripped in my right hand and screamed, "DON'T YOU EVER FUCKING DO THAT AGAIN!"

At first, evil burned in his eyes as he reached the palm of his hand to his face, where a red spot was forming from the impact. Then, he cackled, "Whoo Hooh! You are a feisty little bitch! This ain't no hokey little schoolyard game we're playin' here. We're gonna get dirty—real dirty!"

My heart continued to pound as I put on my best pretense. "GET DOWN ON YOUR KNEES, MOTHER FUCKER! YOU NEED TO BE PUNISHED!" I screamed this, knowing just how dangerous he was and knowing I had to stay on top of the game.

"No!" he defied.

"GET THE FUCK DOWN ON YOUR KNEES, NOW!" I screamed again and slapped him with the riding crop. "You're gonna get PUNISHED!"

A malicious grin spread across his face as he eyed me like a cobra. Then he said, "Yes, mistress," and bent to the floor.

"BEAR YOUR ASS!" I commanded.

He unbuckled his belt and pulled his jeans and skanky underwear down to his knees. The sight of him disgusted me.

"BEND OVER!" I ordered.

He put his arms down on the floor, exposing his nasty bare ass.

I slapped him hard across his ass with the riding crop and fought the urge to go into a ballistic rage. Then, I slapped him harder and again, harder. "You have been VERY VERY BAD!" I screamed. "TAKE YOUR FUCKING PUNISHMENT!" I wanted to grab whatever I could find and start beating him with it. A cast iron skillet still on the nearby stove burner became a potent temptation, but I refrained. I had to play the game to get him tied up in that chair. I had to dominate him but keep him intrigued.

He groaned with every lash, "Yeah, beat me! I've been a bad boy!"

"GET UP!" I commanded after beating his ass until his skin was about to break.

He struggled to get up and braced himself on the oven handle. I knew then he had a weakness. He was still a sick bastard, but age had been unkind to him. Maybe I could use his frailty to my advantage. I felt more confident knowing he was no longer the horrific monster I thought he was when I was a child. I realized that only a weak little man was behind his great and powerful curtian. When he got to his feet, I commanded, "STRIP!"

He fumbled to pull off his shoes and drew his jeans and underwear the rest of the way off. Then he unbuttoned his shirt slowly, glaring at me, thinking he was being sensual and sexy. He stood before me, completely naked. I had always known what he looked like naked, but now, I could see ravages of age around his body.

I looked down at his dick. "YOU CALL THAT A DICK?" I taunted! "THAT'S NOT A DICK! WHAT IS THAT, A LITTLE EARTHWORM? I NEED A REAL MAN! I NEED A MAN WITH A BIG COCK!"

He reached down and fumbled with the same nasty appendage that I had been violated with as a little boy and began to bring it to an erection. "It gets bigger, baby," he moaned.

I had fantasies of pulling out the switchblade and cutting it off. That option was still on the table, but not yet. I needed to get him tied up in that chair, and then I could castrate him before I murdered him.

He continued to stroke it. Then he stepped over and tried to kiss me.

Turning my head to one side, I said, "Oooch, not yet. Get your ass in the living room! I have a surprise for you."

I swished toward the living room with my bare ass cheeks swaying from side to side. He followed as I expected.

I went to the chair and began caressing it up and down, rubbing my tits on it, rolling my tongue over my teeth, and fained my sexiest voice. "Sit down, baby. Momma has a surprise for you."

"What if I don't want to?" he teased.

"SIT YOUR FUCKING NO ACCOUNT ASS DOWN IN THAT CHAIR!" I screamed. Not all of that was play or pretending. I felt the anger as I said it.

He stepped over to me and grabbed my boobs. "Let me feel them tits," He crooned.

I slapped him with the riding crop again and yelled, "I SAID SIT THE FUCK DOWN!"

"Now, why do you want me to do that?" he asked.

"Sit down, and I'll show you," I slipped back into a sultry tone and shimmied my tits.

"Oh," he mused. "I love a good show."

He sat in the chair, and I leaned over eye with him and whispered, "You better behave, or Mamma might have to bring on the real pain." Then I slapped him across the leg with the riding crop. I could see his erection and fought horrible memories. I stepped behind the chair so I wouldn't have to see it. From behind the chair, I leaned over with my tits on his neck and rubbed my hands down his chest.

"Does that excite you?" I crooned. Then I gently pulled his arms around behind him. "Don't move. Cause I've got something extra special for you."

I reached over to the sofa behind him and picked up the handcuffs. I put them on his wrists with his arms bent behind the chair. He could easily have stood up out of the chair at that point. I knew this spider had to pounce, so I grabbed the rope, quickly moved around in front of him, and straddled his lap, trying to avoid touching his nasty dick. "One more thing," I said as I gently wrapped the rope around his neck."

"Now hold on, there," he protested as I continued to wrap several layers of soft cotton rope around his neck. "What are you doing?"

I began to bounce on his lap with my tits flopping up and down, trying to keep him interested. "Ooooh, Daddy!" I warbled with a Shirly Temple voice. "Don't you want to play?" Then I stood up, shimmied my tits, and continued. "You want me to have fun, don't you, Daddy? I promise we're going to have lots of fun."

That brought him back to his lust, as I knew it would. He watched me playfully as I gently and sensually wrapped the rope around him, binding his legs to the chair legs, pulling his torso into the back of the chair. Then I stepped behind him and tied several knots in the rope.

"I'm gettin' uncomfortable with this," he said. I should be tying you up instead of the other way around."

"Oooh, Daddy. You'll get your turn," I crooned in my Shirly Temple voice, "but first, we've got to get you all worked up."

I again tied the rope behind the chair at his shoulder level and placed another strand around his neck. I fought the urge to yank it back and choke him to death right then and there, but I had a score to settle first.

I stepped back around in front of him and played with the tassels over my nipples while I bent over in his direction. "You like that, Daddy? The show is just starting." I reached over and pinched his nipples as hard as my strength would allow.

"Oh, Yeah," he moaned. "Bite 'em too. Put your teeth on 'em."

I stepped back and slapped him hard across the face. "I WOULD RATHER PUT MY LIPS ON A ROTTING DOG, YOU SICK MOTHER FUCKER!"

He still thought it was all part of the game. "Yeah, baby! Hit me again!" he begged. "Take them pasties off and show me them titties!"

I stepped behind him and pulled the switchblade from my boot. Then I grabbed a handful of his scraggly hair and yanked his head back. I flipped out the blade, put it to his neck, and leaned over next to his ear. "How sexy does this feel, mother fucker?"

"What the hell are you doing?" he whimpered as I pressed the blade to his juggler.

"Mother fucker! You are going to die!" I hissed through gritted teeth.

"Wait! What? Is this all part of the show?"

"I said … *you* are going to die." I hissed again.

I stepped back in front of him and put the switchblade under his nose.

"They told me when I bought this that it was sharp enough to shave with," I whispered. "So, I'll bet it's sharp enough to slit a throat. It only takes one little slash across your jugular for you to bleed out. I wonder what one little flick up your nose would do."

Terror filled his eyes, and he realized this was no longer a sex game. It was the real thing. "What do you want?" he pleaded. "I got cash. Let me up, and I'll get it for you."

"No, no, no," I continued to whisper. "It's not cash I want. It's revenge I want."

"What the fuck are ya talkin' bout?"

"You don't know who I am, do you?" I confronted. "You never thought you would ever see me again, but here I am."

"I don't know you!" he desperately implored.

"But you said in the grocery store that I locked familiar." I flicked the knife up slightly into his nostril. "You may not recognize me, but you know who I am. Before I'm through with you, I will make sure you know exactly who I am. Then, I will slit your throat, but you know what? I might like to cut your dick and balls off first!" I moved the knife down his dick and wedged it against his testicles. "Yeah, wouldn't that be a hoot? You ever wonder what it feels like to get castrated? Probably feels a lot worse than getting kicked in the nuts."

I loved seeing the terror on his face. He began bouncing around in the chair and yelling, "Help!"

I grabbed the rubber ball, shoved it in his mouth, pulled the gag around, and tied it behind his head.

"You tip yourself over in that chair," I said, "I can kill you on the floor just as easily as I can while you're sitting up. You're not going anywhere."

He began mumbling through the gag, eyes wide with terror. I reached over between the sofa arm and the end table and pulled out the picture of me with Mable.

"Does this look familiar?" I asked. "Where do you think I found this? See, I know you've got that special little room upstairs. Hmm? How do you think I knew about that? Do you know that woman in the picture, that little boy? Do they look familiar to you?"

I reached over and pulled out the picture that he had taken of Ronza abusing me. "What about this one? Who is that little boy in the picture? What did you and Ronza do to him?"

I pulled out photos of other kids, spread them like a deck of cards, and fanned them before his face. "What did you do to all of these innocent little kids who had no option to escape from your cruelty?"

He couldn't answer, and I didn't care. He knew he had been caught; I wanted him to know that.

"Now, let's take a close look at that picture of that little boy with his mother again, shall we?"

I held the photo up in front of his face. "What's that woman's name, mother fucker? Mable, somebody? Could it be Mable Saunders? And what's that little boy's name? Do you know that little boy? What's his name? Stephen? And what happened to Mable? Hmmm?"

The look on his face was abject terror. I stepped around him, waving the switchblade. Then, I bent over in front of him and licked the back of the knife. "This will feel so good when I slide it deep into your jugular. Don't worry. You'll bleed out quickly. It won't hurt that much, not like it hurt when you molested Stephen Saunders and banged his head into the floor. How old was Stephen then, six, maybe seven years old? You wonder how I know all this?" I leaned over again and looked him straight in the eye. "Take a good look, mother fucker! See any resemblance? Do I kind of look like Stephen Saunders?"

Shock washed over his face, and he again tried to mumble through the gag.

"Yeah," I went on. "Now you recognize me, don't you? But I have another little bone to pick with you. Something else I found. Something I didn't think I was going to find upstairs. I wasn't shocked by all those pictures I found. I knew I would find those, but I was shocked by this. What could it be? Hmmmm?"

I set the switchblade on the seat of an adjacent recliner, pulled the butcher knife and the shoes out of their hiding place, and held them up in front of him. "Recognize these, asshole? I recognized that knife as soon as I saw it. It's a butcher knife that my momma kept in her kitchen. I wonder how it got over here in your house with dried blood on the blade, but whose shoes are these? I wonder whose feet they would fit?"

I set the shoes down, stepped behind him again, yanked his hair back, and put the butcher knife to his neck. "You needed a souvenir after you murdered my mother, didn't you? That souvenir is old and rusty now. I'll bet it's dull, too. I could kill you with that nice razer sharp switchblade over there, but it seems more fitting to kill you with your little souvenir."

He tried to scream, but the ball in his mouth and the gag around his face muffled it.

"Calm down, now," I said. "I'm not ready to kill you yet. I think a little torture might be in order. You know, like you tortured all those helpless kids?"

His mumblings became softer, as though he was trying to say something.

"You got something you want to say? If you don't yell, I'll take the gag off." I offered. "Then, we can have a little conversation, but if you start yelling again, I'll just go ahead and kill you."

He nodded and mumbled.

I stood there momentarily, contemplating whether to take the gag off. Then, I said, "I'm still going to kill you either way." Finally, I untied the gag and took the ball out of his mouth.

After catching his breath, he asked, "How did you? How could you be a woman?" He looked at me like he was seeing a ghost.

"You ever heard of a transsexual? I had surgery and hormones, that simple," I explained. "Yes, I was Stephen Saunders, the little boy, but Stephen Saunders died when Mable Saunders died. That name no longer applies. That name is as dead to me as my no-account mother. None of that changes the fact that YOU FUCKING KILLED HER!" I lunged at him with the butcher knife.

"I'm sorry!" He began weeping and begging. "I'm sorry. It was a different time. I had different feelings. I didn't mean to kill her. I'm sorry!"

"GIVE ME A FUCKING BREAK!" I bellowed. "You didn't mean to kill her? 'I'm sorry, your honor, the murder was an accident.' Are you ever going to stop being full of bullshit? No, wait, you'll stop when I murder your low-life ass. You know who found the body, you sick ass mother fucking piece of shit! I DID! At ten fucking years old, I walked in to find my mother with stab wounds all over her, her throat cut, and her blood rolling across the floor! What the fuck do you think that does to a child's mind? I stepped in that blood! I had my mother's blood on my shoes, and to this day, I can't get the Goddamned smell of her blood out of my head! But you know what?

That was just the fucking cherry on the shit cake that you served me every Mother Fucking week! I suppose you didn't mean to do that either, beat me, molest me, take sick fucking pictures of me and other kids to sell to other perverts! I suppose you can't help it that you still have the cameras up there and negatives of the same shit in your dark room. You have the names and addresses of the creeps you mail that sickness to. I guess the cops will have fun with that when they investigate this murder scene. At least you won't be hurting anyone anymore."

"I'm sorry," he cried. "Please don't kill me."

"Now, why the fuck wouldn't I kill you after all the fucking shit you put me through?" I demanded. "I have more reasons to put an end to your miserable no account fucking life than there are catfish in the fucking Mississippi! I would be doing the world a favor."

"Because I'm your father," He pleaded.

I stepped back in shock. "Because you're my *father*? I don't believe you, but if I did, that would be just one more reason I should kill you! What kind of sick, disgusting, low-life does that to his own child? Never mind! My own Goddamn mother did that to me!"

"Maybe it don't mean nothin' to you." He presented his case. "Maybe you don't believe it, and maybe it makes you want to kill me more, but I'm your real father."

"And why wouldn't you or my mother ever tell me that?" I asked. "That doesn't make any sense."

"We had a deal," he said. "She said she was better off getting a check on you from the government if nobody knew. Then, I was supposed to pay her what we agreed on for child support and other stuff. We figured if you got old enough and knew it, you might spill the beans, and she would lose the check."

"Oh … Well … Isn't that just a couple of snakes in the hen house?" I said. "You were both fucking corrupt. She knew you were molesting me! She knew it! Neither one of you fucking cared about anything but your own Goddamn selfishness."

I went to his dining table, grabbed another chair, sat across from him, and asked. "Why did you kill her?"

"She was gonna cut me off, not let me see you anymore," he replied. "Some jackass had given her some song and dance about how he needed to take you out of Pruitt Igoe and away from her, and I guess he got to her or something. She was scared the government would find out, jerk her check, and make her pay everything back. I was supposed to keep paying her, but she wouldn't let me have you anymore."

My thoughts returned to the day before Mable was killed and memories of Mike standing up for me and wanting to get me out of there. In his own way, he had done precisely that. He didn't know that he had done it, but that day, he started the process that got me out of Pruitt Igoe. Maybe something snapped in Mable, and maybe she had realized what she was putting me through with Jake. Maybe she got scared that they would both get caught. Maybe she stood up to Jake, and the one time in her life that she may have tried to take care of me got her murdered.

"So, you killed her for that," I said. "What was that going to take away from you? No, wait! I know what it would take away from you. You couldn't abuse me anymore. You couldn't sell pictures of me to perverts who want to look at little kids being forced to do things that only adults should even know about. You would be losing some of your income. You have been marketing fucking child pornography since before I was born."

"She threatened to turn me in," he said. "We had a big argument, and she said she would turn me in for child pornography."

"So you killed her."

"Yes."

I dropped my head and stared at the floor. I thought about how my life had changed for the better after Mable was killed. I thought about Miss Mattie, her love, and her wisdom. Then, I thought about what Miss Mattie would say and what she might do in this situation. A tenderness crept into my mind with thoughts of her love, and I no longer felt the urge to slit his throat. Some of the fire was gone out of my rage, and I sat there, continuing to think about Miss Mattie as I looked back up at him. In my mind, I could hear her saying, *You ain't got ta be right ta do de right thing. All you needs ta do is what's the next right thing.*

If I killed him, I was no better than he was. If I killed him, I would have sunk to his level. Miss Mattie had done her best to lift me out of that sewer, and I had to ask myself what I was doing. My hate, alone, meant that I was dropping to Jake's level. By plotting my revenge, my willingness to debase myself for it, set Jarrod aside, and potentially lose him, I had sunk to Jake's level. I had become like Mable. I didn't want to be like her or like Jake. I didn't want to be any of the people who had hurt me. I wanted to be better than that. I knew that I could be better than that.

I sat up and took a deep breath. I knew better. Miss Mattie had taught me better. Mike had taught me better. The McNeils had taught me better. Pastor Simmons and Pastor Dennison had taught me better. The Wilsons had taught me better. Thelma had taught me better. Willard had taught me better, and Jordan had taught me better than what I was doing. I knew better. I just needed to claim it.

I heard Miss Mattie in my memories again, *No matter what peoples do ta you. You ain't gotta be like dem.*

At last, I spoke again. "I'm not going to kill you," I said. "I've got a better idea."

I got up and began blowing out the candles that I had lit. I poured the untouched bottle of wine down the drain in the kitchen and put it and the wine glasses back in the box.

The whole time, he kept asking, "What are you doing? What are you going to do?"

I turned to him, put my finger to my lips, and said, "Shush! It's a secret."

I didn't say anything else but silently went about doing what I would do. I turned on the overhead lights in every room of the house. I put everything back in the box and finished my cleanup. Then, I laid the photos, the shoes, and the butcher knife out on the sofa and turned him around to face them. I shoved the ball back into his mouth and gagged him again. I went into the other room, took off the black leather and changed into jeans, a T-shirt and tennis shoes I had brought. Then, I closed the doors to the downstairs rooms off the living room, ran ropes from his chair to the door knobs of each door, and pulled them tight. I also ran a rope from the chair to other large furniture in the room and secured it. I said nothing as I did all this. Finally, I set my things out on the porch, tied a rope to the knob of the front door, which opened to the inside, and pulled it closed.

He wasn't going anywhere. Pulled tight in almost every direction, those ropes would halt any effort to bounce his chair around or try to get free. I put everything in the van and left. A couple of miles down the road, I pulled in behind a store by a city dumpster and tossed the box and my leather outfit into the dumpster. Then I went to a payphone and called the police.

"St. Louis police department," the person answered.

"May I speak to a detective?" I asked.

"What's the issue?" she asked.

By that time, darkness was beginning to fall.

"I have some information on a murder," I said.

"Okay, what's your name?"

"My name is anonymous. May I speak to a detective?"

"Just a moment."

I was placed on hold, and shortly, a man's voice came online. "This is Detective Patterson, St. Louis P.D. May I help you?"

"I need to report some information about an existing murder," I said.

"What murder?" he asked.

"Nothing recent," I went on. "I have information on the murder of Mable Saunders in 1970."

"That case is closed, and her killer is in prison."

"No, he isn't," I continued. "The man in prison is innocent. I know who the murderer is. If you go to the 3800 block of North 20th, there is a brick house with white trim and columns on the porch. All the lights are on in the house. The house owner is tied and gagged in a chair in the living room. The back door is unlocked. You will find all the evidence you need when you get there. The owner of that house murdered Mable Saunders."

"Is this some kind of prank?" the officer asked.

"I assure you this is not a prank," I said.

"Well, we can't go out to someone's house without just cause," he said, "and that sounds more like a hoax than a legitimate complaint."

This time, I lied. "I placed a candle near a curtain. When it burns down far enough, it will light a waxed string that I have attached to the curtain, and when that happens, the house will catch on fire, and the man I have tied up inside the house will burn to death. I think you had better go."

I figured that would present enough of a threat that they would at least have to do a safety check. I hung up the phone and left. I returned the van to the car rental company and took a cab home. I knew that even if they traced the call, they would only find a pay phone a few miles from Jake's house. By the time anyone got there, I would be gone.

When I got home, I watched TV for a while, got ready for bed, pulled the blinds, and slept comfortably.

The following day, I woke up at about 9:00 a.m. and went to my kitchen to prepare breakfast. I turned on Channel 5 as soon as I got up. I didn't necessarily pay attention to it, but I wasn't sure how long it might take for the police to put two and two together and kept the TV on all day. At about 4:00 p.m., I heard their announcement music for a special report. Then, "This is John Marshall with KSDK, channel 5, and we have breaking news."

I sat up on the couch where I had been half-napping. The TV continued. "We have our field reporter Katherine Warner on the scene. Katherine, what can you tell us about what is going on."

The camera switched to an image of a female reporter standing on the sidewalk in front of Jake's house. The area had been marked off with police tape, and officers appeared to be carrying things out of the house.

"Yes, John," the reporter responded, "Due to an anonymous tip to the police, it appears that a suspect named Jake Carter has been arrested at this residence. It is alleged that he not only has ties to child pornography but may be tied to the murder of Mable Saunders at Pruitt Igoe in 1970. Police have also found the bodies of four young children buried under the house, and investigations continue into those cases."

I gasped. I had not expected that he had also murdered children. A tearful shock went through me, and I grieved for those innocent lives. I wondered if they were kids I had known and grieved that I could have been one of them.

"It appears that there may be sufficient evidence to connect this suspect to the murder of Mable Saunders. There have been repeated appeals by the legal team of Mike Foster, who was convicted of that murder, and there may be new evidence to present regarding his innocence. There were some extenuating circumstances about the anonymous tip that police received. When they arrived at the residence, the suspect had been tied nude and gaged in the living room of his home with much of the evidence, now confiscated by the police, laid out in front of him. The police are unsure what to make of that at this time. Neighbors have been questioned. One reported seeing an unmarked white van parked in front of the house for a couple of hours yesterday but reported no awareness of what may have been on the license plate and could not identify the make or model of the van. John, we will have more for our viewers as this investigation continues."

I flipped off the TV and pushed myself into the back cushions of the couch. I had both grief and peace in me at that moment. I knew that Mike would go free and that Jake could get the death penalty. I also knew that, despite momentarily sinking to Jake's level, I had done the right thing in the end. Ultimately, I had lived up to the morals and ethics that Miss Mattie had taught me. I had been about to sacrifice everything for a while, but I was glad I didn't.

I got up, showered, dressed, and then drove to Domingo's donut shop to buy a dozen donuts. I got home at about 6:00 p.m. Then, I picked up the phone and called Jordan.

"Hello,"

"Hi," I said. "How are you doing?"

"I missed you," he confessed.

"I missed you too," I admitted and realized that even when I was about to lose my mind with obsessive hatred, I still loved and missed him.

"I worked through things a little sooner than I thought I would," I continued.

"I'm glad," he said. "Is everything okay?"

"Everything is very okay," I replied. "I'm sitting here with a box of donuts. Want to come over."

"I thought you didn't do donuts," he said.

"Well, someone told me I should enjoy donuts occasionally, especially when I have something to celebrate."

"Do you have something to celebrate," he asked.

"I think I do," I replied, "Maybe several things. Want to celebrate with me?"

"I'll be right there," he said, and the line went dead.

There is no such thing as the end.

AUTHOR'S AFTERNOTE

Edge of Smoke is purely fiction and created from my imagination as the author. Although I am not transgender, I have tried to imagine walking in the shoes of a transwoman. I tried, unsuccessfully, to find a transgender beta reader for the book, so I continued with the manuscript to the best of my ability trying to walk in the shoes of a transwoman and understand how that would feel, especially during the historical setting of the book. In terms of gender, I'm not sure how to classify myself. I suppose I am non-binary, bordering on cisgender. I am a gay male.

I think transgender and non-binary are a couple of the most misunderstood terms in our society. As well, queer or LGBTQ+ are terms difficult for heterosexual cisgender people to comprehend. Even cisgender queer people (I use queer as an umbrella term) have difficulty understanding what it is like to walk in the shoes of someone who is not cisgender. As a sixty-eight-year-old male, having grown up in a time when gay rights were just beginning, such terms that are applied now did not exist. I have to admit that I have struggled to wrap my head around the new terminology. So, even for some LGBTQ+ people, these terms can be confusing. Many heterosexual cisgender people seem to be very confused about how to comprehend the terms. There is a lot for all of us to learn, but the more we know about each other, the less we fear one another. Yet, learning cannot occur through separation, isolation, and marginalization of anyone. The only way to learn about someone is to spend time with them, and the more we define them as separate, the less we will learn about them and from them, for even those whom society would marginalize have something to teach us.

One of the problems with humanity is that we seem to want a category for everything. We like labels because labels help us define our own and other's identities, but we stick people into those categories without ever trying to learn about who they really are. The problem is that identity is a mental construct that doesn't define anyone. We concoct an idea about ourselves and them that says, "This is who I am, and that is who they are." In truth, none of us are our identities, and the human spirit is much deeper than that. Spirituality would say, "There is no male or female," and we are all one. Still, some people seem to want to categorize, and gender assign even the spiritual realm, which is ultimately beyond human definition.

Regarding *Edge of Smoke*, all my novels so far are written because the protagonist (main character) comes into my head and wants to tell a story. So, I tell their story as they dictate it to me. Nonetheless, part of my reason for writing this book was to bring awareness and understanding about those who are, in my opinion, the most oppressed in human society, especially if they are people of color—transgender. Stephanie is the protagonist and the heroin, not only because she wanted to tell her story but because I want people to understand that, not just in fiction, transgender and other queer people are good people with ethics and integrity.

Stephanie, with proper help, learned to overcome the abuse and trauma of her childhood, but that had nothing to do with her gender. Gender is irrelevant to the development of ethics and a mature morality in which all people are valued for who they are, not as concepts that others impose upon them or objects to be used or discarded. The difference between mature and immature morality is this. Immature morality is based almost solely on authority. It says something is wrong because the rule says it's wrong, and I don't do it because I might get caught or punished. There is no questioning of the rule or whether it even makes sense. It is simply the rule and, therefore, must be obeyed. Mature morality says it is wrong if it hurts someone, and I don't do it because I have compassion and know the act would be harmful. Of course, some of any group, straight, queer, or other, don't seem to care about morality at all or how their behavior might affect others. Some are simply ignorant of themselves. Those who would focus on trying to change someone's gender or sexual orientation demonstrate what the Bible would call straining at a gnat while choking on a camel. All the energy and effort that some in society put into trying to change, demean, degrade and deprive queer people draws attention away from huge problems within society that are far more pressing and in need of our attention. Those who want to marginalize queer people ignore multiple Bible verses that tell them not to behave in hateful ways toward anyone. At the same time, they focus on the few versus that they interpret as defining homosexuality as a sin.

There are a lot of things that I address in *Edge of Smoke*. Still, nothing in this text has been deliberately initiated as an offense to anyone, including fundamentalist Christians. I grew up in a fundamentalist church, and some of the most loving people I ever knew were members of that church, specifically including my grandmother, one of my aunts, and a neighbor. However, that is the same church where, at the age of sixteen, I heard the preacher proclaim, "The sin of homosexuality is worse than the sin of murder."

The Bible verse, "Narrow is the way, and few there be that enter therein," means some people understand that true spirituality is about love, but most probably won't. The role of fundamentalist Christianity in this book is intended to identify the error of focusing on something that is not the real problem while ignoring the most important problem. Being transgender was not Stephanie's problem. Going through tremendous loss, trauma, and abuse, often for being transgender, was her real problem. Again, the Christians in the story were straining at a gnat and choking on a camel. *Matthew 23:24 Amplified Bible (AMP): "You [spiritually] blind guides, who strain at a gnat [consumuing yourselves with miniscule matters] and swallow a camel [ignoring and violating God's precepts]!"*

My depiction of fundamentalist Christians in this text is not about who they are but what they are doing. There is a tremendous difference between what someone does and who they are. Some people have good and loving hearts but are misled and misinformed and do not question beyond the rules they are told they must follow. How we identify ourselves may influence our actions, but awareness would have us see the cause and effect of our thinking and how our actions affect ourselves and those around us. Regardless of our instruction, our need to have meaning, our need to be recognized, or latching our identity onto the perishable world, let us all work on developing awareness and seek to express universal and all-encompassing love. I hope, therefore, that you have realized this is a book about love.

THINGS YOU MAY NOT KNOW (and my comments)

Transgender people are over four times more likely than cisgender people to experience violent victimization, including rape, sexual assault, and aggravated or simple assault, according to a new study by the Williams Institute at UCLA School of Law. In addition, households with a transgender person had higher rates of property victimization than cisgender households.

https://williamsinstitute.law.ucla.edu/press/ncvs-trans-press-release/

Violence against transgender people is significantly higher when the transgender person is someone of color. Justifying the murder of or violence toward transgender people is, in my opinion, a symptom of the underlying misogyny in our culture—hatred of women combined with racism when people of color are attacked at a much higher rate. Women experience violence at a rate of one in three, which is the same statistic for women having been molested as children. These statistics are created by toxic masculinity, misogyny, and male domination, which historically ignores the suffering of those who are perceived to be weak or defined as having little or no value, even if the haters deliberately devalue them through lies and propaganda. Where transwomen are concerned, in the mind of a misogynist, the greatest betrayal of their concept of masculinity would be a man (in their minds) transitioning to or presenting as a woman, even dressing as a woman. The concept of gender outside of genitals is beyond them. They cannot see gender as anything other than a physical manifestation. Males seen as or behaving as feminine has nothing to do with harm that is done to anyone. A person's mannerisms, gender, sexual orientation, color, choice of clothing (unless it is constructed with spikes and blades), or any other difference, harms no one. Hatred is not directed at those who are different because they are dangerous, but innocent people are demonized and dehumanized to justify hatred. It focuses on their nonconformity to expected rules, which they were not allowed to help define. Someone being transgender, queer, black, brown, red, yellow, white, or of a different religion or culture does no harm to anyone. Hatred is a symptom of a gross pathology in society in which the misogynistic ego's lust for control and the illusion of superiority ignores the value of other human lives. This narcissistic hatred is also directed toward gay and bisexual men who are considered to be acting like women for having attraction to men. How dare anyone betray the concocted construct of excessive and toxic masculinity? Some would say that such a betrayal is punishable by death, while they ignore the collapse of their own morals.

LGBT people experienced 5.4 violent hate crimes specifically motivated by sexual orientation and gender identity per 1,000 people, compared to 0.2 victimizations per 1,000 people for non-LGBT people.
https://williamsinstitute.law.ucla.edu/press/lgbt-hate-crimes-press-release/

Hating people for who they are is a pathology created by egocentric people who need an enemy, someone to hate so they can have the illusion of superiority. If queer people didn't exist, a different enemy would be created. In fact, it already has. Alternative enemies are black people, Asian people, Native Americans, Hispanics, migrants, women, Muslims, Jews, etc. Have I left anyone out? None of the violence perpetrated has anything to do with a wrong that was committed against the haters but is associated with a narcissistic need to feel superior. The haters don't realize that those who are confident have nothing to prove. Those who truly know their own worth do not need to attempt to diminish the worth of another.

Research has shown that those who identify as lesbian, gay, bisexual, transgender, or questioning (LGBTQ+) have a 120% higher risk of experiencing some form of homelessness.[1] With up to 40% of the 4.2 million youth experiencing homelessness identifying as LGBTQ+[2] while only 9.5% of the U.S. population[3], LGBTQ+ youth disproportionately experience homelessness compared to their straight and cisgender peers.

https://nn4youth.org/lgbtq-homeless-youth/

The statistics above are because queer people are the only minority at risk of being rejected by their own families, churches, and communities. When LGBTQ+ youth make up to 40% of the population of homeless youth and only 9.5% of the total population, that is about only one thing—hatred toward them perpetrated by their own families. This is partly due to the illusion of choice and the idea that they can stop being who they are and should be punished or shunned if they cannot stop being who they are. Choice is what we do at the moment. The only two elements of life are choice and destiny. Destiny is anything we can't choose or couldn't have chosen. Choice is the only power anyone possesses, but most of life is destiny.

Ask yourself, "Did I choose my sexual orientation? Did I choose my language? Did I choose my parents? Did I choose to be right-handed or left-handed? Did I choose my favorite food or my least favorite food?" Who we are and much of what we experience is not a choice for anyone, and it doesn't matter what "causes" one to be queer. The whole idea of looking for a cause is based on the assumption that it is something wrong, an illness, or abnormality, rather than a natural part of humanity that has existed since the dawn of time. It doesn't matter whether we were born this way or if it developed during our upbringing. We are what we are. I did not choose to be an English speaker. If I had been born in China, there would be a significantly lower chance that I would be able to speak English. Our native tongue, or for some being bilingual, develops in the formative years of our lives when the human brain literally doubles in size after birth. Half of the neural pathways in our brains are formed in the first five years of life. Therefore, language and perhaps things like gender identity or sexual orientation may also be hardwired into us at that time. We don't choose it. It happens to us.

Of course, a homosexual person can choose not to have sex with the same sex, but the alternative would be to either be celibate (which many queer people choose) or to force themselves to deny their feelings and sleep with or marry the opposite sex. Those who insist that queer people do this don't stop to consider if it would be fair if the shoe were on the other foot. What if heterosexual people were either forced to play a gender role that is antithetical to who they are or forced to marry or sleep with the same sex and deny their heterosexuality? How would that feel? Would it be fair?

Choice is an inappropriate term to apply to gender or sexual orientation. We don't choose our language. We can learn a different language as adults, but it is very difficult for most people, and the "foreign" language is never as comfortable to speak as our native tongue. Would it be fair for someone to dictate that you have to learn and can only speak a language unfamiliar to you? Would it be acceptable for someone to force you to eat a food you dislike daily? Trying to push queer people into behaving in conflict with their nature is just as unfair, perhaps more so, and no child should ever have to fear becoming homeless because a parent disapproves of or has difficulty accepting their natural state of being. Behavior is a choice. Who we are is not, and kids who are queer already suffer enough outside the home from bullying and aggression. No child should have to be afraid in their own home.

LGBTQ youth are more than four times as likely to attempt suicide than their peers (Johns et al., 2019; Johns et al., 2020). LGBTQ youth are not inherently prone to suicide risk because of their sexual orientation or gender identity but rather placed at higher risk because of how they are mistreated and stigmatized in society.

https://www.thetrevorproject.org/resources/article/facts-about-lgbtq-youth-suicide/

The Trevor Project (where I got this quote) is an organization to help queer youth who experience homelessness or other ostracization. It has a mission to end suicide among queer youth. It also helps homeless youth and offers other services. I have already said that when I was sixteen, the preacher of our church said, "The sin of homosexuality is worse than the sin of murder." That was in 1971 in rural Arkansas, only two years after the Stonewall riots that began the gay rights movement. We lived ten miles out of town, and the town where I attended school was only two thousand in population. Of course, I knew no other kids who were gay. There was no one I could talk to about it. I had no role models, and I felt completely alone while buying into the concept that being homosexual is the worst possible sin. If I think I am worse than a murderer, why wouldn't I want to kill myself? The other option was to keep my mouth totally shut, lie about it, pretend I was straight, and hope that no one discovered my feelings because, if I'm worse than a murderer, they might try to kill me. Either way, I felt doomed. I grew up listening to people say all kinds of horrible things about gay people and continued to pretend that I was not one of them. Had it not been for my loving grandmother, I might have committed suicide. The thoughts were there.

Youth are especially vulnerable, and I guarantee you that by the time a child is entering puberty, they know their sexual orientation, but what are their choices? If they are rejected by their family, bullied, marginalized and ostracized, the risk increases substantially. We already know that queer youth from loving and supporting families are far less likely to attempt suicide. So, suicidal ideation among queer youth is not about being queer. Wanting to kill yourself has nothing to do with being queer, but it has everything to do with how isolated and lonely you feel and how much you are rejected and degraded for being who you are, especially by your own loved ones. Shunning queer youth is a form of child abuse.

Some say that gay people are attempting to indoctrinate their children. However, the goal is to save those children from going through the torment that we went through. The goal is to give them mentors, role models, and loving support so they can navigate the treacherous waters of growing up queer. Some say that gay people are pedophiles, but do they ever get to know people who are gay or learn about their character? It is true that some queer people are pedophiles, but the vast majority are not, just as the vast majority of cisgender heterosexuals are not pedophiles. It would be constructive if those who believe nonsense such as this would take the time to honestly educate themselves rather than buy into the propaganda of hate. That not only means looking past doctored "research" designed to support the propaganda of hate but spending time with queer people without judging, trying to change them, or forcing your values on them. Take time to simply listen to the content of their hearts.

More than anything else, please understand that no matter who you are, your worth is equal to everyone. There is no one of greater value than you. There is no one of lesser value than you, and no person's thinking, attitude, or behavior can possibly change your worth as a human being.

Okay, that is enough preaching on the subject. If you need help or would like to offer support, below are some available resources. Other resources can be identified through internet search engines, including local groups such as Pride Centers and LGBTQ health organizations in larger cities.

National Center for Transgender Equality:
https://transequality.org/

Trans Lifeline:
https://translifeline.org/

Family Equality:
https://www.familyequality.org/issues/transgender-rights/?gclid=Cj0KCQjw-pyqBhDmARIsAKd9XIPi0-YIP4XVCzd-LoK509UHpLkz-62TSp4-sKvk5unrhl8ygZ-52urgaAsBNEALw_wcB

The Trevor Project:
https://www.thetrevorproject.org/resources/article/facts-about-lgbtq-youth-suicide/

GLAAD (Gay and Lesbian Aliance Against Defimation):
https://glaad.org/

PFLAG (Parents and Friends of Lesbians and Gays):
https://pflag.org/

Human Rights Campaign:
https://www.hrc.org/resources/direct-online-and-phone-support-services-for-lgbtq-youth

Centers for Disease Control and Prevention (LGBTQ health):
https://www.cdc.gov/lgbthealth/youth-resources.htm

ABOUT KARLYLE TOMMS

Karlyle Tomms is a writer who grew up in rural Ozarks poverty. He completed his master's degree in 1981. He has written for different regional magazines and newspapers over the years, and has often been selected to speak at both professional and non-professional events, as well as radio talk shows. However, he had never published fiction until completing his first novel in 2014. His general method for fiction has been to define a character and allow that character to tell his or her own story from first person perspective as though the character is writing an autobiography. Through his characters he explores the psychology of the human condition as well as the various elements and entanglements of personalities. His novels incorporate the social and historical influences surrounding the lifetimes of his characters, and are stories of overcoming social, emotional and spiritual challenges.

Fresh Ink Group

Independent Multi-media Publisher

Fresh Ink Group / Push Pull Press
Voice of Indie / GeezWriter

Hardcovers
Softcovers
All Ebook Formats
Audiobooks
Podcasts
Worldwide Distribution

Indie Author Services
Book Development, Editing, Proofing
Graphic/Cover Design
Video/Trailer Production
Website Creation
Social Media Marketing
Writing Contests
Writers' Blogs

Authors
Editors
Artists
Experts
Professionals

FreshInkGroup.com
info@FreshInkGroup.com
Twitter: @FreshInkGroup
Facebook.com/FreshInkGroup
LinkedIn: Fresh Ink Group

In 1945, ten-year-old Ronald Dennison, the son of a back-woods Arkansas preacher, began having profound dreams about religion and a strange red-haired woman. The dreams follow him for decades with the woman sometimes seducing him, other times calling him to become a televangelist, but eventually berating him for his sins of lust. She holds a secret so dark that he dares never admit it, even to himself. The more famous and wealthier he becomes, the more he struggles with his adultery, his fetish, and his shame until his torment can no longer be contained. Staggering revelations challenge everything he ever believed. Will truth bring him the peace he always craved, or will the woman's demands prove more than he can bear?

Jacketed Hardcover
Softcover
All Ebooks Editions

Family secrets can be deadly. When Lisa visits her parents one fateful Saturday morning, she hugs her father and takes her suitcase to her childhood bedroom. The doorbell rings, and one minute later, her father lies dead on the floor— three bullets to the chest. The death of Eric Holmes sends shockwaves throughout the quiet neighbor- hood. But for the Holmes family, it is devastating. In this fast-paced psychological thriller, Lisa and her brother embark on a quest to solve the mystery of their father's murder. The journey takes them into a secret world where nothing is as it seems. Once the puzzle pieces begin to coalesce, they realize that their father had multiple lives.

As the facts unravel, the siblings discover the true meaning of *Redemption*.

Fresh Ink Group showcases 42 compelling prize-winners from its literary and genre short-story contests. Eclectic, daring, subtle, provocative, diverse—this wide-ranging collection by authors from across the USA and around the world transcends the limits of single-theme anthologies to explore the best of many styles and bold new ideas. Travel through time and space. Experience the Dust Bowl, a dying soldier's love, one distraught boy's mirror, the southern-farm snake, suicidal love lost, politicians run amok, a serial killer's lair, seductive sorcerous charms, a malevolent-house warning, inevitable moon-base death, the vengeful walking corpse, or a Holocaust child's hope, the lament of a life never lived . . . Discerning story-lovers are invited to listen for the voices of these newly favorite authors in Fresh Ink Group Short Story Showcase #1. Keep turning the pages to discover what unexpected delights beckon next.